Chères lectrices,

Nous voilà au plein cœur de l'été, saison des vacances, du farniente… La douceur de vivre s'empare de nous. Tout paraît plus léger et plus intense à la fois. Autour de nous, les arbres nous offrent leur ombre bienfaisante, les abeilles bourdonnent, les lézards prennent le soleil sur une pierre… Capucines, bégonias, fuchsias, héliotropes, impatiens, pétunias, verveine, toutes les fleurs estivales sont au rendez-vous… Oui, il s'agit bien d'une parenthèse, d'une respiration dans nos vies au rythme si souvent effréné. Est-ce le bleu du ciel, l'éclat de la lumière qui nous redonnent cette énergie, cette envie de plonger dans la vie pour nous saisir de ce qu'elle a de meilleur à offrir ?

D'ailleurs, avez-vous remarqué que c'est souvent à cette période de l'année que nous prenons de nouvelles résolutions, que nous faisons de nouveaux projets ? Bien sûr, nous ne les tiendrons pas toutes, nous ne les réaliserons pas tous. Mais ce temps qui laisse place aux rêveries vivifiantes se suffit à lui-même…

Pour vous accompagner dans vos doux songes éveillés, vos romans de ce mois seront, bien sûr, les compagnons idéaux !

Très bonne lecture.

La responsable de collection

La maîtresse cachée

LYNNE GRAHAM

La maîtresse cachée

COLLECTION AZUR

éditions **Harlequin**

Cet ouvrage a été publié en langue anglaise
sous le titre :
THE GREEK TYCOON'S CONVENIENT MISTRESS

Traduction française de
BARNABÉ D'ALBES

HARLEQUIN®

est une marque déposée du Groupe Harlequin
et Azur ® est une marque déposée d'Harlequin S.A.

Prologue

Andreas Nicolaidis raffermit sa prise sur le volant en réprimant un juron. Les pneus de la voiture venaient de patiner sur le bitume verglacé.

Le paysage n'était qu'une suite de champs désolés et couverts d'une mince pellicule blanche, comme les arbres qui bordaient les chemins de terre. Depuis qu'il avait pris cette route de campagne, et il avait l'impression que cela faisait des heures, il n'avait plus croisé un automobiliste. Les bulletins du trafic routier avaient d'ailleurs découragé la population d'entreprendre toute circulation, la journée promettant un brouillard épais et de nombreuses chutes de neige.

Mais il avait relevé le défi. Il entendait bien s'assurer une fois de plus de ses talents de conducteur hors pair au volant de sa nouvelle Ferrari Maranello ! Car même s'il possédait une jolie collection de voitures de sport, il avait rarement l'occasion de prendre le volant lui-même. Certes, il ne savait pas où il se trouvait en ce moment, mais quelle importance ? Tôt ou tard, il finirait par tomber sur un embranchement qui le ramènerait vers Londres et la civilisation.

Pour l'heure, il savourait ces instants volés à une vie parfaitement organisée. Plus que tout, il aimait les challenges et les événements exceptionnels auxquels il devait faire face en personne. N'importe quel imprévu, même le plus ennuyeux, pouvait se régler si facilement ! Ce n'était en général qu'une question d'argent, et pour lui l'argent n'était jamais un problème.

Il n'en avait cependant pas toujours été ainsi.

La dynastie Nicolaidis avait fait fortune grâce à la navigation marchande avant de frôler la faillite complète à l'époque où lui, Andreas, était encore adolescent. Conservateurs et refusant d'admettre la réalité, ses ascendants avaient manifesté bien des réticences quand il avait refusé de poursuivre l'aventure marchande sur les traces de son père et de son grand-père et décidé d'investir le capital familial dans la finance. Néanmoins, au cours des années qui avaient suivi, les murmures de réprobation s'étaient changés en un concert d'éloges. Le succès avait été foudroyant. Ses cabinets de conseils en investissement faisaient référence dans le monde des affaires, et il lui arrivait même d'être sollicité par des chefs d'Etats pour orienter les placements d'un gouvernement.

A l'âge de trente-deux ans, au-delà du fils prodigue qui avait sauvé sa famille de la banqueroute, il incarnait le chef d'entreprise par excellence à qui tout réussit et dont le travail est la seule priorité. Dans sa vie personnelle, aucune femme n'avait réussi à accaparer son attention plus de quelques semaines. Les prétendantes se bousculaient, et nombreuses étaient celles qui auraient aimé le conduire devant l'autel, mais il dominait ses émotions et gardait le contrôle de ses aventures amoureuses grâce à une volonté de fer.

A vrai dire, il ne tenait pas à se retrouver dans la situation qu'avaient connue ses parents : son père, mort trois ans plus tôt, avait été marié quatre fois. Andreas avait été exaspéré par l'incessant ballet de femmes auquel il avait assisté durant son enfance. Non, il ne se laisserait pas prendre au piège, même si les journaux *people* n'hésitaient pas à le dépeindre comme un homme au cœur froid qui collectionnait les fiancées sans

8

états d'âme ! Fier de ses valeurs et de sa détermination, il avait établi une liste des dix qualités que devait à tout prix présenter une femme pour qu'il envisage de passer le reste de sa vie avec elle. Or, aucune de ses maîtresses n'avait su remplir ce cahier des charges — ni même s'en approcher.

Hope Evans remonta ses mains gelées dans les manches de son imperméable et frissonna. Le froid lui gagnait les jambes. Elle n'avait croisé personne à qui demander la direction de l'arrêt de bus le plus proche. Dire que la nuit allait tomber bientôt…

A sa place, n'importe qui aurait été abattu après un tel après-midi.

Néanmoins, elle n'était pas de nature pessimiste. De longues années de privations lui avaient appris qu'il était inutile de jeter autour de soi un regard négatif. Au contraire, elle pensait que rien n'était plus sage que de voir les aspects positifs de l'existence. Par conséquent, même si elle ne pouvait nier qu'elle était perdue sur un chemin de campagne dans le froid et le brouillard, elle gardait espoir. Forcément, elle croiserait bientôt une voiture conduite par une personne charitable qui l'aiderait à se repérer.

A quoi bon se laisser gagner par l'amertume et le désespoir ? Pleurer sur son sort ne l'aiderait pas. Même s'il lui était difficile de ne pas être déçue en se rappelant son enthousiasme lors-qu'elle était partie passer cet entretien d'embauche, quelques heures plus tôt…

A vrai dire, elle se reprochait sa naïveté. Jamais elle n'aurait dû investir autant d'espoirs dans cette affaire. N'y avait-il pas des mois qu'elle était à la recherche d'un emploi ? Ne savait-elle pas mieux que personne à quel point il était difficile de faire ses preuves dans la voie du design et de la mode ? Sur son

CV, son expérience se résumait hélas à quelques lignes, et son brillant cursus universitaire ne suffirait pas à lui ouvrir les portes des créateurs renommés… Dans ce milieu, mieux valait avoir des appuis, des amis, un réseau. Or, ces dernières années, elle n'avait guère eu la chance de sortir de chez elle : à vingt-deux ans, elle avait surtout derrière elle une carrière d'infirmière à plein temps !

C'est tout juste si elle se rappelait un temps où sa mère, Susan, n'avait pas été malade. Le mariage de ses parents s'était délité peu après son douzième anniversaire. Son père avait quitté le domicile familial en les laissant seules, sa mère et elle, et au bout d'un an il n'avait plus donné de nouvelles. Quant à son frère Jonathan, son aîné de dix ans, il était devenu ingénieur et s'était installé en Nouvelle-Zélande. Ses visites annuelles s'étaient espacées depuis qu'il avait fondé sa propre famille, au point qu'elle l'avait à peine reconnu lorsqu'ils s'étaient retrouvés pour les obsèques de leur mère. Son comportement avait alors été celui d'un étranger, jusqu'au moment où il avait osé lui avouer les problèmes financiers qu'il rencontrait. Mais lorsqu'elle avait annoncé devant le notaire qu'elle renonçait à sa part de l'héritage en sa faveur, son attitude avait été bien différente. Soulagé, il lui avait confié que la vente de la petite maison de Susan serait pour lui comme la bouée lancée à un homme en train de se noyer. Dans la mesure où Jonathan était père de trois enfants, elle avait été heureuse que cette modeste succession lui revienne intégralement. Accaparée par son deuil et par le chagrin, elle n'avait pas vraiment réalisé qu'une petite réserve d'argent lui eût été d'un grand secours, le temps qu'elle trouve un travail plus à son goût que celui de secrétaire à mi-temps.

Heureusement, elle n'avait pas de problème de logement pour l'instant : elle partageait un appartement avec sa meilleure amie.

Soudain, le bruit d'un moteur troubla le silence qui pesait sur la campagne enneigée.

Hope se rapprocha du bas-côté. Les congères étaient si épaisses qu'elle ne pouvait pourtant pas trop s'éloigner de la route.

Comme le son striait l'air et devenait plus puissant, ses lèvres s'étirèrent en un sourire de soulagement. Elle tenait enfin le moyen de retourner en ville : elle allait faire signe à l'automobiliste.

Lancé à pleine vitesse dans le virage, Andreas vit trop tard la personne qui tendait un bras vers lui, presque au milieu de la route.

Bon sang ! Il n'y avait qu'une option possible.

Ecrasant la pédale de freins, il tourna brusquement le volant sur sa droite.

Les pneus patinèrent dans la neige avant de crisser dans un vacarme assourdissant. Puis le fracas de la tôle sur un arbre vibra dans l'air, et le silence retomba.

Hope demeura pétrifiée sur le chemin, fixant la voiture de sport enfoncée sur le pin et la fumée noire qui s'échappait déjà du capot.

Instinctivement, elle s'en approcha pour vérifier que l'automobiliste était encore en vie, mais elle n'eut pas fait deux pas que l'homme jaillit hors du véhicule et se précipita sur elle en criant.

— Courez, mais courez donc !

Elle obtempéra mais sentit bientôt un poids terrible s'abattre sur elle et la plaquer au sol. Moins d'une seconde plus tard, elle entendit retentir l'explosion et resta immobile, sonnée, à plat ventre sur le sol malgré le froid qui la transperçait.

Au bout d'un moment, lorsqu'elle recouvra ses esprits, elle sentit les cuisses puissantes de l'homme sur les siennes, son souffle dans son cou, sa main qui avait couvert son front pour la protéger dans leur chute. Elle était trempée : l'homme l'avait précipitée sur un tas de neige à demi fondue… Et ce faisant, il lui avait certainement sauvé la vie, songea-t-elle en ouvrant les yeux.

De sa position au ras du sol, elle apercevait les flammes qui s'élevaient autour du véhicule.

Enfin, l'homme se leva.

— Vous allez bien ? demanda-t-il d'une voix grave et veloutée. Vous n'êtes pas blessée ?

— Non, ça va, dit-elle en acceptant la main qu'il lui tendait pour se relever.

Il était grand et athlétique. Elle devait presque se tordre le cou pour le regarder. Son long manteau gris, très élégant, soulignait sa large carrure. Elle se sentit fascinée dès qu'elle croisa son regard. Dans ses intenses yeux noirs brillait une lueur plus ardente que la braise. Son visage était fin, émacié, mais sa mâchoire imposante d'une virilité toute méditerranéenne mettait en valeur son teint mat et la sensualité de ses lèvres ourlées.

Son charme était tel qu'elle en demeura interdite.

L'inconnu la regarda un instant, visiblement troublé, mais il reprit très vite ses esprits et fronça les sourcils.

— Que faisiez-vous au beau milieu de la route, avec ce brouillard ? C'était extrêmement imprudent de votre part !

— Je regrette, répondit-elle d'un ton penaud.

Il porta une main à son front pour en ôter les traces de neige…

A ce contact, elle frissonna. Il avait une peau très douce, et ses doigts étaient chauds.

— Je voulais simplement vous faire signe, expliqua-t-elle. Je craignais que vous ne m'aperceviez pas si je restais sur le bas-côté.

— Vous m'avez mis dans une situation impossible, grommela-t-il. Je n'avais pas le choix : pour vous éviter, je devais braquer de toutes mes forces.

Embarrassée, elle lança un coup d'œil vers la voiture. A l'évidence, il s'agissait d'un luxueux modèle de sport dont il ne resterait plus dans quelques minutes qu'une carcasse calcinée. Une vague de culpabilité la gagna.

— Je suis vraiment désolée, murmura-t-elle.

A son tour, Andreas se retourna vers la Ferrari et soupira. Il n'aurait guère eu la chance de la conduire : une première fois la semaine précédente, et une dernière aujourd'hui.

Mais il était en vie, et cette jeune idiote aussi !

Il sourit en posant de nouveau les yeux sur elle.

En plongeant dans ces yeux bleu turquoise, il avait l'impression de retrouver la transparence et la profondeur de la mer de son enfance. La blondeur de la jeune femme, la clarté de sa peau diaphane rappelait celles d'une poupée de porcelaine. Elle semblait très jeune. Il y avait une douceur indéfinissable dans son expression, dans la manière dont elle lui souriait. Quelque chose de mystérieux. Son imperméable était trempé, couvert de traces noires, et laissait deviner un tailleur vert.

Il se rappela aussitôt son trouble quand il avait senti ses courbes sous lui. A l'évidence, elle avait la taille fine, de longues jambes fuselées, des hanches bien dessinées et une poitrine généreuse. En fait, elle avait exactement la silhouette de ces actrices hollywoodiennes qui plaisaient tant à son père et lui faisaient dire que les mannequins de mode actuels n'étaient que « d'affreuses planches à pain ».

Pour sa part, lui-même savait également apprécier les formes féminines.

— Quel dommage que vous n'ayez pu éviter cet arbre…, lâcha-t-elle avant de s'interrompre, réalisant sans doute la maladresse de sa remarque.

— Ma priorité était de vous éviter, *vous*, rétorqua-t-il sèchement, en songeant qu'il aurait pu lui-même ne jamais survivre à l'accident.

Néanmoins, dans l'urgence, il n'avait songé qu'à protéger la jeune femme.

Apparemment, aujourd'hui, il n'était vraiment pas dans son état normal. Cette bouffée de chaleur qu'il avait sentie monter en lui quand il l'avait plaquée au sol était franchement déplacée. Inexplicable. Tout comme cette sorte de pouvoir hypnotique qu'avait sur lui ce visage lumineux.

Bon sang, il était en train de regarder partir en fumée plusieurs dizaines de milliers de livres ! Et il aurait pu mourir sur cette route perdue ! Tout cela parce que cette écervelée n'avait pas pensé une seule seconde au danger qu'elle leur avait fait courir…

L'écervelée sourit.

— Dieu merci, dit-elle, nous avons eu de la chance…

— Ah, vraiment ? coupa-t-il d'un ton sarcastique. C'est votre vision des choses ?

— Je vous demande pardon ?

— Eh bien, allez-y ! Expliquez-moi comment vous parvenez à la conclusion qu'aujourd'hui, nous avons eu *de la chance* ! Me voici dans le froid, en plein blizzard, au milieu de nulle part, ma voiture de sport favorite n'est plus qu'un souvenir et mon téléphone portable a disparu avec. Mais comme vous dites, j'ai *de la chance* !

La jeune femme resserra son imperméable sur elle.

— C'est vrai, admit-elle d'une voix douce, mais nous sommes sains et saufs tous les deux.

Ce calme et cet optimisme agacèrent Andreas qui serra les dents.

— Puis-je emprunter votre mobile ?

— Euh, je regrette mais je n'en ai pas.

— Ah. Dans ce cas, je suppose que vous habitez près d'ici. A votre avis, quelle distance devrons-nous parcourir à pied ? Plus d'un kilomètre ?

— Je ne suis pas d'ici, répondit-elle. Je n'ai aucune idée de l'endroit où nous nous trouvons.

Stupéfait, Andreas demeura silencieux quelques secondes avant de reprendre :

— Comment cela ?

— Je vis à Londres, expliqua son interlocutrice. Une amie m'a déposée en voiture ici parce que je devais passer un entretien pour un travail. Ensuite, j'ai décidé de marcher, pensant que je me trouvais non loin d'une agglomération où je pourrais prendre un taxi. Mais avec ce brouillard, je me suis perdue et n'ai jamais retrouvé la route…

— Combien de temps avez-vous marché dans la neige ? demanda-t-il.

— Environ deux heures. Et je n'ai pas vu une seule maison depuis un bon moment. C'est pourquoi j'ai voulu à tout prix attirer votre attention.

Elle claquait des dents et tout son corps tremblait, observa-t-il. Quelques gouttes pendaient au bas de sa gabardine.

— Mais… Vous êtes complètement trempée ? Comment est-ce possible ?

— Il y avait un trou de neige fondue, là où nous sommes tombés, expliqua-t-elle en grelottant.

— Vous auriez dû le dire tout de suite ! ronchonna-t-il.

C'est très dangereux quand la température descend au-dessous de zéro ! Et si vous faites une crise d'hypothermie, comment trouverai-je un médecin ? Comme si j'avais besoin de ça, pour couronner le tout !

— Je ne vous ai pas demandé de veiller sur moi, répliqua-t-elle avec verdeur. Je suis assez grande pour me débrouiller seule.

Il soupira. Le ciel était déjà sombre. Il fallait prendre une décision.

— Ecoutez, j'ai dépassé une grange un peu avant de vous croiser. Elle ne doit pas être très loin. Le mieux serait de nous y abriter au plus vite. Pensez-vous être capable de marcher jusque-là ?

— Oh oui, affirma-t-elle. Dès que nous aurons commencé à marcher, je me réchaufferai.

— Non. Vous ne vous réchaufferez que lorsque vous aurez retiré ces vêtements trempés, dit-il, sûr de lui, en passant son bras autour de la taille de la jeune femme pour la guider.

Ils baissèrent tous deux la tête pour faire front au vent froid.

Frileusement serrée contre son compagnon, Hope fit la grimace en se rappelant les derniers mots de celui-ci.

Quoi qu'il advienne, elle ne se déshabillerait pas devant un étranger ! Mais elle était touchée par sa prévenance. Sans penser à ses propres priorités, il se préoccupait avant tout de son bien-être. Et en un clin d'œil, il avait su comment réagir à la situation. C'était réconfortant. Et nouveau : elle avait rarement pu compter sur le soutien des hommes de sa famille. Or, elle n'en avait guère connu d'autres, ayant consacré tout son temps à ses études et à sa mère. Au fond, elle avait admis depuis toujours l'attitude fuyante de son père et de son frère.

Aussi, cette aide spontanée et inattendue l'étonnait autant qu'elle lui réchauffait le cœur.

Il faisait si froid…

Dans la nuit, elle ne discernait pas la moindre grange à l'horizon.

— Comment vous appelez-vous ? s'enquit-elle. Je suis Hope Evans.

— Andreas Nicolaidis, répondit-il en la conduisant vers une barrière de bois.

Puis, il s'arrêta et l'observa comme elle tentait de la franchir à grand-peine.

Dans ce tailleur étroit, paralysée par le froid, c'est à peine si elle pouvait encore mettre un pied devant l'autre. Alors, escalader une barrière…

Sans mot dire, son compagnon passa la barrière, la souleva dans ses bras et la reposa sur la terre ferme de l'autre côté.

— Oh ! je vous remercie, murmura-t-elle en rougissant, incrédule.

Ses manières de gentleman ne laissaient pas de la surprendre. Aucun homme ne l'avait ainsi prise dans ses bras depuis ses dix ans. Bien sûr, elle avait fréquenté quelques garçons au lycée, mais ses contacts avec la gent masculine s'étaient réduits à quelques baisers et à de rares invitations à des soirées. Et une fois entrée à l'université, elle avait réservé tout son temps libre à sa mère.

La grange se dressait devant eux, une grande bâtisse de brique et de bois probablement abandonnée depuis des dizaines d'années…

— Prenez garde, dit Andreas en désignant le plancher troué.

Comme elle hésitait à entrer, craignant de coincer un talon de ses escarpins dans un trou, il la souleva encore et la conduisit au fond du bâtiment, dans une zone où le plafond, comme les murs et le sol, semblaient en bon état.

— Voyons, je peux marcher, protesta-t-elle. Et je ne veux pas être un poids pour vous.

— Vous êtes plus légère qu'une plume, asséna son compagnon avant de la reposer, et je ne vous laisserai pas vous fouler une cheville.

Et aussitôt, avant qu'elle n'ait eu le temps de s'y opposer, il lui retira son imperméable d'autorité.

— Bon sang ! s'exclama-t-il en regardant son tailleur trempé qui dégouttait sur le sol.

Il ôta son propre manteau et le posa près d'elle.

— Tenez, dit-il. Mettez-le dès que vous aurez retiré tout ça.

Sans attendre sa réponse, il se retourna et fit quelques pas vers le fond de la pièce.

Hope n'avait guère le choix, elle décida de s'exécuter. En tremblant, elle défit son tailleur et, une fois en sous-vêtements, s'enveloppa dans le grand manteau de cachemire. Il était immense, les manches couvraient l'extrémité de ses mains et le bas effleurait ses chevilles. La doublure de soie la fit d'abord frissonner, mais très vite elle sentit son corps se réchauffer. C'était une sensation délicieuse… Les effluves du parfum masculin qui imprégnait le manteau lui chatouillèrent les narines.

Elle ferma chaque bouton et posa soigneusement ses affaires trempées sur le parquet.

— C'est fait, dit-elle.

— Bien. Il y a encore un âtre dans cette bâtisse. Et avec tout ce bois, nous pouvons faire du feu. Auriez-vous de quoi l'allumer ?

— Oui, dit-elle en fouillant dans son sac pour y chercher le briquet qu'elle y gardait tout au fond.

Elle ne fumait pas elle-même, mais elle avait remarqué lors de précédents entretiens d'embauche que les employeurs potentiels appréciaient qu'on leur présente du feu quand ils sortaient une cigarette.

Andreas Nicolaidis prit le briquet et se dirigea vers le mur couvert d'une pile de bois pour y choisir de petites planches et quelques bûches sèches.

Une nouvelle fois, elle s'émerveilla de son sens pratique et de son efficacité. Cet homme semblait plein de ressources. Non seulement il prenait des décisions sans tergiverser, mais il ne perdait pas de temps à gémir sur leur sort ou à pester contre la situation. Même si elle ignorait tout de sa vie, elle aurait pu parier qu'il appartenait à la catégorie des vainqueurs.

Tandis qu'il était agenouillé devant la cheminée, elle admira à la lueur du briquet sa mise soignée, son costume parfaitement coupé. En d'autres circonstances, jamais elle n'aurait osé aborder un homme aussi élégant. Ses mouvements étaient souples et précis. Il était clair qu'il avait déjà allumé de nombreux feux et qu'il savait ce qu'il faisait. Pourtant, sa voiture de sport et sa tenue chic indiquaient plutôt un homme issu de la haute société, passant ses journées dans un bureau plutôt que dans la forêt ?

Intriguée, elle s'approcha et le regarda déchirer et froisser en boules les pages d'un journal qu'il avait trouvé parmi les bûches, poser les planchettes et les bûches dessus en un petit tas et allumer le tout. En moins d'une minute, les planchettes s'enflammèrent et la pièce s'éclaira d'un halo rougeoyant.

Satisfait, Andreas leva les yeux vers sa protégée, guettant son approbation.

Fixant les flammes, la jeune femme souriait. Perdue dans son immense manteau, les mains tendues vers la flamme, elle

19

incarnait maintenant une image étrange, tout droit sortie d'un conte de fées ou d'un roman fantastique.

Pourquoi sentait-il son cœur battre si vite ?

Il se laissa hypnotiser un instant par cette scène magique : les ombres du feu qui dansaient sur le visage de la jeune femme, ses mèches claires qui prenaient maintenant des reflets mordorés. Elle ne ressemblait pas du tout aux femmes qu'il avait coutume de fréquenter, des brunes juchées sur des talons aiguilles et habillées sur mesure par les plus grands couturiers de Londres. Il ne pouvait plus détacher d'elle son regard.

Bon sang, si elle avait retiré son tailleur, elle devait n'avoir gardé sur elle que ses dessous ! La seule idée de son manteau caressant sa peau blanche le troublait... Aussi préféra-t-il détourner les yeux pour se concentrer sur le feu.

Les plus grosses bûches commençaient maintenant à répandre dans la pièce une agréable odeur de campagne.

Elle lui tendit un autre morceau de bois.

— *Efkaristo*, souffla-t-il en l'allumant.

— *Parakalo*. De rien, répondit Hope en souriant. Vous êtes Grec ?

— Oui, acquiesça-t-il en rectifiant l'ordonnancement des bûches, tandis qu'elle s'agenouillait à son tour devant le feu.

— J'adore la Grèce, dit-elle en s'asseyant. Je n'y suis allée qu'une fois, mais ce pays m'a paru sublime.

Il hocha silencieusement la tête, regardant fixement les flammes.

— Vous êtes très doué pour préparer un feu, enchaîna la jeune femme. Je suppose que vous avez l'habitude ?

— Non, répondit-il. Mais c'est un geste instinctif chez un homme.

En son for intérieur, il se demandait si le fameux instinct masculin qui l'avait guidé dans cet exercice expliquait aussi le soudain intérêt qu'il portait à cette inconnue responsable de la perte de sa Ferrari flambant neuve. Certes, la situation était des plus romantiques : la campagne enneigée, cette grange perdue dans la nuit, cette femme presque nue sous son propre manteau et éclairée par ce feu…

— Je vous ennuie, avec mes commentaires, lâcha-t-elle soudain. Excusez-moi, je suis trop bavarde.

Il leva vers elle un regard stupéfait.

— Pas du tout ! Au contraire, vous êtes de bonne compagnie. C'est moi qui ne suis pas très disert. Mais c'est ma nature, je parle peu.

Sa réponse sembla faire plaisir à Hope. Elle se redressa légèrement, effleurant son coude du sien.

— Vraiment ? insista-t-elle.

— Oui, honnêtement, affirma-t-il en s'efforçant de ne rien montrer de sa gêne après ce contact involontaire. Est-ce que vous portez des lentilles de contact colorées ?

Il se reprocha aussitôt cette question stupide, mais l'intensité de ces iris bleus l'intriguait. Ils étaient semblables à la mer Egée par temps d'été…

Etonnée, Hope haussa les sourcils et s'esclaffa.

— Ah, non ! Cela ne me viendrait pas à l'esprit ! D'ailleurs, je porte peu de maquillage.

— Vous avez un teint d'une telle transparence, chuchota-t-il. Vous n'avez pas besoin de maquillage.

Il ne pouvait plus lutter. La jeune femme disparaissait presque sous son manteau beaucoup trop grand pour elle, mais c'était comme s'il pouvait discerner les formes de son corps, les courbes de ses hanches, imaginer sa poitrine…

Il se leva et resta un moment immobile.

Malgré le feu, il faisait encore très froid, sa protégée tremblait de temps à autre.

— J'avais oublié ! s'écria-t-il. Il y a une petite flasque de rhum dans la poche intérieure droite de mon manteau.

— Ah ? fit-elle, déconcertée, en glissant une main dans la doublure tout en veillant à ce que le vêtement ne s'entrebâille pas.

— Rassurez-vous, ajouta-t-il en riant, je ne suis pas un alcoolique. Mais mon grand-père me disait toujours que l'on ne doit jamais sortir en hiver sans un petit flacon d'alcool. Je ne sais pas pourquoi je suis scrupuleusement ce conseil depuis toujours… A vrai dire, une boîte d'allumettes ou un poste émetteur pour les cas d'urgence serait sans doute plus utile !

Hope rit avec lui et lui tendit la flasque.

— Non, dit-il en hochant la tête, je n'en ai pas besoin. Mais vous avez froid, vous devriez en boire une gorgée.

— Je ne sais pas, dit-elle d'une voix hésitante. Je n'ai pas l'habitude…

Il dévissa le bouchon et lui tendit la bouteille.

— Une petite gorgée vous réchauffera sans vous enivrer, reprit-il de son ton le plus persuasif.

Hope céda et porta le flacon à ses lèvres avant de grimacer et de le reposer.

Elle avait l'impression que sa gorge était en feu, et le rhum laissait un goût amer sur sa langue. Mais un instant plus tard, une douce chaleur s'épanouit dans sa poitrine pour l'envelopper complètement.

Andreas rit encore de bon cœur.

— Eh bien, je vois que vous n'avez rien exagéré ! Visiblement, vous n'êtes pas une grande buveuse d'alcool !

— C'est le moins que l'on puisse dire, admit-elle. Mais je ne pensais pas non plus qu'il était possible d'avoir si froid.

Andreas s'approcha d'elle et l'invita à se lever. Quand ils furent face à face, il se mit à lui frotter le dos, puis les bras avant qu'elle n'ait eu le temps de protester.

— Imaginez que vous êtes dans votre lit, bien au chaud sous la couette, murmura-t-il.

Confuse, elle baissa la tête sans répondre. Elle sentait la soie chaude du manteau et les mouvements vifs de ces mains puissantes sur son corps. Même l'alcool n'avait pu lui donner cette intense sensation de bien-être…

Quand elle releva les yeux vers Andreas, leurs regards se croisèrent durant quelques secondes.

Décidément, songea-t-elle en frissonnant, le contact de ces mains viriles sur elle, la proximité du corps de cet homme et son regard faisaient naître en elle des émotions inconnues. A moins que ce ne fût que le froid ?

Mais non. Son cœur battait violemment et elle respirait avec difficulté. Les frissons qui couraient comme une myriade électrique le long de son dos gagnaient sa nuque, et elle se sentait proche du vertige. Il lui semblait que les frictions de son compagnon se muaient en caresses plus lentes…

Durant une seconde, Hope crut qu'elle allait chanceler. Elle soutint le regard noir plongé dans le sien. Des éclats d'or y brillaient, et elle ne put s'empêcher de battre des cils comme si elle était éblouie.

C'était impossible, songea-t-elle. Non, cela ne pouvait pas arriver… Et pourtant, une petite voix lui soufflait qu'il ne pouvait en être autrement. Qu'il était trop tard. Que c'était ce qu'elle désirait au fond d'elle.

Le visage d'Andreas se pencha lentement sur le sien, et l'instant d'après elle sentit ses lèvres avides s'emparer des siennes. Tout son corps vibra tandis qu'elle s'abandonnait à ce baiser. Elle ne sentait plus le froid. Puissantes et douces, les lèvres d'Andreas cherchaient les siennes, et elle répondait à son étreinte avec une ardeur inconnue. Son cœur battait avec une violence inouïe, chaque parcelle de son corps s'embrasait, et un torrent furieux courait dans ses veines. Le temps s'était arrêté, le monde avait cessé d'exister, et elle voulait savourer pour l'éternité ce plaisir qu'elle n'avait jamais connu auparavant.

Enfin leurs lèvres se séparèrent, et Hope, à bout de souffle, reprit lentement sa respiration. Elle était troublée par la manière dont elle s'était abandonnée à l'étreinte de son compagnon sans y opposer de résistance. La confusion gagnait son esprit, et elle fixa le sol sans bouger.

Andreas recula d'un pas et détourna le regard.

— *Theos mou !* soupira-t-il. Je regrette. Je n'avais pas l'intention de… Je n'aurais pas dû, pardonnez-moi.

Elle se mordit la lèvre. Elle se sentait très vulnérable, tout à coup.

Pourquoi se comportait-il ainsi ? Ce qu'elle venait de vivre était un moment d'une intensité qu'elle n'aurait pas osé imaginer. Un instant magique, un baiser plus exquis que tout ce qu'elle avait connu jusqu'alors. Certes, elle n'avait pas fréquenté beaucoup de garçons, mais ce n'était pas la première fois qu'elle échangeait un baiser ! Mais jamais un tel feu n'avait brûlé en elle quand elle avait pressé ses lèvres contre celles d'un homme.

Stupéfaite de sa propre audace, elle se rapprocha de lui.

— Vous êtes marié ? demanda-t-elle.

— Non.

— Fiancé ?

— Non.

— Dans ce cas, je ne vois pas pourquoi vous me présentez vos excuses, déclara-t-elle avec défi.

— Je vous ai choquée, dit Andreas en cherchant son regard.

Elle rougit et détourna rapidement les yeux.

— Non, souffla-t-elle.

Elle ressentait bien des choses, elle était assaillie de

pensées et de sensations contradictoires, mais elle n'était pas « choquée ». Cette rencontre inattendue, cette grange, ce tête-à-tête devant la cheminée lui avaient sans doute fait perdre l'esprit. Pourtant, elle ne regrettait rien.

— Vous savez, j'avais prévu de vous laisser seule ici, avoua Andreas à voix basse.

A ces mots, elle sursauta.

— Quoi ? Pour quoi faire ? Où vous seriez-vous parti ?

— Je voulais trouver une maison avant qu'il ne fasse trop sombre. Mais c'est trop tard, maintenant.

Elle leva les yeux au ciel.

— C'est idiot. Sans votre manteau, vous seriez mort de froid avant d'avoir fait deux cents mètres. Mieux vaut attendre demain matin.

Elle se tourna vers la fenêtre qui donnait sur le chemin qu'ils avaient arpenté ensemble. Il était impossible de discerner quoi que ce fût, pas même un arbre.

Elle retourna sans mot dire près du feu puis s'assit le plus près possible et tendit les paumes vers les flammes.

Andreas l'imita et se tourna vers elle en souriant.

— Parlez-moi de cet entretien d'embauche, suggéra-t-il. De quel travail s'agissait-il ?

— D'un poste d'assistante au département de créations d'un grand magasin de Londres, répondit-elle en soupirant. Une de mes amies connaissait le directeur des ressources humaines du magasin. Quand je l'ai appelé, il était en voyages d'affaires mais avait besoin de quelqu'un très vite. C'est pourquoi j'avais rendez-vous chez lui. Mais l'entretien n'a pas eu lieu. Dès que je suis arrivée, il m'a annoncé qu'il avait déjà trouvé quelqu'un et que le contrat était signé.

Andréas laissa échapper un hoquet de stupéfaction.

— Comment ? Vous voulez dire qu'il n'a même pas eu

la politesse de vous prévenir et qu'il vous a laissée faire le déplacement pour rien ?

— Oui, admit-elle. Il m'a présenté ses plus plates excuses, mais ma déception n'en était pas moins vive. Bah, après tout, c'est la vie…

— Vous êtes très indulgente ! répliqua-t-il, visiblement outré. Comment gagnez-vous votre vie en ce moment, si vous m'autorisez à vous poser cette question ?

— Je travaille à mi-temps dans un secrétariat. Il est très difficile de faire ses preuves dans le milieu du design. Mais je ne perds pas espoir.

Toutefois, sa dernière mésaventure faisait naître de nouveaux doutes en elle. Peut-être ne parviendrait-elle jamais à trouver un emploi dans cette branche ? Peut-être valait-il mieux qu'elle renonce définitivement au design pour chercher un poste dans l'administration ?

Allons, les circonstances ne se prêtaient guère à ce genre de réflexion.

— Et vous, où alliez-vous quand nous nous sommes croisés ? demanda-t-elle.

— Je rentrais à Londres. C'est là que je…

— Pourquoi m'avez-vous embrassée ?

Hope se mordit la lèvre, si embarrassée qu'elle aurait voulu disparaître sous terre.

La question avait jailli de manière si inattendue qu'Andreas garda le silence quelques instants.

Elle-même ne savait pas comment les mots lui avaient échappé. Il était pourtant trop tard pour les effacer.

— A votre avis ? demanda Andreas de sa voix douce et grave en plongeant son regard de braise dans le sien.

Elle haussa les épaules pour signifier qu'elle n'en savait rien.

— A vrai dire, je ne le sais pas moi-même, avoua-t-il. Mais je vous trouve très attirante.

— Vraiment ? s'étonna-t-elle.

— Oui. Votre beauté est singulière. Et je suis un connaisseur.

Elle rougit et réprima le sourire qui lui montait aux lèvres.

Naturellement, un homme tel que lui ne pouvait que collectionner les conquêtes ! Non seulement il avait un charme fou, une élégance à couper le souffle, un regard qui vous faisait tourner la tête, mais ses baisers étaient irrésistibles.

Même si cette révélation n'était pas pour lui plaire, elle était touchée par le compliment qu'il venait de lui faire. Jamais un homme ne lui avait parlé ainsi, de cette manière à la fois directe et sincère. Elle savait qu'il pensait ce qu'il disait, elle le lisait dans ses yeux, elle l'avait senti quand il l'avait pressée contre lui, quand il l'avait embrassée comme si sa vie en dépendait.

Et cette sensation extraordinaire, ce désir fou qui l'avait submergée, elle voulait le connaître encore…

— Hum, reprit-elle en s'éclaircissant la gorge. Vous ne m'avez pas encore dit quel est votre métier.

— Je suis investisseur, répondit-il avec flegme.

— Ah ? Dans ce cas, je suppose que vous passez toutes vos journées enfermé dans un bureau à étudier des listes de chiffres… Ce n'est pas ennuyeux ?

Andreas répondit à la jeune femme par un sourire indéchiffrable.

C'était la première fois qu'une femme osait aborder le sujet de son activité avec cette naïveté, cette franchise. D'ordinaire, il avait droit à des hochements de tête admiratifs qui masquaient un profond désintérêt. Il appréciait le naturel de Hope.

Elle se retourna vers l'endroit où elle avait posé son sac à main.

— Voulez-vous du chocolat ? demanda-t-elle en brandissant soudain une tablette. J'en ai toujours sur moi…

— Oui, je veux bien. Avant qu'il ne soit fondu, précisa-t-il.

La jeune femme écarta son bras du feu et rit.

Amusé, il lui ôta le chocolat des mains pour en casser un morceau. Puis il étudia ce regard turquoise et cette bouche pulpeuse si proches en s'efforçant d'ignorer le désir qui montait de nouveau en lui. Le goût exquis de leur baiser passionné lui revint à la mémoire.

D'une main tremblante, il glissa le morceau de chocolat entre les lèvres de Hope et frissonna quand elle ferma les yeux.

— Mmm, fit-elle.

L'expression de plaisir qui illuminait son visage ajouta à son trouble.

Réagissait-elle ainsi quand elle faisait l'amour ?

Non, il ne se le demandait pas, il voulait le savoir. Il *fallait* qu'il le sache !

— Je crois que je ferais n'importe quoi pour du chocolat, dit Hope à voix basse en rouvrant les yeux.

Quand elle découvrit le regard d'Andreas fixé sur elle et qu'elle y lut l'intensité de son désir, elle déglutit avec peine.

Une étrange bouffée de chaleur monta en elle. C'était comme si son corps obéissait à des pulsions inconnues de son esprit, et les battements frénétiques de son cœur lui disaient qu'elle n'avait plus aucun contrôle d'elle-même.

Elle sentit la main de son compagnon se poser sur sa taille, avant qu'il ne l'attire brutalement vers lui et ne s'empare encore de ses lèvres.

Cette fois, elle chancelait, elle allait tomber... Mais il resserra son étreinte et lui caressa les cheveux tout en approfondissant son baiser.

— Je t'achèterai du chocolat tous les jours, murmura-t-il à son oreille avant de lui déposer une myriade de baisers brûlants dans le cou.

D'un geste d'une douceur infinie, il déboutonna le premier bouton de son manteau pour poser ses lèvres sur sa peau frémissante.

— Il faut que tu me dises de m'arrêter, reprit-il d'une voix rauque. Parce que je ne pourrai bientôt plus contrôler mon désir. Si tu ne veux pas, dis-le-moi maintenant...

Au lieu de la faire réagir, ces paroles avaient un pouvoir hypnotique sur elle, songea Hope. Déjà, elle sentait l'ivresse du plaisir l'envahir et penchait la tête en arrière pour qu'il l'embrasse encore, pour sentir le contact de sa bouche sur sa peau nue.

Elle avait si souvent rêvé du moment où elle ferait l'amour pour la première fois !

La plupart de ses amies avaient déjà connu cette expérience depuis longtemps, et elle avait eu peur de se sentir gauche et timide lorsque ce moment viendrait enfin pour elle. Mais à sa propre stupéfaction, elle n'avait rien imaginé, ne s'y était préparée en aucune façon. Or, tous ses instincts féminins s'éveillaient maintenant en elle avec une ardeur insoupçonnée...

Sans doute parce que son imagination n'aurait jamais pu lui soumettre l'image de cette nuit unique avec un inconnu, dans la campagne enneigée ?

Oh non, elle ne résisterait pas ! Le désir l'embrasait et elle voulait s'y abandonner.

Avec audace, elle défit elle-même le deuxième bouton

du manteau qui l'enveloppait et se cambra sous les caresses d'Andreas. Quand elle sentit ses mains se poser sur ses seins, elle gémit.

Un instant plus tard, celui-ci faisait sauter l'agrafe de son soutien-gorge et laissait échapper un soupir rauque.

— *Theos mou*... Tu es si belle ! C'est la première fois qu'une telle chose m'arrive, balbutia-t-il avant de contempler avec émerveillement les deux globes pâles dont il dessinait lentement les contours de ses doigts.

Puis, d'un geste délicat, il l'allongea sur le sol et déboutonna entièrement son manteau.

Elle était nue devant lui, à peine vêtue de son slip, mais tout son corps vivrait d'ondes violentes, et le désir la brûlait.

— Pour moi aussi, c'est une première, chuchota-t-elle en frissonnant.

Andreas caressa lentement ses jambes et la rondeur de ses hanches avant d'embrasser doucement son ventre.

— Nous sommes complètement fous, souffla-t-il d'un air égaré. Dis-moi de m'arrêter et je te promets que...

— Chut. Ne gâche pas tout, dit-elle tout bas en tirant sur sa veste pour qu'il la retire.

Il s'exécuta et ôta également sa chemise avant de l'embrasser encore.

Ivre de désir, elle laissa ses mains courir sur son torse tiède, découvrant sa peau ferme et lisse, ses muscles parfaitement dessinés, ses épaules puissantes... Glissant ses doigts dans le fin duvet noir qui recouvrait ses pectoraux, elle soupira et sentit une décharge de plaisir en elle comme Andreas venait de prendre un de ses tétons durcis entre ses lèvres. Sa langue avide l'invitait à l'abandon total, ses caresses étaient si exquises qu'elle aurait voulu arrêter le temps pour rester toujours ainsi, toute à lui, offerte à son étreinte.

Comment avait-elle pu se transformer de manière aussi

radicale en quelques instants ? Pourquoi cet homme avait-il le don de mettre ainsi ses sens en émoi, quand elle n'avait jamais connu un désir si violent auparavant ?

Cela n'avait aucune importance, se dit-elle aussitôt. Plus rien n'avait d'importance. Le monde n'existait plus et sa vie tout entière se concentrait dans le plaisir extrême du moment.

— Tu as un corps sublime, murmura-t-il à son oreille tandis qu'il aventurait ses mains entre ses cuisses et frôlait la mince étoffe de son slip.

D'un geste fiévreux, elle déboutonna son pantalon et l'invita avec impatience à le retirer.

Il poussa un grognement et jeta loin de lui ses derniers vêtements avant de lui ôter doucement sa culotte.

Nus l'un contre l'autre, ils tremblaient.

Andreas posa ses lèvres sur le ventre de Hope et descendit vers ses cuisses, qu'elle ouvrit langoureusement.

— Oh, Andreas ! gémit-elle.

— Je ne peux plus attendre, souffla-t-il en caressant une dernière fois la peau satinée de ses cuisses, avant de s'enfouir en elle en une pulsion irrésistible.

La jeune femme poussa un petit cri, étouffé par son propre grognement, mais il interrompit aussitôt son mouvement.

— Tu… Tu es vierge ? s'écria-t-il, la respiration coupée. Mais… Il fallait me le dire !

— Je t'en prie, ne t'arrête pas, dit Hope d'une voix implorante.

Il observa son visage épanoui par le plaisir, plongea son regard dans la profondeur de ce bleu qui menaçait de l'engloutir, et il sut que leur désir était le même. Oui, il devait s'enfoncer avec elle dans ces abîmes vers lesquels ils étaient aspirés.

Dans un lent va-et-vient, ils ondulèrent ensemble sur un rythme envoûtant, jusqu'aù plaisir le plus intense.

Leur extase avait été si violente qu'ils restèrent enlacés plusieurs minutes, le souffle court, incapables de proférer une parole.

Puis, avec tendresse, il déposa un baiser sur le front de Hope.

— Pourquoi ne m'as-tu pas dit que tu étais vierge ?

— Parce que ce sont mes affaires, répondit-elle doucement.

— Désormais, ce sont aussi les miennes, rétorqua-t-il. Tu vis à Londres ?

— Oui. Je partage un appartement avec une amie.

— Ah… Dans ce cas, je crois que tu vas bientôt déménager, si tu le veux bien.

— Comment cela ? interrogea-t-elle en lui décochant un sourire malicieux. Pourquoi aurais-je besoin de déménager ?

Il l'embrassa encore avec voracité avant de déclarer d'une voix assurée :

— Parce que je te le demande et que tu ne pourras pas longtemps me le refuser.

Elle lui sourit, confiante.

1.

Deux ans plus tard

Hope jeta un coup d'œil distrait à sa montre.

Confortablement installée dans un café de Londres, elle attendait Vanessa, sa meilleure amie. Mais ses pensées étaient loin. Tout son esprit était concentré sur Andreas. Elle se demandait comment célébrer le deuxième anniversaire de leur rencontre.

Devait-elle le conduire dans la campagne et retrouver cette grange ? Non, il n'apprécierait pas. Il faisait très froid, et Andreas aimait avant tout le confort.

— Désolée de ce retard ! s'exclama Vanessa d'une voix essoufflée en surgissant soudain devant elle.

Hope sursauta et lui fit la grimace. Après quoi elles s'embrassèrent, puis son amie posa son appareil photo, s'installa face à elle et la dévisagea d'un air mi-moqueur, mi-intrigué.

— Si tu te laisses encore pousser les cheveux, dit-elle, je vais finir par croire que tu nourris le fantasme de devenir une princesse.

Hope haussa les sourcils.

— Que veux-tu dire ?

— Tu sais bien, *La princesse aux cheveux d'or* ! Ce conte

33

de fées dans lequel l'héroïne lance sa natte du haut d'une tour pour que son prince charmant vienne la délivrer…

Elle sourit en glissant une main dans ses longues mèches.

— C'est vrai, admit-elle en riant. Andreas aime que mes cheveux soient très longs… Et je trouve que ça m'affine le visage.

Vanessa opina et se commanda un café.

Comme chaque fois, toutes deux se mirent à bavarder avec animation sans voir passer le temps. Hope était heureuse de revoir celle avec qui elle avait autrefois partagé un studio.

Vanessa était désormais une photographe en pleine ascension et vivait dans un grand appartement de Chelsea. Elle débordait d'énergie et son enthousiasme était communicatif. Sans doute ces qualités lui venaient-elles de l'enfance aventureuse qu'elle avait connue ? Elle avait des parents artistes qui déménageaient souvent et organisaient sans cesse de grandes fêtes auxquelles ils conviaient leurs amis de tout poil, peintres, danseurs, comédiens. Le père de Vanessa, dessinateur, avait légué son talent à sa fille qui avait choisi la photographie pour exprimer sa propre sensibilité. Mais la jeune femme avait également souffert de cette vie instable. Elle déclarait souvent qu'elle ne pourrait jamais quitter Londres et ses amis.

— Et ton prince charmant, demanda Vanessa après lui avoir conté ses dernières frasques. Comment va-t-il ?

Le regard de Hope s'alluma aussitôt d'un éclat particulier.

— Andreas va bien, murmura-t-elle avec ravissement. Il est merveilleux… Oh, bien sûr, j'aimerais le voir davantage. Son travail l'accapare. Mais il me téléphone chaque fois qu'il part à l'étranger pour ses affaires.

— Je vois, répliqua Vanessa d'un ton ironique. Il t'a offert un portable pour t'y enchaîner et vérifier à tout instant que tu lui appartiens complètement.

— Je ne crois pas, répondit Hope en riant. Il aime simplement me parler et savoir où je suis. C'est son côté méditerranéen. Et puis… Te rends-tu comptes qu'il y aura deux ans dans dix jours que nous sommes ensemble ?

Vanessa sembla assez impressionnée.

— Déjà ? C'est formidable ! Mais…

Hope s'étonna de voir son amie serrer les lèvres. Elle hésitait visiblement à poursuivre.

— Mais quoi ? reprit-elle d'un ton encourageant.

— Mais il ne s'engage toujours pas, à ce que je vois, dit Vanessa. Tu adores cet homme, et je ne nie pas qu'il te montre à quel point il est attaché à toi, mais je ne comprends pas comment tu peux accepter cette relation : tu es une femme cachée. Il ne t'emmène jamais dans ses dîners.

— Les médias s'intéressent beaucoup à lui, expliqua Hope avec un soupir. Il préfère éviter de donner l'occasion aux journalistes de voler des photos. D'ailleurs, je n'aimerais pas non plus me voir dans les tabloïd.

Et de plus, elle ne tenait pas à gaspiller le temps précieux qu'Andreas lui consacrait dans des soirées mondaines. Au contraire, elle voulait savourer chacun de leurs tête-à-tête…

— Tu as raison, reprit-elle après avoir observé un court silence. Je suis une femme cachée. Mais je m'en félicite plutôt. Et aujourd'hui, je songe simplement à célébrer notre deuxième anniversaire.

— Il n'a rien fait l'an dernier pour marquer l'événement, n'est-ce pas ? s'enquit Vanessa.

— Oh, tu sais, il n'avait pas conscience que nous étions ensemble depuis une année ! J'aurais dû m'attendre à ce qu'il n'y pense pas spontanément, c'était à moi de le lui rappeler. Les hommes sont rarement doués pour les anniversaires…

— Mais puisque tu n'as rien dit, a-t-il fini par le mentionner ?

Hope hocha la tête en signe de dénégation.

Vanessa soupira.

— Ecoute, laisse-moi te donner un conseil dans ce cas. Si tu veux poursuivre cette relation avec Andreas Nicolaidis, résiste au désir de mentionner votre deuxième anniversaire.

— Pourquoi ?

— Parce que s'il réalise que vous êtes ensemble depuis tout ce temps, il risque de prendre peur.

Mal à l'aise, Hope se tortilla sur son siège et fixa son amie.

— Je ne comprends pas. Qu'essaies-tu de me dire, au juste ?

Vanessa se laissa retomber sur le dossier de sa chaise et laissa échapper un long soupir.

— J'essaie de te dire que tu perds ton temps avec cet homme, lâcha-t-elle enfin. Il n'est même pas venu te féliciter le soir où tu as reçu ce prix de design !

— Ce n'était pas sa faute, rétorqua Hope. Son avion avait été retardé.

— Vraiment ? reprit Vanessa d'un ton lourd de sous-entendus. Il ne semble pas porter un intérêt démesuré à ton travail… Pourtant, il t'a fallu beaucoup de détermination pour devenir responsable des achats d'accessoires pour cette créatrice.

Hope haussa les épaules.

— Il me demande souvent si tout se passe bien. Il est vrai qu'il ne me pose pas beaucoup de questions sur mon métier, mais le design de sacs à main suscite rarement la curiosité masculine. Et puis…

— Il ne t'a jamais présentée à un seul membre de sa famille ! coupa Vanessa. Ni même à ses amis. Quand il t'emmène dîner au restaurant, il choisit toujours un lieu qui ne peut être fréquenté ni par des paparazzi ni par aucune personne de sa connaissance. Sa vie professionnelle et familiale est complètement séparée de celle qu'il mène avec toi, il te garde dans une petite boîte comme si tu lui appartenais corps et biens. Il te considère comme sa maîtresse…

— C'est faux ! s'écria Hope. Andreas ne me considère pas comme sa maîtresse ! D'ailleurs, il n'a jamais cherché à me couvrir de luxueux cadeaux ni à faire de moi sa chose, comme tu sembles l'insinuer. Certes, je vis dans ce magnifique appartement dont il est propriétaire, mais je paie tout le reste seule !

— Voyons, Hope, ce n'était pas ce que je voulais dire. Je te rappelais simplement qu'il ne te présente pas comme sa fiancée à son entourage…

— Mais il tient beaucoup à moi, je le sais ! intervint-elle avec vivacité. Il ne cesse de me le montrer.

Son amie lui lança un regard inquiet, avant de lui sourire pour lui montrer qu'elle la soutenait.

— Je n'en doute pas, reprit-elle. Mais cela paraît bien naturel. Tu lui offres tout ce dont rêve un homme tel que lui : ton soutien, ta chaleur, ton amour… Sans jamais l'interroger sur votre avenir ! Je me demande seulement s'il n'en abuse pas.

— Non ! Il…

— Hope, je t'en prie, cesse de vouloir le défendre et pense un peu à toi. A-t-il jamais prononcé les mots mariage, famille ? Avez-vous évoqué l'idée d'avoir des enfants ?

Vaincue par ces mots directs, Hope ne sut que répondre.

— A tout moment d'une relation, tu as le droit de demander à ton compagnon où vous en êtes, insista Vanessa d'une voix plus douce.

Cette phrase résonna encore longtemps dans l'esprit de Hope tandis que la conversation dérivait sur des sujets plus légers.

Une fois seule, en fin d'après-midi, elle fut incapable de se rappeler ce que Vanessa lui avait dit après ce commentaire.

Elle n'en voulait pas à son amie de s'être montrée si directe : Vanessa ne souhaitait que son bonheur et avait su lui témoigner sa fidélité et son affection en maintes occasions. Au fond, elle aurait pris la même initiative si son amie avait été à sa place. Mais désormais, elle était assaillie de doutes. Depuis deux ans, elle avait l'impression de vivre un rêve. Elle adorait Andreas, qui lui donnait également toutes les preuves de sa tendresse et de son attachement envers elle. Sauf une, elle devait en convenir : jamais ils n'avaient évoqué leur avenir commun.

Et il ne lui avait jamais dit « je t'aime ».

Andreas était un homme très pudique sur ses sentiments. Il savait la serrer dans ses bras et la faire tournoyer quand il rentrait de voyage et qu'ils se retrouvaient. Montrer ses émotions était une chose, mais quand il s'agissait d'en parler…

Pourtant, elle entendait encore chaque mot, chaque remarque de Vanessa.

Son amie avait raison, Andreas ne l'avait jamais emmenée en Grèce. Il avait une jeune sœur, Elyssa, qui s'était mariée trois ans plus tôt et vivait désormais à Londres avec son mari et leurs deux fils. Il ne la lui avait jamais présentée.

Et à la vérité, il n'avait jamais non plus évoqué leur avenir. Le mariage et les enfants étaient des sujets de conversation qu'ils n'abordaient pas.

Elle avait toujours pensé qu'il était préférable de connaître parfaitement l'homme de sa vie avant de s'engager pour toujours. Sa mère lui avait souvent répété qu'un mariage reposait sur la confiance mutuelle et que se marier sans avoir fait l'expérience de la vie commune était une véritable folie. Et elle avait jugé ce discours très sage. Aussi ne s'était-elle jamais inquiétée de la manière dont elle vivait son amour avec Andreas. Ils étaient un couple moderne, ils vivaient ensemble, ils s'aimaient, ces deux années avaient passé à toute vitesse… Mais ils ne songeaient pas au futur.

Hope sentit son cœur s'emballer dans sa poitrine.

Ne pas évoquer l'avenir, voilà qui était une *folie* ! Elle n'allait tout de même pas passer toute sa vie à espérer qu'Andreas se souvienne de leurs anniversaires et faire comme s'ils pouvaient éternellement vivre hors du monde, sans connaître les membres de leurs familles respectives et en faisant comme si le mariage et les enfants n'existaient pas !

Sur le pas de la porte de son immense appartement avec terrasse, elle essuya la larme qui roulait sur sa joue.

Même si Andreas semblait avoir évité la question de l'engagement, cela ne signifiait pas qu'il ne l'aimait pas, elle en était persuadée. Ni qu'il la considérait comme une maîtresse. Elle ne pouvait pas déclarer qu'elle était sa fiancée, mais Elle était… la femme qu'il aimait.

Et il était d'une nature réservée, voilà tout.

Pourtant, si Andreas partageait avec elle cet appartement, il était également propriétaire, en plein cœur de Londres, d'une vaste propriété qu'il ne lui avait jamais fait visiter. Il disait qu'il n'aimait pas s'y trouver parce qu'elle était éloignée de son bureau et que nombre de ses cousins y séjournaient régulièrement. A la vérité, c'était précisément parce que sa famille y venait qu'il ne voulait pas la lui montrer !

Soudain, Hope porta un regard radicalement différent sur les deux années qu'elle venait de vivre avec Andreas. Comment avait-elle pu s'abandonner si naïvement à son bonheur ? Elle avait cru que leur relation était merveilleuse, mais les remarques de Vanessa lui avaient permis d'entrevoir la réalité. Elle était dessillée. Andreas la considérait comme son jouet, rien de plus !

Plongée dans ses sombres pensées, elle sursauta en entendant sonner son téléphone portable.

C'était Andreas, constata-t-elle en voyant s'afficher son nom sur l'écran.

Après un instant d'hésitation, elle décrocha.

— Allô, ma chérie ? Je t'appelle de Genève. Pourquoi ton téléphone était-il indisponible durant des heures ? demanda-t-il d'un ton paniqué. Je commençais à m'inquiéter !

— J'étais avec Vanessa, répondit-elle. J'ai dû oublier de le rebrancher, c'est tout.

— Ah. Je serai avec toi demain soir à 8 heures, ma chérie, poursuivit-il. Dis-moi quelque chose...

Hope soupira, exaspérée. Dès qu'Andreas avait cinq minutes entre deux réunions, il l'appelait. Mais elle comprenait maintenant que c'était par pur ennui. Il comptait sur elle pour le distraire, voilà tout !

— De quoi veux-tu que je te parle ? demanda-t-elle sèchement.

— Eh bien, je ne sais pas, de ce que tu as fait aujourd'hui. Etes-vous allées faire du shopping avec Vanessa ? As-tu acheté une nouvelle robe ? Parle-moi du temps qu'il fait, de ton incorrigible passion pour le chocolat, de la manière dont tu sais voir le ciel bleu et clair même quand il pleut, des gens que tu as croisés dans la rue... De tout, de rien.

Un court silence pesa sur la ligne.

— Je ne comprends pas, enchaîna Andreas. D'habitude, j'ai droit à un splendide, à un merveilleux déluge d'informations !

Hope sentit le rouge lui monter aux joues. Se comportait-elle vraiment ainsi ? Comme une bavarde invétérée qui, à force de parler toute la journée, avait oublié d'ouvrir les yeux sur l'état de sa relation avec l'homme qu'elle aimait ?

— Hope ? Quelque chose ne va pas ?

— Non, tout va bien... Mais j'ai un peu mal à la tête, excuse-moi. Je crois que je vais aller prendre une aspirine.

— Tu m'inquiètes. Si tu es malade, peut-être vaudrait-il mieux appeler un médecin ?

40

— Non, je te remercie, je ne suis pas malade. Ça va passer. A demain soir, Andreas, dit-elle plus doucement avant de raccrocher.

Andreas reposa son portable devant lui et le contempla quelques instants en silence, fronçant les sourcils.

Visiblement, Hope était contrariée. Or, la jeune femme n'était pas sujette aux sautes d'humeur. Avait-il dit quelque chose qui lui avait déplu ? Mais quoi ? Quand elle avait des soucis dans son travail ou dans quelque domaine que ce soit, elle avait l'habitude de lui en faire part. Elle lui avait toujours demandé d'en faire de même, et il lui en était reconnaissant. Quel genre de problème pouvait-elle avoir rencontré pour ne pas souhaiter s'en ouvrir à lui ?

Bien sûr, s'il le voulait vraiment, il pourrait obtenir la réponse tout de suite. Il lui suffisait d'appeler les deux agents de sécurité qu'il avait recrutés et qui ne quittaient jamais Hope d'une semelle. Dans un premier temps, il avait voulu l'en avertir, car il ne s'agissait que de la protéger. Comme la majeure partie des grandes personnalités de la finance, il recevait chaque année toutes sortes de menaces sous forme de lettres anonymes, aussi avait-il sollicité les services d'une agence privée. Pourquoi n'avait-il finalement jamais révélé à Hope qu'elle était surveillée vingt-quatre heures sur vingt-quatre ? Il n'avait pas voulu l'effrayer inutilement… De toute façon, il n'avait jamais posé la moindre question aux deux hommes en mission. C'eût été profiter abusivement de la situation. Et il avait pleinement confiance en Hope.

Pourtant, quelque chose n'allait pas et elle refusait de lui dire de quoi il s'agissait.

Il frémit au plus profond de son être à l'idée qu'elle pouvait être tombée amoureuse d'un autre homme.

A cet instant, une lumière rouge se mit à clignoter sur le mur face à lui, et il soupira. La conférence allait reprendre. Il fallait oublier tout cela...

Hope n'avait pas perdu l'habitude de contempler sa garde-robe pendant des heures quand elle attendait le retour d'Andreas. Elle voulait toujours l'impressionner, lui plaire, lire dans son regard le désir et l'admiration. En dépit des réflexions de Vanessa qu'elle avait ressassées nuit et jour durant les dernières heures, elle se sentait maintenant gagnée par une excitation familière.

Andrea serait là bientôt, enfin...

Sans plus hésiter, elle choisit sa robe de soie bleue et l'enfila avant de vérifier dans le grand miroir qu'elle ne lui arrondissait pas trop les hanches.

Non, décida-t-elle, elle ne laisserait plus tous ces doutes stupides la tourmenter. Dans quelques instants, l'homme qu'elle aimait la serrerait dans ses bras et lui ferait connaître encore cette folle passion qui lui faisait chavirer le cœur...

Vanessa, qui avait hélas connu quelques mésaventures amoureuses, avait simplement voulu la mettre en garde parce qu'elle-même ne parvenait plus à faire confiance aux hommes. C'était bien légitime. Mais elle avait à peine croisé Andreas en deux occasions : elle ne le connaissait pas vraiment et ignorait tout de leur bonheur. En fait, si son amie avait eu la chance de faire plus ample connaissance avec lui, elle aurait compris aussitôt quel homme merveilleux c'était.

Il tenait les paparazzi à distance et faisait tout pour protéger sa vie privée des regards indiscrets. Elle ne pouvait que s'en féliciter, car à plusieurs reprises des journaux avaient ressorti d'anciennes photographies d'Andreas au bras de grandes femmes brunes à la taille mannequin. Elle en avait été blessée, même si elle avait toujours su qu'Andreas avait collectionné les conquêtes féminines avant leur rencontre. Peut-être Vanessa était-elle tombée sur ces tabloïd ? Dans ce cas, elle s'était inquiétée de savoir son amie amoureuse d'un don Juan.

Devant le miroir de la salle de bains, Hope se brossa soigneusement les cheveux.

Andreas était exactement l'homme dont elle avait toujours rêvé, songeait-elle. Il était fort, grand, généreux, attentif, passionné. Il lui arrivait de passer outre ses propres goûts uniquement pour lui faire plaisir. Par exemple, elle adorait les pique-niques. Eh bien, même s'il ne partageait pas son enthousiasme pour les déjeuners sur l'herbe, il avait accepté en plusieurs occasions de se prêter au jeu. Parce qu'il l'aimait. D'ailleurs, il n'aimait pas non plus les promenades, mais il l'avait emmenée à Paris et à Rome, où ils avaient marché ensemble durant des heures pour qu'elle satisfasse sa passion pour l'architecture.

Elle l'aimait de tout son cœur, de toute son âme. Oh, certes, il n'était pas parfait ! Mais elle n'avait pas envie de songer à ses défauts. Non, elle n'allait pas porter un regard négatif sur une relation qui lui apportait autant de bonheur.

Dès que son avion s'était posé, il l'avait appelée.

— Je compte chaque minute, avait-elle soufflé.

Il lui téléphona encore quand sa limousine resta coincée dans le trafic londonien.

— Je n'en peux plus, avait-elle murmuré. Dépêche-toi !

Alors qu'elle lissait sa robe et vérifiait une dernière fois sa coiffure dans le miroir, son téléphone se remit à sonner.

— Tu ne peux pas savoir à quel point tu m'as manqué, dit Andreas.

— Où es-tu ?

— Devant la cage d'ascenseur. J'arrive.

Incapable de réprimer plus longtemps son excitation, elle

43

courut dans le salon et se passa une main fiévreuse sur les bras. Elle frissonnait. Quand la porte s'ouvrit, elle sentit son cœur battre la chamade et se précipita.

— Ma chérie ! s'écria Andreas en lâchant sa valise et ses journaux, avant de la soulever dans ses bras et de la couvrir de baisers.

Ravie, elle caressa ses cheveux noirs, contempla son regard illuminé de joie, passa un doigt sur ses joues râpeuses et ferma les yeux quand elle sentit ses lèvres se presser sur les siennes.

La même vague de chaleur violente montait en elle chaque fois que cet homme la serrait contre lui. Ces moments étaient magiques.

Elle se laissa envelopper par les effluves de son parfum viril et leva encore un regard émerveillé sur son visage si séduisant…

— Que tu es belle, Hope !

— Andreas…

— Je regrette vraiment que tu ne puisses pas voyager avec moi, souffla-t-il à son oreille. Nous aurions plus de temps à partager tous les deux. J'aimerais que tu y penses. Tu pourrais renoncer à ta carrière dans le design, juste pour un moment ?

Elle se raidit sensiblement et fronça les sourcils. Il n'était pas question qu'elle abandonne ce qu'elle avait conquis si difficilement. D'ailleurs, elle était loin d'avoir atteint son objectif : être capable de monter seule sa ligne d'accessoires de mode. Mais l'idée de demeurer près d'Andreas et de visiter tous les pays du monde avec lui était pour le moins tentante.

— Je ne peux pas, répondit-elle.

Comme s'il n'avait pas entendu, il la poussa contre un mur et l'embrassa avec une rage qui la laissa le souffle court.

Elle sentait ses mains courir fiévreusement sur ses hanches, autour de sa taille, et des frissons la parcouraient des pieds à la tête. Ses lèvres sensuelles et douces lui donnaient le vertige, tandis qu'il resserrait son étreinte et pressait son buste puissant sur ses seins. Bientôt, elle sentit l'ardeur de son désir contre son ventre et laissa échapper un soupir. Mais aussitôt, le rituel qui était le leur depuis presque deux ans lui revint à la mémoire. Avant qu'ils ne s'abandonnent à leur désir, il fallait…

— Andreas, coupe ton téléphone, dit-elle.

— Plus tard, grogna-t-il en lui mordant le lobe de l'oreille.

— Non, maintenant, insista-t-elle.

De mauvais gré, Andreas chercha son mobile dans la poche de sa veste et l'éteignit avant de le poser à portée de main sur une console.

Puis il se retourna vers elle.

— Si j'éteins cette machine, lâcha-t-il d'une voix rauque, j'espère que tu seras toute à moi, *pedhi mou*…

La lueur de défi qui brillait dans le regard d'Andreas fit naître une nouvelle bouffée de chaleur en elle.

Lentement, il s'approcha d'elle et défit le Zip de sa robe turquoise avant de contempler la fine lingerie de dentelle qui moulait ses seins.

— Tu es si belle, souffla-t-il d'un ton passionné. Viens…

Il la souleva dans ses bras et poussa la porte de leur chambre.

Elle plongea son regard dans celui d'Andreas et, rassurée, y reconnut le désir qui les consumait tous deux depuis deux ans.

2.

Blottie dans le lit au creux de l'épaule d'Andreas, Hope réfléchissait.

— T'arrive-t-il de penser à moi quand tu pars en voyage ? demanda-t-elle.

— Tu plaisantes ? J'ai été absent quinze jours. Bien sûr que je pense à toi ! Cette semaine, je pensais à toi presque chaque minute. J'avais tellement envie de faire l'amour avec toi…

Elle se mordit la lèvre.

— Ce n'est pas ce que je voulais dire, reprit-elle avec tristesse.

Andreas la fixa droit dans les yeux.

— Ne pose pas de questions aussi folles à un Grec, dit-il avec force. Tu sais à quel point tu m'as manqué.

Puis, comme pour illustrer son propos, il l'embrassa avec passion.

Incapable de résister à ses caresses, elle ferma les yeux et savoura encore la douceur de ces mains viriles sur son corps nu.

— C'est ainsi que je te vois, déclara Andreas comme elle ouvrait les yeux et découvrait son visage penché au-dessus du sien. J'aime me souvenir de la manière dont tu fermes les yeux et souris quand je te caresse.

Il allait encore l'embrasser quand elle détourna le visage.

— Qu'est-ce qui ne vas pas ? demanda-t-il. Ton comportement est si inhabituel…

Il n'avait pas achevé sa phrase qu'elle fondit en larmes.

— Tout va très bien, répondit-elle entre deux sanglots. Je ne sais pas pourquoi je pleure.

Stupéfait, Andreas ouvrit ses bras à la jeune femme qui vint s'y blottir. Doucement, il la berça et lui caressa les cheveux.

Qu'arrivait-il à sa Hope, toujours si joyeuse ? S'il se montrait patient, peut-être arriverait-elle à le lui expliquer ? De toute façon, elle ne lui cacherait pas quelque chose de grave, elle avait confiance en lui…

— Je regrette, lâcha-t-elle enfin. Je suppose que je suis un peu bouleversée à cause de notre anniversaire.

Il haussa les sourcils et se recula un peu pour la dévisager.

— Notre… « anniversaire » ?

— Oui, murmura Hope en séchant ses larmes. Sais-tu que dans quelques jours, il y aura tout juste deux ans que nous nous sommes rencontrés ?

Perplexe, il la fixa. *Deux* ans ? Il y avait deux ans qu'ils étaient ensemble ? Non, c'était impossible… Jamais il n'avait fréquenté une femme durant une si longue période. D'ailleurs, se dit-il en se rappelant la troisième épouse de son père qui avait fait un passage éclair dans sa vie d'adolescent, certains mariages duraient moins de deux ans. Mais pourquoi pensait-il au mariage ? Et comment avait-il pu se laisser ainsi prendre au piège ?

Lui, Andreas Nicolaidis, il partageait tous ses moments privés avec la même femme depuis deux années entières… Décidément, il fallait que Hope soit dotée de toutes les qualités pour que le temps se soit écoulé à cette vitesse sans qu'il en prenne conscience. A la vérité, il devait reconnaître qu'elle était parfaite. Elle rayonnait de joie, lui accordait une oreille attentive, et son ardeur sensuelle n'avait d'égale que la tendresse qu'elle lui prodiguait. Discrètement, elle s'était glissée dans sa vie et y avait fait son nid.

Mais tout ceci signifiait surtout qu'il avait passé deux ans à ne penser qu'à elle, à ne désirer qu'elle !

Une panique insidieuse s'empara de lui.

— Je ne suis pas le genre d'homme qui célèbre des anniversaires, lâcha-t-il avec une froideur délibérée. Ne compte pas sur moi pour te jouer le numéro de l'attendrissement.

Hope sursauta, touchée au plus profond d'elle-même. Ce que venait de dire Andreas la glaçait. Elle aurait voulu qu'il ne prononce jamais ces mots.

Mais c'était trop tard, et elle ne reculerait pas. Cette conversation était entamée, il fallait la conduire à son terme. Savoir si Vanessa avait eu raison…

— Mais pour moi c'est important, dit-elle d'une voix tremblante. Tu fais partie de ma vie depuis deux ans, ce n'est pas anodin !

Andreas se redressa et haussa les épaules.

— Nous passons d'agréables moments ensemble, déclara-t-il. Je tiens à toi, mais il n'est pas question de commémorer quoi que ce soit. Ce serait déplacé.

Puis il se leva et se dirigea dans la salle de bains.

Hope avait l'impression que quelqu'un venait de lui lâcher un seau d'eau glacée sur la tête. Toutes ses illusions venaient de tomber.

S'apercevant qu'elle tremblait de froid, elle se rhabilla. Mais les frissons lui couraient encore le long du dos et sur les bras. Son corps n'était pas moins frigorifié que son âme.

Elle était si choquée.

« Je tiens à toi. » Etait-ce tout ce qu'elle devait espérer obtenir d'Andreas après deux ans, en guise de déclaration ? Pourquoi était-il aussi rétif à l'idée de fêter dignement leur rencontre ?

Il ne l'aimait pas et n'avait aucune intention de le lui laisser croire, voilà tout. Le pire était qu'il semblait si sûr de lui ! Visiblement, il savait parfaitement où étaient ses priorités : il préférait humilier la femme qui lui avait donné deux ans de sa vie plutôt que de l'emmener dîner dans un restaurant pour évoquer avec elle ce premier moment magique... Décidément, elle avait été bien aveugle ! Mais la réalité venait de lui être renvoyée en plein visage, et avec une violence qui la faisait encore trembler.

Incapable de retenir ses larmes, elle s'affala sur le lit et étouffa ses sanglots dans l'oreiller.

Sous la douche, Andreas sentait la colère courir dans ses veines.

Il s'en voulait d'avoir réagi de cette manière, mais les questions de Hope l'avaient pris au dépourvu. Pourtant, il n'aurait pas dû manquer de tact à ce point !

Furieux, il tapa du talon contre le carrelage de la cabine.

Jusqu'ici, sa relation avec Hope était parfaite. Jamais il n'avait rêvé de parvenir à ce degré d'entente avec une femme. Elle lui offrait sa douceur, ses rires, ses baisers passionnés. Chaque moment partagé avec elle représentait un bonheur inespéré. Elle faisait tout pour le rendre heureux et ne lui demandait jamais rien pour elle-même. Son désintéressement et sa générosité suscitaient son admiration. Il était également fier de la manière dont elle accomplissait son parcours professionnel sans l'aide de personne. Dans quelques années, si elle continuait, elle parviendrait sans doute à devenir une créatrice d'accessoires de mode incontournable dans l'univers de la mode. Mais il songeait souvent qu'il eût été plus simple qu'elle ne travaille pas. Lors de ces voyages incessants, elle lui manquait terriblement.

Oui, Hope était merveilleuse, et il ne voulait pas la perdre. Mais jamais il n'avait songé à remettre ses principes en question pour elle. Depuis son plus jeune âge, il avait décidé qu'il ne se marierait pas. Ses parents ne lui avaient que trop montré ce que signifiait le mariage : trahisons, déceptions, ruptures d'engagement… Son désir pour Hope était resté aussi brûlant qu'au premier jour. Dès qu'il lui téléphonait, de l'étranger ou de quelque endroit que ce soit, il sentait son cœur battre à se rompre au seul son de sa voix. Et il y avait une raison à cela : Hope n'était pas son épouse, elle était la femme qu'il souhaitait retrouver pour partager le meilleur avec elle. Et seulement le meilleur.

Il ne devait donc pas la laisser se bercer d'illusions. Célébrer l'anniversaire de leur rencontre ? Quelle folie !

En attachant une serviette autour de ses hanches, il s'inspecta sans complaisance dans le miroir. Il était encore jeune, la vie le comblait de bienfaits, il essayait de rendre Hope heureuse. Mais la seule idée de former un couple le terrifiait et faisait sourdre en lui une colère noire.

Soudain, la porte de la salle de bains s'ouvrit et Hope apparut. Ses beaux yeux bleus étaient baignés de larmes et des traces rouges marquaient sa peau diaphane. Ses cheveux blonds retombaient en mèches désordonnées le long de son visage pâle comme un linge.

— Très bien, dit-elle d'une voix ferme. Si nous ne pouvons pas fêter cet anniversaire, que pouvons-nous fêter ?

Elle paraissait déterminée à obtenir quelque chose. Mais quoi ?

De plus en plus étonné par son comportement, il plongea son regard perplexe dans le sien.

— Je ne suis pas certain de te suivre, répondit-il.

Hope soupira. Une sorte de nausée montait en elle, et elle déglutit avec peine avant d'enchaîner :

— Je suis en train de te demander si tout est fini entre nous.

Impassible, Andreas croisa les bras sur sa poitrine.

— Puis-je savoir pourquoi tu en arrives à cette conclusion ?

Ignorant le tremblement qui la faisait vibrer de tout son corps, Hope serra les poings et soutint le regard froid d'Andreas.

— Un jour, tu m'as dit que rien ne pouvait rester figé et qu'il fallait toujours progresser, déclara-t-elle. Tu as ajouté que ce qui était statique n'était pas vivant. Pourtant, je dois bien constater que nous n'avons pas avancé d'un millimètre depuis deux ans.

Elle n'avait rien prémédité. Ces paroles lui avaient presque échappé, mais elle ne regrettait d'avoir laissé son cœur parler. Elle avait désespérément besoin de savoir à quoi s'en tenir. Il fallait à tout prix qu'elle sache ce qu'elle pouvait espérer de sa relation avec Andreas.

— Eh bien ? Où en sommes-nous ? demanda-t-elle, retenant son souffle.

Elle redoutait la réponse, mais elle n'avait pas l'intention de reculer.

— Où allons-nous ? insista-t-elle.

Andreas ne savait que répondre, des pensées confuses lui assaillaient l'esprit. Il songeait que les femmes avaient une mémoire terrifiante et que Hope lui en faisait la démonstration exemplaire.

Tout en se promettant de garder à l'avenir pour lui ce genre de réflexions qui pouvaient à tout moment se retourner contre lui, il perçut la douleur de la jeune femme. Elle le contemplait avec une sorte de désespoir qu'il n'avait jamais lu auparavant dans son regard.

Il attira brusquement la jeune femme contre lui et l'embrassa avec force.

Surprise, Hope n'eut pas le temps de se refuser à ce baiser.

— Au lit ? suggéra-t-il en souriant, une lueur ardente dans les yeux.

Le visage de Hope se métamorphosa, virant du blanc au rouge. Une colère inouïe la submergeait, comme s'il venait de la gifler.

— C'est ça, la réponse à ma question ? s'écria-t-elle. Je veux sentir que je fais partie de ta vie, Andreas ! Je ne veux pas seulement être ta compagne au lit !

— Mais… Tu fais partie de ma vie ! s'exclama-t-il d'un ton stupéfait.

— Si c'est vrai, comment se fait-il que tu ne m'aies jamais présenté ta famille ni tes amis ? poursuivit-elle en s'efforçant de se calmer. Tu as honte de moi ?

— Comment peux-tu dire de telles bêtises ? J'ai tant de travail… Quand je te vois, je préfère profiter de chaque instant et te garder pour moi seul, *pedhi mou*. Tu peux le comprendre, je suppose. Calme-toi, voyons, tu es à la limite de la crise d'hystérie.

— Pas du tout ! protesta-t-elle. Je suis simplement en train d'éclaircir les choses avec toi !

Il plongea son regard dans le sien.

— Et moi, je n'ai pas envie de me disputer avec toi.

— C'est encore quelque chose qui nous est interdit, peut-être ? rétorqua Hope avec un geste de colère.

Elle heurta le porte-serviettes et frotta aussitôt son poignet meurtri.

— Tu t'es blessée ? demanda-t-il doucement en s'approchant.

Au même instant, le téléphone sonna dans la chambre. Hope en profita pour se détourner et aller répondre.

— Oui, allô ? Ici Hope Evans.

— Bonjour. Elyssa Southwick. Puis-je parler à Andreas, s'il vous plaît ? répondit froidement une voix féminine.

Hope soupira intérieurement.

Quand Elyssa ne parvenait pas à joindre son frère aîné sur son portable, elle appelait ici. Installée à Londres depuis son mariage, elle tenait beaucoup au soutien d'Andreas, et depuis le décès de leur mère survenu quelques mois auparavant, elle voyait également son frère plus souvent. Mais la manière dont la jeune femme s'adressait à elle comme si elle n'était qu'une domestique lui était insupportable.

Elle n'avait jamais révélé à Andreas à quel point elle était blessée de ce qu'Elyssa semble ne pas se soucier de savoir qui elle était. La jeune femme tombait souvent sur elle quand elle appelait son frère, mais elle ne manifestait pas la moindre curiosité à son endroit.

— Je vous le passe, dit-elle en tendant le combiné à Andreas.

Apparemment, Elyssa voulait simplement rappeler à son frère la réception qu'elle avait organisée la semaine suivante. Réception à laquelle elle-même n'était pas conviée, bien entendu.

Pourquoi ? Andreas avait-il honte de la présenter à sa sœur ?

C'était si évident ! Les Nicolaidis formaient une dynastie internationalement connue et admirée. Andreas était un homme brillant, d'une intelligence remarquable, d'un raffinement et d'une élégance rares. Il ne pouvait exhiber à son bras une femme issue d'une famille modeste, aux parents divorcés, qui ne parlait aucune langue étrangère et commençait à peine sa carrière dans le design.

Tandis qu'Andreas poursuivait la conversation en grec avec sa sœur, elle scruta sans aménité son reflet dans le miroir du salon.

Elle y voyait une femme de petite taille, aux longs cheveux blonds qui pendaient tristement sur sa robe froissée, aux yeux rouges. Comment avait-elle pu se laisser griser d'espoirs ? Jamais Andreas ne lui avait fait la moindre promesse, il la considérait simplement comme une compagne agréable... qu'il n'épouserait à aucun prix.

Seigneur, elle n'allait pas encore se bercer d'illusions pendant deux ans ! Non, il fallait qu'elle le quitte. Qu'elle retrouve sa dignité. Elle devait retenir la leçon qu'elle venait de recevoir et partir. Quitter cet homme qu'elle aimait plus que tout.

Elle sentit son cœur se comprimer douloureusement dans sa poitrine en reportant le regard sur la silhouette athlétique d'Andreas. Ses cheveux mouillés étaient plaqués sur ses tempes, soulignant les contours de son visage viril. La serviette autour de ses hanches révélait ses abdominaux, sa peau bronzée, sa musculature parfaite. Et non seulement il était séduisant, mais elle se sentait défaillir chaque fois qu'il posait la main sur elle...

C'était trop dur, elle n'y arriverait pas.

Retenant les larmes qui lui montaient encore aux yeux, elle décida de mettre fin à leur amour ici même, séance tenante.

Andreas raccrocha et se tourna vers elle en souriant.

— Voudrais-tu m'accompagner à la soirée que donne ma sœur la semaine prochaine ? demanda-t-il. Elle serait heureuse de faire ta connaissance. Et tu verras mes neveux. Ils sont très bien élevés.

Estomaquée, Hope s'accrocha au dossier d'un fauteuil pour garder son équilibre.

Andreas la dévisageait, les yeux brillants. Il souriait, comme si leur conversation n'avait jamais eu lieu. Comme si la demande qu'il venait de lui faire était la plus naturelle du monde…

Son soulagement fut tel qu'elle sentit un bien-être incomparable monter en elle. Un sourire se dessina sur ses lèvres.

— Tu es sérieux ? s'écria-t-elle. Oh, oui ! J'en serais ravie.

Elle sentait la culpabilité l'assaillir. Jamais elle n'aurait dû douter d'Andreas ! En une fraction de seconde, il venait de lui rendre tout ce qu'elle croyait avoir perdu. Et à l'évidence, elle aurait été plus avisée de lui ouvrir son cœur plus tôt.

Débordant de gratitude et de tendresse, elle bondit vers lui et l'enlaça avec passion. Il posait déjà ses yeux brûlant de désir sur elle, et elle lui sourit avant de se cambrer et de savourer le goût de ses lèvres sur les siennes…

Andreas répondit au sourire de Hope sans rien lui montrer de l'intense soulagement qui était également le sien.

Pour désamorcer cette dispute, il avait songé à emmener la jeune femme en week-end à Paris ou à Venise. Mais une part de lui-même s'y opposait farouchement : c'eût été une manière de célébrer cet anniversaire dont il ne voulait pas entendre parler. D'ailleurs, *il n'y avait pas* d'anniversaire !

En revanche, présenter Hope à sa sœur était la solution. Les subites craintes de sa compagne en seraient apaisées.

Pourtant, il n'avait aucune intention de multiplier les sorties en société. Cette soirée resterait une exception.

3.

En passant le seuil de la somptueuse villa qu'Elyssa et Finlay Southwick avaient fait décorer par une architecte d'intérieur très connue, Hope sentit la timidité la gagner.

Elle ajusta nerveusement le décolleté en V de sa petite robe noire, qui révélait sa poitrine pulpeuse et sa taille fine sans trop la mouler.

La soirée était plutôt une fête : les gens dansaient dans la salle de réception où un orchestre jouait des airs de samba. La plupart des femmes étaient parées de bijoux clinquants, des serveurs en livrée circulaient à travers les groupes en portant des plateaux de petits-fours… Bref, l'ambiance évoquait les réceptions de la haute société.

Cela augmenta le trouble de Hope. Elle eut envie de s'accrocher au bras d'Andreas et de rester collée à lui durant toute la soirée.

Elle avait eu si peur de ne pas savoir choisir la bonne tenue qu'elle avait opté pour un classique, mais elle jetait désormais des regards embarrassés sur toutes ces femmes vêtues d'ensembles extravagants, à l'évidence taillés sur mesure par les plus grands noms de la mode.

Soudain, une petite blonde s'arrêta devant elle et la dévisagea avec stupeur.

— Mais… C'est vous ! s'écria-t-elle. Vous êtes la femme qui

vendait ces charmants sacs à main sur le marché de Camden l'an dernier, avant Noël !

— Vous devez faire erreur, intervint Andreas d'un ton froid.

Hope se sentit soudain très mal à l'aise, et elle s'aperçut que leur interlocutrice n'était pas moins gênée qu'elle.

— Oui, c'est moi, admit-elle à voix basse.

Puis elle sourit à la jeune fille qui, moins crispée, reprit sa mine réjouie.

— Ma mère adore ce sac que je vous ai acheté ! Il est extraordinaire. D'ailleurs, toutes ses amies voudraient avoir le même et ne cessent de la harceler de questions. J'ai gardé votre carte, je vous appellerai bientôt, ajouta-t-elle avant de s'éclipser.

Andreas prit la main de Hope et l'entraîna un peu à l'écart de la foule, dans un long corridor, avant de lui lancer un regard courroucé.

— Qu'est-ce que c'est que cette histoire ? gronda-t-il. Tu as fait la vendeuse sur les marchés ?

Elle soupira et soutint son regard.

— Ecoute, tu sais bien que je veux créer un jour ma propre collection de sacs ! Je t'ai montré mes premiers prototypes. Je suis très heureuse de mon poste de responsable des achats d'accessoires pour cette jeune créatrice de Soho, mais si je ne me fais pas connaître, je ne parviendrai jamais à réaliser mon rêve. D'ailleurs, c'est aussi grâce à cette vente à Camden que j'ai reçu ce prix de design, l'an dernier. Je peux comprendre que l'idée que je vende des sacs sur un marché ne te plaise pas, mais…

— En effet, coupa-t-il, cela ne me plaît pas. Comment oses-tu me mettre dans une telle situation, chez ma propre sœur ?

Elle serra les poings, sentant la colère monter en elle.

— Je ne suis peut-être pas issue de la haute société, mais

j'entends aller au bout de mes ambitions ! déclara-t-elle. Vendre des sacs sur un marché, ce n'est pas mon activité favorite. Mais si je dois en passer par cette étape pour me faire connaître, je n'ai aucune hésitation. Il n'y a rien de honteux à cela ! C'est toi qui n'es qu'un snob !

— Je ne suis pas snob, rétorqua Andreas avec hauteur.

— Ah ? fit-elle en le toisant d'un regard narquois.

— Pourquoi ne m'as-tu jamais parlé de cette activité ? reprit-il d'un ton accusateur.

— Parce que cela n'a duré que quelques jours. Tu étais à l'étranger…

« Encore une fois ! » ajouta-t-elle en pestant intérieurement. D'ailleurs, même si elle l'avait voulu, elle n'aurait pas pu lui parler de son métier. Il ne s'y intéressait pas. Ses propres affaires l'accaparaient. Et elle savait qu'il aurait condamné cette idée de vendre ses sacs sur un marché.

Andreas s'efforçait visiblement de conserver son calme.

— Je suis navré que tu te sois abaissée à un tel niveau, lâcha-t-il avec mépris. Et j'espère qu'à l'avenir, cela ne se reproduira pas.

Hope fit un effort surhumain pour ne pas lui crier d'aller au diable. Son attitude l'humiliait et la rendait folle de rage. Mais le lieu était mal choisi pour lui dire qu'elle ne laisserait personne lui dicter ce qu'elle avait à faire et qu'elle se moquait bien de ses avertissements.

Andreas ne savait plus comment mettre fin à cette conversation déplaisante. Une étrangère croisée à une soirée en savait plus sur les activités de sa compagne que lui ! C'était plus que vexant : c'était intolérable.

Il connaissait les ambitions de Hope. Il savait qu'elle consacrait toute son énergie dans son travail, et c'était précisément ce qui le blessait. Il se sentait exclu de son univers. Le fait qu'elle vende des sacs sur des marchés ne le choquait pas : tout travail bien fait était un travail honnête, ainsi que le lui avait enseigné ses parents et ses grands-parents, qui avaient eux-mêmes été des marchands. Mais il avait l'impression que le travail de Hope était en concurrence avec leur relation. Si elle n'avait pas travaillé, elle l'aurait accompagné dans tous ses voyages. Et jamais elle ne lui avait dit qu'elle avait vendu des sacs à Camden. Pourquoi ? A l'évidence, elle considérait son métier comme un refuge dans lequel il n'avait pas sa place. Il avait le sentiment qu'une porte venait de s'entrebâiller : Hope lui avait caché cette histoire...

Comment être certain qu'elle n'en faisait pas de même avec tous les événements qui rythmaient sa vie quotidienne ?

Après tout, il était si souvent loin de Londres... Il ignorait tout des gens qu'elle fréquentait ou des conversations qu'elle échangeait avec ses collègues. Il y avait deux ans qu'ils se connaissaient. Il avait peine à le croire, mais c'était ainsi, même s'il lui semblait que leur rencontre remontait à la semaine précédente. En deux ans, elle avait eu le temps de lui cacher bien d'autres informations !

Une jeune femme vêtue d'un fourreau de taffetas rose s'avança vers eux. Son port de tête était majestueux et sa démarche avait quelque chose d'empesé.

Hope, qui avait à maintes reprises contemplé des photos d'Elyssa dans la presse, reconnut aussitôt la sœur d'Andreas. D'un geste machinal, elle repoussa une mèche blonde derrière son oreille et sourit.

Mais Elyssa fixait son frère en évitant soigneusement de la regarder. Parvenue à leur hauteur, elle l'embrassa avec chaleur tout en lui reprochant d'être arrivé si tard.

60

Hope eut envie de se pincer. Se trompait-elle, ou Elyssa s'adressait-elle vraiment à Andreas comme s'il était seul ?

Enfin, Andreas se dégagea de l'étreinte de sa sœur et tendit un bras vers elle.

Mais alors qu'il allait les présenter l'une à l'autre, un homme de haute taille l'aborda et l'abreuva d'un flot de paroles ininterrompu.

— Veuillez m'excuser un instant, dit Andreas en s'éclipsant avec l'homme, les laissant seules.

Hope sourit encore et tendit la main.

— Bonsoir, Elyssa, dit-elle. Je suis Hope. Je suis très heureuse de faire enfin votre connaissance.

Elyssa accepta avec réticence sa poignée de main.

— Pas moi, répondit-elle froidement. Andreas n'avait jamais osé jusqu'ici me présenter l'une de ses poupées. Car c'est bien ce que vous êtes, aux yeux de mon frère : un jouet.

Puis elle tourna les talons et retourna vers la salle de réception, laissant Hope bouche bée et rouge d'humiliation.

C'était incroyable ! Comment cette femme pouvait-elle se comporter ainsi, avec l'éducation qu'elle avait reçue ? Et pourquoi lui témoignait-elle une telle hostilité ?

Pourtant, en se rappelant les appels téléphoniques d'Elyssa à l'appartement, elle se dit qu'elle en avait déjà reçu tous les signes d'une animosité profonde. Si cette jeune femme richissime et apparemment comblée l'accueillait ainsi, il ne pouvait y avoir qu'une explication : elle ne tolérait pas qu'une femme se glisse dans la vie de son frère.

Mais elle n'avait pas l'intention de laisser Elyssa savourer sa victoire. Elle était ici pour sa première soirée en société avec Andreas, et elle ferait tout pour oublier cet incident, qu'elle garderait secret.

Retournant dans la salle de réception, elle aperçut de l'autre côté de la pièce un homme d'une trentaine d'années aux yeux bleus rieurs et aux cheveux blonds lui faisait signe de la main.

Au moment où elle lui répondait, Andreas revint vers elle, lui prit la taille d'un geste possessif et se pencha à son oreille :

— Qui est cet homme ?

— C'est Ben Campbell, le cousin de Vanessa, répondit-elle avec un sourire forcé. Je l'ai croisé une ou deux fois.

Le terme « poupée » lui résonnait encore aux oreilles.

— Vraiment ? Je ne savais pas qu'ils étaient parents, reprit sèchement Andreas. En tout cas, je ne veux pas que tu fréquentes ce Campbell.

Fronçant les sourcils, elle leva les yeux vers lui.

— Et pourquoi cela ? En tant que proche de Vanessa, je…

— Il est réputé pour hanter toutes les soirées londoniennes et pour ses talents de séducteur. Il n'est pas fréquentable. A partir de maintenant, tu ne le connais plus, asséna-t-il d'une voix ferme.

Hope en eut le souffle coupé. Depuis le début de la soirée, Andreas ne cessait de lui dicter ce qu'elle avait le droit de faire et surtout de ne pas faire. Pensait-il vraiment qu'elle allait obéir à ces injonctions arbitraires comme une… « poupée » ?

Au moment où elle allait protester, une femme d'une soixantaine d'années couverte de diamants attrapa le bras d'Andreas et l'entraîna vers le buffet.

En silence, Hope regarda Andreas s'éloigner. Puis, elle l'observa échanger quelques mots avec une très jeune femme brune moulée dans une robe très courte et qui exhibait de longues jambes de gazelle.

A côté de ce top-modèle, se dit-elle, elle n'était rien. D'ailleurs, il y avait plus d'une vingtaine de jeunes femmes sublimes dans cette soirée : de véritables reines de beauté, qui pouvaient faire tourner la tête aux hommes les plus puissants de la planète. Sans doute était-ce la raison pour laquelle il s'adressait à elle comme à une domestique ! Il avait tout loisir ce soir de comparer la femme avec laquelle il partageait sa vie avec ces jeunes stars des podiums qui ne demandaient qu'à céder à son irrésistible charme…

Blessée dans son amour-propre et gagnée par un terrible élan de jalousie, elle battit en retraite dans un coin de la salle en sirotant tristement un verre de jus de pamplemousse. Elle n'aimait pas l'alcool et ne se sentait plus d'humeur à faire la fête.

Elyssa, la seule personne à qui elle avait voulu faire bonne impression ce soir, lui avait jeté son mépris à la figure. C'était plutôt raté !

— Bonsoir, je crois vous avoir aperçue avec Andreas tout à l'heure… Vous êtes Hope ? demanda quelqu'un derrière elle.

Elle se retourna, surprise.

L'homme, en élégant costume beige, ne devait pas avoir plus de trente ans. Pourtant, dans son visage long et fin, son regard semblait fatigué. Ses cheveux blonds grisonnaient déjà sur les tempes.

— Oui, admit-elle, intriguée. Et vous êtes… ?

— Finlay Southwick, dit-il en lui serrant la main. Le mari d'Elyssa.

— Oh ! Enchantée.

Encore troublée par l'incident qui venait d'avoir lieu, Hope s'efforça de n'en rien montrer. Et Finlay, s'il avait perçu une certaine tristesse dans son attitude, fit comme si de rien n'était.

— Andreas est si secret sur sa vie privée que je suis vraiment heureux de découvrir enfin la charmante jeune femme qui partage sa vie, poursuivit-il en souriant. Il a si longtemps qu'Elyssa et moi espérions vous connaître ! Je regrette que vous ne puissiez voir nos enfants ce soir. Mais ils sont couchés à cette heure-ci, comme vous pouvez le comprendre.

Rassurée par les manières de gentleman de son hôte, elle se détendit.

— Je suis moi-même flattée d'assister à cette soirée, répondit-elle avec prudence, préférant éviter de mentionner sa désastreuse rencontre avec Elyssa.

Finlay sourit d'un air navré.

— Vous savez, déclara-t-il après avoir observé un court silence, Elyssa est beaucoup plus jeune qu'Andreas. Elle a été très gâtée par ses parents, qui se sont séparés alors qu'elle n'avait que quatre ans. Trop gâtée, sans doute. Ceci explique son caractère un peu... difficile.

Hope ne sut que répondre et baissa la tête.

— Le frère et la sœur ne se ressemblent guère, enchaîna son interlocuteur en jetant un coup d'œil vers Andreas, qui, bavardait à l'autre bout de la pièce avec deux jeunes Grecs.

— Ah non ? demanda Hope avec intérêt.

— Non. Andreas est pudique, ambitieux... Il travaille avec la même équipe depuis dix ans. C'est un homme fidèle, ajouta-t-il.

Alors que Hope se demandait où Finlay voulait en venir et ce que signifiait ce commentaire, deux femmes le saisirent chacune par un bras et l'entraînèrent au loin. Il se retourna vers Hope avec un petit geste d'excuse, et elle lui sourit : il était le maître de maison et se devait d'accorder la même attention à tous ses invités.

Elle resta seule encore quelques instants, à réfléchir aux propos de Finlay Southwick.

Selon celui-ci, Andreas et sa sœur ne se ressembleraient pas ? Il devait faire référence à leurs caractères respectifs, car physiquement les similitudes étaient frappantes : ils avaient

64

le même teint mat, des yeux noirs et profonds, des cheveux lisses et une démarche aristocratique.

Visiblement, Finlay avait souhaité évoquer le métier d'Andreas avant d'être interrompu...

Lasse de cette soirée déroutante et gagnée par une sorte d'agoraphobie à force de subir le brouhaha ambiant, elle posa son verre vidé sur le buffet et quitta la pièce.

Elle avait besoin d'un peu de solitude et de calme pour oublier que rien ne se déroulait comme elle l'aurait souhaité. Andreas l'avait abandonnée à tous ces inconnus. Certes, il connaissait bien les invités de sa sœur et devait lui aussi souscrire aux mondanités de rigueur, mais elle avait tant espéré qu'il la présente à tous ces gens comme sa compagne...

Cherchant un lieu tranquille, elle se perdit dans le dédale de l'immense villa et décida de pousser la première porte venue pour s'asseoir quelques instants.

Il s'agissait d'un petit salon où toutes les lumières étaient éteintes.

Elle demeura immobile sur le seuil, figée.

Devant elle, Elyssa, affalée sur un canapé, embrassait un homme qui ne ressemblait pas du tout à Finlay. Même si Hope ne pouvait que l'entrapercevoir dans le rai de lumière du couloir, elle distinguait ses cheveux bouclés, ses épais sourcils bruns et sa chemise violette.

Les deux amants ayant levé les yeux, elle referma précipitamment la porte.

Elle s'apprêtait à retourner vers la salle de réception quand elle entendit derrière elle des talons d'escarpins qui martelaient le sol de marbre.

Elyssa surgit derrière elle et, la prenant par le bras, la contraignit à se retourner.

— Je ne vous conseille pas de dire à mon frère un mot de ce que vous venez de voir ! menaça-t-elle en pointant vers elle son index verni de rouge. Je vous promets que si Andreas en entend parler, vous le regretterez !

Surprise par cette agression, Hope rassembla néanmoins tout son sang-froid et soutint le regard furieux de son hôtesse.

— Vous n'avez aucune raison de me menacer, répliqua-t-elle d'une voix calme. Je…

— Oh, si, j'ai la meilleure des raisons ! s'écria Elyssa avec fureur. Que faisiez-vous à fureter ainsi ? Vous m'espionniez !

— Bien sûr que non, rétorqua Hope, choquée. Je cherchais simplement un peu de calme. Je pensais que la pièce était vide, et…

— Vraiment ? demanda Elyssa d'un ton sarcastique en posant ses mains sur ses hanches.

Hope parvint difficilement à ne pas s'énerver.

— Ecoutez, reprit-elle, je n'ai pas l'intention de révéler ce que je viens de voir à qui que ce soit. Tout cela ne me regarde pas et m'est égal.

Et, sans attendre la réponse d'Elyssa, elle tourna les talons et reprit le corridor dans l'autre sens.

Seigneur, cette soirée tournait au cauchemar ! Comme elle plaignait le malheureux Finlay ! Il avait épousé une peste, une enfant gâtée et mal élevée, qui n'avait aucun sens des valeurs. Mais cette peste était également la petite sœur adorée d'Andreas… Après tout, tout cela ne la concernait pas. Elle devait être folle d'avoir tant voulu rencontrer la famille de l'homme qu'elle aimait. Elle ne songeait plus qu'à une chose : rentrer chez elle le plus tôt possible.

Elle courait presque lorsqu'une main se posa sur son bras.

Elle reconnut Ben Campbell, qui venait de sortir d'un salon dont la porte était ouverte sur le corridor. Quelques personnes discutaient là, en petit comité.

— Où courais-tu ainsi ? demanda-t-il. Tu as l'air essoufflée… Et tu es toute pâle ! Tu as vu un fantôme ?

Elle reprit son souffle, se força à sourire et suivit Ben dans le petit salon, où il l'invita à s'asseoir dans un grand fauteuil.

— Eh bien, que se passe-t-il ? insista-t-il. Tu as l'air bouleversée.

Elle poussa un profond soupir.

— Elyssa me hait ! lâcha-t-elle d'une voix où perçait le désespoir. Tout se passe mal depuis que je suis arrivée ici.

— Bravo ! s'exclama Ben avec un enthousiasme étrange.

— Comment ça, bravo ?

— Cela prouve que tu conserves ta personnalité au milieu de ces gens sinistres auxquels tu veux tant plaire !

Elle haussa les épaules. Ce commentaire ne la touchait pas. Sinistres ou pas, ces gens étaient les proches d'Andreas.

— Quant à Elyssa, poursuivit Ben, tu ne devrais pas lui donner la satisfaction de te soucier de ce qu'elle pense. C'est une héritière gâtée, snob et méprisante. Elle a eu beaucoup de chance d'épouser Finlay Southwick. Je me demande d'ailleurs comment un homme si subtil et si intelligent a pu tomber sous son charme. Mais dis-moi tout. Elle a été désagréable avec toi ? Que t'a-t-elle dit ?

Mal à l'aise, Hope croisa les jambes. Il lui était impossible de répondre.

— De toute façon, quoi qu'il soit arrivé, enchaînait Ben, tu peux te confier à ton compagnon.

Elle le dévisagea avec étonnement.

— Oui, il est évident que tu as beaucoup d'influence sur lui. Je ne connais pas très bien Andreas Nicolaidis, mais nous avons quelques fréquentations en commun, et tout le monde s'accorde à dire qu'il a beaucoup changé depuis qu'il vit avec sa « charmante et secrète petite amie ». Il est détendu, visiblement heureux… Si Elyssa s'est montrée déplaisante, tu devrais t'en ouvrir à lui.

— Vraiment ? demanda-t-elle, peu convaincue.

Ben haussa les épaules.

— Si Elyssa a décidé d'être ton ennemie, tu n'as pas le choix !

Comme elle baissait les yeux sans répondre, Ben fronça les sourcils.

— Hope, est-ce plus grave que ce que je croyais ? Où est passé ton merveilleux sourire ? Tu peux me parler en toute confiance, tu sais. D'ailleurs, Vanessa me tuerait si je ne faisais pas tout pour te remonter le moral !

Incapable de retenir plus longtemps ses larmes, Hope se leva. Elle n'allait pas pleurer devant les gens qui riaient non loin d'eux dans le salon.

Inquiet, Ben l'imita et l'invita à le suivre dans le couloir. Il ouvrit la porte d'une pièce de service qui devait conduire aux cuisines.

— Il n'y a personne ici, dit-il d'un ton encourageant, tandis qu'elle essuyait une larme. N'aie pas peur, tu peux me parler… A moins que tu ne préfères que je te raccompagne chez toi ?

— Non, c'est gentil de ta part, Ben, mais…

— Je suis un excellent conducteur et je n'ai presque pas bu, poursuivit-il. Je déteste voir une femme souffrir. Quand je pense qu'Andreas te laisse ainsi… Penses-tu que j'aie une chance de te séduire et de te faire oublier ton millionnaire grec ?

Elle secoua vivement la tête.

— Personne ne peut y parvenir, affirma-t-elle.

— N'en sois pas si sûre ! répondit-il. Tu es une personne merveilleuse, Hope. Tu es belle, généreuse et gaie. Tu mérites un homme qui sache te rendre heureuse.

— Je… Je te remercie, balbutia-t-elle en quittant la pièce et en se dirigeant une nouvelle fois vers la salle de réception.

Seigneur... Tout allait de mal en pis ! Même si Ben se contentait de se montrer serviable, ses flatteries étaient déplacées. Que serait-il arrivé si Andreas avait surpris ce qu'il venait de lui dire ?

Soudain elle sursauta en sentant une main l'enlacer.

— Enfin te voici, *pedhi mou* ! s'écria Andreas en l'attrapant par la taille. Je te cherche depuis un long moment. Viens, rentrons. Quel temps perdu ! J'aurais préféré cent fois dîner tranquillement avec toi et nous mettre au lit...

Hope lui sourit et se blottit contre lui. La douceur de sa voix l'enveloppait d'une chaleur familière et rassurante.

Comme ils se dirigeaient vers l'entrée, une voix les arrêta.

— Andreas ! cria Elyssa. Un instant, s'il te plaît. J'ai quelque chose à te dire avant que tu ne partes.

Andreas soupira et se retourna vers Hope.

— Attends-moi dans la limousine, dit-il, je reviens tout de suite.

Hope observa Elyssa qui, sans lui avoir adressé un regard, venait de prendre le bras de son frère et l'entraînait à l'écart. Il n'y avait plus dans sa voix l'hystérie qu'elle témoignait un moment plus tôt, mais un calme et une sérénité étranges.

Elle sortit sur le porche de la villa, attendit que le chauffeur s'arrête devant elle puis s'installa à l'arrière de la limousine pour attendre Andreas.

Durant cinq minutes, elle songea à l'attachement d'Andreas pour Elyssa et à ce que lui en avaient dit Ben et Finlay. Un homme du tempérament de son amant ne pouvait que protéger à l'excès une petite sœur privée trop tôt de l'affection de ses parents.

Au bout d'un long quart d'heure, Andreas revint enfin. A peine installé à côté d'elle, il donna l'ordre au chauffeur de démarrer et fixa le paysage droit devant lui. Il semblait très contrarié.

Hope n'osa lui demander quelle avait été la teneur de son entretien avec sa sœur. Elle craignait de le deviner : la jeune femme avait certainement préféré prendre les devants et tout avouer à Andreas de peur qu'elle ne lui en parle auparavant.

Or, elle connaissait la position de son compagnon à l'égard de l'infidélité. Il n'avait aucune indulgence pour les femmes qui se montraient volages.

Tout le long du chemin, Andreas ne desserra pas la bouche. La limousine s'arrêta enfin devant l'immeuble.

Devant l'ascenseur, Hope contempla avec inquiétude le visage fermé de son compagnon.

— Tu ne veux pas me dire ce qui ne va pas ? demanda-t-elle avec douceur.

— Qu'est-ce qui te fait croire que quelque chose ne va pas ? rétorqua-t-il d'une voix impassible.

— Tout, répondit-elle. Et surtout ton comportement depuis que nous avons quitté la réception.

Elle entra dans la cabine de l'ascenseur sans cesser de fixer le regard faussement calme d'Andreas. Comme ils parvenaient devant la porte de l'appartement, elle sortit les clés et le précéda pour entrer. Mais lorsqu'elle s'aperçut qu'il demeurait immobile sur le seuil, elle fronça les sourcils et se retourna vers lui.

— Eh bien ? Tu ne rentres pas ?

— Si, dit-il en faisant un pas dans la pièce et en plongeant son regard dans le sien.

Un regard noir, qui lançait des éclairs de fureur.

— As-tu quelque chose à me dire à propos de ce qui s'est passé ce soir, Hope ?

70

4.

Stupéfaite par ce ton glacial et plein de sous-entendus, Hope soutint avec une perplexité croissante le regard de son compagnon.

Pourquoi Andreas se comportait-il comme si elle avait commis un crime ? Lui reprochait-il d'avoir surpris sa sœur avec un autre homme ? Non, c'eût été absurde. De toute façon, il n'avait pas voulu aborder le sujet avec elle dans la voiture…

Savait-il déjà qu'Elyssa s'était montrée odieuse avec elle ? Mais elle avait décidé de ne pas s'en plaindre.

— Non, répondit-elle enfin. Je ne vois rien de particulier à dire.

— Dommage, répondit-il froidement en se versant un verre d'alcool. Tu as été surprise alors que tu étais seule avec Ben Campbell.

Déconcertée par ce commentaire, elle haussa les épaules.

— Oui, c'est exact. Nous avons bavardé un moment.

— Paul, le meilleur ami de mon beau-frère, vous a vus, poursuivit Andreas d'une voix égale.

Hope eut soudain la chair de poule.

L'attitude d'Andreas était inquiétante. Il était impossible qu'un innocent entretien avec Ben provoque cette colère, Andreas devait songer à autre chose… Qui était ce Paul ? Elle ne lui avait pas été présentée. Néanmoins, il avait visiblement convaincu Andreas que sa conversation avec Ben était de nature à exciter à sa jalousie.

— Je ne comprends pas, assura-t-elle. Il ne s'est rien passé qui justifie ta colère.

— Vraiment ? tonna-t-il en se retournant vers elle et la dévisageant avec fureur.

Hope sentit des frissons lui courir dans la nuque.

Andreas était grec, il avait un tempérament passionné et se montrait possessif, mais il ne lui avait jamais fait de scène de jalousie. Or, en cet instant, il était manifestement hors de lui et luttait pour ne pas exploser.

Ne sachant comment désamorcer cette attitude toute nouvelle chez lui, elle inspira profondément et essaya de sourire.

— Voyons, Andreas ! C'est ridicule. Pour commencer, il y avait une bonne douzaine de personnes autour de nous. Et Ben ne cherchait pas du tout à me séduire !

— Dans ce cas, pourquoi Paul l'a-t-il vu t'entraîner dans un lieu désert ?

Déterminée à cacher la raison pour laquelle elle s'était mise à pleurer, elle ne pouvait lui expliquer que Ben cherchait seulement à la consoler.

— Andreas, Ben m'a probablement conduite hors du salon parce qu'il y avait trop de bruit et que nous ne pouvions plus nous entendre. J'ai peine à croire que nous ayons cette conversation !

— Nous avons cette conversation, maugréa-t-il entre ses dents en s'approchant d'elle, parce que cinq minutes après que Paul t'a vue sortir du salon, Elyssa t'a surprise en train d'embrasser Ben dans un recoin sombre de la buanderie.

Incrédule, Hope le fixa.

— Quoi ? Tu veux me répéter cela ?

Andreas lui opposait toujours une expression hostile et avalait son verre à petites gorgées, d'un air faussement dégagé.

— Non, je n'ai pas besoin de te répéter cela, dit-il avec flegme.

Puis, il abattit violemment son verre sur une console et se tourna vers elle avec une moue de dégoût. Des éclairs de rage traversaient le noir de ses yeux.

— Vous vous êtes jetés l'un sur l'autre dans un coin tranquille… C'est ignoble. Et c'est indigne de toi ! Alors je t'en prie, ne nie pas, ce serait le comble ! Tu as été prise en flagrant délit. N'invente pas d'excuses ou de mensonges.

— Je ne mens pas et je n'ai pas à présenter d'excuses, s'insurgea Hope. Je n'ai rien fait !

— Tu embrassais Ben Campbell, et il te caressait…

— Arrête ! C'est faux ! Ta sœur a…

— Ne me mets pas davantage en colère en mettant en cause l'intégrité de ma sœur, hurla Andreas en levant un doigt menaçant. Tu lui as fait honte dans sa propre maison, tu l'as humiliée ! Je crois que c'est bien assez !

— Mais… Tout ceci est ridicule. Cette histoire est fausse ! répéta Hope en tapant du poing sur la table. Je te le jure !

Elle parvenait mal à concevoir comment un être humain pouvait se comporter comme l'avait fait Elyssa Southwick. Son machiavélisme la rendait physiquement malade. Une nausée la gagna tandis qu'elle tentait de trouver un moyen de convaincre Andreas qu'elle disait la vérité.

L'homme qu'Elyssa avait entraîné dans son mensonge ne pouvait être que son amant, c'est-à-dire… le meilleur ami de Finlay.

— Ce Paul, reprit-elle tout à trac, portait-il une chemise violette ce soir ? C'est un grand brun ?

— Oui, admit Andreas en fronçant les sourcils. Mais il s'agit bien de lui !

— Puisque lui et ta sœur prétendent que…, commença-t-elle.

— Elyssa était affreusement désemparée ! la rabroua Andreas. Elle a longuement hésité avant de m'en parler. Elle en a discuté avec Paul et a préféré laisser son mari en dehors de tout cela, ce qui est tout à son honneur. Enfin, elle a conclu que j'avais le droit de savoir avec quelle sorte de femme je partageais ma vie !

— Mais ce n'est pas vrai, reprit Hope d'un ton où perçait le désespoir. Cette histoire est inventée !

— Je veux t'entendre m'avouer la vérité avant de partir, coupa Andreas. Tu me dois bien cela.

Tandis que son univers s'écroulait sans qu'elle puisse l'en empêcher, Hope réalisait combien Elyssa avait manœuvré avec habileté. Non seulement il lui était désormais impossible de convaincre Andreas qu'aucun geste équivoque n'avait eu lieu entre elle et Ben, mais la diablesse s'était protégée de toute attaque.

— J'ai été terriblement naïve, souffla-t-elle d'un ton amer. Depuis toujours, je cherche à ne pas juger la conduite des autres, parce que je sais que je ne suis pas parfaite moi-même. Et j'ai oublié de prendre garde à un danger bien réel… Ta sœur est très intelligente. Aussi vive et ingénieuse que toi, Andreas. Et de toute évidence elle a décidé de détruire notre relation…

Il lui lança un regard assassin.

— Ce que tu dis est absurde. Aie la décence de ne pas reporter tes fautes sur ma sœur, s'il te plaît.

— Je ne crois pas que ce soit possible, rétorqua Hope, prête à révéler ce qu'elle avait vu.

Mais en une fraction de seconde, elle réalisa qu'il était trop tard. Jamais Andreas ne voudrait la croire. Plus maintenant. Si elle avait parlé dès le début de la soirée, c'eût peut-être été différent. Hélas, tous les arguments qu'elle avancerait désormais seraient balayés avec mépris.

Elle était prise au piège.

— Andreas… Tu me connais mieux que cela ! implora-t-elle.

— Réponds-moi, Andreas, insistait la jeune femme. Tu crois vraiment que j'aurais pu faire une chose pareille ?

Aussitôt, la colère le reprit et ses yeux brillèrent d'une lueur menaçante.

— Je ne vois pas ce qu'il y a d'impossible à cela ! rétorqua-t-il. Tu es bien tombée dans mes bras en une soirée, dans cette grange…

Blessée, Hope se mordit la lèvre pour ne pas pleurer.

Andreas avait tout gâché. Oh oui, elle s'était donnée à lui cette nuit-là ! Parce qu'elle avait cru qu'il était l'homme de sa vie… Devait-elle le lui rappeler ? Pour qu'il se moque d'elle ? Comment pouvait-il salir ainsi le souvenir de leur rencontre, ce moment magique entre tous où leur amour était né ?

— Il faut que tu m'écoutes, reprit-elle en s'enjoignant au calme.

— Non. Je n'ai plus envie de t'écouter, répondit-il d'un ton las.

— Seigneur ! C'est insensé ! s'énerva-t-elle. Je n'ai rien fait, ce soir ! Je ne t'ai pas menti ! Et je n'ai pas embrassé Ben Campbell.

Ces paroles semblèrent attiser de plus belle la colère d'Andreas qui répondit en serrant les dents :

— C'est fini, Hope. Je souhaite que tu trouves un autre logement dès le mois prochain.

Il attrapa ses clés posées sur une table basse et les mit dans sa poche avant d'enfiler son manteau.

Terrifiée, Hope réalisa qu'il allait partir. Sans doute avait-il l'intention de retourner dans sa grande maison, le temps qu'elle quitte elle-même l'appartement.

— Mais… Tu ne peux pas partir ! s'écria-t-elle d'une voix paniquée.

Il haussa les épaules et se dirigea vers le dressing.

Hope le suivit et le regarda avec ébahissement sortir un sac de voyage et y glisser quelques vêtements.

— C'est… C'est impossible, balbutia-t-elle. C'est un cauchemar. Cela ne peut pas nous arriver. Pas à *nous* !

Avec tristesse, Andreas plongea le regard dans les yeux intensément bleus de la jeune femme.

Ces yeux dans lesquels il s'était perdu tant de fois avec bonheur, sans retenue, et qui semblaient maintenant le supplier… Mais elle l'avait trahi, alors qu'il lui avait accordé toute sa confiance. En une soirée, tout avait été détruit !

Jamais auparavant il n'avait pris conscience de la puissance des liens qui les unissaient. Il réalisait maintenant ce qu'il allait perdre. Il avait commis une erreur avec Hope. Il l'avait laissée occuper trop de place dans sa vie. La preuve en était ce qu'il sentait se déchirer en lui…

Ce visage radieux, cette bouche pulpeuse, ce regard magique…

C'était fini. Elle venait de briser à jamais le petit monde qu'ils s'étaient créé et au sein duquel il avait cru trouver le bonheur.

— Il n'y a plus de nous, répondit-il de sa voix la plus dure, en ignorant la douleur qui l'étreignait au plus profond.

Après avoir jeté chemises et costumes dans le sac, il se releva et fit quelques pas vers la porte d'entrée.

— Si tu ne me crois pas, pourquoi n'interrogerais-tu pas Ben ? demanda Hope.

— Pourquoi m'abaisserais-je à ce niveau ? rétorqua-t-il avec une feinte indifférence.

En réalité, s'il recroisait jamais ce Ben Campbell, il l'em-

76

pêcherait définitivement de faire la cour à une femme engagée ailleurs.

— Tu me déçois beaucoup, lâcha Hope.

— C'est un comble ! ironisa-t-il en ouvrant la porte, avant de la claquer derrière lui.

Hope n'aurait su dire depuis combien de temps elle demeurait immobile au milieu de la pièce, à fixer la porte refermée. Elle avait écouté le pas d'Andreas dans le couloir, guetté le chuintement de l'ascenseur...

Finalement, Andreas ne l'avait jamais aimée. Il avait suffi qu'il se persuade qu'elle en avait embrassé un autre pour la quitter. La jalousie l'avait amené à claquer la porte sur leur amour...

C'était effroyable. Elle en était autant choquée que blessée.

Dire que durant une fraction de seconde, elle avait été sur le point de lui dire qu'elle l'aimait. Quelle folie ! Andreas avait un cœur de pierre, pour oublier si vite deux ans de bonheur parfait. Elle ne pouvait y croire.

Pourtant, il l'avait fait ! Il était parti.

Encore quelques heures plus tôt, elle revêtait cette robe en songeant avec joie qu'Andreas allait enfin la présenter aux membres londoniens de sa famille. Mais cette relation qu'elle avait crue solide, fondée sur des bases inaltérables, s'était effritée sous ses yeux en une soirée. D'ici à quelques jours, elle commencerait une autre vie, devrait trouver un autre logement et... oublier celui qu'elle avait considéré comme l'homme de sa vie.

Car il était inutile de lutter. Même si de folles impulsions lui traversaient l'esprit, comme d'aller trouver Elyssa pour la supplier de dire la vérité à son frère, elle savait que tout était fini.

Non, elle s'épargnerait cette inutile humiliation. De plus, elle sentait son amour-propre lui souffler qu'elle devait à tout prix éviter de tenter de rattraper Andreas. Ne venait-il pas de l'abandonner avec une facilité déconcertante ? Comment pouvait-il refuser de l'écouter, alors qu'elle partageait sa vie depuis deux ans ? Pourquoi était-il demeuré obstinément sourd à ses tentatives d'explications ?

Au fond, jamais il ne lui avait fait confiance. N'importe qui pouvait intervenir dans leur vie et tout gâcher en moins d'une heure...

Le chagrin et la révolte bouillaient en elle.

Elle courut dans la chambre et s'effondra en larmes sur le lit. Un T-shirt d'Andreas était posé près de l'oreiller. Elle y enfouit son visage pour donner libre cours à ses pleurs, se soûlant de ce parfum familier qui, déjà, s'évaporait.

Dans la limousine qui le conduisait vers son hôtel particulier de Chelsea, Andreas était assailli d'émotions contradictoires. La douleur et la rage lui étreignaient le cœur.

La scène dont Elyssa avait été le témoin involontaire ne laissait hélas pas le moindre doute sur la nature des relations de Hope avec Ben Campbell. Il y avait peut-être des mois qu'ils se fréquentaient et qu'elle était sa maîtresse, et il n'avait rien soupçonné...

Plus que tout, l'attitude de Hope le rendait fou de colère. Comment avait-elle l'audace de nier ? Ah, si seulement elle avait avoué, si elle lui avait demandé pardon, peut-être aurait-il trouvé la force de tout oublier ! Mais elle l'avait insulté en le prenant pour un imbécile. Ses mensonges avaient eu raison de ses dernières résistances.

En tout cas, il saurait rapidement depuis combien de temps elle le trompait : il lui suffirait de passer un coup de fil aux deux agents qui la suivaient.

Dès le lendemain matin, le compte rendu précis de toutes les activités et de tous les déplacements de Hope durant les derniers mois le délivrerait au moins de cette question torturante.

5.

Le lendemain matin, au réveil d'une nuit agitée, Hope se souvint que sa vie venait d'être bouleversée.

Au moment où elle avait cru faire pleinement partie de la vie d'Andreas, alors qu'elle se réjouissait de rencontrer cette sœur qu'il chérissait tant, tout s'était effondré, comme dans un cauchemar. L'homme qu'elle aimait avait préféré croire les accusations d'Elyssa plutôt que de lui accorder sa confiance à *elle* !

Comme la veille, elle se sentit écartelée entre la douleur et la colère.

Mais il ne serait jamais qu'un homme au tempérament bouillant, songea-t-elle en enfilant le superbe peignoir de soie ivoire qui, selon Andreas, la faisait ressembler à une héroïne hollywoodienne.

Elle ne le verrait plus. Vanessa avait eu raison…

Comme les larmes lui montaient aux yeux, elle chercha la boîte de mouchoirs sur la table de chevet de son compagnon et aperçut un petit écrin de velours noir orné d'un ruban doré. Elle se souvint qu'il l'avait posé là le soir de son retour de Genève.

Cela ne pouvait être qu'un cadeau pour elle, sinon il ne l'aurait pas posé ici. Il avait dû lui rapporter un ballotin de chocolats suisses : il connaissait sa passion pour le chocolat mais savait aussi qu'elle veillait sur sa ligne.

Intriguée, elle l'ouvrit.

Ce n'étaient pas des chocolats. Il s'agissait d'une chaîne d'argent sur laquelle brillait, en pendentif, un ravissant trèfle à quatre feuilles. Sur chacune des feuilles était gravée à la main une des quatre lettres : H, O, P, E.

Reposant l'écrin d'une main tremblante, elle se moucha bruyamment. Comment était-ce possible ? Comment Andreas avait-il pu songer à lui faire ce charmant cadeau pour la quitter si brutalement quelques jours plus tard ?

Un rapide coup d'œil à la pendule lui rappela qu'elle devait partir dans une heure au travail.

Décidant d'oublier provisoirement l'incompréhensible attitude d'Andreas Nicolaidis, elle alla savourer le jet chaud de la douche et les vapeurs bienfaisantes d'huiles essentielles dans cette salle de bains qui ne serait bientôt plus la sienne.

Dans la voiture qui le conduisait à l'aéroport, Andreas espérait que le long vol en jet vers New York lui permettrait de se reposer. Et de se calmer.

Non seulement il n'avait pas fermé l'œil de la nuit, mais les documents dont il venait de prendre connaissance ce matin avaient ravivé sa colère de la veille.

Dès la première heure, sa secrétaire lui avait transmis par fax le compte rendu des deux agents de sécurité qui suivaient Hope depuis des mois.

Jamais il n'avait senti une telle rage bouillir en lui. C'était tout simplement incroyable.

Il hésita un instant avant de prendre sa décision. De toute sa carrière dans les affaires, pas une fois il n'avait repoussé un rendez-vous ni annulé un vol. Mais il se sentait incapable de partir pour New York sans avoir confronté Hope à son ignoble trahison.

— Faites demi-tour, ordonna-t-il. Nous rentrons à Londres.

Devant le miroir de la coiffeuse, Hope lissait sa longue chevelure blonde en un sage chignon. Elle venait d'enfiler un tailleur beige à rayures qui lui allongeait les jambes et faisait ressortir la couleur de ses yeux. Exactement le genre de tenue qu'Andreas appréciait.

Quelle importance ? songea-t-elle en exhalant un long soupir. Tout cela était fini… Mais une part d'elle-même ne parvenait pas y croire.

Soudain, le bruit d'une clé dans la serrure de la porte d'entrée la fit sursauter.

Son cœur se mit à battre à coups redoublés dans sa poitrine et elle se leva, tremblante d'espoir. Il était revenu ! Bien sûr ! Après une nuit de sommeil, il avait réalisé au matin que cette histoire était ridicule !

— Hope ?

— Je suis dans la chambre ! cria-t-elle en se dépêchant de vérifier son maquillage dans le miroir.

Puis, elle se leva et retint son souffle en attendant qu'Andreas apparaisse devant elle.

Lorsqu'il poussa la porte à la volée, elle sentit les effluves de son eau de Cologne lui chatouiller les narines. Il avait revêtu l'un de ses costumes préférés. Avec sa chemise blanche et ses cheveux parfaitement coiffés, il était plus séduisant que jamais. Mais elle vit dans son regard la même lueur de rage que la veille au soir et elle crut défaillir.

Son sourire s'évanouit et elle demeura interdite.

— Quelle honte ! explosa Andreas, brandissait une liasse

de papiers. Comment as-tu osé me trahir à ce point ? Il y des mois que tu me trompes !

Stupéfaite, elle posa ses mains sur ses hanches et le dévisagea avec autant de sang-froid qu'il lui était possible.

— Je ne comprends pas de quoi tu parles, Andreas.

Il leva encore sa liasse de documents et cria :

— Tu es allée chez Ben Campbell plusieurs fois ! Tu as même passé une nuit chez lui, alors que j'étais en voyage !

Hope s'efforça d'ignorer l'indignation que suscitaient en elle ces accusations ridicules.

— C'est absurde, répondit-elle avec calme. Je n'ai jamais mis les pieds chez Ben. Je ne sais même pas où il vit.

— Quoi ? Tu… Tu nies ? balbutia Andreas, qui suffoquait visiblement de colère. Mais j'ai les preuves ! Toutes les preuves !

Comme il lui tendait sa liasse, Hope fronça les sourcils et s'approcha. Avant de lui prendre les documents des mains, elle leva un regard soupçonneux vers lui.

— Des *preuves* ? demanda froidement. Mais de quoi s'agit-il, au juste ?

— Surprise ! lâcha-t-il d'un ton cinglant. Depuis près d'un an, tu as fait l'objet d'une enquête de sécurité. Et voici les rapports les plus récents concernant toutes tes activités, heure par heure.

Hope se mordit la lèvre tandis que le sens de cette révélation l'envahissait peu à peu.

Sans rien perdre de son calme, elle toisa Andreas.

— Es-tu en train de m'annoncer que tu m'as fait surveiller pendant un an ? demanda-t-elle d'une voix altérée par le choc.

— En réalité, je me suis assuré de ta protection, expliqua-t-il. Il était important que…

— *Qui* m'a surveillée ? demanda-t-elle, livide.

Un tourbillon de visions écœurantes s'était mis en mouvement dans son esprit : chaque fois qu'elle avait cru être seule, chaque fois qu'elle était allée faire ses courses au supermarché ou qu'elle avait emprunté le métro, le moindre de ses faits et gestes était enregistré ! Elle en avait la nausée. Aucun être humain ne pouvait être ainsi rabaissé au rang d'un objet, pensait-elle. Depuis toujours, elle respectait la liberté d'autrui et croyait qu'une relation devait se fonder sur la confiance réciproque.

— *Qui* m'a surveillée ? répéta-t-elle.

— Des professionnels, répondit Andreas avec détachement. Des agents très efficaces, qui travaillent pour une agence avec laquelle je collabore depuis longtemps. Et par conséquent, n'essaie pas de vouloir me faire croire qu'ils ont inventé ce qu'ils ont vu, parce que…

— Je peux à peine croire que tu aies pu me faire cela, coupa-t-elle d'une voix forte. C'est ignoble ! Tu as payé des gens pour qu'ils me suivent partout ? Tu m'as fait espionner ! Cela dépasse tout.

Andreas resta un instant interdit avant se reprendre.

— C'était pour te protéger, assena-t-il d'un ton glacial. J'avais reçu des menaces anonymes et craignais pour ta sécurité. C'est une démarche malheureusement banale dans le milieu des affaires…

Hope n'écoutait pas ce qu'il disait. La fureur montait en elle, plus intense à chaque seconde.

— Depuis hier soir, s'écria-t-elle, je réalise que tu ne m'as jamais fait confiance. C'est inouï ! Jamais je ne t'aurais cru capable de ce coup bas. Aucune relation ne peut s'établir sur de telles bases. Je ne suis ni ta chose, ni un criminel en puissance qu'il convient de surveiller à chaque instant !

— C'est le monde à l'envers ! explosa Andreas, furieux. J'ai peine à croire que tu uses de cet argument pour te défendre. Tu m'as trompé ! Comment peux-tu t'offusquer d'une simple surveillance de routine, quand tu t'es comportée de cette manière avec moi ? Comment oses-tu m'accuser, *moi* ? Jusqu'à la nuit dernière, il ne me serait pas venu à l'idée de demander à lire ces rapports ! Je respectais ta vie privée. Mais puisque tu niais l'évidence, il a bien fallu que je trouve des preuves. Or, tu t'es rendue à maintes reprises chez Ben Campbell, ce qui corrobore parfaitement ce que m'a dit ma sœur !

Ignorant son cœur qui battait la chamade et la confusion de son esprit, Hope arracha des mains d'Andreas les feuillets qu'il brandissait et les parcourut fiévreusement.

Elle reconnut aussitôt l'adresse familière qui correspondait, sur la même ligne, au nom de Ben.

Elle lança à Andreas un regard où perçait l'ironie.

— Cet appartement est celui de Vanessa, dit-elle en lui rendant les feuillets. J'avais oublié ce détail, mais il appartient à son cousin. Ben en a acheté un autre il y a environ un an, et il a alors proposé à Vanessa de lui louer celui-ci à un prix très intéressant. Désolée, mais tes « preuves » tombent à l'eau.

— Tu me prends pour un imbécile ! rétorqua Andreas. Ton amie s'empressera de confirmer tout ce que tu voudras lui faire dire, mais cette histoire ne tient pas debout. La coïncidence serait trop belle ! Tu as embrassé ce garçon hier soir, et tu voudrais me faire croire que son appartement n'est pas vraiment le sien… C'en est trop !

Il éructait de rage et se dirigeait déjà vers la porte d'entrée.

— Je ne suis pas étonnée que tu ne veuilles pas me croire, s'emporta-t-elle, désespérée. Tu ne m'as jamais fait confiance. Pourquoi commencerais-tu aujourd'hui ?

Andreas se retourna et lança à Hope un regard noir.

Durant une fraction de seconde, il se demanda si elle ne

disait pas la vérité. Dans son charmant tailleur, avec ses cheveux relevés, elle avait l'air d'un ange. C'était bien ainsi qu'il pensait à elle quand il partait au loin : ce visage, ce regard bleu et ardent, ces cheveux soyeux qu'il aimait tant caresser avant de s'endormir…

Décidément, il avait abandonné toute prudence. il avait trop longtemps oublié qu'il ne devait pas permettre à une femme de prendre tant d'importance dans sa vie. Ses parents l'avaient payé cher, et il devait rester fidèle à la décision qu'il avait prise une fois pour toutes : ne jamais s'engager ni ouvrir son cœur.

Il posa un regard triste sur le grand lit dans lequel il avait tant de fois contemplé Hope endormie, sans qu'elle le sache.

— Quand je pense que tu as certainement fait venir cet homme ici… Je suis écœuré, lâcha-t-il.

Hope sursauta comme si une guêpe venait de la piquer. Sa fureur resurgit aussitôt.

— C'est facile à savoir, cria-t-elle. Tu n'as qu'à le demander à tes agents soi-disant chargés de me protéger !

Sans même se donner la peine de répondre, il claqua la porte derrière lui.

Dans la salle de bains, Hope soupira en regardant son visage bouffi de larmes. Elle avait cette nuit encore pleuré toutes les larmes de son corps.

Il y avait pourtant sept semaines qu'elle était installée chez Vanessa, occupant la chambre d'amis que celle-ci avait mise à sa disposition dès qu'elle avait appris le drame. Elle se remettait très mal de sa rupture avec Andreas. Elle pensait à lui sans cesse. A tout moment de la journée, elle se remémorait leur terrible dispute et les mots cruels qu'ils avaient échangés.

Après une douche, elle enfila un pantalon noir et un pull

blanc et se maquilla soigneusement pour cacher les marques de chagrin.

Elle ne parvenait pas à retrouver le sourire. Vanessa lui avait dit qu'après une semaine de larmes et de laisser-aller bien légitimes, il devenait indispensable de se remettre d'un chagrin d'amour. Elle était reconnaissante à son amie de lui témoigner tant de chaleur et de générosité et se reprochait de ne pas être une colocataire de très bonne compagnie. Aussi cachait-elle sa profonde souffrance autant que possible. De toute façon, il fallait qu'elle aille travailler chaque matin et qu'elle présente un visage souriant aux clients… Mais cet effort lui coûtait, et elle se sentait souvent épuisée quand elle rentrait. Elle dormait mal et avait souvent mal au ventre. Parfois, au petit matin, de violentes nausées l'assaillaient et elle se tournait et se retournait dans son lit en attendant qu'elles passent.

N'était-il pas normal que ce soit si difficile ? Durant deux ans, Andreas avait été au centre de sa vie. Elle avait accompli chacun de ses gestes les plus familiers en fonction de lui : elle ne choisissait que des vêtements susceptibles de lui plaire, se hâtait de prendre le métro pour le retrouver plus vite, rêvait de partir en week-end avec lui à Paris ou à Rome…

Sortant de la salle de bains, elle se dirigea vers la cuisine où elle trouva Vanessa en jean et en T-shirt en train de prendre son petit déjeuner, ses longs cheveux châtain clair en désordre.

— Pourquoi es-tu déjà maquillée ? lui demanda son amie en la dévisageant avec curiosité. Et pourquoi es-tu habillée comme si tu allais travailler ?

— Mais… Je pars travailler ! répondit Hope en jetant un coup d'œil à sa montre.

— Un dimanche ? demanda Vanessa en riant. Tu as vraiment l'esprit ailleurs, Hope.

Elles rirent ensemble, et Hope s'assit près de son amie.

Vanessa porta sa tasse à ses lèvres, une lueur d'inquiétude dans le regard.

— Tu veux un *bagel* à la confiture ? demanda-t-elle.

— Non, je n'ai pas faim, répondit Hope en se servant une tasse de café.

— Mais tu as complètement perdu l'appétit ! protesta Vanessa. Tu as maigri, tu sais… Il faut que tu manges quelque chose !

— Oui, plus tard, c'est promis, acquiesça Hope.

Elle se sentait l'estomac noué et n'aurait pu avaler quoi que ce fût. Vanessa venait d'avaler un paquet de biscuits entier, et Hope se demandait toujours comment cette fille au corps de liane pouvait tant manger sans prendre de poids.

— Tu sais, reprit Vanessa, j'ai parlé avec Ben hier, et je crois que tu devrais le laisser t'aider à monter ta propre entreprise. Les banques sont un peu frileuses en ce moment, et Ben sait qu'il faut donner sa chance à un artiste.

Hope haussa les épaules. Même si elle ne pouvait rien reprocher à Ben, celui-ci avait été mêlé à sa rupture avec Andreas. L'idée qu'il puisse prendre une part active à sa nouvelle vie la mettait mal à l'aise. De plus, elle préférait trouver seule le moyen de réaliser son rêve.

Néanmoins, c'était un fait, elle craignait de ne jamais parvenir à réunir les fonds nécessaires à l'ouverture de sa propre enseigne.

— Je ne crois pas que ce soit une bonne idée, répondit-elle faiblement.

— Pourquoi ? insista Vanessa. Tu as vu cinq banquiers qui ont refusé de financer ton lancement. Mon cousin a de l'argent, et il serait heureux de t'aider dans ta carrière. Je crois que tu devrais y réfléchir avant de refuser son offre.

Hope approuva d'un signe de tête et avala une gorgée de café en silence.

Depuis qu'elle vivait chez Vanessa, elle avait croisé Ben plusieurs fois. Il s'était montré charmant et avait évité toute allusion à Andreas. De plus, il n'avait pas cherché à profiter de la situation, ce dont elle lui était reconnaissante. Elle se rappelait ce qu'il lui avait dit au cours de cette affreuse soirée chez Elyssa :

« Penses-tu que j'ai une chance de te séduire et de te faire oublier ton millionnaire grec ? »

Mais Andreas hantait sans relâche ses pensées…

— Je crois que Ben est très sensible à ton charme, reprit Vanessa en lui adressant un clin d'œil.

Hope haussa les épaules.

— C'est un séducteur. Il aime plutôt que les femmes se montrent sensibles à *son* charme.

— Non, il a changé. Autrefois, il aimait beaucoup sortir, c'est vrai, mais il est devenu plus sérieux. Et j'ai l'impression qu'il apprécie avant tout tes qualités humaines. D'ailleurs, nous avons passé une très bonne soirée tous les trois, la semaine dernière…

— C'est vrai, admit-elle. Pourtant, je crois surtout qu'il se sent coupable d'avoir été mêlé à ma rupture avec Andreas. A mon avis, c'est la raison pour laquelle il est si gentil avec moi.

Son amie leva les yeux au ciel et s'esclaffa.

— Mais non, voyons ! Il pense qu'Andreas s'est conduit comme le dernier des idiots, et je suis bien d'accord avec lui. Mais tu sous-estimes l'attachement qu'il a pour toi.

— De toute façon, ça n'a pas tellement d'importance, opposa Hope en soupirant.

Vanessa demeura silencieuse quelques instants. Puis, sans cesser de la fixer, elle déclara :

— Tu sais, Andreas est parti pour de bon. Et Ben ne t'attendra peut-être pas durant des décennies. Tu devrais essayer de passer à autre chose...

— Je sais cela ! s'écria Hope. Mais...

— Non, je ne crois pas que tu en sois consciente, coupa Vanessa. Je m'inquiète beaucoup à ton sujet, Hope. Tu ne crois pas qu'il serait temps de quitter ta bulle et de revenir dans le monde réel ?

— Bien sûr que si. Mais Andreas...

— Récapitulons, enchaîna Vanessa. Cet Andreas t'a accusée d'avoir entretenu une aventure avec Ben mais il ne t'a pas laissé aucune chance de t'expliquer...

— Parce qu'il a voulu croire sa sœur, intervint Hope en soupirant. Et même si je suis blessée, je ne peux pas haïr un homme parce qu'il prête crédit aux propos de sa sœur. Ce n'est pas un crime.

— Ecoute, dit Vanessa en lui prenant la main. Je ne cherche pas à faire d'Andreas un démon. Il est vrai qu'Elyssa porte une lourde responsabilité dans votre séparation. Mais je ne peux plus supporter que tu le défendes ainsi. Il s'est trop mal conduit. Et surtout, tu dois songer à toi et à ton avenir. Alors...

Elle sembla hésiter, puis elle se leva et alla dans sa chambre prendre un magazine qu'elle jeta sur la table.

— Regarde ceci. Je ne te le montre pas pour que tu aies du chagrin, mais pour que tu comprennes que pour *lui*, la vie ne s'est pas arrêtée...

Hope regarda le sommaire que son amie lui désignait de l'index et découvrit une photo représentant Andreas dans un cocktail au bras d'une grande femme brune.

Le visage rayonnant, Andreas levait une coupe de champagne, et la jeune femme semblait tout aussi heureuse que lui.

Le choc fut violent. C'était comme si Hope s'était tenue au bord d'une piscine et que quelqu'un l'avait poussée sans lui laisser le temps de prendre son souffle.

90

Le pire, c'était qu'il emmenait sa nouvelle compagne dans ses soirées et ses réceptions… Alors qu'il ne lui avait pas seulement permis de fréquenter ses amis, du temps où ils étaient ensemble ! Non seulement elle sentait son cœur se déchirer, mais son amour-propre recevait par là-dessus une gifle mémorable. Quelle humiliation !

Vanessa lui entoura les épaules d'un bras protecteur.

— Je regrette de te causer cette peine, mais il faut que tu comprennes que cet homme ne mérite pas l'amour que tu lui portes, dit-elle. Cela fait des semaines que je veille à ce que tu ne tombes pas sur ces magazines où il est visible dans des soirées organisées à Londres ou à New York. Tu vois bien qu'il ne se lamente pas et ne reste pas enfermé chez lui…

— Oui, oui, le message est très clair, admit Hope, agacée. J'ai compris.

— Je regrette, répéta Vanessa.

La sonnette retentit.

En soupirant, la jeune femme se dirigea vers la porte d'entrée.

— Tu sais, reprit-elle en se retournant, je voulais seulement te faire comprendre qu'Andreas est sorti définitivement de ta vie…

Hope approuva d'un hochement de tête et regarda par la fenêtre le ciel gris.

Vanessa avait raison, il fallait qu'elle se ressaisisse.

Mais avec qui parlait elle ?

— Oui, nous nous sommes croisés une ou deux fois, mais vous n'avez pas annoncé votre visite à Hope…

Elle tendit l'oreille. De l'autre côté du couloir, son amie parlait assez fort, sur un ton étrange. Comme si elle voulait l'avertir.

— … Et elle a tant fait la fête ces derniers jours que je ne sais pas si elle peut vous voir maintenant. Il faut que je lui pose la question. Elle est rentrée tard de sa soirée, hier…

Que signifiait cette avalanche de mensonges ?

Doucement, Hope se leva et s'avança dans l'embrasure de la porte de la cuisine pour apercevoir le visiteur.

Elle resta pétrifiée en reconnaissant Andreas.

Aussitôt, elle sentit son cœur battre à se rompre, ses mains trembler. Des frissons glacés la parcouraient. Elle ne savait plus que penser ni que sentir…

Cependant, décida-t-elle en traversant à son tour le couloir pour aller à sa rencontre, il fallait qu'elle reprenne le contrôle d'elle-même. Même si elle défaillait en retrouvant ces cheveux noirs, ce regard intense, cette silhouette imposante et familière, elle voulait savoir ce qu'il faisait là.

Au moment précis où Vanessa lui disait qu'il était définitivement sorti de sa vie… La coïncidence ne manquait pas de piquant !

6.

Vanessa se tenait toujours devant la porte d'entrée, bloquant le passage, mais quand Andreas aperçut Hope, il poussa la porte et fit d'autorité un pas sur le seuil.

— Merci beaucoup, dit-il d'un ton sec à Vanessa.

Celle-ci se croisa les bras sur la poitrine et le dévisagea non sans perplexité.

— Je ne m'attendais pas à te voir, lança Hope.

Il regarda avidement la jeune femme.

En examinant son visage, il fut d'abord frappé par sa pâleur. Et puis, malgré les ombres à paupières et le mascara, par le fait qu'elle avait les yeux fatigués. Comme si elle avait pleuré. A moins qu'elle n'ait fait la fête très tard, comme venait de l'annoncer Vanessa ? Mais le bleu turquoise de ses iris était toujours aussi lumineux, aussi profond, observa-t-il avec un battement de cœur.

Elle n'avait pas bonne mine.

— Hem... Veux-tu que je reste avec toi ? demanda Vanessa en se penchant à l'oreille de Hope.

— Non, je te remercie. Je vais inviter Andreas à me suivre dans ma chambre. Ne t'inquiète pas.

Vanessa approuva d'un signe de tête et lança un regard de soutien à Hope avant de s'éclipser. Cette dernière précéda Andreas dans le couloir et le conduisit vers sa chambre.

Il jeta un regard embarrassé tout autour de lui.

La chambre occupée par Hope était une pièce spacieuse, pourvue d'un petit balcon et meublée avec un goût tout féminin.

Il lui était désormais évident que cette Vanessa était bien l'occupante de l'appartement. Dans le hall de l'immeuble, il avait vainement cherché une boîte aux lettres portant le nom de Ben Campbell. En revanche, son regard s'était arrêté sur la mention « Vanessa Fitzsimmons et Hope Evans ». Pourtant, si les doutes s'étaient insinués dans son esprit ces derniers temps, il ne pouvait croire que Hope n'avait pas entretenu une liaison avec Ben Campbell. La scène à laquelle sa sœur avait assisté n'était guère ambiguë, hélas…

Mais tout cela était si étrange ! Durant deux ans, il avait connu une femme désintéressée et sensible, spontanée, gaie, incapable de mentir. Hope n'était pas le genre de femme à retrouver régulièrement un amant à la dérobée et à mener double jeu. Peut-être avait-elle simplement succombé aux avances de Ben Campbell lors de la soirée donnée par Elyssa ?

— Tu veux t'asseoir ? proposa Hope, visiblement nerveuse, en désignant un fauteuil.

Pour se donner une contenance, elle s'assit elle-même sur une chaise et leva machinalement la main à son chignon, laissant retomber ses cheveux sur ses épaules dans les rayons du soleil matinal.

Il perçut le parfum de son shampoing et se rappela le plaisir qu'il prenait à glisser ses doigts dans cette chevelure soyeuse dont les reflets l'aveuglaient.

Il soupira et s'assit à son tour.

— Veux-tu que j'aille nous chercher une tasse de café ? suggéra-t-elle.

— Non, je te remercie… Je ne vais pas rester long-temps…

— Ah ?

Embarrassé, il s'efforça d'ignorer le violent désir qui montait en lui. Ces yeux, cette bouche… comme il aurait voulu prendre Hope dans ses bras et l'embrasser ! Elle lui manquait tant. Toutes les femmes qu'il avait croisées depuis lors dans ces soirées mondaines interminables l'avaient ennuyé. Aucune d'elles n'avait un visage doux et lumineux comme celui de Hope. Lorsqu'il s'endormait le soir, il ne voyait qu'elle…

La jeune femme le fixait avec obstination. Elle attendait qu'il poursuive.

Il prit une longue inspiration avant de déclarer :

— Je suis venu prendre de tes nouvelles, mais pas seulement. Je voulais savoir comment tu allais, et… Qu'est-il arrivé à ton téléphone portable ?

— Je l'ai jeté.

— Il semble que la ligne ait été définitivement coupée…

— Oui, je n'en avais pas un besoin indispensable, admit Hope avec une pointe d'impatience.

Il hochait la tête, sans mot dire.

Il aurait pu se douter qu'elle ne conserverait pas un téléphone qui ne lui avait jamais servi qu'à communiquer à lui ! Et il venait de dire qu'il y avait une raison précise à sa présence ici…

— Tu voulais me joindre, si je comprends bien, relança-t-elle.

— Oui. Ton frère a laissé plusieurs messages sur le répondeur de l'appartement. Il va venir à Londres la semaine prochaine et souhaite te voir. Ne pouvant te joindre ni là-bas ni sur ton portable, il a commencé à s'inquiéter…

Hope se mordit la lèvre. Elle n'avait rien espéré, se rappela-t-elle. Mais la manière dont Andreas venait de lui annoncer qu'il n'était venu la voir que pour lui transmettre un message de son frère était assez humiliante.

Et décevante.

— Je n'ai pas songé à l'avertir tout de suite de mon déménagement. Jonathan m'envoie tout juste une carte une fois par an, à Noël.

— Il faut que tu le rappelles, la ligne de l'appartement sera bientôt coupée.

Elle haussa les sourcils.

— Ah ? Pourquoi ?

— Je l'ai mis en vente, lâcha-t-il à contrecœur.

Il aurait préféré ne pas lui divulguer cette information. La raison pour laquelle il se séparait de cet appartement très confortable et idéalement situé ne crevait-elle pas les yeux ? Il ne supportait plus de s'y trouver sans elle. Le lieu avait perdu sa chaleur, sa magie. Dès qu'il y mettait les pieds, il sentait un poids de tristesse s'abattre sur lui.

— C'est dommage, souffla doucement Hope. C'était un appartement agréable.

Elle avait formulé cette remarque d'une voix distraite, comme si elle pensait à autre chose.

Aussitôt, il fut piqué au vif. Quelle indifférence ! Elle ne l'avait même pas remercié d'être venu jusqu'ici pour l'avertir des appels de son frère ! Et visiblement, elle n'avait eu aucune difficulté à se détacher de cet appartement où ils avaient vécu durant deux ans.

— C'était aussi l'avis de Ben Campbell ? demanda-t-il d'un ton acerbe.

Hope le dévisagea avec colère.

— Tes agents sont visiblement bien placés pour connaître tout des goûts et de la vie privée de Ben Campbell ! rétorqua-t-elle. Tu devrais leur poser directement la question.

— C'est à peine croyable, rugit-il. Tu me trompes avec cet homme, et tu me reproches la manière dont je l'apprends ! Mais ma sœur aussi, a vu…

96

— Ta sœur a menti ! cria Hope. C'est elle qui embrassait un autre homme que son mari. Je les ai surpris, et…

— Comment peux-tu t'abaisser à accuser ma sœur de tes propres fautes ? coupa-t-il en se levant d'un bond. C'est indigne ! Laisse Elyssa en dehors de tout ça. Tu ne vas quand même pas t'étonner qu'elle m'avertisse des infidélités de la femme avec laquelle je vis ? Ce Campbell a tenté de me prendre ce qui m'appartenait, et…

— Je ne suis pas un objet ! Je n'appartiens à personne ! s'écria Hope en se levant à son tour et en ouvrant la porte de la chambre, l'invitant par ce geste à sortir.

Ils gagnèrent tous deux l'entrée dans un silence lourd.

— Je te prie de sortir d'ici, déclara sèchement Hope en ouvrant la porte.

— Avec plaisir, dit-il en franchissant le seuil.

Il s'immobilisa aussitôt : Ben Campbell se tenait devant lui, un bouquet de fleurs à la main.

Durant une fraction de seconde, tous deux se fixèrent sans mot dire.

Puis, Andreas se retourna vers Hope et lui lança un regard mi-outragé, mi-triomphant, qui semblait signifier : « Je le savais bien. »

— Va-t'en ! hurla Hope. Je te déteste !

— Vous ne devriez pas importuner Hope, intervint Ben d'un ton froid. Je crois qu'il vaut mieux que vous la laissiez.

Fou de rage, Andreas serra soudain les poings et lui décocha un violent crochet dans le menton.

Surpris, Ben chancela avant de s'effondrer sur le sol.

— Tu es fou ! s'écria Hope.

— *Theos !* Je lui devais bien ça, déclara Andreas entre ses dents, en posant un regard glacial sur Ben.

Puis il traversa le palier et dévala l'escalier.

Andreas ne s'était pas même retourné, songea Hope, frissonnant à l'idée qu'elle venait sans doute de le voir pour la dernière fois de sa vie.

Vanessa, qui était accourue, l'aida à soutenir Ben et à le relever. Furieux, celui-ci semblait sur le point de se lancer à la poursuite d'Andreas.

— Ne sois pas aussi mesquin que ce pauvre type, souffla Vanessa, viens. Hope va prendre tes fleurs, allons nous installer dans le salon…

Depuis plus d'un quart d'heure, Hope était enfermée dans sa chambre, prostrée dans un fauteuil.

Trop bouleversée par cette rencontre avec Andreas, elle n'avait pas encore pu rejoindre Vanessa et Ben qui prenaient le thé dans le salon.

L'homme qu'elle aimait de tout son cœur venait de lui rappeler qu'ils avaient vécu sur un malentendu : il était encore persuadé qu'elle lui avait été infidèle malgré tous les témoignages d'amour et de tendresse qu'elle lui avait donnés durant deux années. Il avait suffi que sa sœur affirme qu'elle l'avait vue embrasser un autre homme pour qu'il croie à ce scénario.

Il fallait qu'elle cesse de se tourmenter avec cette histoire. N'avait-elle pas contemplé quelques minutes plus tôt une photo représentant Andreas au comble du bonheur, accompagné d'une top-modèle, dans l'une de ces soirées réservées à la jet-set ?

Si seulement elle était capable de penser à autre chose…

On frappa à la porte.

— Entrez, dit-elle en se redressant.

C'était Ben. Une ombre rouge lui voilait le menton, mais il ne semblait pas avoir trop souffert du coup qu'il avait reçu.

— J'espère que cette confrontation n'a pas été trop éprouvante pour toi, dit-il gravement.

— Oh, Ben ! Je suis vraiment désolée que tu aies été mêlé à tout cela !

— Cela n'a aucune importance, Hope, répondit-il en s'asseyant près d'elle et en posant sa main sur la sienne d'un geste protecteur. En revanche, je n'aime pas te voir si affectée par le comportement de cet homme. Je crois que tu as besoin de te divertir un peu.

Elle soupira.

— Oui, sans doute... C'est aussi ce que dit Vanessa.

— Ecoute, je serais vraiment heureux si tu acceptais de venir avec moi dans notre cottage de famille, à moi et à Vanessa, le week-end prochain. Il n'y aura personne, tu seras libre de te reposer et de respirer le grand air.

Certes, deux jours au grand air, loin de la ville, lui feraient le plus grand bien...

— Oui, mais... Nous irions là-bas en *amis*, n'est-ce pas ? demanda-t-elle en plongeant son regard dans celui de Ben.

— Oui. Si je peux t'embrasser en *ami*, bien sûr, dit-il en déposant un baiser sur son front.

Elle lui sourit.

Elle avait perdu Andreas, mais elle pouvait compter sur l'amitié de Vanessa et le soutien de Ben. C'était réconfortant.

— C'est entendu, lança-t-elle. Et pour fêter cela, nous allons déjeuner tous les trois dans un très bon restaurant.

Au cours de la semaine qui suivit, Hope parvint à recouvrer un peu de sa bonne humeur.

Elle avait du mal à trouver le sommeil en se remémorant sa dernière conversation avec Andreas, mais la perspective de passer deux jours à la campagne la réjouissait, et de plus elle était parvenue à contacter son frère, qui avait insisté pour dîner avec elle au plus vite.

En se rendant au restaurant où elle allait le retrouver, elle songea qu'ils ne s'étaient pas revus depuis les obsèques de leur mère. Elle avait hâte de le retrouver !

Jonathan lui fit signe depuis la table où il était installé.

Hope traversa la salle de restaurant en souriant et ils s'embrassèrent chaleureusement, mais elle fut surprise de voir ensuite son frère l'examiner de pied en cap et la dévisager gravement.

— Hope… Qu'est-ce qui se passe ? demanda-t-il. Tu as quelque chose à m'annoncer ?

Interloquée, elle baissa les yeux sur son manteau.

— Je ne comprends pas, dit-elle enfin. Que veux-tu dire ?

— Tu es si pâle ! Et tu as maigri. En revanche, il me semble que ton ventre est un peu rond… Excuse-moi, mais quand je t'ai vue, j'ai pensé que tu étais peut-être enceinte.

Hope blêmit et s'assit face à lui sans mot dire.

L'épouse de Jonathan était une femme très maigre, se rappela-t-elle, cherchant à comprendre ce commentaire. Bon, elle se sentait un peu à l'étroit dans ses vêtements ces derniers temps… Mais c'était parce qu'elle s'était empiffrée de chocolat après la pénible visite d'Andreas. Et puis… Non, son ventre n'était pas si rond ! se dit-elle en le jaugeant du plat de la main.

— Bon sang, quelle réflexion stupide de ma part ! Je regrette, Hope, enchaîna son frère, rouge de confusion.

Ils oublièrent vite l'incident. Jonathan, le regard brillant de joie, lui expliqua que ses affaires se portaient maintenant au mieux. Il avait réussi à remonter la pente et avait désormais toutes les raisons de croire que son entreprise d'architecture allait prospérer.

— Et c'est la raison pour laquelle je tenais à te voir très

vite, expliqua-t-il en sortant un chèque de son portefeuille. C'est pour toi, Hope.

Eberluée, elle baissa les yeux sur le chèque. Le montant correspondait à la part de l'héritage qu'elle avait cédée à Jonathan, augmentée de 15 %.

— C'est à mon tour de t'aider à faire tes preuves dans ta carrière, ajouta-t-il. C'est bien le moins que je puisse faire ! Et je n'oublierai jamais ta générosité, au moment où j'étais dans le besoin.

— C'est très gentil, mais…

— Il ne s'agit pas d'un prêt, Hope. C'est *ton* argent. J'espère que ta ligne d'accessoires de mode verra le jour avant la fin de l'année ! Mais je reste persuadé que tu devrais commencer un petit régime…

Folle de joie, elle sauta au cou de son frère.

Déjà, elle prévoyait qu'elle garderait encore quelque temps son emploi dans la boutique de Soho où elle travaillait. Mais bientôt, elle pourrait créer une nouvelle collection de proto-types et les présenter à de grands créateurs.

— Je me souviens de sacs que tu m'avais montrés, reprit Jonathan d'un ton enthousiaste. Ils étaient superbes. Tu les as vendus ?

— Oui, et ils ont remporté un certain succès. Mon amie Vanessa les avait également photographiés. D'ailleurs, si tu as un peu de temps demain, j'aimerais que tu assistes au vernissage de son exposition. Tu sais, c'est une artiste très connue, désormais !

— Et tes sacs connaîtront bientôt la même renommée, c'est clair, affirma Jonathan en trinquant joyeusement avec elle.

7.

D'un geste agacé, Andreas repoussa la revue d'art dans laquelle quatre pages étaient consacrées à l'exposition londonienne de Vanessa Fitzsimmons.

Le journaliste qui avait signé l'article expliquait que la jeune photographe avait dédié toute une série de photos de mode à son amie Hope Evans, la talentueuse créatrice des accessoires dont étaient parés les mannequins, laquelle venait de lancer sa propre collection. Une adresse Internet indiquée en bas de page permettait aux lecteurs intéressés d'accéder au site de Hope et de commander les objets. D'autres photos prises lors du vernissage représentaient Hope souriante, entourée de Ben et de Vanessa. Ses cheveux blonds tombant en cascade sur ses épaules nues, le regard vif, la jeune femme semblait parfaitement heureuse.

Andreas était fou de rage. Il ne s'était donc pas trompé : ce Ben avait toujours rôdé autour d'elle. Sur chacun des clichés, il lui tenait familièrement le bras. Bon sang ! Il était *aussi* venu lui offrir des fleurs, le jour où Andreas était allé chez Vanessa, et il avait osé embrasser Hope lors de cette soirée chez Elyssa…

Par conséquent, peu importait qu'il n'ait jamais occupé l'appartement où se rendait Hope du temps de leur vie commune.

Si elle ne le voyait pas à cette adresse à l'époque, elle se laissait forcément séduire ailleurs.

Mais pourquoi ne parvenait-il pas à oublier cette histoire ? Pourquoi sa vie était-elle sans saveur et ennuyeuse depuis que Hope n'en faisait plus partie ?

Hope referma doucement derrière elle la porte du bureau du gynécologue qu'elle venait de consulter.

Dans la salle d'attente du cabinet, Vanessa feuilletait distraitement un magazine. En la voyant, elle bondit sur ses pieds et vint à sa rencontre.

— Tu es livide. Tu te sens bien ? demanda son amie en la guidant vers la sortie.

Hope se contenta de répondre par un hochement de tête affirmatif et la suivit dans un café à côté du cabinet.

Quand elles furent confortablement installées devant une tasse de thé, Vanessa plongea son regard dans le sien.

— Alors ? demanda-t-elle d'un ton grave. C'est positif ? Tu es enceinte ?

— Oui, murmura Hope d'une voix à peine audible. De trois mois. Bientôt quatre.

— Comment, bientôt quatre mois ? Mais c'est impossible ! Ton ventre est à peine arrondi ! Et puis, tu t'en serais rendu compte avant !

— Non, expliqua-t-elle en secouant la tête. Même si cela peut paraître curieux, il est normal de peu grossir avant la fin du quatrième mois. Cela arrive souvent, au point que la grossesse est indiscernable à l'œil nu. De plus, j'ai maigri après ma rupture avec Andreas.

— Mais… Tu n'as pas réalisé que ton cycle était interrompu ? balbutia Vanessa, incrédule. Je ne comprends pas.

— Je sais, dit Hope en haussant les épaules. C'est étrange

comme on peut s'aveugler sur tout, quand on est préoccupé. Je n'ai pensé qu'à mon chagrin et à Andreas. Une perte de poids ou un stress provoquent aussi parfois une interruption de cycle, alors je ne m'en suis pas inquiétée.

Vanessa se tut pendant quelques instants en fronçant les sourcils.

— Je déteste cet homme, déclara-t-elle. Le fait que tu aies ignoré les avertissements de ton corps durant des semaines en dit long sur ta détresse. Et non seulement il a été injuste avec toi, non seulement il a frappé Ben, mais il te met dans une situation impossible ! Mais aussi, pourquoi n'as-tu pas pris tes précautions ?

Hope rougit.

— Eh bien, Andreas utilisait des préservatifs. Mais il est arrivé plusieurs fois que nous fassions l'amour dans des circonstances un peu… imprévues. Dans sa voiture, par exemple.

Malgré la gravité du moment, Vanessa sourit, amusée, et lui prit la main de dans la sienne.

— Bon. Ce sont des choses qui arrivent. Que comptes-tu faire ?

Sans hésiter, Hope fixa son amie.

— Il faut que je l'annonce à Andreas.

Dès le lendemain, Hope téléphona à Andreas. Il était injoignable, aussi laissa-t-elle un message sur son répondeur.

Trois heures plus tard, il la rappelait.

— Que se passe-t-il ? demanda-t-il d'un ton sec. Pourquoi voulais-tu me joindre ?

— Il faut que je te parle le plus tôt possible, déclara-t-elle avec fermeté. Mais ce que j'ai à te dire ne peut pas être dit au téléphone.

— Je suis très occupé, répondit-il, agacé. De plus, je

pars demain pour la Grèce. Dis-moi ce que tu veux me dire maintenant.

— Non. Il faut que je te voie. C'est important.

Andreas soupira.

— Très bien. Dans ce cas, passe me voir demain matin à 7 heures, à la salle de gym. J'y suis pour mon entraînement.

En raccrochant, Hope se demanda comment elle allait annoncer à un homme aussi peu désireux de la voir qu'elle attendait leur enfant.

Pourtant, elle n'avait guère le choix !

Durant la nuit, elle avait retourné cent fois dans son esprit les images de son avenir et de celui de son enfant. Elle allait être mère. Quelle que soit la réaction d'Andreas, elle entendait garder ce bébé et lui donner toute son affection. Dans le meilleur des cas, Andreas accepterait de tenir son rôle de père et de s'occuper de son fils ou de sa fille comme le faisaient les parents séparés, un week-end sur deux et la moitié des vacances scolaires… Ce n'était pas ce dont elle avait rêvé quand elle avait pensé devenir mère, mais ce serait mieux que rien. Dans le pire des cas, la fureur d'Andreas serait telle qu'il ne voudrait jamais entendre parler d'elle ni de cet enfant, et alors ce serait *son* enfant à elle.

La luxueuse salle de sport où Andreas pratiquait la musculation était située au cœur du quartier des affaires. Elle disposait également d'une piscine et d'un SPA.

A la réception, un vieil homme chauve toisa Hope d'un œil suspicieux et lui demanda sa carte d'identité avant de décrocher son téléphone, de dire quelques mots à l'un des entraîneurs, et de l'autoriser à emprunter l'ascenseur.

Le cœur battant, Hope traversa une première salle de gymnastique. Heureusement, ses nausées du matin avaient cessé. Elle n'avait pas boudé son petit déjeuner et se sentait prête à affronter le regard hostile d'Andreas.

Celui-ci se trouvait dans une plus petite salle, installé sur une machine de musculation. Son T-shirt moulait ses pectoraux en exercice.

Hope s'approcha et demeura debout, à quelques mètres de lui, ne pouvant s'empêcher de poser sur ce spectacle un regard admiratif.

— Ah, tu es venue ? dit Andreas en haussant les sourcils, comme s'il avait oublié cette visite.

Hope serra les poings, décidée à ignorer cette entrée en matière destinée à la vexer.

— Oui. J'ai *vraiment* quelque chose d'important à te dire, lança-t-elle en le regardant droit les yeux.

— Très bien. Je t'écoute.

Il s'était assis sur un banc et l'invitait à l'imiter.

Mal à l'aise, elle préféra rester debout.

— Eh bien ? reprit-il d'un ton pressant. Je n'ai pas toute la matinée et je ne vais pas jouer aux devinettes ! De quoi s'agit-il ?

— Ce n'est pas très facile à dire, répondit-elle en soupirant.

— Peu importe. Je t'écoute.

Elle hésita.

— Je préférerais que tu *devines*, justement, mais… Il vaut mieux que je te donne quelques indices.

Hope le fixait sans ciller, et Andreas lui lança un regard éberlué.

Que signifiait ce discours tortueux ? Elle ne l'avait pas habitué à ce genre de tergiversations. D'ordinaire, elle allait droit au but.

106

— Qu'est-ce qui se passe ? s'enquit-il d'une voix plus inquiète. Tu es malade ?

Soudain, il imagina le pire. Son rythme cardiaque s'emballa. Il était prêt à se lever à envelopper de son bras les épaules de la jeune femme.

— Non, souffla-t-elle, je ne suis pas malade…

Il poussa un profond soupir.

— Mais alors, vas-tu enfin parler ?

— Je suis enceinte, annonça-t-elle.

Sous le choc, il manqua tomber du banc et se leva avant de se passer nerveusement la main dans les cheveux.

— Si c'est une plaisanterie, elle est de très mauvais goût ! s'écria-t-il.

— Ce n'est pas une plaisanterie, rétorqua-t-elle. Ça n'aurait rien de drôle.

Il la dévisagea avec attention avant de fixer son ventre. Oui, il était arrondi…

Son cœur se remit à battre avec violence, et une colère inexplicable monta en lui. Elle était enceinte… Des œuvres de Campbell, évidemment. Eh bien ! Ils n'avaient pas tardé à donner à leur amour le plus fort des symboles ! Peut-être étaient-ils également sur le point de se marier ? Décidément, Hope ne manquait pas de culot. Elle venait le lui annoncer, ici, dans *son* club de sport…

— J'ai besoin de prendre une douche, lâcha-t-il après un silence.

— Tout de suite ? s'étonna la jeune femme. C'est tout ce que trouves à me dire ?

Il plongea son regard dans ces yeux bleus qui avaient sur lui un pouvoir de fascination si dérangeant.

Cette femme l'avait trompé, elle refaisait désormais sa vie avec un homme qui serait bientôt le père de son enfant. Leur avenir était tout tracé. Elle était sortie de sa vie brusquement et avait tôt fait d'effacer leur relation de sa mémoire. Une relation de deux ans, comme elle le lui avait rappelé alors qu'elle se donnait déjà à cet autre homme.

Alors, pourquoi venait-elle le voir, *lui* ? Pour le narguer ? Ou parce que Ben Campbell refusait d'assumer ses responsabilités ? Venait-elle quémander de l'aide ? De l'argent ? Non, Hope n'avait jamais été de ce genre...

— J'imagine que c'est un choc pour toi, enchaîna-t-elle. Moi aussi, j'ai été très surprise de l'apprendre de la bouche du médecin. Mais il faut bien envisager la suite des événements. Et au fond, je suis très heureuse de...

— Je m'en doute ! coupa-t-il. Tu avais les meilleures raisons du monde de vouloir cet enfant !

Hope fronça les sourcils et considéra Andreas avec perplexité. Qu'était-il en train d'insinuer ? Qu'elle avait fait en sorte de tomber enceinte ? Qu'elle lui avait tendu un piège ?

— Ce que tu dis est ridicule, protesta-t-elle. Et offensant. Je ne crois pas que...

— Je regrette d'avoir élevé la voix, marmonna-t-il. Assieds-toi.

Perplexe, elle obéit et s'assit près de lui.

Après tout, il était normal qu'il réagisse de manière un peu irrationnelle. Quelles idées pouvait-il nourrir, en cet instant ? De toute façon, elle devait écouter ce qu'il voulait lui dire. Autant qu'elle, il avait le droit de donner son avis sur l'avenir de leur bébé.

Au bout de quelques instants, Andreas émergea de ses songes et releva les yeux vers elle.

— Qu'attends-tu de moi exactement ? demanda-t-il.

— Rien, dit-elle en ignorant le frisson qui la parcourait. Je voulais seulement que tu connaisses la situation. Il me semble que c'est important.

— Eh bien… Je te remercie, lâcha-t-il doucement. Il est vrai que je n'aurais pas aimé l'apprendre par le biais d'une autre personne. Et surtout pas par Ben Campbell. D'ailleurs, comment a-t-il réagi ?

Elle fixa son interlocuteur avec ébahissement.

— Ben ? Mais… Il n'est pas au courant. Pas encore.

Andreas haussa les sourcils, visiblement choqué.

— Tu veux dire que tu as préféré me le dire *à moi*, avant de le lui annoncer ?

— Oui, bien sûr ! s'exclama-t-elle. C'est évident ! Que vient faire Ben dans cette affaire, finalement ?

— Tu parles ainsi du père de ton bébé ? s'étonna Andreas, en lui jetant un regard interloqué.

Hope ne pouvait croire ce qu'elle venait d'entendre.

Andreas avait-il perdu l'esprit ? Il croyait donc que… Comment pouvait-il s'imaginer qu'elle entretenait une relation intime avec Ben ?

— C'est trop fort ! s'écria-t-elle en se levant d'un bond et en fusillant Andreas du regard. Comment oses-tu proférer de telles insinuations ? Je regrette de te décevoir, mais le seul responsable de mon état, c'est *toi* !

Andreas éclata de rire.

— Impossible ! Il y a trois mois que nous ne sommes plus ensemble.

— Et je suis enceinte de trois mois et demi ! assena-t-elle.

— Peut-être. Mais tu étais déjà avec Ben à la fin de notre relation, rétorqua-t-il.

Blessée en plein cœur, elle lança à l'homme qui lui faisait face un regard de colère et de détresse mêlées.

— Je ne peux pas croire que tu sois si cruel ! C'est *ton* bébé ! Je n'ai jamais fait l'amour avec Ben Campbell, enfin !

— Tu me prends pour un imbécile. Tu voudrais que je croies cela ?

— J'aurais préféré que cet enfant soit de Ben ! cria-t-elle, tandis que ses yeux lançaient des éclairs. Il aurait au moins un père pourvu d'un peu de décence ! Cette fois, Andreas Nicolaidis, tu passes les bornes ! Adieu.

Andreas voulut la retenir en lui prenant le bras, mais elle se dégagea d'un geste brusque.

— Lâche-moi ! Je te plains !

— Mais…

Déjà, elle traversait la salle sous le regard médusé des dizaines de sportifs qui n'avaient pas perdu une miette de cette scène édifiante.

Pour la seconde fois en trois mois, Andreas ordonna à son chauffeur de faire demi-tour alors qu'il se rendait à l'aéroport.

Il avait pourtant des affaires urgentes qui l'attendaient en Grèce. Et Elyssa se trouvait à Athènes. Visiblement, elle traversait une crise conjugale avec son mari et avait besoin de se retrouver parmi ses cousins, ses oncles et ses tantes. Elle l'avait supplié de les rejoindre au plus tôt, elle et ses fils. Il ne pouvait rien refuser à sa sœur : elle était si charmante, si vulnérable… Elle avait besoin de lui.

Pourtant, il céda à ce qu'il considérait comme une priorité personnelle : voir Hope de toute urgence et savoir de quoi il retournait dans cette affaire.

Elle était bouleversée… Mais pouvait-il croire que Ben n'était pas le père de l'enfant qu'elle portait ? Non, c'était impossible ! Hope ne pouvait être enceinte que d'un ou deux mois, il fallait examiner attentivement son ventre pour s'apercevoir qu'elle attendait un bébé. Pourquoi semblait-elle persuadée qu'il était le père ? Peut-être parce qu'elle ne voulait pas épouser Ben ? Il ne la rendait peut-être pas heureuse…

De toute façon, il n'avait pas supporté de voir son charmant visage, d'ordinaire illuminé de vie et d'enthousiasme, ravagé par la détresse. C'était sans doute en partie sa faute : sa colère était telle, chaque fois qu'il songeait à la trahison de Hope, qu'il ne parvenait pas à conserver son calme en sa présence. Néanmoins, il lui fallait éclaircir cette affaire. Hope devait lui dire pourquoi elle tenait tant à lui faire croire — et à se persuader elle-même qu'il était le père de son enfant.

— Tu es sûre que je peux aller m'installer pour quelques jours dans le cottage ?

Hope préparait son sac de voyage avec l'aide de Vanessa, et la panique courait encore dans ses veines après son entrevue du matin avec Andreas.

Elle avait besoin de repos. Son bébé ne devait pas souffrir de toute cette instabilité émotionnelle. Dans une demi-heure, elle partirait pour la gare et prendrait le premier train en direction d'Oxford.

— Bien sûr ! répéta son amie en la serrant encore une fois dans ses bras. Nous y allons rarement. Mais est-ce une impression, ou tu fuis Londres ?

— Je veux simplement rester quelque temps au calme et réfléchir. Loin d'ici, et surtout loin d'Andreas.

— Dans ce cas, tu ne peux pas trouver un lieu plus approprié, conclut Vanessa. J'ai averti Ben de ta situation. Je sais, cela ne me regarde pas, mais je pense qu'il a compris qu'il ne pourrait pas te séduire. Du moins, pas en ce moment. Il t'aime beaucoup, et tu peux compter sur son amitié. C'est important, non ? Il m'a dit qu'il te rejoindrait peut-être pour veiller sur toi…

Hope soupira.

— Ben est très gentil, mais…

La sonnette d'entrée retentit, et elles se regardèrent.

— Je ne serais pas étonnée que cette visite soit pour toi, déclara Vanessa. Tu devrais aller toi-même ouvrir.

Hope se leva et traversa le couloir en espérant qu'Andreas n'aurait pas eu l'audace de revenir ici. Mais lorsqu'elle ouvrit et qu'elle découvrit la haute silhouette qu'elle avait quittée une heure plus tôt, elle fronça les sourcils.

— Que veux-tu ? demanda-t-elle brièvement.

Elle avait à peine entrebâillé la porte.

— Que tu me laisses entrer, répondit Andreas.

— Pas question. Nous n'avons plus rien à nous dire. Laisse-moi tranquille.

Andreas réprima visiblement la fureur qui montait en lui.

— Jamais tu ne m'aurais parlé ainsi, du temps où nous vivions sous le même toit ! Je suppose que c'est le cerbère de cette maison qui t'incite à agir ainsi ?

— Je ne te permets pas de parler ainsi de Vanessa, rétorqua-t-elle sèchement. C'est mon amie.

— Une amie qui consacre le plus clair de son temps à te monter contre moi, lâcha-t-il.

Indignée, Hope ferma les yeux un court instant et inspira une longue goulée d'air. Ce que venait de dire Andreas la mettait hors d'elle. Il avait d'abord accusé Ben d'être son amant… Avait-il l'intention d'offenser sa meilleure amie, maintenant ? Alors qu'il était incapable d'entendre la vérité au sujet de sa sœur et qu'il la défendait avec une énergie inouïe ?

Pour la première fois de son existence, elle dévisagea Andreas d'un regard de glace.

Cet homme prétendait qu'elle l'avait trompé, qu'elle ne lui

112

avait jamais été fidèle. Non content de l'avoir fait suivre durant près d'un an à son insu, il avait toujours refusé d'entendre ce qu'elle avait à dire pour sa défense. Il avait déjà détruit tous ses rêves sans un remords. Il était le père de son enfant, elle l'aimait profondément, mais elle ne lui permettrait pas de parasiter sans cesse sa nouvelle vie.

Pourquoi était-elle si compréhensive ? N'avait-elle pas le droit de se mettre en colère, elle aussi ?

— Andreas, je te prie de t'en aller, articula-t-elle d'une voix blanche. Je ne sais pas ce que tu es venu faire ici. Nous n'avons *rien* à nous dire.

— Ça alors ! C'est toi qui es venue au club de sport ! C'est toi qui voulais me parler de toute urgence !

— Et je t'ai dit tout ce que j'avais à te dire, rétorqua-t-elle. Ecoute, je suis pressée. J'ai un train à prendre…

— Et moi ! s'écria-t-il, je devais prendre un avion pour Athènes mais je suis revenu pour te parler ! Tu ne crois que cela mérite que tu m'accordes quelques instants ?

— Non, tonna-t-elle. Je me fiche de tes urgences, de tes rendez-vous et de tes affaires. Maintenant, dehors ! Je ne veux plus te voir.

Sur ces mots, elle lui claqua la porte au nez et rejoignit son amie qui, de l'autre bout du couloir, n'avait rien perdu de la conversation.

Médusée, Vanessa la regarda avec admiration.

— Ça alors ! Tu viens de congédier l' « homme de ta vie » ! « Celui que tu ne pourras jamais oublier » ! J'ai peine à le croire.

Hope haussa les épaules.

— Mes sentiments pour Andreas et mon état de fatigue sont deux éléments distincts. Le médecin m'a avertie : porter un bébé est un véritable travail. C'est épuisant, et je ne dois

113

pas laisser quelqu'un qui me perturbe me harceler. Même s'il s'agit du père de mon enfant.

— Félicitations ! s'écria Vanessa. Andreas Nicolaidis avait besoin que quelqu'un lui tienne tête ! Et maintenant, je vais appeler un taxi et t'accompagner à la gare.

8.

Durant le voyage en train, Hope s'était endormie. Puis, dans le taxi qui la menait vers le cottage de la famille Fitzsimmons-Campbell, elle avait admiré le paysage des Cotswolds.

La grande bâtisse était couverte de lierre et bordée d'un jardin planté d'arbres centenaires. Les oiseaux chantaient.

Emerveillée comme chaque fois à son arrivée, elle fit quelques pas entre les bougainvilliers et longea la rivière qui serpentait sur le terrain. Puis elle visita la charmante demeure où trônaient dans chaque pièce de confortables fauteuils victoriens.

Elle s'installa dans une grande chambre aux murs recouverts d'une tapisserie rose, qui donnait sur le jardin.

La vieille dame qui venait deux fois par semaine entretenir la maison avait rempli le réfrigérateur de victuailles sur l'instruction de Vanessa, et sur la table de la cuisine trônait un panier de fruits et de légumes frais.

Hope s'étira. Heureusement qu'elle pouvait compter sur la chaleur et la générosité de ses amis. C'était si réconfortant ! Enfin, elle allait pouvoir respirer.

Le soir, elle se prépara une omelette aux champignons accompagnée d'une soupe de légumes. Puis, bien au chaud dans son grand lit, elle se plongea dans un roman policier et s'endormit, un sourire aux lèvres.

Le lendemain matin, à son réveil, c'est pourtant le souvenir de sa dernière discussion avec Andreas qui l'assaillit.

Une tristesse insistante s'empara d'elle. Elle se demandait comment elle allait élever son enfant, sans père… Bien sûr, elle aurait les moyens de lui donner une bonne éducation. L'argent que son frère lui avait rendu et la récente publicité que lui avait valu l'exposition photographique de Vanessa l'autorisaient à être plus optimiste quant à son avenir professionnel. Mais elle aurait tant voulu qu'Andreas assume un peu ses responsabilités…

Elle soupira et décida de se donner le temps d'y songer, tout en profitant du grand air de la campagne. Un merle gazouillait dans le jardin, et elle se hâta d'aller prendre une douche et de s'habiller avant de descendre dans la cuisine se préparer son petit déjeuner.

Elle était attablée devant une tasse de thé et des toasts quand le bruit d'un moteur dans l'allée la fit sursauter. Non, elle ne rêvait pas, une voiture venait de se garer devant le cottage.

Etait-ce Ben ?

Ecartant le rideau de l'entrée, elle découvrit avec stupéfaction une Lamborghini rouge. Un instant plus tard, Andreas en descendit et se dirigea vers le porche.

Que faisait-il ici ? se demanda-t-elle, non sans colère.

Mais son cœur s'était emballé, et elle sentait dans tout son corps cet étrange trouble qui la saisissait chaque fois qu'elle était à proximité de l'homme qu'elle aimait.

Non ! se rappela-t-elle. De l'homme qu'elle ne *devait plus* aimer.

Elle baissa les yeux sur sa tenue : elle avait enfilé une robe légère qui soulignait la rondeur de son ventre et des espadrilles. Le temps printanier de la campagne l'avait incitée à quitter ses gros pulls. En rencontrant son reflet dans un miroir posé sur un buffet, elle s'aperçut qu'elle avait les joues roses.

Tant mieux, songea-t-elle. Andreas verrait bien qu'elle était heureuse et épanouie. Elle n'avait pas besoin de lui et le sommerait de s'en aller sur-le-champ.

Oui, mais… S'il avait enfin admis qu'il était le père de leur enfant ?

Elle hésita. Une part d'elle-même lui soufflait qu'elle devait se protéger des attaques d'Andreas. Il la blessait chaque fois qu'il prétendait qu'elle avait entretenu une relation avec Ben. Mais il fallait bien qu'il comprenne un jour que son enfant était aussi le sien ?

A contrecœur, elle alla ouvrir la porte au deuxième coup de heurtoir.

Les mains sur les hanches, elle lui décocha un regard noir.

— Comment as-tu découvert que j'étais ici ? demanda-t-elle.

— C'est Vanessa qui me l'a dit, répondit-il tranquillement.

— Vanessa ? répéta-t-elle, incrédule.

— Oui. Je lui ai expliqué que je m'inquiétais pour toi. Ça l'a déstabilisée. Elle a pensé qu'il était sans doute utile que nous parlions, toi et moi.

Hope leva les yeux au ciel et soupira.

— Je ne suis pas de cet avis. Mais après tout, puisque tu es là, entre.

Andreas suivit la jeune femme dans le salon tout en jetant un regard appréciateur autour de lui. Il aimait ce genre de maisons typiquement anglaises, qui ont à la fois quelque chose d'accueillant et d'élégant. Ces murs bleus, ces meubles de chêne, ces sols en tommettes… Le décor était charmant. Il faisait chaud, et un parfum de feu de bois emplissait la pièce.

Soudain, alors que Hope lui désignait un grand canapé pour qu'il s'y installe, Andreas repéra une veste d'homme posée sur une chaise. Ben Campbell !

D'un geste du menton, il indiqua le vêtement.

— Ben est avec toi, à ce que je vois…

le visage de Hope se ferma.

— Cette maison appartient à la famille de Ben et de Vanessa, déclara-t-elle d'un ton glacial. Cette veste peut appartenir à l'un de leurs oncles ou cousins… Ou à Ben lui-même, en effet. D'ailleurs, il viendra peut-être ici bientôt. C'est son droit le plus strict.

— Certes, maugréa Andreas entre ses dents.

Il contenait mal sa colère.

— Hope, je veux savoir si tu fréquentes toujours Ben, reprit-il. J'ai le *droit* de le savoir !

— Ça alors ! s'exclama-t-elle, offusquée. Tu n'as aucun droit sur ma vie privée…

— Bon sang, coupa-t-il, c'est moi que tu es venu voir hier. Pas Ben ! Je peux donc en conclure que votre relation n'est pas au beau fixe.

— Andreas, répondit-elle en s'efforçant visiblement de rester calme, Ben est mon ami, rien de plus, et je suis venue te voir *toi* parce qu'il s'agit de *ton* enfant !

— Impossible, répliqua-t-il. C'est absurde. Nous sommes séparés depuis trop longtemps. Et ton ventre est presque plat. Tu es enceinte d'un mois, pas davantage.

Blême de rage, Hope s'avança vers lui et le regarda intensément.

Troublé, il reconnut la détresse qui s'était allumée la veille dans ses yeux bleus.

— Non seulement tu es le père de cet enfant, mais tu es le

seul responsable de cette situation, expliqua-t-elle. Si tu veux vraiment connaître le stade de ma grossesse, je t'autorise à appeler mon médecin et à en parler avec lui. Il parviendra peut-être à te faire comprendre qu'à quatorze semaines, une femme peut ne pas avoir un ventre énorme. C'est ainsi, et c'est très banal. Ensuite, je te prie de te souvenir de la vie qui était la nôtre. Tu avais choisi d'assumer la contraception… Tu ne te souviens pas de cette nuit où nous avons fait l'amour dans ta limousine ? Ni de ce matin où, en sortant de la douche, tu m'as enlacée dans la salle de bains et m'as murmuré que tu n'avais pas eu le temps de racheter des préservatifs ?

Les yeux rivés à ceux de Hope, Andreas écoutait en silence.

— Si, je m'en souviens, chuchota-t-il. Comment pourrais-je oublier ce moment dans la limousine ?

Son regard descendit pour se poser sur le ventre de la jeune femme. Etait-il possible que… Etait-ce vraiment son enfant ?

— Dans ce cas, reprit-il, il faudra pratiquer un test A.D.N. quand le bébé sera né.

Mais déjà des émotions contradictoires jaillissaient en lui, dominées par une joie étrange, inconnue.

Ainsi, il allait être père ! Un petit Nicolaidis allait faire son apparition dans ce monde. Préférait-il un garçon ou une fille ? Il ne saurait le dire. Quoi qu'il en soit, il était intolérable d'imaginer que cet enfant puisse être élevé par Ben Campbell. Non, il ne le supporterait pas !

Déjà lasse, Hope songeait avec désespoir que cet homme ne lui accorderait jamais sa confiance. Ne venait-il pas d'exiger un test A.D.N. ? C'était si humiliant !

— Hope, dit Andreas, je *dois* savoir quelles sont tes relations avec Campbell. Il faut que tu me le dises !

Elle haussa les épaules avec mépris.

— Je te l'ai déjà dit, je te signale. Ben est mon ami. Il me soutient.

— Parce que je ne t'ai pas soutenue ? protesta-t-il. Je ne demandais qu'à te garder près de moi…

— Comme ta maîtresse ! coupa-t-elle. Merci bien.

L'étonnement se lisait maintenant sur le visage d'Andreas.

— Pourquoi employer de tels mots ? demanda-t-il en se levant et en lui prenant les mains. Je n'ai jamais cherché à te ranger dans une catégorie. Notre relation allait bien au-delà… Tu étais la femme avec laquelle je partageais ma vie, c'est tout. Et aujourd'hui, je veux bien croire ce que tu me dis : que je vais être père. Sache que j'assumerai mes responsabilités.

Hope sentit son cœur battre à se rompre. Elle allait défaillir, la tête lui tournait.

Etait-il possible qu'Andreas veuille enfin l'écouter ?

Même s'il semblait toujours persuadé qu'elle fréquentait Ben, son attitude était soudain plus rationnelle… et plus douce. Le regard dont il l'enveloppait en cet instant était celui qui lui avait fait perdre la tête tant de fois par le passé, du temps où ils partageaient ces moments si heureux…

Elle reconnaissait enfin l'homme qu'elle n'avait cessé d'aimer.

Il s'approcha d'elle et murmura à son oreille :

— J'ai envie de toi, *pedhi mou*.

Fermant les yeux, elle se cambra et le laissa l'enlacer, avant de sentir ses lèvres se presser contre les siennes. Bientôt, il resserra son étreinte, et elle savoura le goût de ce baiser fougueux dont elle avait tant rêvé depuis trois mois. Cela lui avait tant manqué…

Avec délices, elle sentit ensuite sa bouche d'une douceur enivrante sur son cou. D'une main tremblante, elle défit un à un les boutons de la chemise d'Andreas, qui tomba sur le sol. Puis, la respiration courte, elle glissa ses doigts dans le fin duvet qui recouvrait son torse.

Andreas laissa échapper un grognement rauque lorsqu'elle effleura ses pectoraux de ses lèvres.

— Attends, souffla-t-il en relevant lentement sa robe.

Tâtonnant d'une main, il défit le Zip qui la fermait et laissa le vêtement tomber à ses pieds.

— Tu es si belle, si belle… Et ce ventre te rend si sexy.

Dans le silence de la campagne environnante, seul le murmure de leur respiration saccadée rythmait leurs gestes.

Hope sentit sa gorge se serrer douloureusement. Elle demeura immobile, comme pétrifiée de timidité, et la puissance de son désir pour Andreas la submergea. Comme lors de leur première rencontre, dans la grange.

Quelque chose de magique était en train d'arriver. Malgré elle, malgré sa peur, malgré tout ce qu'elle avait encore à reprocher à cet homme, elle voulait sentir sa peau contre la sienne, elle voulait qu'il l'embrasse encore avec passion, à en perdre haleine. Son cœur s'emballait quand elle percevait la lueur du désir dans son regard envoûtant. Chaque caresse attisait en elle un feu irrépressible.

Un frisson d'angoisse la parcourut. Oui, elle avait peur de ce qu'ils allaient partager. Peur d'engager son cœur trop loin. Car elle savait ce qu'elle ressentait pour Andreas. Elle parvenait à peine à respirer. Sa gorge était sèche et son corps en feu. Elle avait l'impression qu'elle allait s'enflammer, avant de tomber en tas de cendres sous ses yeux. Ses jambes se dérobaient sous elle, et elle maintenait difficilement son équilibre en s'appuyant contre le mur.

Etait-elle en train de perdre la tête ?

Reprenant sa respiration, Andreas s'efforça d'articuler :

— Ce n'est pas dangereux… Pour le bébé ?

— Non, il ne risque rien.

Le regard de Hope rencontra le sien. C'était un regard confiant, complice, rassurant. Ils étaient ensemble, même dans cette appréhension.

— Je serai très doux, *pedhi mou*…

Fébrile, il fit glisser sur l'épaule de la jeune femme une des bretelles de son soutien-gorge, puis l'autre. Enfin, sans cesser de la regarder, il passa une main dans son dos et fit sauter l'agrafe.

Lorsque le mince bandeau de soie tomba sur le sol, il savoura le spectacle de cette poitrine nue et offerte. Les pointes des seins étaient dures, et il les caressa du bout des doigts en un mouvement circulaire, faisant jaillir un soupir de désir des lèvres de la jeune femme. Mais il interrompit sa caresse pour glisser une main dans le triangle de tissu qui cachait son bas-ventre.

— Oh ! Andreas, s'exclama-t-elle avant de gémir.

D'un baiser fiévreux, il lui couvrit les lèvres, tandis que Hope écartait les cuisses, lui permettant d'approfondir sa caresse.

Avec douceur mais non sans exaltation, il explora l'antre humide et chaud de sa féminité et écouta le plaisir qui s'échappait par murmures de sa bouche entrouverte.

Elle était si belle ! Ses yeux couleur de Méditerranée s'illuminaient avant de se refermer quand le plaisir montait. Elle le serrait très fort, comme si son équilibre ne tenait qu'à un fil.

Hope avait visiblement envie de le caresser aussi. Au moment où il fit glisser son slip sur ses chevilles, elle le renversa brusquement sur le sol et le débarrassa à son tour de ses vêtements. Ses gestes étaient enfiévrés, rageurs. Quand il fut nu au-dessous d'elle, les caresses passionnées qu'elle lui prodigua lui arrachèrent des marmonnements presque bestiaux.

Il aurait voulu que tout se passe très lentement, mais maintenant qu'elle avait posé ses mains sur lui et qu'il sentait la chaleur de leurs corps nus pressés l'un contre l'autre, il ne savait plus comment retenir l'éruption qui sourdait en lui, menaçant de tout emporter.

S'appuyant contre le mur, il roula sur Hope et l'embrassa jusqu'à ce qu'ils soient incapables de respirer. Sentir cette peau douce et satinée contre lui était la plus exquise des tortures. Il ne pouvait plus nier la puissance de son désir, qu'il allait devoir assouvir sous peine de devenir fou.

Il la souleva pour la porter jusque sur le canapé, à l'autre bout de la pièce, mais à mi-chemin il s'arrêta pour l'embrasser encore. Il en avait besoin, il ne pouvait se passer du contact de ses lèvres, ne fût-ce qu'une seconde…

Il tomba alors à genoux sur le parquet. Une indescriptible chaleur montait entre eux. La gorge sèche, il écarta le buste de la jeune femme du sien et posa les mains sur ses seins gonflés, admirant leur rondeur et leur fermeté, savourant le plaisir de les sentir si parfaitement galbés dans ses paumes. Ivre de désir, il en agaça les pointes dressées du bout des lèvres, tandis que Hope se cambrait sous lui, s'abandonnant à sa bouche affamée.

Gémissant, elle enfonça les doigts dans ses cheveux, l'invitant à poursuivre encore et encore sa caresse qui la secouait d'ondes délicieuses.

— Je ne peux plus attendre, souffla-t-il, la voix rauque.

— Viens, murmura-t-elle d'un ton suppliant.

D'une main tremblante, elle chercha son membre dressé et le guida entre ses cuisses.

Alors, ils poussèrent ensemble un long soupir.

Tandis que Hope collait ses hanches contre les siennes, Andreas entra doucement en elle et imprima son rythme à son corps. Ondulant dans un même élan, ils se soudèrent l'un à l'autre et sentirent un feu lancinant s'allumer en eux.

Il n'y avait plus que leur étreinte et leur plaisir incandescent.

— Oh, ma chérie ! murmura-t-il en cherchant son regard, comme il sentait monter du plus profond de lui-même une vague de jouissance inouïe.

Elle lui sourit, et il noya ses yeux dans les siens avant de se laisser porter par un flux de sensations aussi douces que violentes et de basculer avec elle dans un ciel sans fin.

Enlacés l'un contre l'autre sur le parquet du salon, ils demeurèrent longtemps silencieux avant qu'Andreas ne dépose un baiser sur le front de Hope.

— Je veux que tu rentres avec moi à Londres, déclarat-il.

Hope ne répondit pas tout de suite. Elle songeait à ce qu'elle venait de vivre entre les bras d'Andreas. Elle avait tant rêvé de se blottir encore au creux de son épaule ! Mais le désir l'avait étourdie, elle n'aurait sans doute pas dû y céder.

Car rien n'avait changé, Andreas ne voudrait jamais faire d'elle sa femme. Son cœur se déchirait chaque fois qu'elle y songeait : il la voulait près de lui, comme un objet. Or, plus jamais elle ne l'accepterait.

— Je regrette, répondit-elle en poussant un profond soupir. Mais j'aime la campagne. Je suis heureuse d'être ici.

Andreas sursauta comme s'il venait d'être frappé en plein visage. Stupéfait, il se redressa et la considéra avec insistance.

— Es-tu en train de me dire que ce qui vient de se passer ne signifie rien pour toi ?

— Non, souffla-t-elle. Je ne dis rien de la sorte. Mais il est trop tôt…

— Si cet enfant est bien le mien, reprit-il d'une voix plus forte, nous sommes liés pour la vie.

— C'est vrai. Mais je ne veux pas être ta maîtresse, répondit-elle.

— Ce qui signifie que tu comptes épouser Ben Campbell ?

— Non ! s'écria-t-elle. Cela suffit ! Ben est mon ami, rien de plus ! Oh, combien de fois devrai-je te le répéter ?

Elle porta une main à son front et alla ramasser ses vêtements pour se rhabiller.

— Que se passe-t-il ? demanda-t-il en l'imitant. Ça ne va pas ?

— Non, ce n'est rien… Mais j'ai besoin de calme.

— Je vais appeler un médecin !

Il sortait déjà son téléphone de la poche de sa veste quand elle l'arrêta d'un geste.

— Je n'ai pas besoin de voir un médecin, affirma-t-elle. Je suis enceinte, c'est tout.

— Je t'en prie, reviens à Londres avec moi, insista Andreas. Je n'aime pas l'idée de te laisser seule ici…

Hope secoua fermement ses mèches blondes.

Elle resterait au cottage.

Depuis quelques jours, elle se sentait plus forte. Son bébé l'aidait à prendre les bonnes décisions.

Elle aimait Andreas, elle l'aimait de toutes ses forces et ne cesserait jamais de l'aimer. Mais jamais elle ne pourrait le lui avouer, et elle avait eu tort de céder à ce désir d'une puissance incompréhensible. Au-delà du fait qu'il l'accusait encore de l'avoir trompé avec Ben, elle ne voulait plus partager comme autrefois sa vie avec cet homme, sans engagement, sans avenir. Or, Andreas Nicolaidis ne voulait pas se marier. Et

125

certainement pas avec une femme à laquelle il n'avait jamais fait confiance.

Par conséquent, ce qui venait d'arriver resterait un merveilleux souvenir.

Elle sentit son cœur se contracter douloureusement en levant les yeux vers ce visage qui lui souriait avec persuasion. Avec un peu de chance, Andreas et elle parviendraient au moins à faire de bons parents.

— J'ai besoin de calme, Andreas, reprit-elle avec douceur. Je préfère que nous reparlions de tout cela dans quelques jours.

9.

Hope avait besoin de vivre hors de la ville, songeait Andreas au volant de sa Lamborghini. C'était manifeste.

Eh bien, aucun problème ! Il allait trouver une belle maison à la campagne puisqu'elle refusait de rentrer à Londres. Il avait déjà contacté son agent immobilier, et avec un peu de chance, celui-ci dénicherait la perle rare en moins de vingt-quatre heures…

Car il n'y avait pas une minute à perdre.

Il avait toujours admiré le courage de Hope. En toute circonstance, elle était prête à affronter l'adversité. Ne lui avait-elle pas tenu tête, la veille, quand il lui avait rendu visite ? Elle venait d'apprendre qu'elle était enceinte, mais elle protégeait déjà son enfant. Et la manière dont elle venait de s'abandonner à leur étreinte lui avait rappelé l'ardeur de leur passion…

Si seulement elle ne l'avait pas trompé avec Ben, tout eût été si différent ! Si seulement elle avait évité de lui mentir, au sujet de ce baiser échangé avec lui lors de la soirée chez Elyssa… Et cette veste ? Bien sûr, ce ne pouvait être que celle de ce type. En revanche, il voulait bien croire que le bébé était le sien, et non celui de Campbell. Il se sentait honteux en se rappelant les moments extraordinaires qu'il avait vécus avec Hope dans la limousine, dans la salle de bains…

Il avait été irresponsable, d'accord, mais cet enfant aurait tout ce dont pouvait rêver un Nicolaidis.

Pourtant, l'attitude de la jeune femme l'inquiétait. Où était la Hope qu'il avait connue ? Elle était toujours d'une beauté à couper le souffle, avec ce regard vibrant et cette chevelure lumineuse, et le plaisir qu'il ressentait dès qu'il posait ses lèvres sur les siennes était plus puissant que tout ce qu'il avait connu avec d'autres. Mais elle semblait distante.

C'était comme si elle pouvait désormais envisager de vivre sans lui. Impensable !

Il s'aperçut alors que ce qu'il ressentait n'était pas de la colère. La rage qui était d'ordinaire sa défense en toute circonstance avait disparu.

A la place, il souffrait. Et il avait peur. Peur d'avoir définitivement perdu Hope.

Alors que la panique s'insinuait dans ses veines, son téléphone portable se mit à sonner, et il activa le haut-parleur du tableau de bord.

— Andreas ? C'est moi, Elyssa. Pourquoi n'es-tu pas venu à Athènes comme tu l'avais promis ?

Il soupira. Sa sœur avait aussi besoin de lui, et il lui avait fait faux bond.

— Je regrette, répondit-il. J'ai eu un empêchement, et…

— Je suis à Londres, coupa-t-elle d'un ton agacé. Il faut que je te voie le plus vite possible ! Peux-tu me rejoindre chez moi ?

— Oui. Calme-toi, Elyssa, j'arrive dans une heure.

En mettant fin à la communication, il se demanda pourquoi la jeune femme semblait si affolée. Il avait toujours admiré le couple qu'elle formait avec Finlay. Son beau-frère était un homme d'une remarquable intelligence. Discret et sensible, il semblait très amoureux d'Elyssa. Quant à leurs deux fils, ils étaient adorables. En quoi consistait cette crise conjugale ?

Lorsqu'il parvint devant la propriété de sa sœur, il gara sa Lamborghini devant le porche et en franchit les marches quatre à quatre.

Depuis quelques mois, il n'aimait plus entrer dans cette maison. Elle lui rappelait cette soirée fatale qui avait entraîné sa rupture avec Hope. Il se rappelait aussi avec malaise les propos qu'il avait tenus en présence de cette jeune admiratrice de Hope au sujet de la vente des sacs sur le marché de Camden. Uniquement parce qu'il était jaloux du temps qu'elle consacrait à son travail...

Une fois encore, ne s'était-il pas laissé dominer par son tempérament irascible en oubliant que Hope était sensible et vulnérable ? Ce soir-là, n'aurait-elle pas au contraire mérité de sa part encouragements et compliments, quand elle consacrait tant d'énergie à faire connaître son talent ?

Ses pensées furent interrompues par Elyssa, qui se jeta à son cou et l'entraîna dans le parc.

— Finlay est parti, lui dit-elle d'un ton perplexe. Il a déclaré qu'il avait besoin de prendre l'air et qu'il allait passer quelques jours à la campagne dans la maison du Sussex de sa mère. Et il a emmené les enfants !

Andreas réprima le sourire amer qui lui montait aux lèvres. Sa sœur et lui se trouvaient dans la même situation !

— Pourquoi ? demanda-t-il. Que se passe-t-il entre vous ?

— Je ne sais pas, geignit-elle.

— Voyons, Elyssa, tu le sais forcément, insista-t-il d'un ton grondeur. Sinon, tu ne serais pas si inquiète. Que crains-tu, au juste ?

— Je... J'ai peur que Finlay ne demande le divorce, lâcha-t-elle. Et qu'il ne répande les pires ragots sur moi pour obtenir la garde des enfants !

Andreas considéra le visage courroucé de sa sœur avec étonnement. Mais il garda le silence et glissa son bras sous le sien, comme ils traversaient une longue allée bordée d'arbres.

— Quel genre de ragots ? demanda-t-il enfin.

Elle haussa les épaules.

— Oh ! Tu sais… Ce que disent toujours les hommes dans ces cas-là. Que je ne m'occupe pas assez des enfants. Uniquement parce qu'il m'est parfois arrivé de les confier à leur gouvernante pour quelque temps…

En y réfléchissant, il est vrai que pour une jeune mère, sa sœur sortait beaucoup. Elle aimait un peu trop les fêtes et les réceptions.

— Combien de temps as-tu laissé les enfants seuls avec leur gouvernante ?

— Oh, je ne sais pas, dit-elle d'un ton agacé. Finlay part souvent en voyage pour ses affaires avec les banques suisses. J'ai besoin de prendre l'air, moi aussi ! Durant quelques week-ends, et… pour un court voyage à Paris.

Choqué, Andreas s'efforça de ne rien montrer de sa surprise et de s'exprimer avec tact :

— Je comprends que Finlay s'en soit inquiété, Elyssa ! Ne pouvais-tu emmener les enfants avec toi ?

— Andreas ! J'ai seulement vingt-cinq ans ! protesta-t-elle. J'ai bien le droit de m'amuser avec des gens de mon âge sans avoir les petits dans les jambes ! De toute façon, tu sais, ils sont trop jeunes pour faire la différence entre leur gouvernante et moi…

— Je vois, répondit-il sèchement après avoir observé une pause, abasourdi. Maintenant, dis-moi pourquoi ton mari est parti.

Il chercha son regard et s'aperçut qu'elle le fuyait.

— Eh bien, Elyssa, reprit-il en lui prenant le poignet et en la contraignant à lui faire face. Pourquoi ?

— Promets-moi que tu ne me feras pas de sermon, supplia-t-elle d'un ton infantile.

— Cesse de jouer à la petite fille. Alors ?

— Très bien, soupira-t-elle. J'ai eu… une liaison.

Andreas en eut le souffle coupé. Il ne se serait jamais attendu à cette révélation. Sa propre sœur ! Et l'infidélité lui avait toujours été insupportable.

Pourtant, une nouvelle fois, il tenta de conserver son sang-froid.

— Tu es amoureuse de cet homme ? demanda-t-il.

Elyssa secoua la tête d'un air dégoûté en signe de dénégation.

— Non. C'est la raison pour laquelle je ne comprends pas pourquoi Finlay en fait une telle histoire ! Enfin si, il a une autre raison…

Elle s'interrompit en se mordillant la lèvre.

— Quelle autre raison ? demanda-t-il, agacé.

— C'était son ami Paul, murmura-t-elle. Je n'y peux rien, les hommes ne peuvent pas me résister…

Andreas avait l'impression de tomber de Charybde en Schylla. Toute une partie de son monde était en train de s'écrouler.

La manière dont la jeune femme avouait son comportement inadmissible le choquait plus que tout. Elle était si complaisante avec elle-même, si peu consciente de ses fautes et de leurs conséquences ! Elyssa, sa charmante Elyssa, sa petite sœur adorée, était une femme adultère, narcissique et immorale !

Toutes sortes d'images lui traversaient maintenant l'esprit. Il revoyait ce Paul, avec ses cheveux mi-longs et sa chemise violette, le soir de cette fameuse réception… Soudain, un doute terrible lui serra le cœur.

— Elyssa… Paul était bien là, le soir où Finlay et toi avez donné cette réception, il y a environ trois mois ?

— Euh, oui. Pourquoi ?

— Tu m'as affirmé alors que tu avais surpris Hope en train d'embrasser Ben Campbell, enchaîna-t-il d'une voix blanche. Est-ce que c'était vrai ?

La jeune femme rougit.

— Pourquoi me poses-tu cette question ?

Il la toisa.

— Tu as tout inventé, c'est ça ?

Sa sœur se mordit la lèvre et baissa la tête avant de murmurer :

— Oui. Comment as-tu deviné ?

Ignorant le courant électrique qui le traversait des pieds à la tête, il insista :

— Pourquoi as-tu fait cela, Elyssa ?

Elle haussa les épaules.

— Cette fille ne m'a pas laissé le choix. Elle nous avait surpris, avec Paul. J'ai décidé de me protéger. Pour éviter qu'elle ne fasse peser le discrédit sur moi, je l'ai accusée d'avoir flirté avec ce garçon que vous connaissiez tous les deux.

Andreas sentit le sol se dérober sous ses pieds. Il se cacha le visage entre ses mains.

— Jamais je ne te pardonnerai cela, lâcha-t-il enfin, glacial. As-tu seulement conscience de la gravité de ton mensonge ? Et de ses conséquences ? Tu as profondément blessé Hope.

— Ce n'est pas juste ! geignit-elle. Tu m'as poussée à avouer, et…

— Parce que toi, tu as été « juste » vis-à-vis de Hope ?

— Tu voulais peut-être que je l'apprécie ? rétorqua la jeune femme avec colère. Dès la minute où tu as rencontré cette Hope Evans, tu n'as plus eu une seconde à me consacrer ! Tu l'as emmenée à Paris et à Rome, tu l'aurais peut-être même épousée, à la longue ! J'ai bien vu la manière dont tu la regardais… Je ne voulais pas qu'une vulgaire marchande de sacs devienne ma belle-sœur !

132

Andreas serra les poings.

Sa sœur venait de tomber définitivement du piédestal sur lequel il avait trop longtemps voulu la garder. Il réalisait qu'il partageait avec elle la responsabilité du chagrin de Hope. Par leur faute à tous les deux, la jeune femme était passée par des tourments aussi cruels qu'inutiles.

Bon sang, il avait commis tant d'erreurs ! Pourquoi ne l'avait-il jamais crue quand elle lui avait dit et répété qu'elle n'avait jamais entretenu de relation avec Ben ? Durant deux ans, elle lui avait témoigné sa tendresse, sa générosité, peut-être même son amour… Et il lui avait jeté tout cela à la figure, préférant avaler les sornettes de cette sœur qu'il ne reconnaissait plus ! Hope n'avait pas eu une chance de se défendre. Pourtant, il se rappelait vaguement qu'elle avait tenté d'expliquer que c'était Elyssa qui avait embrassé un autre homme… Et Vanessa occupait bien l'appartement de Ben à l'époque où la jeune femme s'y était rendue, suivie par les agents de sécurité.

Hope lui avait *toujours* été fidèle !

Il secoua la tête, atterré. Il s'était comporté avec une cruauté et une bêtise qui lui faisaient honte. Désormais, tout était peut-être perdu…

— Tu me dégoûtes, lança-t-il à sa sœur en la fixant d'un regard noir.

Puis, la laissant interdite, il tourna les talons et retourna vers sa voiture.

Le lendemain matin, Hope attendait avec appréhension l'arrivée d'Andreas dans le salon du cottage.

Il l'avait appelée très tôt pour lui demander de l'accompagner visiter une maison qu'il souhaitait acheter. Elle avait d'abord été plutôt réticente. L'idée lui paraissait incongrue, et le ton d'Andreas était étrange. Et quand il lui avait annoncé qu'ils se rendraient sur place en hélicoptère, sa perplexité n'en avait été que plus grande. Mais il l'avait presque suppliée, et elle avait fini par accepter.

Elle craignait surtout qu'Andreas ne croise Ben : ce dernier avait annoncé qu'il passerait au cottage pour préparer un excellent déjeuner.

— Je dois aller visiter une maison avec Andreas, avait-elle répondu. Je regrette, mais je ne serai pas là…

— Visiter une maison ? Pour y vivre ? Tous les trois, avec le bébé ?

— Non, avait-elle répondu en soupirant. Apparemment, une maison pour Andreas tout seul.

— Ah… Dommage que vous ne soyez pas réconciliés. Il est évident que tu l'aimes toujours. Mais je passerai tout de même. Je dois récupérer une veste que j'ai laissée au cottage.

Elle avait acquiescé et attendait maintenant avec fébrilité l'arrivée des deux hommes. Elle se reprochait toutefois ses craintes : après tout, elle n'était pas responsable de la jalousie d'Andreas.

Le téléphone sonna, et elle espéra aussitôt qu'Andreas n'allait pas lui annoncer qu'il serait en retard. Elle n'avait pas le courage d'assister à une autre querelle avec Ben !

— Hope ? C'est Vanessa. J'ai une excellente nouvelle pour toi !

— Vraiment ? Laquelle ?

— C'est ex-tra-or-di-naire ! reprit Vanessa avec un enthousiasme débordant.

Son excitation était telle qu'il lui fallut plusieurs minutes pour relater de manière compréhensible sa rencontre avec Leonie Vargas, une grande créatrice de mode : celle-ci avait remarqué les sacs réalisés par Hope dans l'exposition consacrée aux photos de Vanessa. Elle avait été si impressionnée qu'elle voulait à tout prix la rencontrer le plus vite possible et souhaitait qu'elle dessine sa nouvelle ligne d'accessoires.

En écoutant, le cœur battant, les précisions que lui donnait Vanessa, Hope sentait une confiance toute nouvelle la gagner. Enfin ! Elle allait réaliser son rêve.

— Il faut que tu sois à Londres dès demain, reprit Vanessa. Elle va te rappeler pour te donner un rendez-vous. Tu te rends compte ? Leonie Vargas !

— C'est merveilleux ! Je vais demander à Andreas de me déposer en ville dès que nous aurons visité sa maison.

— Il… Il t'emmène visiter une maison ? Pour vous ? demanda Vanessa d'une voix où perçait la stupéfaction.

Hope soupira. Pourquoi Ben et Vanessa voyaient-ils dans cette démarche anodine le signe d'une réconciliation ? Ne savaient-ils pas qui était Andreas Nicolaidis ?

— Non. Une maison *pour lui*, expliqua-t-elle. Oh ! L'hélicoptère est là, je dois te laisser. Mais je reviens dans l'après-midi !

Par chance, Andreas était arrivé au cottage à l'heure dite : non sans soulagement, Hope avait donc échappé à une confrontation avec Ben. Le voyage en hélicoptère avait été très amusant. Durant le vol, elle avait posé un regard fasciné sur les Cotswolds et les environs de Londres tout en admirant les talents de pilote d'Andreas.

Un parc immense s'étendait maintenant devant eux. La « maison » que son compagnon l'emmenait visiter était située à quelques dizaines de kilomètres de Londres. Il s'agissait presque d'un château.

En traversant une enfilade de salles et de couloirs, en admirant les plafonds à caissons et les lustres à pampilles de cristal, elle pouvait à peine en croire ses yeux. Cette demeure était digne d'un conte de fées ! Des escaliers semblaient émerger de toute part, menant à des suites sans fin de pièces plus vastes les unes que les autres, ornées de cheminées de pierre et donnant sur de petites terrasses à balustrades…

— C'est… magnifique ! souffla-t-elle en se tournant vers Andreas qui la fixait d'un regard inquisiteur.

— C'est vrai ? Cela te plaît ?

Il venait de poser la grosse mallette de cuir qu'il transportait avec lui depuis qu'ils étaient sortis de l'hélicoptère, et Hope y jeta un coup d'œil intrigué.

— Bien sûr. Mais c'est immense !

— « La propriété est située dans un parc de vingt hectares dont les chênes centenaires et les vergers garantissent une vue imprenable sur la vallée », récita gravement Andreas, citant mot pour mot la brochure de l'agence immobilière.

Elle le dévisagea avec perplexité.

Que lui arrivait-il ? A quoi jouait-il ? Son comportement était si étrange depuis qu'il était venu la chercher au cottage ! Il la regardait comme si elle était un objet de porcelaine susceptible de se briser au moindre coup de vent et ne cessait de lui sourire avec une tendresse inhabituelle. Lorsqu'elle lui avait appris qu'elle allait rencontrer Leonie Vargas, il avait semblé ému et lui avait serré les mains en murmurant : « Tu peux être très fière de toi, *pedhi mou*. J'ai toujours su que tu réussirais. » Elle en était restée bouche bée.

— Que se passe-t-il, Andreas ? Tu te sens mal ? demanda-t-elle, de plus en plus étonnée.

Il baissa la tête, fit quelques pas vers la grande fenêtre devant laquelle ils se tenaient et revint vers elle.

— Oui. Je me sens très mal, Hope. Je ne pourrai jamais trouver les mots pour te dire combien j'ai honte de ma conduite.

Elle haussa les sourcils. Comme elle s'approchait pour lui

136

prendre la main, Andreas l'attira et la serra très fort contre lui.

Comme un marin qui retrouverait sa femme après des années d'absence, songea-t-elle, incapable de respirer. Que lui arrivait-il ? Quoi qu'il en soit, elle sentait son cœur battre la chamade et savourait l'instant.

Il se contenta d'abord de la garder contre lui. Puis, la relâchant, il plongea son regard grave dans le sien. Alors, il lui exposa la manière dont il avait découvert l'odieux mensonge de sa sœur.

— J'aimerais pouvoir te dire qu'elle regrette. Ou au moins, qu'elle a conscience de la gravité de son geste… Mais ce n'est pas le cas, apparemment. Quant à moi, je n'avais jamais soupçonné qu'Elyssa te considérait comme une menace.

Hope hocha la tête en silence, gagnée par un intense soulagement.

Durant des semaines, elle avait repassé cent fois dans son esprit cet épisode insupportable. Maintenant, tout était éclairci, Andreas avait enfin appris la vérité.

Enfin… Mais bien trop tard.

— Je savais que tu l'adorais, répondit-elle d'une voix altérée par l'émotion. C'est pourquoi je me doutais que jamais tu ne croirais que c'était elle qui avait embrassé ce soir-là un autre homme que son mari.

— Je l'ai idéalisée, admit-il. Mais ce n'est pas à Elyssa que je pense désormais. Et elle n'est pas la seule fautive, hélas. J'ai été bien plus injuste qu'elle. Car moi, je te connaissais, *pedhi mou* ! Oh ! Je suis si désolé de tout ce que j'ai pu te dire, ce soir-là et après ! Je ne sais par où commencer pour te présenter mes excuses. Ma colère m'a aveuglé. Et par malchance, la même semaine, tu m'avais dit que tu n'étais plus satisfaite de notre relation. Cela a fonctionné comme un déclic pour moi :

j'ai pensé que, comme je ne te rendais plus heureuse, il n'était pas étonnant que tu sois tombée amoureuse de ce Ben.

Hope ouvrit de grands yeux. Elle réalisait pour la première fois que cette conversation au sujet de l'anniversaire de leur rencontre avait sans doute considérablement envenimé la querelle qui les avait opposés. D'une certaine manière, elle comprenait maintenant comment Andreas avait pu échafauder, dans sa jalousie, un scénario aussi invraisemblable. Loin de ne lui avoir jamais fait confiance comme elle s'était obstinée à se le répéter, il était au contraire tombé de très haut en découvrant que la femme qui partageait sa vie ne lui avait pas parlé de ses frustrations, de ses attentes déçues. Dans cette perspective, elle avait donc pu trouver le réconfort dans les bras d'un autre homme.

— Je m'en veux beaucoup, Hope, reprit Andreas. Davantage que je ne saurais le dire. Et je veux aussi présenter mes excuses à ton ami Ben.

— Co… Comment ? balbutia-t-elle, stupéfaite.

— Oui. Pourquoi sembles-tu si étonnée ? J'ai conscience que tu le connaissais à peine, le soir de cette réception. Et je vois aussi à quel point tes amis t'ont été précieux quand tu ne pouvais plus compter sur l'homme qui t'aimait.

Pétrifiée, Hope resta silencieuse, le regard plongé dans celui d'Andreas.

— Qu'est-ce que… Qu'est-ce que tu viens de dire ? lâcha-t-elle dans un souffle.

Celui-ci lui prit la main pour y déposer un baiser d'une douceur qui la fit frissonner et sourit.

— Je viens de dire que tu as les amis que tu mérites. Des amis fidèles et bienveillants, qui t'ont apporté leur soutien. Je serais très heureux de mieux les connaître, si tu m'en donnes la chance.

— Mais tu disais aussi…

— Que je t'aime, Hope. Oui. Je t'aime comme un fou. Ou plutôt comme un idiot, puisque je n'ai pas voulu le reconnaître durant tout ce temps. Hope… Depuis que nous sommes séparés, ma vie n'a plus aucun sens.

Sans voix, elle le dévisageait, incrédule.

Etait-elle en train de rêver ? Ou bien Andreas avait-il perdu l'esprit ? Après tout, en trois jours, il avait appris qu'il serait bientôt père et que sa sœur n'était pas l'ange qu'il avait toujours vu en elle mais un véritable démon. Devait-elle le croire ? Ne risquait-elle pas encore de souffrir si elle se berçait d'illusions pour être ensuite rattrapée par la réalité ?

Comme elle demeurait silencieuse, Andreas souleva la mallette et lui sourit.

— Viens avec moi.

Elle le suivit à travers le dédale d'escaliers et sortit avec lui dans le parc, pleine de curiosité. Que pouvait-il bien y avoir dans cette mallette ?

Le soleil brillait et l'air était tiède. Il l'entraîna et l'invita à s'asseoir sur l'herbe, près de lui.

— Ouvre, dit-il en lui tendant l'objet.

Hope s'exécuta et découvrit… un fabuleux nécessaire à pique-nique !

Des assiettes en porcelaine de Limoges ornées de rossignols et de roses, de charmants petits verres en cristal de Bohème, des couverts ciselés, une nappe. Une salade, des sandwichs et des jus de fruits frais préparés par le meilleur traiteur de Londres.

— Oh, Andreas ! s'exclama-t-elle, ravie. C'est… C'est la plus charmante des attentions ! Et c'est exactement ce dont j'avais besoin. J'ai une de ces faims !

Il s'esclaffa.

— Moi aussi. Et le bébé aussi. Du reste, il faut que j'ai l'estomac plein pour t'annoncer encore deux ou trois choses…

10.

Allongée sur l'herbe, Hope admirait la majesté du parc qui les entourait.

Elle avait encore le cœur battant au souvenir des mots qu'Andreas avait prononcés. « Je t'aime ». Enfin, il le lui avait dit ! Et elle se sentait bercée par un sentiment inconnu de sécurité et de bonheur...

Pourtant, elle n'avait pas répondu. Malgré l'amour qu'elle portait à Andreas, elle s'était sentie incapable de lui faire cette déclaration à son tour. Devait-elle croire que plus rien ne s'opposait à ce qu'Andreas et elle vivent heureux ensemble ? Ou bien son compagnon était-il seulement sous le choc de l'aveu d'Elyssa ?

— Nous pourrons refaire un tour dans la maison un peu plus tard, proposa-t-il en posant son verre. Mais j'aimerais connaître ta première impression sur ce domaine. Il s'appelle Knightmere.

Elle lança un regard circulaire autour d'elle et soupira.

— Je trouve que c'est sublime. Comment as-tu trouvé cette propriété ?

— Mon agent y a tout de suite pensé quand je lui expliqué ce que je recherchais. Le manoir de Knightmere a été bâti au XVIIᵉ siècle et a appartenu à la même famille pendant plus de deux cent cinquante ans. Mais le dernier héritier, incapable de faire face aux investissements et aux rénovations nécessaires l'a vendu à un homme d'affaires américain, qui a fait installer le chauffage central et restauré la toiture. Il s'est finalement aperçu qu'il n'avait pas l'occasion d'y vivre et l'a mis en vente.

— En tout cas, c'est une merveille d'architecture !

Andreas sourit.

— Mais pourquoi songes-tu à l'acheter ? reprit-elle. C'est un peu loin de Londres, non ?

— C'est vrai, admit-il. Mais en hélicoptère, le trajet représente moins d'une demi-heure. Depuis que j'ai appris à piloter, j'apprécie beaucoup cet appareil. Plus encore que les voitures de sport ! Et puis, Knightmere est le lieu idéal pour vivre en famille.

Elle haussa les sourcils.

— Tu veux vendre ta maison de Londres et faire venir ici tes cousins ?

— Non. Pour le moment, je pense seulement à trois membres de la famille Nicolaidis.

— Ah ? Lesquels ?

Andreas leva les yeux au ciel avant de la fixer avec insistance.

— Tu ne comprends pas ? Je suis en train de te demander de m'épouser et de venir vivre ici avec notre enfant.

Hope sentit sa gorge devenir soudain très sèche. Elle déglutit difficilement et crut que son cœur avait cessé de battre.

Avait-il réellement prononcé ces mots ? Andreas Nicolaidis, l'homme qui avait juré de ne *jamais* se marier, lui demanderait-il de l'épouser ? Non, c'était impossible.

— Pou… Pourquoi ? balbutia-t-elle. Pourquoi me fais-tu cette demande ?

— Ce n'est pas évident ?

— Parce que tu ne veux pas qu'un Nicolaidis naisse en dehors des liens du mariage ? suggéra-t-elle.

Andreas s'esclaffa.

— C'est ainsi que tu me vois ? Comme un homme dévoré d'orgueil qui ne songe qu'à la fierté de sa famille ? Hum, ce n'est pas complètement faux. Mais penses-tu sincèrement que je te ferais cette demande si je n'étais pas follement amoureux de toi, *pedhi mou* ?

Il l'attira à lui et l'installa confortablement, la tête sur sa poitrine, avant de continuer.

— Tu sais, mes parents ont divorcé alors que j'étais très jeune. J'en ai été blessé. A compter de ce moment, j'ai voulu croire que l'amour et le mariage étaient des notions volatiles et dangereuses. Pourtant, comme tu le sais, je n'ai jamais supporté l'infidélité et je crois en l'engagement. Après la trahison de ma sœur, j'ai réalisé que j'avais fait fausse route. Durant deux années, tu m'as offert un bonheur parfait. J'avais rencontré la femme la plus belle, la plus tendre, la plus excitante et la plus fidèle. N'importe quel homme moins buté que moi t'aurait demandée en mariage… Il est si évident que tu es la femme de ma vie, Hope. Je ne peux pas vivre sans toi. Plus jamais je ne commettrai l'erreur de laisser filer ce que j'ai de plus précieux sur terre !

Tandis que Hope écoutait Andreas, une délicieuse chaleur la gagnait. Elle avait tant rêvé de l'entendre un jour prononcer ces mots ! Durant des semaines et des mois, elle avait consacré ses nuits blanches à imaginer le bonheur d'un tel moment… Jusqu'à se convaincre qu'elle s'étourdissait d'illusions, que cela n'arriverait pas et qu'Andreas ne l'avait jamais aimée. Elle aussi, songeait-elle maintenant, elle avait été injuste. Pendant les deux ans de leur vie commune, Andreas s'était montré attentif, tendre, plein d'attentions. L'attachement qu'il lui avait témoigné était incontestable. Quand elle lui avait reproché de ne pas vouloir fêter leur second anniversaire, elle avait probablement manqué de diplomatie. Et cette fatale conversation avait été déterminante dans le malentendu qui avait entraîné leur rupture.

Mais tout était changé aujourd'hui. Enfin, tout redevenait possible…

Elle leva la tête vers lui.

— Andreas, murmura-t-elle avec ferveur, je t'aime.

L'émotion se lisait dans le regard noir de son compagnon, et il l'attira violemment vers lui.

— *Pedhi mou*, répéta-t-il en l'embrassant avec passion.

Etourdie par ce baiser, elle reprit lentement ses esprits. Puis elle déclara :

— Je serai ravie de m'installer ici avec toi le plus tôt possible. Mais pour le mariage, je préfère prendre le temps d'y réfléchir.

Six semaines plus tard, dans le lit de la plus grande chambre de Knightmere, Andreas tentait d'arracher des mains de Hope un magazine *people*.

— Non, non, non, je ne veux pas que tu regardes cela ! s'écria-t-il.

— Pourquoi pas ? se défendit la jeune femme en s'enfonçant dans ses oreillers, tandis qu'il faisait tomber le drap, découvrant son ventre très rond.

— Parce qu'il est question de nous dans une rubrique. Tu ne vas pas accorder ton attention à ces bêtises !

Comme elle haussait les épaules, il parvint enfin à lui prendre le magazine, ignorant ses protestations choquées.

— Rends-le-moi ! s'écria-t-elle.

Il jeta le magazine sur le sol et lui décocha son sourire le plus irrésistible où brillait ce désir qui les consumait chaque nuit depuis leur installation.

— Non, murmura-t-il d'une voix rauque en l'embrassant fiévreusement.

Hope se mit à rire et déposa une myriade de baisers sur son front avant de lui adresser un clin d'œil.

— C'est un peu facile, mais tu ne m'auras pas si aisément ! Je veux savoir de quoi il est question dans cet article. Et surtout, je veux que tu me dises pourquoi tu ne veux pas que je le voie !

— Voyons, *pedhi mou*, susurra-t-il, le médecin t'a dit de rester calme…

— Et si tu ne me rends pas le magazine immédiatement, je serai obligée d'aller en acheter un autre au village, menaça-t-elle en croisant les bras sur sa poitrine.

Devant son air malicieux, il préféra céder. Elle serait capable de faire des kilomètres pour récupérer ce maudit magazine.

Il soupira, le ramassa et le lui tendit à contrecœur.

Quand elle eut fiévreusement tourné les pages et trouvé l'article qui les concernait, Hope laissa échapper un hoquet de stupeur.

Le sous-titre proclamait : « La styliste qui triomphe chez Leonie Vargas refuse la demande en mariage de l'héritier des Nicolaidis. »

Tout l'article relatait ensuite leur liaison, rappelant que l'un des célibataires les plus séduisants et convoités de la planète venait d'être rejeté par la nouvelle coqueluche du monde de la mode londonien. L'information, selon l'auteur, provenait d'un proche.

— Kostas doit être aux anges, soupira Andreas. Il adore intervenir dans la presse.

— Ton grand-père ? s'étonna Hope en se retournant vers lui. C'est lui qui a alerté les journaux ?

Elle était rouge de confusion.

— Je suis désolée, Andreas, murmura-t-elle. Ce ne doit pas être très agréable pour toi, en effet…

— Non, répondit-il d'un ton tranquille, cela m'est égal. Mais je dois partir au bureau.

Il déposa un baiser sur le front de Hope et se dirigeait déjà vers la salle de bains quand elle le rappela :

— Tu rentres bien à 19 heures, ce soir ? s'enquit-elle.

— Oui.

— Tu me le promets ? insista-t-elle en le fixant.

— Oui, je te le promets, si tu veux.

Le sourire avec lequel la jeune femme accueillit ses paroles lui fit battre le cœur.

Même s'il regrettait qu'elle ait refusé sa demande en mariage, il était heureux. Il vivait avec la future mère de son enfant, dans cette somptueuse demeure… Que demander de plus ?

« Le mariage », lui souffla une petite voix qu'il ignora, comme il poussait la porte de la salle de bains.

Toute la journée, Andreas s'était demandé pourquoi Hope refusait de devenir sa femme.

Il craignait surtout qu'elle ne se soit persuadée qu'il tienne au mariage uniquement pour le bébé. Or, rien n'était plus faux ! Certes, le fait que son fils ou sa fille naisse au sein d'un couple uni par ces liens sacrés lui tenait à cœur…

Bah, songea-t-il en quittant son bureau, peut-être finirait-elle par changer d'avis s'il se montrait persévérant. L'idée de demander la jeune femme en mariage tous les matins à son réveil ne lui déplaisait pas. Même s'il aurait préféré qu'elle dise oui sur-le-champ.

En survolant la ville alors que la nuit tombait, il ressentit cette impatience qui le faisait vibrer de tout son corps quand il s'apprêtait à retrouver Hope et à la serrer dans ses bras. Il se souvint des quelques mois durant lesquels ils avaient été séparés : il s'était immergé dans le travail pour éviter de penser à ce qu'il avait perdu. A cette époque, quand il assistait à des réceptions et des cocktails, il sortait accompagné d'une top-modèle qu'il était presque incapable de regarder. Le regard bleu de Hope le hantait, et il savait qu'elle était seule à pouvoir éveiller son désir. En fait, il avait espéré provoquer la jalousie de la jeune femme en laissant quelques paparazzi s'approcher de lui… Cette jalousie qui avait failli le priver du plus grand bonheur du monde.

En se posant à l'arrière de la propriété, il remarqua tout de suite la lueur des bougies qui scintillaient dans la grande salle du rez-de-chaussée.

Hope leur avait-elle préparé à tous deux un dîner romantique ?

En toute hâte, il gravit les marches du perron et poussa la grande porte, puis il traversa le long corridor lambrissé de chêne et entra dans la salle à manger, un sourire confiant aux lèvres.

— Surprise ! s'écrièrent plusieurs voix.

Il sursauta en voyant jaillir Vanessa et Ben derrière deux fauteuils. Il y avait aussi une femme et un homme qu'il n'avait jamais rencontrés. Mais quand il aperçut Hope, il crut carrément que son cœur allait cesser de battre.

Elle était vêtue d'une longue robe de soie bleue brodée de fleurs blanches qui soulignait avantageusement les rondeurs de sa poitrine et de son ventre. Ses cheveux blonds tombaient en boucles libres sur ses épaules nues. Elle était splendide.

— Bienvenue à la maison, mon chéri, déclara-t-elle en s'approcha lentement de lui, avant de se hisser sur la pointe des pieds pour déposer un timide baiser sur ses lèvres.

Stupéfait, il la contempla sans mot dire avant d'articuler :

146

— Mais, qu'est-ce que…

— Permets-moi de te présenter Chantal, l'amie de Ben, coupa-t-elle en se tournant vers une jeune femme brune.

Andreas lui sourit et lui serra la main.

— Et voici Richard, poursuivit Hope en se tournant vers un homme blond qui posait une main sur la taille de Vanessa.

— Enchanté, dit-il.

— Andreas, reprit Hope en lui prenant la main et en l'entraînant vers la cuisine, j'ai besoin de toi un instant pendant que Vanessa fait visiter Knightmere à nos hôtes. Tu veux venir avec moi ?

Incapable de s'y opposer, Andreas suivit sa compagne tandis que Vanessa, d'un ton enthousiaste, entraînait les convives de l'autre côté de la maison.

— Vas-tu enfin m'expliquer ce qui se passe ? demanda Andreas en entrant dans l'immense cuisine qui donnait sur les jardins. Tu es habillée comme une princesse, Ben et Vanessa sont également vêtus comme s'ils allaient assister à un mariage, et je…

— Tu es merveilleux ! coupa-t-elle en lui sautant au cou. Tu as tout deviné ! Mais le mariage n'aura pas lieu ce soir.

— Quel mariage ?

— Le nôtre ! Si tu veux toujours que je devienne ta femme, bien sûr.

Andreas manqua en tomber à la renverse.

— Quoi ? Tu… Tu acceptes de m'épouser ?

Hope s'approcha de lui avec un sourire malicieux.

— Oui, murmura-t-elle. Ce soir, c'est moi qui te demande d'accepter de m'épouser. Et si tu dis oui, nous pourrons célébrer nos fiançailles devant nos amis… Ou plutôt, devant nos témoins. Qu'en dis-tu ?

Il parcourut encore des yeux la merveilleuse robe de la

jeune femme puis plongea le regard dans ses yeux bleus et l'attira à lui pour l'embrasser avec fougue.

— *Pedhi mou !* Tu fais de moi le plus heureux des hommes. Mais pourquoi maintenant ? Quand as-tu changé d'avis ?

— Oh, Andreas… J'ai toujours voulu devenir ta femme, plus que tout au monde. Je n'ai jamais changé d'avis, ni dans un sens ni dans un autre. Mais quand tu m'as fait cette demande, le jour où nous avons visité Knightmere, j'étais sous le choc : tu m'avais annoncé en vrac que ta sœur t'avait tout avoué, que tu m'aimais, que tu voulais m'épouser et que tu allais acheter cette propriété ! C'était trop, je pouvais à peine le croire… De plus, j'avais appris ce matin-là que j'allais travailler avec Leonie Vargas. C'était le plus beau jour de ma vie, le plus incroyable. Nous étions assis sur l'herbe, devant ce château de conte de fées… Il me semblait que c'était un rêve. Mais le soir même, quand je suis rentrée à Londres, j'ai demandé à Vanessa si elle acceptait d'être mon témoin. Et j'ai songé à organiser ce dîner où je te dirais solennellement, devant mes plus chers amis, que je t'aime et que je veux consacrer ma vie à te rendre heureux.

Emu, Andreas serra Hope dans ses bras et la fit virevolter autour de lui.

— Attention, cria-t-elle en riant, tu vas te faire mal au dos ! Cet enfant n'est pas né, mais il pèse déjà lourd !

— « Vous êtes plus légère qu'une plume », murmura-t-il. Tu te souviens ? C'est ce que je t'ai dit en te soulevant dans mes bras pour la première fois, quand nous sommes entrés dans cette grange, une certaine nuit d'hiver…

— Tu m'avais caché que ton fiancé était si romantique, déclara Vanessa en entrant dans la pièce. Hope, je ne peux plus attendre ! Alors, vous êtes fiancés ?

Andreas prit la main de Hope dans la sienne et la porta doucement à ses lèvres avant de répondre :

148

— Nous sommes fiancés... Et vous êtes tous invités à assister à un mariage grec inoubliable !

Dès la fin de la semaine, Andreas présenta Hope à l'ensemble de sa famille. Ils passèrent un week-end à Athènes et commencèrent à préparer la cérémonie. La jeune femme eut l'occasion de réviser ses connaissances de grec et de susciter l'admiration de tous les oncles et tantes d'Andreas.

Trois semaines plus tard, le mariage fut célébré dans une charmante église d'Athènes. En instance de divorce, Elyssa ne put y assister. La mariée portait une robe dessinée pour l'occasion par Leonie Vargas et un petit sac en forme d'hippocampe en guise de porte-bonheur. Ben et Vanessa prirent à cœur leur rôle de témoins et prononcèrent un discours qui provoqua le fou rire de Kostas, le grand-père d'Andreas, lorsqu'ils évoquèrent les caractères enflammés des deux mariés.

— Ma nouvelle petite-fille est déjà une vraie Grecque ! s'écria le vieil homme en serrant Hope dans ses bras.

Les fêtes s'étendirent sur plusieurs jours au cours desquels Andreas fit plus ample connaissance avec Ben. Ils découvrirent qu'ils étaient tous deux passionnés de poker et décidèrent d'organiser des parties hebdomadaires en compagnie de Richard et de quelques autres, pendant que les « femmes » pourraient échanger des conversations à bâton rompu sur leurs diverses activités artistiques.

— Knightmere est immense, rappela Andreas, nous ne risquerons pas de les déranger.

Après le mariage, les jeunes mariés rentrèrent à Knightmere, et la petite Karisa Nicolaidis naquit cinq semaines plus tard.

Fou de bonheur, Andreas se transforma aussitôt sous le regard attendri de Hope en père attentif et amoureux de sa fille.

Quelques mois plus tard, ils s'envolèrent tous trois pour

Paris. Le soir de leur arrivée, Andreas emmena Hope dîner au restaurant tandis qu'une nurse veillait sur la petite.

— J'ai peine à croire que tu laisses Karisa seule quelques heures, déclara-t-elle en riant.

— Il s'agit d'une occasion exceptionnelle, *pedhi mou* ! répondit-il en l'embrassant. C'est le troisième anniversaire de notre rencontre, rappelle-toi.

Emue, elle plongea son regard dans le sien.

— Je suis si heureuse ! murmura-t-elle.

— Et j'ai l'intention de m'assurer que tu le seras pour le reste de nos jours, promit Andreas, tandis que ses yeux noirs s'allumaient d'un désir brûlant.

LA FIANCÉE TROMPÉE, *Daphne Clair* • N°2711

Quatre ans plus tôt, Sorrel a fui, le jour même des noces, l'homme qu'elle devait épouser. Aujourd'hui de retour en Nouvelle-Zélande pour le mariage de sa cousine Elena, Sorrel doit affronter Bruce pour la première fois depuis toutes ces années. Dès qu'elle croise son regard, elle comprend qu'il éprouve toujours une intense colère à son égard, ainsi qu'un désir qui la bouleverse…

RETOUR À VENISE, *Susan Stephens* • N°2712

Venue à Venise pour mettre en place un partenariat entre l'hôpital de la ville et l'association qu'elle dirige, Nell découvre, stupéfaite, que le directeur de l'hôpital n'est autre que le Dr Luca Barbaro, qu'elle a rencontré deux ans plus tôt dans des circonstances douloureuses. Très vite, elle doit affronter l'hostilité du médecin à son projet… et le désir intense que cet homme fait naître en elle.

UN CHANTAGE INACCEPTABLE, *Sara Craven* • N°2713

Si elle veut sauver le quartier populaire des Docks, Cally va devoir céder à l'ignoble chantage de son mari, qui n'est autre que le promoteur en charge du dossier de démolition, et dont elle vit séparée depuis un an… Celui-ci exige qu'elle revienne vivre avec lui pendant un an. Si elle refuse, le quartier des Docks sera détruit. Désespérée, Cally accepte, même si elle sait qu'elle va vivre un enfer auprès de celui qu'elle n'a jamais cessé d'aimer, mais dont le cœur est pris par une autre…

POUR L'AMOUR D'UN PATRON, *Maggie Cox* • N°2714

Lorsque le grand patron du cabinet d'architectes pour lequel elle travaille vient visiter les bureaux londoniens, Morgen tombe aussitôt sous le charme. Mais jamais, elle le sait, cet homme plein d'ambition ne pourra envisager une relation durable avec une simple assistante. Et quand il lui aura signifié que tout est terminé entre eux, ne la chassera-t-il pas aussi de l'entreprise ?

Et les 4 autres titres…

LA CAPTIVE REBELLE, *Jane Porter* • N°2715

Depuis qu'elle a été enlevée par les rebelles du cheikh Tair, Tally a l'impression de se retrouver en plein cauchemar. Cet homme rude et autoritaire, qui vit dans un univers aux antipodes du sien, ne lui a-t-il pas signifié qu'elle était à présent sa femme ? Pourtant, malgré l'absurdité de la situation, Tally sent un désir irraisonné s'emparer d'elle... Et si le cheikh du désert était un homme très différent de ce qu'il laissait paraître ?

UN BOULEVERSANT SECRET, *Emma Darcy* • N°2716

Pour sauver son école de danse, Nicole se voit contrainte de solliciter l'aide de Joachin Sola, l'homme qu'elle a quitté cinq ans plus tôt quand elle a compris qu'elle n'était à ses yeux qu'une simple maîtresse. Mais Joachin lui propose un odieux marché : pendant trois mois, elle devra passer deux nuits par semaine avec lui. Nicole sent la panique l'envahir : si elle accepte, parviendra-t-elle à lui cacher qu'elle a une petite fille, une petite fille dont il est le père ?

AMOUR ET TRAHISON, *Kate Walker* • N°2717

Par naïveté et par amour, Sarah a cru à la sincérité des sentiments de Damon quand celui-ci lui a demandé de l'épouser. Mais son beau-père, le terrible patriarche du clan Nicolaides, lui révèle très vite les véritables motivations de Damon : s'emparer grâce à cette union des terres de la jeune femme, des terres que les Nicolaides convoitent depuis toujours. Terriblement blessée, Sarah préfère fuir...

L'HÉRITIER DES SCORSOLINI, *Lucy Monroe* • N°2718

3 Princes à marier

Lorsqu'elle apprend qu'elle ne pourra donner à Claudio, l'héritier du trône d'Isole dei Re, l'enfant qu'il attend d'elle, Therese comprend qu'elle va devoir renoncer à l'homme qu'elle aime depuis toujours...

Collection Azur
8 titres le 1er de chaque mois

69 L'ASTROLOGIE EN DIRECT
TOUT AU LONG
DE L'ANNÉE.

(France métropolitaine uniquement)
Par téléphone 08.92.68.41.01
0,34 € la minute (Serveur JET MULTIMÉDIA).

Composé et édité par les
éditions Harlequin
Achevé d'imprimer en juillet 2007

BUSSIÈRE
GROUPE CPI

à Saint-Amand-Montrond (Cher)
Dépôt légal : août 2007
N° d'imprimeur : 70949 — N° d'éditeur : 12962

Imprimé en France

Poppy Day

AMANDA PROWSE

SC 1/14

All royalties due to the author shall be donated to
The Royal British Legion for the support of troops
returning from recent conflicts and also the families of
those who sadly lost their lives. Many will need the support
of The Royal British Legion for the rest of their lives.

First published and printed in 2011 by TIP Limited

Registered Office: Unit 3 Glovers Court, Bury Mead Road, Hitchin, Hertfordshire, SG5 1RP United Kingdom
www.tipltd.com

Cover design, editing and typesetting by Peachy Creative Ltd
www.peachycreative.co.uk

ISBN: 978-1-906382-06-3

How far would you go to bring home the one you love?

Foreword — Poppy Day

Mandy Prowse is the wife of a serving soldier and my very best friend. Her husband Simeon is one of the bravest of the brave, a Bristol man who began his army life 26 years ago as a Private and is now a Major. Amongst many medals, Simeon has received an MBE for his inspirational leadership in the face of overwhelming adversity while deployed on active service. Mandy and Simeon live in an army house in Bristol with their two boys Josh and Ben.

Mandy wrote *Poppy Day* as a way to say 'thank you' to her extraordinary husband and his colleagues who serve their country selflessly every day.

Mandy is an army wife who has written about an army wife, and while *Poppy Day* is a work of fiction, she understands life beneath the uniform; what it's like to be the one left at home, ticking off the days until your loved one returns, and what happens when there is the knock on the door that every Forces' spouse, parent and lover dreads…

The times when Simeon is deployed in areas of violent conflict (and those times are frequent) are tough for Mandy and the boys. I witness her pain and worry; the anguish she has to bear, concern that most of us will never have to live through.

The two of them, husband and wife together, manage to get through those times largely relying on a lot of laughter and the fact that they are hopelessly in love.

The interest in *Poppy Day* has taken them completely by surprise. Mandy has been writing in her spare time and keeping the house going. Simeon supports her as he loves her, she is unpublished until now. In spite of that, Mandy and Simeon are giving all of the proceeds from sales of *Poppy Day* directly to the Royal British Legion.

They are overwhelmed by the thought of possibly being able to help others in a significant way.

Simeon has known many of the men and women who have needed help. He's been with them on the battlefields, he has witnessed death in many forms and he knows that the work of the Royal British Legion is invaluable. All of the money which goes to the Royal British Legion will fund the operations of four new Personnel Recovery Centres, offering the very best in rehabilitation care for the wounded: adapting a home to make it suitable for a disabled young soldier, or providing support such as pension advice or bereavement counselling to those who need it most – welfare work which is a lifeline for thousands of serving and ex-Service people and their families.

She will go mad with me for saying it, but I believe that Mandy and Simeon are two of life's special people and we live in a safer and better world because they are in it.

So, on behalf of Major Simeon Prowse MBE and his wife Mandy, my best friend, thank you for buying *Poppy Day*. By doing it, you have made a difference.

By Carol Vorderman

One

The Major yanked first at one cuff and then the other, ensuring three eighths of an inch was visible beneath his tunic sleeves. With his thumb and forefinger he circled his lips, finishing with a small cough, designed to clear the throat. He nodded in the direction of the door, indicating to the accompanying Sergeant that he could proceed. He was ready.

'Coming!' Poppy cast the sing-song word over her shoulder in the direction of the hallway, once again making a mental note to fix the front door bell as the internal mechanism grated against the loose, metal cover. The intensely irritating sound had become part of the rhythm of the flat. She co-habited with an orchestra of architectural aliments, the stars of which were the creaking hinge of the bedroom door, the dripping bathroom tap and the whirring extractor fan that now extracted very little.

It was probably Jenna, who would often nip over during her lunch break. Theirs was a comfortable camaraderie, arrived at after many years of friendship; no need to wash up cups, hide laundry or even get dressed, they interacted without inhibition or pretence. Poppy prepped the bread and counted the fish fingers under the grill, working out how to make two sandwiches instead of one, an easy calculation. She felt a swell of happiness. The front door bell droned again, 'Alright! Alright!' Poppy licked stray blobs of tomato ketchup from the pads of her thumbs and laughed at the impatient digit that jabbed once more at the plastic circle on the outside wall.

Tossing the checked tea towel onto the work surface, she stepped into the hallway and looked through the safety glass at the top of the door. Poppy slowed down, until almost stationary, squinting at the scene in front of her as though by altering her viewpoint, she could change the sight that greeted her. Her heart fluttered in an irregular beat. Placing a flattened palm against her breastbone, she tried to bring calm to her flustered pulse. The surge of happiness disappeared, forming a ball of ice that sank down into the base of her stomach, filling her bowels with a cold dread. Poppy wasn't looking at the silhouette of her friend; not a ponytail in sight. Instead, there were two shapes, two men, two soldiers.

She couldn't decide whether to turn and switch off the grill or continue to the front door and let them in. The indecision rendered her useless. She concentrated on staying present, feeling at any point she might succumb to the maelstrom within her mind. The whirling confusion threatened to make her faint. She shook her head, trying to order her thoughts. It worked.

She wondered how long they would be, how long it would all take. There were fish fingers to eat, and she was due back at the salon in half an hour with a shampoo and set arriving in forty minutes. Poppy thought it strange how an ordinary day could be made so very extraordinary. She knew the small details of every action, usually forgotten after one sleep, would stay with her forever; each minute aspect indelibly etching itself on her memory. The way her toes flexed and stiffened inside her soft, red socks, the pop and sizzle of her lunch under the grill and the way the TV was suddenly far too loud.

She considered the hazy outlines of her as yet unseen visitors and her thoughts turned to the fact that her home wasn't tidy. She wished she wasn't cooking fish. It would only become curious in hindsight that she had been worried about minutiae when the reason for their visit was so much more important than a cooking aroma and a concern that some cushions might have been improperly plumped.

Columbo was on TV. She hadn't been watching; it was instead a comforting background noise. She had done that a lot since Martin went away, switching on either the TV or radio as soon as she stepped through the door; anything other than endure the silence of a life lived alone. She hated that.

Poppy looked again to confirm that there were two of them; thus reinforcing what she thought she already knew. It is a well-known code; a letter for good news, telephone call for minor incident, a visit from one soldier for quite bad, two for the very worst.

She noted the shapes that stood the other side of her door. One was a regular soldier, identifiable by his hat; the other was a bloke of rank, an officer. She didn't recognise either of their outlines, strangers. She knew what they were going to say before they spoke, before one single word had been uttered; their stance was awkward and unnatural.

Her mind flew to the cardboard box hidden under the bed. In it was underwear, lacy, tarty pieces that Martin had chosen. She would throw them away; there would be no need for them anymore, no more anniversaries, birthdays or special Sunday mornings when the world was reduced to a square of mattress, a corner of duvet and the skin of the man she loved.

Poppy wasn't sure how long she took to reach for the handle, but had the strangest feeling that with each step taken, the door moved slightly further away.

She slid the chain with a steady hand; it hadn't been given a reason to shake, not yet. Opening the door wide, it banged against the inside wall. The tarnished handle found its regular groove in the plasterwork. Ordinarily, she would only have opened it a fraction, enough to peek out and see who was there, but this was no ordinary situation and with two soldiers on the doorstep, what harm could she come to? Poppy stared at them. They were pale, twitchy. She looked past them, over the concrete, third floor walkway and up at the sky, knowing that these were the last few seconds that her life would be intact. She wanted to enjoy the feeling, confident that once they had spoken, everything would be broken. She gazed at the perfect blue, daubed with the merest wisp of cloud. It was beautiful, really beautiful.

The two men appraised her as she stared over their heads into the middle distance. It was the first few seconds in which they would form their opinion. One of them noted her wrinkled, freckled nose, her clear, open expression. The other considered the grey slabs amid which she stood and registered the fraying cuff of her long sleeved tee shirt.

Their training told them to expect a number of varied responses, from fainting or rage to extreme distress, each had a prescribed treatment and procedure. This was their worst scenario, the disengaged, silent recipient with delayed reactions, much harder for them to predict.

Poppy thought about the night before her husband left for Afghanistan, wishing that she could go back to then and do it differently. She had watched his mechanical actions, saw him smooth the plastic-wrapped, mud-coloured, Boy Scout paraphernalia that was destined for its sandy desert home. A place she couldn't picture, in a life that she was barred from. She didn't notice how his fingertips lingered on the embroidered roses of their duvet cover, the last touch to a thing of feminine beauty that for him meant home, meant Poppy.

Martin was packing his rucksack, which was propped open on their bed, when he started to whistle. Poppy didn't recognise the tune. She stared at his smiling, whistling face as he folded his clothes and wash kit into the voluminous, khaki cavern. He paused to push his non-existent fringe out of his eyes. Like the man that's lost a finger, but still rubs the gap to relieve the cold, so Martin raked hair that was now shorn.

Poppy couldn't decipher his smile, but it was enough to release the torrent that had been gathering behind her tongue. Any casual observer might have surmised that he was going on holiday with the boys, not off to a war zone.

'Are you happy Mart? In fact, ignore me, that's a silly question, of course you are because this is what you wanted isn't it? Leaving me, your mates and everything else behind for half a year while you play with guns.'

Poppy didn't know what she expected him to say, but she'd hoped he would say something. She wanted him to pull her close, tell her that this was the last thing he wanted to do and that he didn't want to leave her, or at the very least that he wished he could take her with him. Something, anything that would make things feel better. Instead, he said nothing, did nothing.

'Did you hear me Mart? I was asking if you were finally happy now your plan is coming together, the big fantastic future that you've been dreaming of.'

'Poppy please...'

'Don't you dare 'Poppy please', don't ask me for anything or expect me to understand because I don't! This is what you signed up for; this is what it means Mart, you pissing off to some godforsaken bit of desert, leaving me stuck here. This is what I've been trying to tell you since you walked through the door in your bloody suit with your secret little mission complete!'

'It won't be forever,' his voice was small; his eyes fixed

on the floor.

Poppy noted his blank expression, as if it was the first time it had occurred to him that she might need him too. This only made her angrier because it might have only just occurred to him, but she had been thinking of nothing else.

'I don't care how long it's for. Don't you get it? Whether it's for one night or one year, it's too long. You are leaving me here with the junkies on the stairs and the boring bloody winter nights. All I've got to look forward to is sitting with my bonkers nan. So you go Mart and get this little adventure out of your system, prove whatever it is that you need to prove. Don't worry about me. I can look after myself, but you know that right?'

She didn't want to argue, preferring instead to clamp her arms around his neck and hang on. She wanted to press her lips really hard onto his and kiss him, storing those kisses away for the times when she would miss him the most. Her ache had grown so physical that she shook; the tremors fed a growing anger.

In the aftermath of Martin's departure, Poppy felt some small relief that he had gone. The dread of his imminent exodus disappeared, replaced with the reality of his absence which, initially, was somehow easier to bear. She re-played the words of their argument, considered their actions... She did that, knowing the only person that suffered because of her obsessional recalling of the details, was her.

Martin called it sulking, but for her, the silent musings were a way of trying to figure out what happened and why, looking for an answer or at least some kind of rational explanation. Sometimes of course there wasn't one, a row just happens because of tiredness, an irritation or a million other inconsequential things.

Their fight couldn't be attributed to anything so

transparent. He hadn't failed to hoover the carpet properly, left the loo seat up or not put the milk back in the fridge. It was much more than that. They were frightened, yet too scared to admit to that fear.

It would be difficult to put in order the many things that they were afraid of. Being parted for such a ridiculous length of time was right up there, the possible lack of communication and the loneliness; these were all contenders for the top spot. There was also the unspeakable fear that Martin might get hurt or killed. It was too awful a scenario to share or say out loud, but think about it they did, separately and secretly.

Poppy had wanted to tell him that if he got injured, think loss of limb or blindness, that it wouldn't make any difference to her. She knew that it would be tough, but she also knew that she would not have loved him any less, confident that they would find a way through it; that they could find a way through anything, at least that's what she believed.

One of her many 'if-only' scenarios, saw her telling Martin over a glass of wine that he was the one thing that had made her life worth living for so many years. The only constant that she could rely on and she would never regret a single second. She wanted him to know that she would rather have had him for a shortened length of time, than fifty years of average. She hoped he knew that she would miss him every second of every day, that she would never let another man touch her. It was only him, always him, the very thought of anything else made her feel sick. She would be content to grow old alone with her memories; the biggest sadness of course, would have been that she never got her baby.

After brooding unhindered for a few days, Poppy was

then swamped with guilt. How dare she have fought with him, not given him physical comfort when he was now so far away, facing an enemy in a hostile environment, devoid of love, affection and human touch?

When these sharpened emotions blunted through the passing of time, she was left with the dull ache of loneliness. Half a year, one hundred and eighty days, it didn't matter how many times she pictured an event six months previously and thought how quickly that time had passed; it still felt like an eternity, a sentence.

The officer coughed into his sideways bunched fist, drawing her into the now. She waited for him to speak, not wanting to prompt; there was no hurry. Similarly, she didn't want to make it easy, hoping he might feel a little bit of the pain that she was starting to feel. Poppy stood rigid, imagining what came next. She heard his unspoken words in her head, wondering which phrase he had chosen, rehearsed. 'Martin is dead'; 'Martin was injured and now he is dead'; 'something dreadful has happened Poppy, Martin is dead'; 'Mrs Cricket, we have some terrible news. Are you alone?'

She'd always imagined what this visit would be like. Try to find an army wife, husband, mother or father that hasn't played out this scenario. You won't be able to because this is how they live. Every time there is a lull in contact or a late night when a promise to call is broken, pulses quicken, car keys are mentally located. Muscles tense as if on starting blocks, in readiness to get to wherever they might be needed with the first waves of grief lapping at their heels. Each unexpected knock at the door, or post nine pm telephone call, causes palms to break sweat until the moment passes and breath returns in a deep sigh. The various salesmen mistake the euphoria for buying signals and not simply the relief of those left behind to watch the clock and tick off the days. For the loved ones of these warriors, it is a sweet relief that it's not their turn, not today.

Poppy used to practice her reaction in her head. She pictured herself sinking to her knees with fingers shoved into her scalp, 'Oh no, not Mart! Please tell me it's not true!' She thought her practised reaction was very convincing, having once performed it in front of the mirror in the salon. Some might question the need to rehearse, but Poppy worried that if and when it came to it, they might not know how devastated she was, figuring it was best to have this pre-prepared reaction in reserve. She didn't need it.

In his early forties, the officer was the younger by a couple of years, but his position gave him confidence over and above his colleague's experience. He removed his hat as he stepped forward.

'Mrs Cricket?' his tone was confident, without any hint of nerves. Poppy noted tiny beads of perspiration peppering his top lip; he might have mastered the neutral voice, but would have to work on that sweat thing if he was to be totally convincing.

She nodded.

'May we come in?' he spoke as he entered the hallway, turning the question into a statement.

'I am Major Anthony Helm, this is Sergeant Gisby,' he put his hand out in the direction of the soldier stood behind him. Poppy stepped forward and placed her limp fingers against his palm, she wasn't used to this shaking hands lark. It made her feel awkward.

In a controlling role reversal, the officer filled her home with his presence, making Poppy feel confused and slightly angry. He guided her by the elbow. She didn't like the stranger touching her. She felt queasy and embarrassed.

He led her into the lounge. The other man walked over to the TV and turned it off. Columbo had been in the middle of his big summing up speech, raincoat flapping; a cigar clamped between his teeth.

She sat on the edge of the sofa and cast a fleeting eye around the room, the walls needed more pictures and the dried flower arrangement held a latticework of cobwebs. A minute spider was suspended on invisible thread. A tiny abseiler, his destination the ring stained wood of a pine shelf. She closed her eyes and wished she could go home, only therein laid her dilemma.

The officer perched on the chair opposite, his colleague stood rigidly by the door. In order to prevent her escape or to facilitate his, she wasn't sure. Poppy could hear the blood pulsing in her ears with a drum like beat. Her hands felt cold and clammy, they had finally found their tremor.

She exhaled loudly and deeply like an athlete preparing to perform, flexing her fingers and nodding, her gestures screamed, go on then, tell me now!

'Are you alone Mrs Cricket?'

'Yes,' her voice was a cracked whisper, strained, the voice she sometimes had when speaking for the first time after a deep sleep.

The Major nodded. He was a plain, flat-faced man, made all the more unattractive by his confident stance. There was the hint of a North East accent that he tried desperately hard to erase, concentrating on delivering neutral vowels and the right pitch. Anthony Helm was a good soldier, respected by those who served under him and relied upon by those he reported to. His reputation was for straight talking, a man that tenaciously did it by the book and did it well. Ironically, the traits that enabled him to climb the ranks with ease, did not necessarily equip him for a carefree existence in the civilian world. The vagaries of modern life were hard for a practical man like Anthony Helm to negotiate, when the structure and rules of his regime were removed, he was somewhat adrift.

She smiled nervously at the Sergeant and bit her tongue. Her smile was fixed and unnatural. She could feel an inane statement wanting to escape from her mouth, 'Sergeant, is that better than Private, but not as good as Colonel? Mart has tried to teach me, but I can never remember the order...' She didn't know why she wanted to say this. To ease the tension? Fill the silent void? Or was it simply manners, shouldn't she be making conversation?

Poppy didn't warm to the Major. Her ability to read people told her that whilst he was doing his duty, he would rather have been anywhere else. Mr Gisby smiled back at her, as if reading her thoughts. He had sincere eyes that crumpled at the edges. She was glad that he was there.

Then Helm began, just as she had known he would, with the phrase she had dreaded every day and night since her beloved husband had stepped into that bloody recruiting office. The words that she had considered with trepidation from the first time he came home with his letter telling him to report to the training department at Bassingbourn and bizarrely a cheque, which Martin had been delighted with, but she had seen as a bribe, the modern day Queen's Shilling. What was it he had said as he waved the piece of paper in front of her? 'You knew what joining the army meant Poppy! None of this is a surprise. I know I should have told you first about joining up, but when I did, you knew that this would be my job. And don't tell me you won't like it when we get the house with a garden and the extra pay, or the chance to live abroad. You won't be moaning then will you!'

Poppy couldn't believe his words; she was stunned that he had fallen back on a shallow argument. He knew she couldn't care less about houses and possessions. She wasn't made that way. It made no sense to her; he was choosing to go away, to leave her alone for months, if not years, and had reached this decision without discussion or consultation. Martin had been a maximum of an hour away from her since she was a little girl and the idea of him being out of reach horrified her. The thought of him being in a different city was something she couldn't comprehend, let alone a different country. Poppy never bought the supper without asking for his preference, yet he had done this thing alone, furtive, duplicitous. She felt excluded and betrayed.

'Mrs Cricket?' for the second time the officer used his tone to anchor her in the present.

Poppy nodded to show that he had succeeded, he had her full attention. Her teeth shook against her bottom lip; she bit down, trying to gain composure.

'I'm afraid I have some bad news.' He paused, pursing his lips, remembering his training, allowing the information to be received slowly in bite-sized chunks.

She wanted to say, 'For God's sake hurry up. We all know what comes next!'

Again, he coughed, 'As you know, Martin is currently deployed in Afghanistan.'

Poppy tried to control her quivering legs and nodded to show understanding.

'We are here because we have some news about your husband and it isn't good news... I am very sorry to have to tell you that Martin is missing.'

It took a second for his words to reach her brain and a further second to digest the fact, two seconds longer than usual.

'D'you mean dead?' she prompted, loudly. Her wide eyes told him her abruptness was a symptom of shock. Her body wasn't wasting precious reserves on pleasantries.

'No, not dead. Not at this stage. He is missing.'

His response only served to confuse her more; not at this stage? So dead, but not confirmed? Dead; but not discovered? Dead, but not yet? All permutations had him very definitely dead. The rest was semantics.

'But that means dead doesn't it?'

'No. Not dead, he is missing,' he glanced at Sergeant Gisby, silently asking if he had any better suggestions on how to clarify the facts.

'Isn't that just because you haven't found him or had it confirmed yet or something?'

Major Anthony Helm visibly coloured. She had accurately called the situation and similarly was asking him the question that he'd dreaded the most. Had Poppy looked closely, she would have seen the vaguest twitch to his right cheek; he wasn't a man that knew how to respond to questions from a girl like her. Despite his years of service, these encounters would always be outside of his comfort zone. It was alien to Anthony, sitting in a council flat in Walthamstow on a muggy Tuesday with fish fingers under the grill, telling Poppy that Martin was possibly dead whilst being subjected to questions that he couldn't answer. It was an element soldiers rarely considered when enlisting; the pastoral responsibilities, the pressing of the flesh, the human face of the MoD machine. It was a world away from kicking in doors and crawling through undergrowth with a gun in your hand.

Poppy felt his unease and might have felt sorry for him, were it not for the fact that she had decided to blame him. Well, she had to blame someone, didn't she?

His tone was clipped, not through any lack of compassion, but because that was how he operated; whatever the task in hand he retained absolute control.

'No, that is not the case at all. Martin at this stage is missing. We have no other useful facts, but we do believe in keeping you informed of every development as soon as we have it. At the moment, that is all the information we have.'

'I appreciate that Major...' she hesitated as his surname slipped from her memory, 'Major Thingy, but what exactly does it mean?' Poppy hadn't intended to be rude, but she did want to know what was going on.

Major Helm licked the sweat from his top lip, lizard-like in his dexterity. 'It's Anthony.' His smile was fleeting. It had taken one slip up of his name for him to reach a point of intolerance; he was not about to be known as 'Major Thingy' especially in front of the Sergeant. It had been twenty-four years, eight tours and a clutch of service medals since he had answered to a name he disliked.

Sergeant Gisby stepped forward. He bent low in front of Poppy, addressing her while resting on his haunches, his fat thighs pressed against the double seam of his combat trousers. 'What it means Mrs Cricket...'

'No one really calls me Mrs Cricket. I'm Poppy.'

'What it means Poppy is that he was on patrol in Helmand province and he didn't come back when he was expected to. He went out on patrol in a group of twelve and so far, only ten have returned to base. That's all we know at this point. We are trying to get information for you from those that did come back and as soon as we have more we'll pass it straight on to you. What we do know, is that something went very wrong on that patrol. Martin and one other infantryman are missing.'

'So he could be dead?'

Sergeant Gisby didn't flinch. He held her gaze, giving Poppy the impression that he was on her side, 'Yes Poppy that is a possibility.'

She nodded, grateful for his honesty. There was a minute of silence, each gathering thoughts. 'When did it happen?' Poppy addressed the Sergeant. She wanted to try and picture what she was doing while her husband was getting into trouble, possibly even killed.

'It was yesterday, yesterday afternoon.'

Yesterday afternoon, where had she been? In Sainsbury's, oblivious. Poppy had always thought that if anything happened to Martin she would know. Like the twins you read about in the *National Geographic*, when one breaks a leg and the other feels the pain even though they are hundreds of miles apart. Poppy thought it might have been like that, but it hadn't. She hadn't felt a thing. Instead, she'd been perusing the three-for-two offers, trying to choose between Pepperoni and Hawaiian, while her man was being killed, going missing.

'What was he doing in that Helmans Province, or whatever it's called? I thought he wouldn't be in any danger.'

The Major piped up, 'You should be very proud of him Poppy. He had been selected to aide an American patrol as part of a special task force.'

She looked at him long and hard. Her thoughts went briefly to what her husband had put up with every day of his childhood, how he had joined up to give them a better life.

When they were little, Martin would knock for Poppy after school and the two would head to the 'Recreation Area', a rather grand term applied to the dilapidated swings in the central courtyard next to the car park. There, they invented games like collecting a stick off the floor while swinging, or daring each other to shout things out. It used to feel really brave when it was cold, dark and everyone else was inside safe and warm, having their tea. They would take it in turns to shout out 'BUM!' louder and louder until someone would hang over a balcony and tell them to 'Shut it!' That used to make them laugh even more. Poppy's mum never came to check that she was ok, if she was warm enough, where she was or who she was with. Sometimes it got really late, but still she never appeared. Martin's mum never came to find him either, she probably thought he was safer out on the streets, taking his chances with the paedophiles and pushers than he was in his own house.

Poppy and Martin thought about it sometimes and agreed that if they had a little girl, or a little boy for that matter, they wouldn't let them wander about with no idea of where they were for hours on end. They would instead have them safe by their side or they'd be outside with them, teaching them the pick up the stick or the shout out 'bum' game.

'Oh I am proud of him, very proud, but not because he was helping some Americans doing God knows what, God knows where. And what do you mean special task force? He only finished his training five minutes ago!'

Major Helm smiled, but kept his eyes downcast, making it hard for Poppy to read his expression, 'They only select the best. He was a very good soldier Poppy.'

'Was? So you think he's dead too?'

'No... I... Is... He *is* a good soldier.' He was scarlet.

Poppy didn't wait for the Major to start uttering further clichés, 'I haven't got any more questions right now.' Her voice sounded sharper than intended, like she was conducting an interview and didn't know how to wrap it up. It was her polite way of saying go. Please go now. She wanted to be by herself; well, she did and she didn't.

The silent tableau was fractured as Poppy leapt from the sofa, alerted by the acrid scent of burning, 'Oh shit!' She ran into the kitchen. Pulling the grill pan from the cooker, she watched the tray and its blackened content clatter into the water filled sink and then almost instantly, was sick on the floor, retching until her gut was empty.

Sergeant Gisby's voice came from the doorway, 'Can I call anyone for you Poppy? Is there someone that can come and sit with you?'

Poppy shook her head, no on both counts. She remained at a right angle, trying to free strands of hair that were glued to her face with vomit. There was only one person she wanted and he was missing, probably dead, in some dusty landscape on the other side of the world. 'I don't even know what he is doing out there. It's so far away.' She addressed the black and white chequered lino. The Sergeant ran her a glass of cold water and steered her back to the safety of the sofa.

Major Anthony Helm sat awkwardly, rearranging his hands again and again until they were comfortable. He looked like an unwanted guest that knew as much.

'So, what happens now?' Poppy prompted.

'We'll assign you an information point of contact that will be in regular touch, keeping you up to date with any developments, no matter how small.'

'Can it be Sergeant Gisby?' she interrupted him; once again throwing his rehearsed rhetoric into touch.

'Well, I don't see why not.'

Sergeant Gisby looked at her. He had one of those bushy moustaches that looked like it must be irritating. She decided that the letters 'R' and 'W' were the most likely to tickle.

'Please call me Rob. I'd be happy to keep you informed with any news.'

Poppy counted three tickles.

'Mrs Cricket, we are here to help you in any way that we can. I only wish that our meeting was under different circumstances.'

She smiled at his comment and thought that if circumstances were different, they would not be meeting in a million years. Their worlds would not have overlapped were it not for this bloody awful situation, and if he had known anything about her he wouldn't be calling her Mrs Cricket. 'Thank you. Please call me Poppy. Mrs Cricket always makes me think of Martin's mother and she's a right old cow.'

He nodded, not sure of how to respond. Logistics and support were discussed before the military men left quietly and quickly.

Rob Gisby drove as the Major sat in quiet contemplation on the back seat. Rob figured he was feeling as sad for Poppy's situation as he was. Anthony was preoccupied with Poppy; her lack of ambition and seeming acceptance of her humble circumstances were beyond his comprehension. He wondered if her acceptance was down to low intellect. Thank God he wasn't similarly afflicted or he might still be living under his mam's roof. The thought made him shudder. He ran his fingers over the shiny buttons of his tunic, tangible proof that he was an officer, a fact that still delighted and amazed him. Anthony carried with him a furtive air as if at any moment he might get found out. 'Fortitude Fortunately Forgives'; he mentally practised the sounds that helped eradicate the Geordie accent, banishing it to another time, a different person.

Anthony Helm was wrong. Poppy's expectations *were* small, her horizon within reach and her world navigable by foot; a mere eight hundred metres from her front door in any direction. But she was clever. Not Mensa, PhD, rocket science genius, but more able than most and smart enough to know what made people tick.

Poppy left school when she was sixteen as realisation dawned that staying on to get qualifications was pointless for someone like her. The standard question was, 'If she's so clever, how come she didn't go to university and gather an armful of degrees to see her on her merry way?' There was a single response she gave to the teachers, heads of year and careers advisers that she sat in front of on more than one occasion, 'There was absolutely no point!'

They sighed on cue, tapped the rubber-stoppered ends of pencils on their clipboards and looked at her with vexed expressions, imploring her to recognise that they knew better, if not best. She stood her ground because actually they did not know what was best for Poppy Day. She did.

Poppy's role in life was to make sure that no one fell out of the net that kept her strange little family snug and safe.

This, she could never have made the academic hierarchy understand. The simple fact that had she gone off to university, there wouldn't have been anyone to collect Dorothea's many and varied prescriptions. No one to make sure she took the daily drugs that stopped her wandering off down the High Street with her knickers on her head. No one to keep the fridge stocked with food and pay the bills. On and on the list went. The demands and responsibilities were endless; Poppy was needed at home several times a day.

Of course the standard argument was, 'If she went off and got qualified, think medicine or the law, she could then secure a wonderful future for herself and her family.' This was probably true, but still failed to answer Poppy's question of who was going to wash her nan's soiled bed linen, sober her mum up enough to collect her benefit and lock the door every night while she was off securing their future? Poppy was smart enough to know that this was her life and there was naff all she could do about it.

Her sunny disposition meant she wasn't bitter. She did sometimes think about a life with a different kind of luck. A life that had seen her born into a circumstance that allowed her the freedom to study and become whatever she wanted! This was not bitterness; try to find one person on the planet who doesn't also ponder some aspect of their life, a different choice, a different person, a different career that might have kept their husband safe from harm...

Poppy pulled her knees up under her chin and sat back on the sofa, feeling surprisingly numb. She had expected hysteria, or at the very least, anger. What she couldn't have predicted was the anaesthesia that now gripped her. She rubbed the back of her wedding ring with the thumb of the same hand and found herself repeating his name, 'Mart... Mart...' She tried to invoke his image with the self-soothing mantra. The room was once again silent, as if the soldiers had never been there.

Is that what it would be like now for Martin? As if he had never been there at all? The flat was now quiet and empty, without the telly on for background noise and without the two men that had filled the small space only a few minutes before. It had been four years since the space had been home to a family; a rather unconventional one, but a family nonetheless. Death and desertion had seen the group eroded, leading up to that moment, when it was just Poppy, alone.

Her mum, Cheryl, had never been cruel, intentionally neglectful or deliberately spiteful. Similarly, she had never been affectionate or proud of her little girl. Never glad to see her or interested to know about her day. Never shared an event with her, told her a secret or cleared her clothes from the end of the sofa so that her child could sit down. Never brushed her daughter's hair if it was ratty or trimmed her nails so she wouldn't have to bite them. Whether Poppy was fed or not, whether she was in bed asleep or sitting alongside her mother on the settee at eleven o'clock on a school night with no clean uniform, weren't important to Cheryl, so they had to be important to Poppy.

Wally, her grandad, was a professional snoozer. His dozing form fascinated Poppy; she wondered what the point of Wally was. He slept all night in his bed and all day in his chair. His skinny frame permanently concertinaed into a snoring 'z' shape, a human onomatopoeia. His slumber took precedence over all other household activity; he sat like a queen bee whose activity and lifestyle is supported by all those around her. Wally held court over his kingdom of Somnambular. In this dreary realm, many restrictions were put in place to curb the behaviour of a growing, inquisitive girl, 'Keep the noise down Poppy Day, your grandad is sleeping'; or 'Turn your music off Poppy Day your grandad is sleeping'; or 'Stop hitting the floor with that bloody yo-yo your grandad is...'

'Yeah, yeah I know... he's sleeping!'

Wally's death was a strange non-event in Poppy's life; the most memorable consequence being that there was now an empty chair with an indent of his dead arse in it. She felt no sadness at his passing; figuring that Wally must be delighted to be permanently turning up his toes in readiness for the ultimate snooze...

The main difference for Poppy was that now when her mum or nan wanted her to be quiet they said, 'Turn that bloody racket off Poppy Day,' or 'Keep quiet Poppy Day!' In her head she heard, '...your grandad is sleeping' and had to fight the urge to shout out really loudly, 'Yes! I know he is sleeping, but my yo-yo banging sure as hell isn't going to wake him up now!'

Poppy's nan, Dorothea, had always been slightly nuts. She watched the tumble dryer instead of the telly, and made jelly with peas in it instead of fruit because it looked nicer; as opposed to now when she is completely crazy, proper full-blown bonkers.

Poppy lived with her mum and nan in the flat until her mum went off to the Canaries with her latest beau. There was no discussion concerning the new domestic arrangements, largely because Cheryl made the decision, packed her bags and was Heathrow-bound within a twenty-four hour period. It was assumed by all that Poppy would continue in her unofficial role as Dorothea's nursemaid, jailor and confidante. If anything, her life was easier without her mum's drunken presence and the procession of wastrels that followed in her unsteady wake.

Dorothea and Poppy plodded along amicably until the old lady's mental health deteriorated and her behaviour became increasingly odd. Poppy came home one lunchtime to find her sitting on the loo, wearing nearly all of her clothing including coats, hats, scarves and gloves, clutching a rolling pin as a weapon.

'The bloke in the flat upstairs has been crawling through a hole in the ceiling and trying to turn our water off, the bastard!'

Poppy tried to hide her disbelief, 'Who Nan? Mr Bennett? The eighty-four year old with the double hip replacement and the Zimmer frame?'

'That's him.'

'Let me get this straight. He's been crawling through a hole in the ceiling and scurrying around the flat while we sleep, trying to turn our water off?' she needed clarification.

'Yes Poppy Day, did you not hear me the first time girl?'

'I heard you Nan and I understood, but what I don't get is why are you sat in the loo wearing all your clothes?'

Dorothea looked at Poppy, shaking her head slightly as if it was her granddaughter without full understanding. She bent forward conspiratorially, 'I'm guarding the stop cock.' She winked at Poppy, who smiled in response.

Her nan quickly went from being slightly unsettled to quite frightened; at this point, Poppy found it hard to cope. As her nan's primary carer, it was tough. If Poppy was on top of things, she would find her nan's little adventures or wanderings funny; but when tired, finding Dorothea at three in the morning sitting in the kitchen, with a full packet of flour, a jar of coffee and three pints of milk tipped into a slippery heap on the floor as she 'made the Christmas cake' was very wearing. Especially when it was June, far too early to be thinking about bloody Christmas.

Poppy could have managed her nan's decline were it just about her own ability to cope, but it wasn't, it was about what was best for Dorothea as well. She needed to be somewhere that she could be watched and supported twenty-four hours a day.

Poppy came home from work one wintery evening to find her sitting in the dark crying and bewildered. She had no way of knowing if Dorothea had been in this state of distress for ten hours or ten minutes; it was a moment of realisation. Not that it made what came next any easier; it was the toughest decision of Poppy's life, at that point.

She and Martin found the home after weeks of trawling through brochures and trudging the streets. Some were rejected on price, others on location and one before the front door had even been opened, after hearing expletives bellowed from within.

Poppy considered the Major's words and thought that she should cry. She tried pushing some tears out, but none came. For some reason this made her giggle; she pictured someone watching her and saying, 'What *are* you doing Poppy? Why are you sat there with your eyes screwed shut, digging your nails into your palms?'

'I'm trying to push some tears out. I thought it might make me feel better because I feel a little bit guilty that I haven't cried yet, despite those two soldiers watching and expecting me too whilst secretly hoping that I wouldn't, especially Major Tony Thingy. It's as if I have read about this story in the paper or seen it on the news. It feels like someone else's life, not mine, not real. Where are those darn tears when you need 'em?'

She was sure that whoever she delivered this monologue to would probably shake their head in a kind of 'she has finally lost the plot just like her grandma' way.

Two

It was a big day for Martin Cricket. He had been chosen as part of a select task force supporting the Americans on an all-day sortie. It was not without a certain amount of trepidation that he acknowledged the order. Other than being on patrol; the plan was a bit sketchy. He had no option other than to trust in the powers that be. Martin was used to this, the abdication of choice, a life of submission and capitulation; it was the nature of his work as a soldier.

Despite his level of fitness, his joints groaned in remonstration. The two stone of body armour and equipment that he donned each and every morning didn't get any lighter as the tour wore on. It was early in the day, yet the heat was intense and not the pleasurable warmth of a sun-soaked holiday; more akin to being foil wrapped and placed on the top shelf of an oven. He and his colleague, Aaron, prepared to climb up into the second Jackal; a high-mobility, cross-country vehicle; not exactly comfortable, but no one minded so much about comfort as long as they were safe.

Aaron stood aside, 'After you, short arse.' He waited for his friend to scramble aboard. At five foot seven, Martin was at least six inches shorter than his mate; a constant source of amusement to both them and their unit.

'Mate, a short arse I might be, but it's not my head that'll be stuck above the parapet like a sitting duck when we get out there.'

Martin indicated towards the open-backed truck and the desert with his thumb. Twelve soldiers were to travel in three vehicles. Any more than four in each car would make movement en route difficult, as the bulk of their kit took up the space of two men. Any fewer than four and a feeling of vulnerability would kick in, which was never good.

The Jackal drove for two hours from the base. The lead vehicle, at least a hundred metres in front, kicked up a trail of dust as it ventured into the sandy abyss. Gone was the easy banter of the first half an hour. Once the camp was out of sight their mood became sombre. The men were contemplative, each concentrating on his defined role; an arc to watch, gun ready, senses alert. Martin jerked in the direction of every flash of light or quick movement. They were exposed, each trying not to think of the probability. 'Improvised explosive device' and 'sniper fire' were words that tripped off the tongue with alarming ease, only out here they were not mere phrases, they were possibilities.

At that time in the Afghan conflict, over the course of a six-month tour, the numbers of dead and injured were higher than anyone could have anticipated. The deaths of soldiers were so frequent that the public were suffering from compassion fatigue, unable to mourn yet another name on an ever-growing list. The odds for all deployed military personnel were terrible; more than odds, they were faces etched in their minds, names engraved in stone and the flag-draped coffins paraded through a silent Wiltshire town.

Martin's SA-80 rifle felt hot and heavy, slipping against his sweaty palm. Nervous energy was palpable, partly because they were with the Americans whose approach and methods were so different to the British. Martin was able to witness what an abundance of resource and equipment meant in terms of strategy. Their allies could do what they considered most effective in theatre, untethered by the constraints laid down by parsimonious politicians. It gave them confidence that bordered on cockiness, complacency almost, and this too was never good.

The collective jitters were justified; the convoy was

headed into dangerous territory, bandit country. Previous contact and activity meant Martin could feel the imaginary, yet intense, gaze of a thousand pairs of hidden eyes; each belonging to the nameless owner of a ready weapon, a Kalashnikov with its muzzle trained on him. Bravado was easy within the compound walls, but out there in the mountains it was different. He wanted the operation to be over as soon as possible, back for tea and a shower. Some of the lads had been talking about organising a game of five-a-side. Martin tried to think of that more than anything, wondering if he'd get lumbered in goal again.

The landscape was barren, remote villages surrounded by mountains and a smattering of scrubby shrubs. These settlements to the untrained eye were desolate and abandoned. Martin studied the ramshackle buildings, each with a shimmering heat halo. He was intrigued by the flutter of coloured silk beyond the dun-coloured bricks, the floating wicker baskets that rested on heads and the furry legs of dogs that disappeared around corners. He mulled private thoughts. For him to be comfortable at home meant the TV, clothes, central heating, a decent fry up, the pub and a day trip to Southend. These villagers existed with a single cooking pot, one outfit that hung by threads and a roof of some description for shelter. There was no sanitation, no electricity and no comfort. It was a harsh environment and one that Martin, covering the desert in his armoured bouncing cage, could not imagine living in.

It would be difficult to piece together exactly what happened in the next hour and in what order. Every man present would give you a different perspective of events.

The leading American vehicle slammed its brakes on, coming abruptly to a halt; the brake discs squeaked against the pads in rebellion. Martin was instantly aware of shouting, more specifically, shouts in English and Arabic of some sort, possibly Pashto. The stop was unscheduled and unplanned, which meant either some minor interaction with the locals or big trouble. His pulse quickened and his heart beat loudly in his ears just the same. The shouting was getting boisterous. Martin and Aaron looked at each other and without saying a word; they unbuckled their seat belts and jumped out of the Jackal.

At least fifteen men surrounded the lead vehicle. The same number again rushed forward, swarming around Martin and the others. He didn't see where they came from. His eyes darted from man to man, trying to assess the situation. Hostile or neutral? Friend or foe? His training told him that he had a few seconds to decide whether it was a handshake or bullet that awaited him. The group wore clothes spattered with mud and food; gaping sleeves had been worn shiny through age and lack of detergent. They were dressed the same, with identical straggly beards that hung beneath tightly wrapped shemaghs. They were a variety of age and stature, but all bore the same desperate, bloodshot eyes. It was impossible to ascertain their motive. Martin saw at least one child among the group, boy or girl he couldn't tell, but enough of a distraction to cause his trigger finger to recoil in hesitation. Sweat trickled into his eyes; he didn't have a free hand to remove the irritation.

The Afghanis kept their faces covered, surging forward; some with outstretched hands, others with fists clenched. Coiled around what? Grenade or gift? Martin tried to read the intention as the crowd breached the gap between them. A caricature American, with chiselled jaw, flat-topped, cropped hair and visibly chewing gum, pulled a pistol from the holster strapped to his thigh and raised it above his head. Martin waited to hear the warning shot.

Instead, the American brought his arm up high over his head and smashed it down across the nose of a man standing within striking range, 'Back off! Back off!' he barked his instruction to the throng.

Martin watched the man stagger backwards into the arms of his countrymen. Blood snaked towards his mouth from a nose that was smashed, flattened. Martin, as ever, had one eye on the underdog. Here it was the unarmed, but not so long ago it was a little girl in the playground called Poppy Day, who wanted to disappear into her shoes.

'Hey, pal! Go easy!'

The American flashed Martin a look that told him to keep his mouth shut, this was not his patrol and he was a guest.

The crowd held their rigid stance, staring wide-eyed with adrenalin pumping, rocking on heels, arms stiff, jaws locked, ready to go. It was the same posture witnessed in the wee small hours on any Saturday night, at any taxi rank, in any British city. There was a moment of stillness before the outbreak of pandemonium. Guns appeared from beneath garments, transforming the crowd of locals into soldiers with a desire to fight that shone from unflinching eyes. Martin smelt the sharp tang of sweat emanating from the group. They were unpredictable and close.

The mob around both cars pitched forward, shouting louder, some screaming. It was impossible to figure out what was going on with so much noise and movement.

Suddenly, there were gunshots; both the rapid fire of the insurgents and the single aimed shots of allied guns. The deafening crack of gunfire filled the air. Martin couldn't gauge which weapons the shots were coming from. It would be nice to say that every combatant knew what to do; comforting for the relatives of those affected to believe the level of training and battle competence meant the soldiers knew how to keep themselves safe when it mattered. It would be nice to say, but it wouldn't be the truth. No amount of training or textbook theory could have prepared Martin for that single moment of madness. In the movies, individuals fall into place with planned perfection, but it wasn't like that at all.

Whenever Martin felt frightened, he was sure that he shrunk to the size of his six-year-old self. This was one of those times; his helmet felt large, his chin strap loose and his jacket voluminous. The movement of so many feet and some vehicles caused clouds of dust to billow in every direction. The team lost its bearings. In the midst of the melee, they didn't know which way was up. Martin didn't have time to fire, he couldn't think clearly. The faces of the insurgents were contorted with hatred, lips curled, teeth bared. He stared at the crowd, each one a stock representation of a baddie.

Martin looked to his right; less than thirty feet away, two of the bearded men held Aaron by his arms, which were bent up behind his back. One of his captors was tall; one short. Martin registered the parallel. Aaron was silent. Martin shouted at Jonesy, who was twenty feet to his left, 'Over here!' his voice quavered. He had been separated from the group; instinct told him that they were coming for him next. He felt his colon spasm and fought to control his bowels.

There was renewed shouting; this time with an identifiable tone of panic, both in English and Pashto. Individuals tried shouting louder than the next man, presumably firing off instructions to their own men. The words, however, were lost, swallowed up in the fray. There was yet more gunfire. An unseen fist punched Martin full in the stomach, winding him. He tried to draw breath, to speak; he wanted to tell the owner of the unseen fist that they had hurt him. Martin forgot he was in the guise of a soldier and believed that he'd been struck in error. Why would anyone want to cause *him* pain? What was any of this to do with him? In a more rational moment, he would have fully understood what his uniform represented.

He dropped to his knees, eyes watering. Terror and pain fought for space inside his head. His breath began to return in shallow pants. Foreign hands yanked roughly at his chin strap until his helmet crashed to the floor. Something was placed on the top of his head; at the same time his wrists were secured behind his back with a plastic cable tie. A second before they pulled the cover over his head, he looked up and could see Aaron; all else was blurred, but his friend was visually clear and sharp.

Martin tried to call to him, but no words came. Aaron too was on his knees; the short captor held him fast by the arms. Martin thought about Aaron's son, Joel, and a picture that he had drawn his daddy, received in the post only hours earlier. As Martin considered the child, the other, taller one, who was holding Aaron's hair, pulled out a knife and cut his throat...

Martin's senses refused to acknowledge that he had just seen his friend murdered; killed without preamble or ceremony, without consideration.

Martin heard angry bursts of instruction issued in a foreign tongue. Hands gripped him under the arms as he was dragged ten feet across the floor. Still bound and hooded, he was thrown against the wheel of a car. He heard a spring groan as the tailgate opened. His breath became low, panicky gulps; he did not want to be put into the boot of a car. Would there be any oxygen?

How could he possibly escape?

His carriage was an old saloon; he had noted as much before being hooded. His amateur-mechanic eyes had glimpsed the white paintwork, flecked with rust around the wheel arches and doors. At least two pairs of hands hauled him upwards, grappling with his ankles and shoulders. He bucked, trying to struggle free, but something heavy landed right in his balls, possibly the butt of a gun. He yelled; tried shouting to Jonesy again for help, his desperate sounds muted by the cloth covering over his head.

As a teenager he'd travel in his mate's dad's car of similar make and model. Three sports bags would fill the boot, the space that he now occupied. Despite his overwhelming fear, he felt indignant at having been bundled into the boot of a car. It was a strange combination of distress and anger. One second he felt like crying; the next he flailed his legs within the confined space, a physical manifestation of his fury. He understood that was the moment he stopped being a person to his captors. The boot isn't for people; it's for bringing the shopping home after a trip to the supermarket, rubbish going to the tip and bags of football kit when teenage boys are playing away.

He could see very little from within the dark space. The air was stifling. Each hot breath taken through his hessian mask left his lungs unsatisfied. With no means of cradling his head or protecting himself, his bones and skull were at the mercy of every bump or sudden brake that jarred him against the metal, which was hot where it touched against bare skin.

Martin closed his eyes, alternately cursing and praying to a God whose existence he had always been sceptical of, 'Help me, Lord help me, don't let me die,' 'What the fuck is going on? Why are you doing this to me?' and repeating,

'This is real' in his head over and over. He blocked out thoughts of Aaron. Martin was with it enough to know that if he let himself mourn, there would be no room left to think about his own survival and the one thing he had to do was concentrate on staying alive. No matter what, he had to get back to Poppy. At some point on the journey, he lost consciousness. Regardless, the car bounded along its dusty path in the midst of a convoy of similarly rusted desert run-arounds.

When Martin came to, he was lying on a mattress. His arms hurt; they were secured above his head, tied to a metal bed frame. His body armour had been removed. He broke into a sweat, knowing that having been transported and imprisoned he had very likely missed the best opportunity he had of escape. Getting away would be that much harder now he was incarcerated. The muscles on his arms and back were beginning to cramp. He had wet himself, the shame of which was acute. Despite the heat in the room, he was shaking. He reasoned that he couldn't be cold and, once he recognised that he was shaking with fear, was able to control it slightly.

His overriding need was for water. His spit was thick; his tongue, larger than usual, rasped against the roof of his mouth. The walls of his throat felt as if they were sticking together.

With the cover still over his head, Martin couldn't see. He determined it was sacking by the texture. He tasted blood in his mouth, but didn't know exactly where or how he was injured. Opening his mouth wide, he felt the unnatural pull of skin and the sting of a fresh wound. He remembered his face skimming the rim of the car boot, the rubber seal having long since perished. He pictured the deep gash that ran from mouth to cheek. The plastic strip that bound his wrists bit into the skin; he desperately wanted to rub the sore areas.

Martin's head twitched from side to side in an effort to hear, to figure out his environment. The room was at least big enough to accommodate a double bed, it was hot and there wasn't a single sound to break the silence. These were the three things he knew to be true. He felt dazed and so edgy that it was difficult to think about anything for a significant length of time. His mind flitted from one thing to another. He lay still, but inside his head there was panic. Conflicting suggestions leapt into his mind, 'Shout, move, scream, get away, kick out, lay still, be quiet, listen, pray…' he tried his best to ignore them. Martin gave up trying to get comfortable. There was so much wrong with his physical situation he didn't know what thing to concentrate on first. Despite the silence, it was as if he was being bombarded with information, most of which he was unable to process. 'Think like a soldier. You've been taken! What should you do? Shout now! Jump up, try and stand. Stay still, keep safe, be invisible, don't antagonise. Help will be on its way, someone will come Martin, someone will come. Reason with them, shout loudly, try something, anything!'

Martin tried to remember his training. The whole unit had been given a session on what to do if you were taken. 'Conduct Under Capture' was now, however, a dim and distant memory. The one element he recalled was 'think about loved ones and the joy of reunion'; this was to help you focus on the thing that would give you mental strength, a reason to survive. His mouth twitched into a small smile behind the cloth. That was the one thing he didn't need to be trained on, thinking about Poppy was automatic, like breathing. He mouthed a silent prayer, an apology, 'I'm so sorry Poppy, I should never have left you. I'm sorry…'

The sack over his head had been pulled back and held taut, causing his nose to press upwards; the prickly cloth irritated his whole face. It stank of old dust and cooking smells. He could blink, but as his eyelashes skimmed the rough hessian, tiny fibres were pushed into his eyes. He was unable to move his hands to scratch the itch or release the fabric.

His breath was warm inside the covering. Tiny drops of spit and sweat gathered in the space around his mouth. He could feel the fabric rubbing his wet jaw, causing a rash. He was desperate to gulp air unfiltered by the filthy sack.

It felt as if bugs, lice or similar were crawling down his face, over his hair and skin. It could have been something as innocuous as sweat trickling, but he was convinced it was the marching feet of insects. With his hands restrained and unable to bring his fingers up to his brow, he surrendered to a silent rage. With every muscle coiled in angry response, his impotence caused tears to pool, which ironically offered some relief. There was worse to come for Martin Cricket, but it was the first few hours that were the hardest to bear.

Martin took a deep breath, and was trying to think how he could make his face more comfortable, when he heard a small cough. He realised for the first time that he was not alone. His body convulsed. The breath stuttered in his throat. Narrowing his eyes into slits, he tried once again to look through the sacking, but could only make out tones of light and dark. There was a stranger in the room, possibly several strangers. He couldn't see them, but they could see him. He knew they wanted to hurt him, they had already hurt him and he had seen them… poor Aaron.

He spoke for the first time, 'My name is Martin Cricket. I am a British soldier with the Princess of Wales's Royal Regiment!' The words sprang from him unrehearsed.

The sound was muffled, uttered through dry, uncoordinated lips. He was aware that he should try to make contact, believing in the possibility that the whole thing was a terrible mix-up. Did they think he was someone of influence? Was it a simple case of mistaken identity? Surely they knew that he was only doing his job? He thought that maybe his captors would hear that he was a British citizen and let him go.

Three

Poppy locked her front door. The ceremony was familiar, turning the key and then pushing the frame with the heel of her palm not once but twice, to check it was secure. Having decided to go back to work, Poppy ambled towards the lift, figuring it would better for her state of mind to be immersed in an afternoon of nits, suds and gossip than to sit on the sofa in silence considering all the possibilities.

No one noticed her enter the salon; it was business as usual for everyone except Poppy, who felt ethereal. She donned her blue and white striped, polyester tabard, the uniform of the menial. Its front, patch pocket was sewn up the middle making two sections; the fabric sagged under the weight of curlers, combs and her emergency Polo's. She had been issued with the garment on her first day, hating it on sight. Now, however, putting it on was an integral part of her working ritual. Without the scratch of the nylon stitching against her skin and the static crackle it created when she touched metal, she didn't feel physically equipped to perform her role. She rollered and pinned Mrs Newton's hair while her mind tried to sort through the various scenarios regarding her husband's disappearance.

Option one, Martin was dead, she just didn't know it yet. Poppy rejected this; her brain would not allow her to consider this or even process it as a possibility.

Option two, he had been briefly separated from his mates and was now safely back at the base, possibly injured, maybe with a broken arm or dislocated shoulder. She liked this option the best so far. Oh my goodness! If this were the case, then he would be coming home! Oh thank God! He would be coming home, her beautiful husband. She smiled at the prospect.

'Y'alright gel?' her customer could see she was miles away.

'Yup, I'm fine Mrs Newton,' Poppy mumbled against the four hair pins between her lips.

The old lady nodded, lifting her ample bust with her folded arms. Mrs Newton did not want to be trotting off to bingo with a lopsided do.

Option three, he really was missing. What did that mean, missing? It was a bloody desert for God's sake! Where could he have got to? Poppy knew he had a crap sense of direction, like the time they had to go up West and ended up in Brent Cross, twice. All because of a dodgy roundabout and the fact that he refused to consult the A–Z or phone his mate who was a cabbie. Not even Martin could get lost in a load of sand, could he? If he had fallen off the back of a Land Rover or tumbled off a tank, surely his mates would have noticed and gone back for him… Unless… Unless…

Poppy felt her knees sway slightly; her head felt cold, the pins tumbled to the floor from her open mouth. The true picture of option three came into perfect focus; her breath lost its natural rhythm. She felt the instant covering of perspiration, chilly against her skin. What if they didn't mean 'missing', what if they meant 'taken'? An image flashed into her mind, Martin was wearing what she called his summer uniform. She thought about school, when in the summer term you were allowed to ditch your jumper and skirt in favour of a little gingham dress, not that she ever had one. Instead, her mum used to make her roll up her sleeves and go without socks… well, she always thought of the pale desert camouflage as the equivalent of his little gingham dress.

Poppy saw it clearly, Martin had a helmet on with a strange chin strap and what looked like a microphone sticking out. His face was more tanned than she had ever seen it and he was shouting, 'Over here! Jonesy! I'm over here!' He sounded desperate to be heard. His eyes were wide. She could see the whites around his iris exposed. He looked frightened. Was he frightened? He then made a strange noise as though he had been winded. It was a deep, short, guttural exhale, the like of which you sometimes hear on the sports field when someone takes a blow to the stomach; quite literally as though the breath has been knocked out of them. Then it went dark and quiet. The picture disappeared and there was only blackness.

Poppy knew then. She knew that he had been taken, she had seen it. She saw it then and she could see it whenever she needed to. It lasted no more than five seconds, but she knew that it was real; could *feel* that it was real. Poppy wandered out on to the street in a daze, not sure what to do next, who to tell or what to tell them. She doubted that even the *National Geographic* would have taken her seriously. How could she explain to anyone what she had seen? She would be laughed at. She trod, nimble-footed over the pavement until she hovered on the broken white line in the middle of the road, sandwiched between white vans and the speeding, Lycra-clad couriers on bicycles. Caught midstream, Poppy was oblivious to the abuse mouthed at her from road users, urging her to 'get out of the bloody road!'

She stood at the halfway mark, having forgotten all about her customer and the fact that she had a shampoo and set to finish, when the phone on the reception desk rang. It became a focus for Poppy above the groan of the traffic. Christine answered it in her usual fake telephone voice. She had an irritating way of going up at the end and over pronouncing the letter 's', her voice an octave higher than usual.

She sounded to the uninitiated like little Miss Sunshine, permanently happy and sweet, but this was a false impression. The reality was that she was miserable and miserly. Christine would rather be counting the takings with a fag clamped between her lips while the dirty smoke swirled up into her hair, giving her fringe a permanent tinge of yellow. Her face would twist as she spoke through a mouthful of cigarette, the side opened slightly to allow the words to escape; her teeth were brown and crowded, with smoke swirling around in there too.

She had no children, which Poppy thought was a blessing. She would have been as crap as her own mother, if not worse, and that's saying something. She was fond of telling Poppy, 'you're the daughter I never 'ad,' and Poppy would think, thank Christ for that. The main difference between her mum and boss was that Cheryl was as ingenuous as Christine was divisive. If Poppy had to choose between the two... They would both get nil points, a draw. In Eurovision terms they would be Luxembourg and Latvia.

Poppy stuck with it for one simple reason; it suited her. The salon was situated on the ground floor of the flats where she lived, making her commute non-existent. She was two roads away from where her beloved nan now resided and she used to be a short stroll away from the garage where Martin worked, until he made other decisions about his career.

Poppy's whole world was within five minutes of where she woke each morning, fabulous. What's the expression; the best laid plans of mice and men?

Christine dropped fag ash all over the appointment book. On the wrong side of sixty, she dressed as though she still had the pert body that she was gifted with as a teenager; one of those women who had the makings of pretty if circumstances had been a little kinder, with a little less grime, a little more class, a little less poverty and a lot more fruit and veg (preferably organic).

Christine had a face and a voice that she used for customers, a different one for her staff and a COMPLETELY different set of faces and voices that she used when talking to a man, any man. Whether the male in question was sixteen or eighty-six, she spoke to them as though they were prey. Poppy had, over the years, watched burly East End builders, who came to pick up their wives from the salon, cower like baby girls as Christine made her move.

She carried with her an ingrained whiff of body odour that, no matter how many showers she took or how much she scrubbed and sprayed, wouldn't shift. It was the kind of smell you sometimes experienced at the end of the day, having worn man-made fibres while you laboured away. She disguised the grim odour with a liberal application of sweet scent, which did nothing to help, only adding to the heady cocktail.

'Snipz Unisex Salon, Christine the proprietor speaking. How may I help you?'

It made Poppy cringe every time she heard the phone answered in that manner. She cringed without fail even though she knew what was coming. Christine answered the phone up to ten times a day. Having worked at Snipz for six years, an average of three hundred and thirteen days a year, meant Poppy had endured a little fewer than nineteen thousand cringes to date.

'Poppyissforyou!' she bellowed, her volume cutting across the road noise, confident the voice on the end of the line was not a customer.

Poppy wandered back towards the salon. Her boss's

dulcet tones had reached her down the street and probably half the people in the next street as well. Her client was still engrossed in a magazine with her hair half pinned up. Poppy didn't think she had noticed her absence; she may even have nodded off, judging by her slumped posture. Either that or she was dead. Whichever.

Christine jabbed the phone towards Poppy, extending a painted nail in her direction, "'urry up!'

Poppy ignored her. Sometimes this worked best for both of them. She knew it was Sergeant Gisby before he spoke.

There was a silence. It was as if the two verbally danced in silence, skirting the issue, unsure how to begin, twisting and passing each other in well-choreographed moves.

'How are you Poppy?'

'I'm...' she felt lost for words quite literally; not knowing how to describe what she was feeling or how she was. *'Poppy has a fourteen-year-old reading age despite being only six and an excellent grasp of the English language and its vocabulary'* [sic]. This was one of the few comments she could recall from her school reports – it couldn't have been less accurate than at this moment. She didn't have the words because she didn't have the understanding, '...fine.'

'Good. I am glad that you're alright. No more news I'm afraid, but I'd like to come and see you when you finish work. Would that be convenient?'

Would that be convenient? It wasn't as if she had other plans, or that anything she may have planned could have been half as important as anything he might want to tell her, like whether or not her husband was alive or d... d... not.

'That would be fine Rob. I'll be home at about six-ish.'

'Great Poppy, I'll see you then.'

Christine pounced, 'Oooh, Rob is it? See you about six-ish? And what might I ask, would your Mart think about you entertaining gentleman callers of an evening while he's off fighting for his country, God knows bloody where?' She delivered the whole speech without drawing breath. She did that a lot, talked until she ran out of air rather than pause, as though she was on a timer.

Poppy looked her squarely in the eye, 'What would Mart think? Mmmn... he would think, thank God my Poppy isn't like Christine and, therefore, not likely to shag the first thing that she sees in trousers the moment her husband's back is turned.'

'Oh Poppy love, I was only joking!' she patted the girl's thin arm with her talons, attempting a girlish giggle.

Poppy continued to look her in the face, her expression stony, 'So was I!'

Christine chose to swallow the lie. Both glad the conversation was over.

It had been a very long day. Poppy sat on the sofa in the dark. The silent gloom suited her, enabled her to think without distraction. She replayed the five seconds of vision that she had encountered earlier, trying to see around the corner, to hear more, feel more. There was nothing else, but it was enough.

It wasn't often that she wished she had someone to talk to, but this was one of those times and her mate would not have sufficed. Jenna had been in Poppy's life since junior school, they looked and sounded similar. Jenna was her surrogate family, in fact not surrogate, she was family.

She had always been there for Poppy when things were bad at home, helping in the small ways that children can. She was still there for her now, not that Poppy was so afflicted or inept that she needed constant care and attention. There was no rota, but Jenna was protective, knowing what she had been through. In this instance, however, Poppy wanted to talk to someone who had life experience, like a mum, Ha! Or more specifically a dad, Poppy wished that she could talk to her dad. Having never spoken to or met her father that would have been an interesting inaugural conversation.

Poppy's biological father was a 'No Hoper.' For years she thought the 'No Hopers' were followers of a bizarre religion, like the 'Jehovah's whatstheirname' or the 'brethren of the thingy' that you see on the High Street. The ones with the scarves and the kids that look too old to be wheeled around in buggies.

Every time her dad was mentioned or asked after, her nan, quick as a flash, would say by way of excuse or justification that he was a 'No Hoper' and came from a family of 'No Hopers'.

Poppy used to wonder what the significant behaviour of his sect was. She recognised that the Jews had their particular Sabbath, the Latter Day Saints didn't do Christmas, or was that the other lot? Anyway, she figured that her dad's particular religious group must have been against having anything to do with daughters, illegitimate or otherwise, because she had never seen him, heard from him or had so much as a birthday card in her whole life. As her mother was fond of pointing out when questioned, 'Your dad? You wouldn't know him if you shat him. In fact, I'm not sure I would!' Nice.

Poppy rather liked the idea of her dad being a bit mysterious, living in his unusual sect. She even learned a hymn, *Onward Christian Soldiers*, thinking that if ever she was to go and live with him, she didn't want to turn up completely ignorant.

She saw exactly how it would happen in her mind, thinking about it before she fell asleep some nights.

He would live in a huge church, obviously, and when she walked in he would say to her, 'Do you go to church Poppy?'

'Only at Christmas and Harvest Festival, but I do know a lovely hymn.' She would then break into a tuneful rendition of the above and bang! She would be in, a fully paid up, scarf-wearing-buggy-pushing member.

Her dad would then hug her, in a proud, 'I love my daughter even though she is illegitimate and only knows one hymn' kind of way.

One of Poppy's earliest memories was standing in the playground when Jackie Sinclair screamed in a fit of anger, '...just 'cos you've got no dad!' She spat out her venom, the very words contagious and a verbal disease that marked Poppy. Jackie's tone suggested it was Poppy's fault, as if she had done something wrong, misplaced this precious family member. Poppy shouted at the top of her voice, 'I have got a dad actually Jackie Sinclair, but I can't see him and he can't see me! It's not his fault; it's because of his religion. He's a 'No Hoper'!'

She could hear a ripple of laughter spreading across the tarmac. It started at the wiggly painted snake puzzle and finished at the middle school girls' toilet block.

Poppy's face felt hot and sweaty, her heart boomed and shook in her chest. She couldn't figure out why they were all laughing, but she wished they would stop. Twisting her leg, she tried to burrow deep down into her scuff-toed shoes. She wanted to disappear.

Martin Cricket didn't laugh. Instead, he pulled her to one side, gave her a slow hug and two slightly tacky cola bottles, peppered with fluff, that had been nestling deep in his pocket. He told her it wasn't a good idea to tell people that her dad was a 'No Hoper'. She told him it was the truth, it was his religion. Martin shook his head.

He looked her in the eye and told her that it wasn't his religion, her dad was just a useless bastard, but she wasn't to worry because his dad was a useless bastard too. He suggested that they stick together. She popped the sour cola bottles on her tongue. A bargain had been struck.

Poppy would never forget standing with her head under the crook of Martin's arm; he was solidly built, a pre-cursor to the short, stocky man that he would become. It was the only time in their life when he was significantly taller than her. She surreptitiously sniffed his jumper; it smelt like food, a school dinnery smell of wool that needed washing. He noticed for the first time how her straight, freckled nose wrinkled when she concentrated. How her toffee-coloured hair hung limply against her pale complexion; yet when the sun found it, a myriad of colours was revealed from red to gold. It reminded him of Bonfire Night. He thought she was beautiful; sixteen years later, he still did.

Poppy changed his world. She had a certain look about her. Martin was a little boy, yet old enough to recognise her expression as the one that stared at him every morning from the mirror as he cleaned his teeth. She, like him, was frightened, confused and constantly looking over her shoulder to see where the next blow or disappointment was coming from. He loved her instantly without measure and knew that, no matter what, he wanted to look after her.

Martin's revelation made Poppy grow up and wake up all at once. She knew then that her dad didn't see her because he didn't want to. Even though she was only six and had never seen him, she suddenly felt very sad, rejected and lonely. She didn't know that was how she was feeling at the time because she didn't have the words. She only knew it when she got older and was able to identify that feeling of hunger that is nothing to do with food and that cold ache inside you that can't be warmed.

Up until the point that Martin told her the harsh truth, she thought that maybe one day she would meet her dad and he would take her in and take her away from her mum, the constant stream of different boyfriends and her sleeping grandad.

Poppy had already given up on her mum so this made her mythical dad her last hope of a decent, respectable family. Like the one in *Little House on the Prairie*, with the mum baking bread, occasionally wiping her floury hands on her pinny and carrying her little wicker basket, while the dad chopped logs, drove his wagon and played the fiddle in his red checked shirt.

Now that hope was gone and ironically her dad did become a 'No Hoper', only now it meant no hope of ever seeing him and no hope of rescue from her shitty life. Until Martin offered her friendship and love, Poppy's life had indeed been shitty.

The doorbell clattered its familiar herald. Poppy flicked on the lamp before poking her head through the gap between the safety chain and frame. Bloody pointless those chains; she had seen many a bloke in anger kick a door similarly tethered and they snapped like the multi-coloured paper chains that you made at playschool.

'It's me Poppy.'

She knew it was him, but still no harm in making doubly sure. She nodded, slipped the chain from its mooring and opened the door fully.

He came into the hallway and took off his beret, still in uniform, 'How you doing?'

Again she offered the moronic response, 'Fine'. Why she kept repeating it she didn't know. It was so far from the truth. It was the same response she had given her whole life, even when she was little. Whether she was hungry, cold, miserable or lonely, whoever was asking and wherever they asked it, 'How are you Poppy?' the stock response was always, 'fine.' What was the alternative? 'Thanks for asking, lady in the lift. Actually, I haven't eaten since yesterday lunchtime. I haven't got any clean pants for tomorrow. I'm frightened to go to sleep because my mum is always out somewhere and I need to be awake in case we get burgled, or the house catches fire, or in case Nan does something stupid or dies...' 'Fine,' was definitely easier.

Rob followed her into the lounge. Sitting on one end of the sofa, Poppy placed a cushion over her chest, a subconscious gesture to shield her from the information, protect her from the blows. He sat at the other end.

'Have you told anyone Poppy? Have you got someone that could be with you?' Rob seemed genuinely concerned that she was not surrounded by tea and tissue-toting relatives.

She shook her head, again, no on both counts. She thought about Jenna, but decided against mentioning her. Poppy now understood that some things were so unbelievable even though you knew them to be true, that you had to keep them contained until you could make sense of them. Only then might you be able to explain them to others.

'We've had a bit more information come through Poppy.'

She nodded, hurry up, hurry up! Tell me what you know!

'As we told you earlier, Martin went out in a patrol of twelve and only ten men came back,' he paused, 'we can now account for eleven of the men on that patrol.'

Poppy placed the nail of her index finger between her front teeth and ripped. The pain was a welcome momentary distraction. She hated the way Rob was trying to disguise the facts. She wanted clear and concise information; it was frustrating, but she knew that he was just following procedure, 'Is it Mart?'

The expression on his face told her that the news was not positive, 'No. It isn't Martin.' There was more to come, 'It was Aaron Sotherby, Martin's colleague. I am sorry to say that he is deceased. His next of kin have been informed.'

Poppy exhaled through bloated cheeks, unaware that she had been holding her breath.

'We expect the details to be released to the media tomorrow. There's a news blackout on it at the moment, but we can only do that for so long, then the world will want the details. What we must do, Poppy, is make sure that you know as much as we do so that there are no surprises for you.'

'Was he killed by the people that have taken Mart?' the words tumbled out, unplanned.

Rob gasped, she watched him trying to order his thoughts, 'How..? Poppy we...' It was his turn to be lost for words.

'I saw it Rob. I know it sounds completely crazy, but I saw him. I know that he has been taken.'

Rob groaned as he pushed his thumbs into his eye sockets, trying to figure out what to do next. Poppy had no way of knowing that Rob had been thoroughly briefed; he not only knew that Martin had been taken, but also by whom, and the answer to Poppy's question was yes, the people that had killed his colleague had taken Martin. He faced a terrible dilemma; who in his organisation would believe that he hadn't given her the facts that she appeared to be in possession of?

'Poppy,' she could see that he was trying to think, fast, 'there are reasons why information is given out in the way that it is. I am going to ask you to trust me. I know it's a big thing to ask you at a very difficult time, but you can trust me. I promise that I will tell you everything that I can, when I can.' They were silent for some seconds, equally matched chess players considering their next moves.

'Are you married Rob?' she could see him thinking about his family, his wife. They had wanted children, but had not been so blessed. His wife was his family, his life.

'Yes, yes I am married, to Moira,' he smiled broadly when he said her name aloud. Poppy would learn that this was always the case; it was a reflex, the very mention of her name, the woman who was his wife, made him happy. She knew what that felt like.

Poppy's had been an unremarkable wedding, lower than low key, but, despite the lack of pomp, Poppy and Martin made a solid and binding commitment to each other. Poppy knew instantly that she felt differently. She loved being married, finding herself unexpectedly excited and comforted by it. Three years later, she still glanced down at the little gold band on the third finger of her left hand and smiled with a rush of exhilaration in her stomach because she was someone's wife and someone was her husband. It made her feel special; someone had wanted to marry her! Her; Poppy Day.

'Can you imagine what this is like for me Rob? Imagine something had happened to Moira, something terrible and people knew what had happened. They knew where she was, whether she was dead or alive, and what was likely to happen to her. The only person that didn't know was you, her husband, the person she loves. The person that she exchanged wedding vows with...'

Rob looked away, envisaging just that; his Moira, his wife and a buttoned up Major like Anthony Helm, who would conduct himself in accordance with the rule book, withholding that information. It was an unbearable thought; unbearable for him, for any man, for any person.

'Please Rob. I'm not stupid, and I want to tell you that even though you don't know me either, you can trust me too. I will not reveal what you have told me until you tell me I can. I promise you.'

Poppy could tell that at that precise moment Rob hated his job, hated the fact that she was being forced to negotiate, to bargain, when it was she that was the victim. He looked at her like she was a brave little girl who had every right to know about her husband, the person that she had exchanged vows with.

'Poppy, I can see that you are far from stupid, but you must understand that it's not only my career that is on the line here, but possibly other people's safety; maybe Martin's safety. Do you understand the implications of that?'

She nodded, understanding that this was real. He did have more information. This was no bluff; her instinct was right, Martin was still alive, but he was in danger. Her Mart, her beloved. Hang in there baby...

Rob shook his head as though he couldn't believe that he was going to fly in the face of his superiors and against all he had been trained to do. He was doing it to give information to Poppy Day, a young girl, on nothing more than a hunch. She was very glad that he did.

'When Martin's patrol went out, it was with an American sortie into the mountains. The Americans knew that it was a hot spot, a recognised enclave for insurgent activity, they had all been fully briefed.'

'You make it sound exciting, like Mart would have wanted to go, but I bet he was shit-scared.'

Rob smiled at her, drawing from experience, thinking

back to his last tour, 'You're probably right. It's difficult to describe exactly what it's like in theatre. You are shit-scared sometimes, but it's also exciting, and if it it's not exciting then it's usually boring, so you almost welcome the excitement to escape the boredom. Ultimately though, you are doing what you are trained to do and you feel invincible...'

'Shame no one told that to Mart's colleague, the one that's deceased.'

Rob nodded. Touché.

'So what happened on this mission or whatever it's called?' Poppy felt her face flush, embarrassed to be using army terms. It made her feel like she was hamming it up in some crappy American war movie, or was one of those nutters who live with their mum until they are fifty, who love guns and combat magazines. She started to chew the nails on her other hand. Her stomach was in knots.

'They were in a convoy or vehicles. The one in front got surrounded by locals and contact was made...'

'They made contact?' Poppy pictured the soldiers and locals shaking hands and swapping details, 'Hello there! Lovely day!'

'...contact as in exchanged fire.'

'Oh.' Rob's clarification caused the images of the hand shakers to turn red and slip Dali-like until they formed a pool of blood.

'The soldiers from some of the other vehicles dismounted and went to the aid of the first, but it was a carefully planned ambush. The group were surrounded and two soldiers were taken, Martin and one other, Aaron. It seems the purpose was to take hostages. The feeling is that one soldier has been killed to show they mean business, but that means, Poppy, that Martin is alive and they will keep him alive as he is their bargaining chip.'

She tried to filter the information. Hostage. Prisoner. Captive. Try as she might to make sense of it, the words felt alien, especially when referring to her husband. She once again, saw the image of Martin shouting and then winded as they struck him. She could guess that much, but what with? Was he hurt? 'Who are they, the group that has taken him, do you know?' she wanted the detail; knowing this would help her understand and that she wouldn't sleep until she knew as much as the army did.

'It is a group that's named after its founder Zelgai Mahmood – the ZMO, or Zelgai Mahmood Organisation. We know that they are extremists who are feared, well-funded and organised, but currently we don't know exactly why they have taken Martin or what it is that they want.'

'It's probably money though right? Or if he is a bargaining chip as you say, then maybe they want to exchange him for some of their prisoners?' Poppy was trying to think of all the possibilities knowing that this would be where the answer lay. She was already thinking of a solution; there had to be something that could be done.

Rob smiled at her again and was glad that she was thinking along the right lines, 'That's probably about the sum of it, yes Poppy.'

She felt exhausted, but needed to keep alert, needed to know more, 'And do you know where they are holding him Rob?'

He shook his head, 'We don't. It is very likely that he is still in the region that he was taken, as moving him around would be deemed too risky.'

'That's a good thing isn't it? Can't we just send in those Special Forces blokes, or Ross Kemp, or whatever, and get him back?' Poppy's fatigue allowed her to fuse the fiction with the reality. She regretted sounding naive, young.

'It's not that simple Poppy. The region where Martin was taken is mountainous and dangerous, even without the possible threat from ZMO supporters.'

'I can't believe people actually support them when they do such bloody horrible things.'

'It's hard for us to understand, but the people that live there are so poor, they have nothing. The ZMO looks after them in exchange for loyalty and help; it's a system that works. Even if we could get close enough to take him, he might be moved or sold on quicker than we could get to him. It's better that neither of those things happen.'

'Better why?'

He didn't answer.

Poppy accepted his silence, trusting him enough to assume if he thought it better that she didn't know, then maybe it was, 'I don't know what I should be doing Rob. It's like I'm in a horrible dream and I wish I'd wake up.'

'I know it's easy to say Poppy, but try not to worry.'

She smiled; yes, it was easy to say...

'Poppy, I don't think that you should be here alone. Is there someone that you can call? I'm happy to wait with you until they arrive,' he was insistent.

It was her turn to shake her head, 'There's no one, but I am going to visit my nan now, so I won't be alone.'

Rob visibly brightened. She didn't spoil the illusion, but rather let him picture her sitting in front of her nan's fire, being fed fruitcake from a doily laden plate, while the two drank tea from dainty, floral china cups. The reality was Poppy changing her nan's pants for the umpteenth time that day and helping to brush her dentures, while her nan rummaged in her knitting bag for stray mints and plucked at invisible lint on her cardigan.

The residential home for the elderly is called The

Poplars, which Dorothea pronounced 'The Populars' and which quickly became known as 'The Unpopulars' as she hates it there, or so she says. Poppy's not so sure. It is owned and run by Mr Akwal and his family, at least twenty members of which Poppy has met over the last few years. Mr Akwal calls her nan 'Dorothy,' which drives her crazy, no pun intended. It makes Poppy laugh, the things that bother her, the moments when she is completely lucid and the things that slip through her ever-widening net of reality.

The old lady, in whatever state the day might find her, always, always knows Poppy; she knows that she loves this gift of a granddaughter and that her love is reciprocated. For this, Poppy is entirely grateful. Dorothea also has a strange, misguided belief. This is one of those bits of information that to anyone outside of their immediate circle, sounds bizarre, humorous even, but isn't at all strange to Poppy. This is either because she is used to it, or she too is one currant short of a bun. Either way, Poppy's nan, Dorothea Day, is utterly and totally convinced that her daughter is Joan Collins. Poppy doesn't know when this belief first manifested itself or where it came from. The fact is, she will tell anyone that will listen how tough it was bringing up a wilful character like her Joan. As far as Poppy can tell, the only connection between Joan Collins and her mother is that they have both played *The Bitch*.

Dorothea is also convinced that Mr Akwal and his entire retinue are trying to poison her. Despite this ingrained belief, she polishes off the food they present her with each mealtime, ending with, 'Ha! You didn't get me this time!' Often followed by, 'Any more of that apple pie going spare?'

She is also in love. Nathan, the object of her affection, is the nineteen-year-old gay nursing assistant, who tends to her every need. She tells him every day, several times a day,

'...such a good boy, you need a nice girlfriend.' To which he replies, several times a day, 'I don't need a girlfriend Dorothea. I've got you.' But she doesn't remember.

Poppy visits her nan daily without fail. It is the highlight of the day for both of them. If Nathan is around, Dorothea will introduce them, 'Nathan, this is my Poppy Day.'

Nathan shakes her hand and says, 'I am pleased to meet you Poppy Day' even though it's probably the millionth time that they have met.

She then says, on cue, 'Poppy Day, I want to leave Nathan something in my will. Can you sort it out for me?'

'Certainly Nan. What would you like to leave him?'

To which she replies, 'I think about a million pounds.'

'Consider it done.'

Nathan smiles, thinking for one second about what he could do with that million pounds.

They both know the reality. Her total wealth sits somewhere between four and sixty eight pounds, depending on what she has in her purse and the few sentimental possessions that are scattered around her room.

Rob left, telling Poppy that he would be in touch in the morning. She walked along the road to 'The Unpopulars,' finding it difficult to think about the situation. Unable to picture Martin, where he was or what had happened to him. She thought about normal things, like whether her nan might need anything, wondering if the fridge needed defrosting, anything to fill her thoughts.

She rang the doorbell, to be greeted by Nathan.

'Hello gorgeous'.

'Hello yourself. How's Dorothea?'

'Oh Poppy Day she has been a complete nightmare today! Threw her breakfast across the room first thing, by eleven am we had a dirty protest and after lunch she tried to bite Mrs Hardwick on the arm.' Poppy loved Nathan, the way that he made even the most awful day sound almost funny, almost.

'Is Mrs Hardwick alright?' She was used to having to apologise or mop up for her nan, the Reggie Kray of the house.

'Yes, she is fine. I gave her an extra custard cream with her cuppa tonight to soothe away any angst over the whole sordid incident.'

'Thanks Nath.'

'You are welcome Poppy Day,' he had picked up Dorothea's habit of calling her both Christian and surname. 'You look shattered honey, tough day at the office?'

'Mmmnn, something like that.'

Poppy made her way along the corridor to her nan's room. She scanned the TV lounge, which was crowded as usual. Fourteen mismatched, high-backed chairs in various floral and vinyl finishes formed a u-shape around the perimeter; these seats the bequest of residents long dispatched. The pea soup-coloured walls absorbed the fetid, foul breath of the decaying occupants. The linoleum floor caught drips from lax muscles, splashes of tea from shaky hands and tears shed at memories that refused to budge. The room and the people in it were fused into an amorphous mass of decrepitude. Even when empty, the ghosts and scents of the dead and not yet dead, tangibly lingered. The residents of the 'Unpopulars' had similar backgrounds, native East Enders that had witnessed the Blitz, all of whom had been around long enough to see their lives and landscapes transformed beyond recognition. They were strangers bound by common ancestry and the shared choice of their final postcode; the last place they would call home.

Poppy watched Nathan tuck a blanket around the legs of an ancient woman, who's tiny, birdlike frame, he lifted with ease. The woman reached up with knobbly fingers and touched the keys that hung from his belt, 'Keys,' she offered.

'Yes, my house and office keys, oh and a car key, bit of a jailers bunch!' he tried to lighten the mood with a touch of joviality.

'I don't have keys anymore,' she looked at him through a long grey fringe, a curtain from behind which she could study the strange world and simultaneously hide. Nathan stared; he didn't know what to say to make it better. She was right; of course, no keys meant no property, no vehicle, no belonging and no freedom. A bit like Mart.

Dorothea was, as usual, sitting in her little room, in front of the TV with the volume and heating both turned a little too high for comfort. She was obsessed with cookery programmes; any format, any recipe, at any time of the day or night. This, despite the fact that she had never made any effort in her own kitchen, other than the occasional roast dinner on a Sunday and the ready supply of bacon sandwiches that kept Wally the miserable sleeper from starvation. A chef with a booming voice was giving explicit instructions on how to stuff and roast a loin of lamb. Poppy bent low and kissed her forehead.

'Ah Poppy Day!'

'Hello Nan. How are you tonight?'

'They are trying to poison me. I had shepherd's pie tonight and it smelt very funny!'

'Did you manage to eat it?'

'Yes I did. In fact, I had two portions. I'm not going to give them the satisfaction of watching me starve. I am not afraid of their poison!' she turned her head to shout the last few words in the direction of the corridor.

'Quite right too Nan. Apart from your near death by poisoning experience, anything else happen today?'

'Now you come to mention it, yes, I've had a terrible day. That Mrs Hardwick's been causing trouble again.'

'So I've heard.'

'Was it on the news?'

'Yes it was; it was the headline: *That Mrs Hardwick causes trouble again!*'

'Well I'm not surprised, she is a right cow. Ah Poppy Day, there is someone that I would like you to meet!'

Nathan stepped into the room.

'Nathan, this is Poppy Day, my granddaughter. Poppy Day, this is Nathan.'

Nathan shook her hand, 'Pleased to meet you Poppy Day.'

'I want to leave Nathan something in my will. Can you sort it out for me?

Poppy and Nathan recited their lines until Dorothea was content...

'What did you do today Poppy Day?'

'I had some bad news actually Nan.'

'Oh no! It's not Wally is it?' Dorothea's breath came in short bursts as she clutched at the front of her cardigan, her anxiety evident.

Poppy thought of Wally, who had died well over a decade ago, and wondered what could have happened to him that would be so bad now? Maybe he had given a worm acute indigestion, 'No Nan, it's not Wally.'

Her fingers unfurled, 'Did I tell you about that Mrs Hardwick? She's been causing trouble again.'

'No you didn't mention it. Mrs Hardwick you say?'

'Yes, someone told me it was on the news!'

'Did they? I think that was someone pulling your leg Nan.'

'No, it was definitely on the news.'

'Who told you Nan?'

'Mrs Hardwick told me. She'd seen something about our Joan, she's in trouble again.'

Poppy stroked the back of her Nan's hand. This was how her evening went, verbally going around in circles, trying to find the beginning and end of a moving piece of thread, without crying, screaming or both. No matter how frustrating, this was her lovely nan and, at that point, she was all the family Poppy had and she needed her.

The hour passed slowly for Poppy, tiredness crept into her joints, and tugged at her eyelids, 'Right then Nan, I'm going to make tracks. Do you need anything before I go?'

'Yes I do! I need you to go and have a word with that Mr What'shisname; he is trying to poison me! I fed some of my shepherd's pie to the cat and it rolled over and died! That's proof Poppy Day!'

'Nan, I will get right onto it I promise. I love you.'

'...and I love you. I just hope that I am still here in the morning and that they don't poison me in the night!'

'I think you'll be ok Nan, just don't eat anything!'

Poppy walked home slowly. Despite her exhaustion and the lure of her bed, she didn't want to arrive. She twisted the key in the lock and walked into the shadowy, hushed space.

Bedtime was now Poppy's least favourite part of the day. Like most married couples, she and Martin had fallen into a steady night-time routine over the years, with well-established habits. Swapping trivia about their day as they took turns to clean teeth, passing in the hallway with pyjamas slung over arms, fetching glasses of water that would remain untouched on bedside tables, only to be discarded in the morning. Poppy would then submerge herself under the duvet, curled into a ball, trying to muster warmth while she waited for her husband whose job it was to switch off the lights, lock the door and unplug the telly...

On one occasion Martin donned his wife's pink nightdress and entered the bedroom performing an elaborate mock ballet move. Poppy watched her hairy man with his arms aloft and a dozing puppy on his chest. They had laughed like children...

Poppy now completed her night-time ritual in silence, without the easy chatter that the two exchanged. She'd lock the door early and re-check it at least twice. The bedroom was always tidy. She missed retrieving the pool of dirty linen that gathered on the floor seven days a week; the pants, jeans, t-shirt and socks; evidence of a life lived in harmony with hers.

In the half an hour or so before falling asleep, she wondered what her man was doing, where he was sleeping, what he was thinking. Holding his pillow against her chest, she imagined his protective arms around her. She would talk to him about her day, how she was feeling, ask about his. She would hear his response and it was as good as chatting. 'Goodnight baby, sweet dreams,' as if he was dozing by her side. It gave her comfort. She could sometimes fool herself that he was there, keeping her safe. To wake in the night and reach for him, only to find him gone meant a night of cold and lonely musings. It didn't get any easier.

She would often re-read the one letter Martin had written her in reply; an innocuous three sheets, penned in haste by torchlight, using his knees as a desk. It would become a talisman, a thing so precious that Poppy would keep it close, fingering the pale blue airmail paper and learning each loop of script by heart.

She no longer needed to unfold the sheets and feel their feather-light weight in her palm; she could simply close her eyes and visualise each pen stroke and each smudge.

Well Poppy,

Here is a surprise for you, a letter from your old man! I miss you baby, more than you can imagine.

Time passes very slowly or very quickly, depends if I'm mega busy or bored stupid. When I'm mega busy its fine, but when I am bored and missing you, it's bloody miserable.

I want to come home Poppy, I want to come home and be with you in our flat. I want to take you to bed and hold you tight and feel your arms around me. I hate sleeping on my own and I always reach out for you in the night.

I want to make our baby with you Poppy, I want our little family. I want to see you with our baby.

I know we are solid and that's the one thing that keeps me going and stops me going mental.

I think about you every minute.

I love you Poppy, always have an I always will. I think about the wedding a lot.

Sometimes I am homesick Poppy and I imagine you holding my hand and it helps. I can hear your voice in my head and it's as good as sitting with you on the settee.

Got to go now baby, never forget how much I am loving you and missing you.

Mart xxxxxxxxxxxxxxxxxxxxxxxxxxxxxxxxxxxxx

It had become increasingly difficult for Poppy to write with any originality. She found herself repeating the content of previous letters, always trying to think of new and different ways to tell him about her boring life.

Self-censorship meant she avoided telling him anything that would make him miss home too much, make him worry or jealous, not that Martin was the jealous type. It was more out of consideration than self-preservation.

Poppy carried with her a low-level guilt. It wasn't always at the forefront of her mind, but was more of a hum, like distant motorway traffic; the more you strained to hear it, the louder it became. She never exactly lied to Martin, but, rather, doctored the facts to make for more palatable reading. She would neglect to mention an evening at home with the girls and a Chinese takeaway, as they watched the football and drank plonk. It didn't feel fair, doing the stuff that he loved. Instead, she kept to neutral topics, particularly her nan. Pages could be filled with the wonderful conversations that took place at 'The Unpopulars' and some of Dorothea's more crackers ideas. She knew these insights would make him laugh, as well as keeping him updated. It was good for Poppy too, to be able to share her worries and thoughts.

She neglected to tell him that she'd seen his mum and dad, who had ignored her. Poppy had been perusing the fruit and veg in the supermarket, when she looked up from the shrink-wrapped broccoli and caught his mum's eye. She knew that they had seen her; could tell by the way his mum concentrated on looking the other way to prove that she hadn't seen her, when it was really obvious that she had... Poppy felt embarrassed, what did they think? That she might want something from them? God forbid.

There was little point in sharing this with Mart, it would

only have angered and possibly upset him. It wouldn't be pleasant to know that they had not wanted to find out if there was any news on their son. Was he well? Alive? That sort of thing.

Poppy looked through the open door into the kitchen, where she spied the burnt fish fingers stuck to the grill pan, dumped in the sink. She slid down the door until her back was pushed against the wood. Her legs finally submitting to fatigue, crumpled beneath her and she started to cry. She didn't have to pretend or think about her prepared reaction, it was real. Fat tears ran from her eyes, clogging her mouth and nose, 'Mart...' she whispered through her distress, 'Mart...' she willed him to hear her calling to him across the sea and sand. Her heart ached with longing for her husband, her man, her best friend, 'Where are you?'

Four

Martin lay in captivity, still tied to the bed, trying to work out how many hours had passed since he had woken safe and happy in the camp. He figured it was the same day, but without the guidance of daylight and no way of knowing how long he had been unconscious, he could only guess.

As with anyone that's suffered trauma, it's not only the incident, but the whole of that day that takes on significance. There is a temptation to analyse the surrounding events, looking for clues that might help you understand how a day can start off in such an ordinary way, yet end so unexpectedly.

On his final morning in camp, Martin had woken early and whistled his way to the shower block. The Portakabin housed a row of showers along its back wall, several sinks to the left of the central door and a long, slatted, wooden bench that ran across the middle of the room. It reminded Martin of the changing room in the public swimming baths he had frequented whilst at school; although here there was marginally less towel whipping and no one dared nick your clean pants. Martin stashed his body armour and helmet on the long bench, whilst standing inside the cubicle; hoping it was a day when water was available and dreaming of the privacy, fluffy towels and sparkling tiles of home, where after a shower, he would join Poppy on the sofa. There, they'd drink tea and watch the news, her knees curled up against his thigh, her head on his shoulder...

Unlike some, Martin didn't mind the routine of camp life. He'd divided his time away into chores, having calculated that when he had completed one hundred and eighty-six ablutions, he'd be heading home. As his eighty-fourth shave dawned, he reflected that there was only one hundred and two to go before he would be packing his kit, shipping out.

The day of his capture had indeed started out routinely. Wearing his towel as a scarf he pulled his chin with his left hand into a taut and unnatural angle, whilst scraping at the whiskers with the razor in his right. He knew that Poppy liked to watch him shave, finding the nature of the task intimate and sexy. At home, he would speak to her pyjama-clad reflection as it hovered over his right shoulder. Standing in the Portakabin, his eyes darted to that space in the mirror's corner, hoping to catch a glimpse of her face. Every touch to his skin of the razor's blade took him one step closer to Poppy.

The previous night had been relatively peaceful, one siren and subsequent attack meant he had enjoyed six consecutive hours of sleep. He was in good spirits.

Martin and Aaron stood side by side, exchanging small talk that would with hindsight, become significant. The men tended to keep their conversation to the current or amusing; safe, gossipy topics that kept emotions in check. Aaron had only mentioned his son maybe once or twice before, yet uncharacteristically, he wanted to discuss him that morning.

'I got a picture from Joel today, not really sure what it's supposed to be, but it's a bloody masterpiece. I'll keep it safe in case he's ever a famous artist. I mean look at what those *Sunflowers* fetched! I can't believe he's nearly two already. I really miss him Mart.'

Martin nodded, unsure of what to say or how to make it better. He didn't know what it felt like to miss anyone other than your wife. It was especially hard for him to envisage a happy father and son relationship. He considered the love between Aaron and Joel with fascination and something close to envy.

Martin, like Poppy, had lived in E17 all his life. The

Crickets' maisonette, situated in a block adjacent to Poppy's, was a decorative homage to the 1960s. The lounge boasted swirly patterned carpets, a Pepita clown print over an electric fire and a glass-topped, kidney-shaped bar that gathered dust, pizza flyers and out-of-date copies of the yellow pages. His mum, a nervous chain smoker, had been a dinner lady at their school and his dad was... his dad was a complete bastard. Martin couldn't imagine his dad hanging onto one of his works of art. He was one of those men that in his whole life never went anywhere or achieved anything, yet was able to confidently mock and correct those that had. He knew better than anyone about everything! It was quite a talent for a shithead that had only ever sat in the front room, throwing his weight around, dispensing wisdom from his grotty chair in front of the telly.

He was a big man, fat and slovenly, who wore remnants of his last meal on his exposed vest and whose grey stubble sat as a dark shadow, designer-like in its uniformity. He carried with him the sour odour of fried food and sex. Martin grew up knowing that his dad was mean, unable to fully explain how frightened he was of him. When he looked back, he realised that for most of his childhood he held his breath. This, he did in the belief that it made him feather-light, undetectable and Martin Cricket wanted to be invisible.

For the first decade or so of his life, Martin could not have told you the colour of his dad's eyes, having never looked him directly in the face; his gaze always either averted or downcast. He became a quiet child; experience taught him not to offer his opinion. On the few occasions he shared a viewpoint his dad had laughed, mocking his childlike suggestions, guffawing loudly and repeating his son's words with a feminine lilt to his booming voice, 'Do what you useless little poof? How would that work? You bloody idiot!' He would then bring back his hand, sometimes to hit him, but just as often he would raise his hand quickly as though he was going to hit the boy, then let it fall to his side. Martin would never know if this gesture was going to end in a smack or not, he would flinch and yelp just the same. This his father would find funny, in fact, not just slightly funny, but absolutely HILARIOUS!

The fear of violence became so acute that Martin's dad could move his hand a fraction too quickly and the boy would jump out of his skin. When the man did actually hit his son it was almost a relief, confirmation that Martin wasn't mad. He would think, 'See Mart, you were right to be scared, he does hit you; you didn't imagine it and it does really hurt.'

His nicotine-addicted mum did nothing to stop her husband. Martin didn't blame her; whilst not exactly thanking her for the life he had, he understood that she had her own battles to win, her own struggle every day. Martin would hear her cry out in the night, the pitch informing that it was a cry of pain, not pleasure. He would put the pillow over his face and sob into it, trying to make it all go away. It made him feel worthless. He would think, 'Look at you Mart, lying under your pillow crying, not doing anything to help Mum. He's right; you are a useless little poof.'

It was in this atmosphere of tension, dread and cigarette smoke that Martin lived; he couldn't see an escape, exit hatch or light at the end of any tunnel. Poppy, however, proved to be all three. She liked listening to him and she didn't laugh. He would never forget the day in school when he had opened the door as she approached the dining hall, stepping slightly ahead to get to the handle before her. He couldn't explain why he did those things, he just knew that he wanted to do every little thing that he could to make her happy, make her life better. Before stepping through the door she looked at Martin, wrinkling her nose and shaking her head to move her fringe from her eyes, 'You make me feel very safe.'

Martin thought he might burst. It was as if she had given him the moon in a box, something so wonderful, rare and unbelievable that he didn't want to share it with anyone. He walked home from school as though gliding. He reasoned that if he made someone as smart and beautiful as Poppy Day feel safe, he wasn't a useless little poof after all. He was twelve years of age.

Martin walked into the flat that same afternoon; his dad was in the usual spot, rooted to the chair and TV. Without looking up from the set, he greeted his son, 'Oh, here she is back from school, how was netball?'

Martin stood between him and the telly. His dad flexed the beer can in his hand; the aluminium popped under the pressure, 'Getoutothebleedinway!' Martin didn't flinch, didn't move. He stared at his dad, noticing that his eyes were of the palest blue. His fingers balled into fists, twitching with temptation, ready to launch an assault, but Martin, the bigger man, stayed calm, his hands remained by his sides.

Mr Cricket was strangely silent, no clever comment or insult. He looked at his son and knew that there had been a change, enough was enough. Martin wasn't going to take his shit anymore. It was all down to loving Poppy. She made him feel like he could take on the world and win.

The next time the two were sitting on the swings, gripping rusted chains, 'You're my best friend in the whole world Martin.' It was dark, but Poppy knew that he was smiling, 'And I would be very sad if ever you moved away or couldn't play with me anymore.'

'That's never going to happen Poppy. Where would I go?'

She had shrugged in response, unable to picture where he might disappear to.

'I promise you Poppy that I will always be your best friend. It's like we are joined together by invisible strings that join your heart to mine and, if you need me, you just have to pull them and I'll come to you...'

Poppy had laughed out loud, loving the idea of their invisible heart strings, 'And if you pull yours, I will come to you Martin. That way, I'll always know if you need me.'

He reached out a hand in the shadows until he found Poppy's small fingers and placed them inside his own.

Martin glanced at Aaron's foam-covered jaw and thought about what it might be like to have a little boy of your own who would draw you a picture. He and Poppy had so much to look forward to; it was all ahead of them, out there for the taking.

Breakfast, like everything else inside the camp, quickly became routine for Martin. His footfall was no longer hesitant along unfamiliar paths, it was now normal for him to tread duckboards wearing heavy armour in the middle of the desert in search of Weetabix. At first, he found life in theatre exciting; there was a particular thrill in everyone being dressed the same and looking the part. He felt like a member of the ultimate gang, exactly as he had seen in countless films and magazines. Martin felt bonded to his unit in a way that no one at home could begin to understand. The routine, rules and privation governed everything from when he and his unit used the loo to how they worshipped, and the only people that could relate to that were his comrades.

For the first couple of weeks, Martin was tense waiting

for something to happen, one ear permanently cocked for that bloody siren. The odd rocket attack kept him on his toes, especially in the middle of the night. Blissful dreams of Poppy would be shattered in seconds as his instinct kicked in. When his body hit the deck with his face buried in the ground, he would hold his breath, waiting to see if he was in luck or out of it.

He lived with an expectancy that wasn't dissimilar to the feeling he had as a child on Christmas Eve. He didn't know whether the next day all his dreams were going to come true, or whether it would be a rubbish day like any other. Christmas for Martin was usually a rubbish day like any other, but that didn't stop him being excited. There was always the smallest possibility that the rumours were true, that if you'd been good you would get lots of great stuff.

Martin was always a smart child, quickly learning that the whole Santa thing was a lie, but for an hour or two before bed time, the anticipation would be almost painful. He liked the possibility that there might be some magic, somewhere. The first few weeks of his tour were a bit like that, the rumours and the possibility of danger.

After a fortnight, however, reality sunk in. His job and his life in that place were going to be monotonous and predictable. There was nothing glamorous, thrilling or fun about being bombarded with rockets and possible injury at any hour of the day or night. It wasn't vaguely exciting; it was, in fact, totally shit. He was stuck. There was no way to leave without giving a year's notice, no pulling a sicky, no going slow, no walking out on the job. Martin also believed that the future for him and Poppy would be rosy if he could just get through this bit, get some service under his belt. Promotion would mean a house, a garden, possibly a posting somewhere hot. It would make up for all the holidays that they had never had...

Martin's arm muscles spasmed, yanking him from his recollections into the present. He twisted his body, trying to get comfortable on the mattress. He saw the irony that he now longed for the monotony and fatigue of life in camp. Whatever it threw at him, it was one million per cent better than where he was now, wherever the hell that was.

There was a sudden surge in his bowels. 'Oh no!' he howled, louder than he had intended, 'Please, I need a bathroom! I need to move, please...' His begging fell on indifferent ears.

Two silent guards, as yet unseen by Martin, sat either side of the door with their guns in hand. They had only hours before dumped a decapitated body at the gates of the base. A note with their demands was stuffed inside the mouth; the release of four hundred prisoners loyal to their cause, incarcerated across three continents, in exchange for the soldier they had in their possession. The British government had twenty-four hours to respond. The couriers, sitting with their feet on the bundle in the back of a car, had cared little for the twenty-one year old father of Joel, whose corpse they had hauled inside a rolled carpet for most of the journey. Long sausages of ash from their cigarettes had fallen onto his remains. They cared even less that Martin Cricket needed the loo.

It was another couple of hours of watching Martin lie in his own waste before his captors were convinced he wasn't much of a threat. An unseen hand cut the plastic tie around his neck, easing the cloth over his head. The skin of his chin was nicked by the knife that freed him. Martin could feel the warm trickle of blood running down, but with his hands tied, there was very little that he could do about it.

His breath came in large bursts, dry sobs of relief as he

blinked without hindrance or the musty smell that had been his companion. He was inhaling air that was thick with a particularly male aroma, a combination of sweat, piquant breath and musk. It was the stale atmosphere of a fetid room, but compared to having to draw each breath through the filthy sack cloth, it was wonderful. It took a few minutes for his eyes to adjust to seeing without their filter; they darted everywhere, trying to establish the environment.

The room was approximately a fifteen foot square. The walls were whitewashed with an orangey-brown painted stripe from the floor to approximately three feet up. They were pitted, damaged. Chunks of plaster had fallen away beneath the unmistakeable peppering of bullet holes. On the far wall, someone had scrawled some Arabic text in a sloping hand.

Martin would over time study the loops and lines, trying to decipher the dots and dashes of the ornate script. He would, however, end his days without ever interpreting the ancient phrase or appreciating the irony of, 'The secret of happiness is freedom. The secret of freedom is courage'.

A trailing loop of electrical flex hung ominously from the ceiling; a reminder of the electricity that had been promised by benevolent benefactors, but never materialised. A small, high window had been shuttered with the remnants of an old wooden crate. The cheap slats were nailed randomly across its frame, in the same haphazard way that a cartoon character might bar a door in haste, only to turn around and find their nemesis already in the room. Martin studied the square eighteen inch opening. Could he fit through? How would he reach it and remove the wood? What was on the other side?

Apart from the bed, the only other furniture were two plastic chairs, the kind you find stacked in DIY hypermarkets at the start of barbeque season. They were positioned either side of the door frame, both empty, their occupants standing in front of Martin. When his eyes stopped running, he was able to study the two men. Their identical garb meant they looked similar at first, but were in fact quite different. 'Thank you,' it was the first time he had spoken without an obstruction in quite a few hours; his voice sounded strange to his ears.

His relief was instantly replaced by fearful questions. Why had they taken the sacking off? What came next? Were they going to hurt him? What should he do? Say? Did Poppy know he was missing?

His face was raw, eyes watering. The guards and their captive studied each other with equal interest. The men had beards and wore traditional Afghan hats. One was significantly older, toothless, and looked as if life had got the better of him on more than one occasion. Scars and ingrained dirt indicated an existence with little comfort. The other was better groomed with brushed hair and a neatly trimmed beard. He gave Martin some water and treated his charge with indifference, both aspects for which Martin was extremely grateful.

He removed the ties from Martin's wrists. After the initial agony of the blood rushing back down to his limbs from their vertical position, it was wonderful to be able to run his hands through his hair, to scratch his face and rub his eyes. His hands were numb bundles of flesh on the end of clumsy arms.

Martin shifted his weight until he was in a sitting position, propped against the wall. He pulled at the material of his combat trousers, unsticking it from his skin. He was a mess. Instinct told him not to make a request, but simply to be thankful for the small freedom that he had been given.

The guards ignored him, retaking their places either side of the door, continuing their conversation in the guttural Arabic that excluded him.

Martin closed his eyes, relishing the change of position. He had never believed that he would find himself in this predicament; aware that it was one of Poppy's biggest fears, he used to laugh at her as the odds were so much against it. He'd spent a large part of his leave over the last year trying to convince her that the chances of him being taken were practically non-existent. He had to concede that maybe it was him and not her that had been naive.

His life in the military was very different from what he thought he was signing up for. Until the night before he joined up he had never thought about the army, army life or what being a soldier might mean. He had never met anyone that had been in the army, apart from the old men that had done their bit and, quite frankly, he found their recollections a bit boring.

There was only one reason that he even considered joining up; he thought it was a way that he could do better for him and Poppy. He hated the flat they lived in, the noise from the traffic, the graffiti and the junkies in the corridors. He disliked the fact that her job was in the precinct, a stinky lift ride away from home, where she stood for eight hours a day washing and placing rollers in old ladies' hair.

Martin worried that the life that she had, the life that he had given her, might not be enough, that maybe he wouldn't be enough. She was worth so much more than standing in a grotty salon every day, working for a daft tart, and he wanted to give her more.

He had seen adverts on the telly and in the papers, might even have read some literature, but if you asked him why he *actually* joined up, his first answer would be that he didn't know. The truth was, he did know, but avoided thinking about the reasons why.

When he first left school Martin took a job in his local garage. He had visions of becoming a mechanic and, in more fanciful moments, could picture himself running the place. His was not a conscious career plan, but rather a path that offered the least resistance, an opportunity that had presented itself when alternatives were sparse. He eventually realised after a couple of years of making the tea, running back and forth to the bookies for the owner, answering the telephone and sweeping up the crap at the end of the day that he wasn't going anywhere.

Martin worked hard, really hard, in the way that a shire horse does, blinkered and no matter what the conditions, ploughing on. He did it willingly, because he thought it was his future, and he honestly thought that he would be rewarded.

The boss kept telling him, 'In about six months' time your training will start.' Like an idiot, he believed him. He wanted to believe him, he needed to believe him. One winter morning, something happened to change all that.

The owner's son, aged sixteen, started work at the garage. On the lad's first day, he was given his very own overalls and a set of tools in a blue, metal carry box. It was a box that Martin coveted, with little compartments and a mini padlock. He was also given a peg on which to hang his clothes and coat. Not like Martin's peg on the back of the door in the office, but a peg in the garage with all the mechanics' and body shop repairers' pegs.

Martin watched the gang pat him on the back at the end of his first day. He saw the lad admire the tell-tale ring of black grease under his finger nails. Martin looked at his own soft, clean hands that had filed invoices and answered the phone all day and he knew. He knew what he had been trying to deny for the last two years; he was never going to get that pat on the back, his training was never going to start and he was never going to get a peg in the garage. He felt sick and more than a little bit stupid.

That night, he walked home slowly and quietly with the taste of bitterness filling his mouth; it ran down his throat, seeping into his veins. He was crying on the inside, angry and let down, his dad's words filled his head, 'useless little poof.' This was the second reason he joined up; to show his dad, his nasty crappy dad that he was something, that he was capable of being someone. There was a third reason; he wanted to show his Poppy that he could be a better man, a man that could provide the house in the country that she wanted, a man that could earn enough for them to start their family.

He walked down the High Street, not noticing much, his shoulders hunched over, his mouth turned downward at the corners. The recruiting office stood out. Martin must have walked past it a thousand times without really noticing it, but tonight the whole building seemed to pulse, lit up against the gloom. In the middle of the rain soaked street, the grey concrete and litter, the sign called to him. '*Be the Best*' it said, and it was as if it had been written just for Martin, that was exactly what he wanted; to be the best that he could be.

He pushed his nose against the window, captivated by pictures of people in exotic, sunny places and a list, 'Learn one of these trades.' His eyes drank the words written in alphabetical order; everything from Chef to Mechanic and hundreds of roles in between. Martin couldn't believe it! It was the answer to his prayers.

He ran home, literally, ran all the way, full of energy and

anticipation. He burst into the flat. Poppy was standing in the kitchen with her back to her husband. Her hair was pulled back in a ponytail, with pointy tendrils that had worked their way loose hanging down against her pale skin. He grabbed her by the waist and spun her around. He looked into her eyes that were so clear he could see his image perfectly reflected in them.

Martin felt like he could explode with all the possibilities, 'I love you Poppy. Things are going to start getting a whole lot better for us!' He kissed her on the lips.

'Well I am glad to hear that, Mart. Now, wash your hands because your tea's ready. ' She continued to retrieve cutlery from the murky depths of the sink, wiping it with the tea towel. Poppy was calm and unflustered, despite her husband's uncharacteristic display of enthusiasm for their future. It was how she worked, remaining cool until the detail unfolded and she would then decide whether to get excited or not. Poppy had learnt that if you contained your enthusiasm until you were absolutely sure that there was something to be excited about, it avoided a lot of unnecessary disappointment. Martin bumped her out of the way with his hip and washed his hands, pushing the soap under his clean finger nails, no longer irritated by their softness and cleanliness. Instead, he was happy because he had a plan and a future. Tomorrow he would take the first steps to sorting it all out.

Martin leapt out of bed, jumping up as soon as the alarm went off. The day started without the usual groaning or wishing for an extra ten minutes' grace. He'd slept lightly in anticipation of the beeping of his clock, eager for the day to begin. He felt as if he was on the verge of something amazing; the start of all good things for him, for them.

He decided against phoning the garage to say he wasn't

going in. He had never been unreliable, but wanted to show them that he couldn't be pushed around. It was a meagre protest, pathetic really, but it was important to make a stand, no matter how small.

Martin left the house in his suit, feeling ten feet tall, swaggering down the High Street, smiling at anyone that caught his eye. He felt powerful, fantastic, like one of the cocky blokes down the pub who stand at the bar and never get out of the way, who know everyone and always have enough cash. He felt like them, like he knew all the answers.

The recruiting office, now open, was again lit up, a beacon. He walked through the door with confidence, thinking about all the men that had ever joined up; he was about to become part of something unique and important.

Two men in uniform sat behind two desks. Martin walked to the one on the right. What would have happened if he had chosen the one on the left? A different regiment? A different posting? Where would he be at that point? Playing five-a-side within the compound walls? Quite possibly, but contemplating what-ifs didn't help anyone.

It was as though the recruiting Sergeant had been expecting him. Three newly sharpened pencils sat to the right of his hand on top of a pristine white pad.

He smiled at Martin, gesturing to the chair in front of the desk, 'Please take a seat.' Before asking his name or why he was there, he was treating Martin with respect and he liked it. He liked it a lot.

'I'm Sergeant Keith Edwards, of the Princess of Wales's Royal Regiment or the PWRR for short. Can I take your name?'

'I am Martin Cricket,' he waited for the usual smirk, raised eyebrow or full-blown laugh, but there was none, as though being called 'Cricket' was nothing out of the ordinary, nothing to mock. This was a serious business. The Sergeant's lack of response gave Martin the confidence to stay put, no one was laughing, his plan was right on track.

'What can I do for you today, Mr Cricket?'

What could he do for him? Martin wanted to leap across the table, hug him and shout, 'Take me away from this shit life! Make me into something better! Make me into 'The Best!' Give me a life that Poppy and I can be proud of! Give me a peg in the garage, let me get grease under my finger nails, let me train to be a mechanic, let me prove that I am not a useless little poof!'

Thankfully for them both, he did neither of these things. Instead, linking his hands together at the knuckles, he laid his fingers across the back of the opposite hand and placed them in his lap. Primarily this was to stop them shaking, but it was also an unconscious act, giving the whole exchange gravitas.

Before Martin had time to hesitate, contemplate or run, he looked Sergeant Keith Edwards squarely in the eye, 'I am thinking of becoming a soldier.' His voice sounded more confident than he felt.

The Sergeant didn't laugh, but nodded his head slowly as though he had been given the correct answer, the answer he was expecting. He had encountered thousands of blokes that were desperate and didn't know where to go, or what path they should be treading. Blokes that only saw the value of school once its gates had been locked behind them forever. The army could provide that second chance, an opportunity to start over. That was exactly what he was looking for, a bloke just like Martin. The process was relatively quick and administrative, like renewing your passport or registering a death.

Martin didn't tell Poppy where he was going or what he

was planning. He wanted to show her that he could use his initiative, could take control of a crappy situation and turn it around. Having left the flat suited and booted, Poppy knew that it was something or somewhere important. Suspecting a job interview, Poppy played along like a wise parent, letting him keep his secret, allowing the suspense to build, not wanting to spoil the big surprise.

When Martin arrived back at the flat and told her where he had been and what he had done, Poppy couldn't believe it, asking over and over like a broken-down robot, 'What? You have what? Why? Why, Mart?' Her smile collapsed as she folded her arms around her middle. His answers were full and honest, yet she kept repeating, 'You have what?' followed by, 'Why?' as though he spoke in a foreign tongue.

Martin couldn't hide his disappointment, his confusion. He thought she would be as happy as he was and that she too would see it as the answer to their prayers instead of the beginning of their nightmare.

The moment he walked through the door beaming and excited, Poppy saw one word, 'separation'. To her it was obvious and instant. They were going to be apart, isolated, alone.

She felt swamped by a wave of sadness. Worse still, she couldn't believe that he didn't get that! It was as if it hadn't occurred to him *exactly* what this would mean for them. Poppy bit her bottom lip to avoid calling him a useless idiot, knowing that it would remind him of his dad. Besides, it wasn't true.

Martin was stunned. It was as if she didn't know him at all, didn't understand why he had done it, couldn't see that it was all about getting a better life for them. He gripped her arms, 'I want to become someone that you can be proud of.' In his head he added, '...so you don't find anyone better, so you never leave me. I want a career that pays us enough to start our family. I don't want to sweep up anymore Poppy, it's killing me.' These words would have made all the difference to Poppy, but they were not easy for Martin to say. So much more than a collection of syllables, they were an admission of unhappiness, a statement of insecurity.

'But Mart, I'm already proud of you.'

He knew she meant it, making him feel guilty and a little bit sad.

She shook her head, 'Why Mart, Why?'

They stood facing each other, bit players in a low-budget drama, playing strangers. It was awkward, embarrassing, all the things you don't expect to feel when you are with your spouse, your soul mate. Martin could hear the faintest whisper of a little voice on his shoulder, 'Nice one, Mart, you've really ballsed things up, just when you had it pretty perfect.'

Martin thought he'd get a house with a garden, be well paid and learn a trade. He planned on taking that skill and setting up for himself somewhere. He was undecided between plumbing and mechanics. He thought wrong. His spur-of-the-moment decision meant there had been little time for research. He was an infantryman; the pay was low, barely enough, less than he was getting at the garage. He had been told that he could transfer to another trade at a later date. Martin hoped that this was not another empty statement, designed to lure him. There were no houses, or even flats, available for them; not in their area, not yet and moving away was out of the question for Poppy. Unlike other army wives, she couldn't set up home in barracks close to where her husband trained, not when she was needed elsewhere. They were stuck in their council flat, albeit with the army paying some of the rent.

Martin was used to being treated like dirt, it was how he had grown up, yet he didn't expect it now. Not at his age, not now that he was someone's husband, someone that had been tasked with protecting Queen and country. He was out of practice at taking crap. He quickly got used to it again.

The basic training was repetitive and physical; designed to flex his will if not break it, to help him see that doing what he was told when asked was the most important thing in the world. He learnt that lesson fairly quickly, taking orders and literally keeping his head down. It was only when deployed in theatre that Martin understood the full value of his instruction. The last one to follow an order, the last one to react, and the man that questioned the task, was the one that risked not only his own safety but that of his entire unit.

Martin wasn't interested in being the funniest, the most outrageous or the one that pushed the boundaries until they almost got thrown out, although he worked very closely with the aforementioned three. His agenda was different. He wasn't looking to make friends, but that happened by default. He wasn't searching for a replacement family like some of the loners and weirdoes; Poppy was all the family that he would ever need. Instead, he wanted to see where being good at something might take him. Martin smiled when he thought of where it had taken him, where he had arrived. So much for that theory.

Martin's date to leave for Afghanistan had been set. At every encounter during his basic training it sat between him and Poppy like an invisible tumour, never mentioned, yet acutely felt, in the vain hope that it would somehow disappear through neglect. The day arrived sooner than either of them was prepared for; hitting them squarely on the breast bone with such force, it left them breathless. Unspoken angst bubbled behind every sentence, rendering normal speech and action impossible. A new and awkward formality had existed between them for some weeks; both were so concerned with avoiding the topic, it became a verbal dam that stopped words and sentiment from flowing freely.

He knew that Poppy made a conscious decision to try and put things right, to try and make it as special as she could. She had bought a bottle of wine, washed her hair and liberally applied perfume. He was grateful, wanting to somehow bridge the gap from anger and despair to a place of calm acceptance. It was not to be.

Their arguments were so infrequent that Martin could recall them all, word for word. In the weeks ahead, he wouldn't remember exactly how it started, but would recollect what was said and how it ended.

Martin was far from happy. He was scared, anxious and would have given anything not to have been packing for a trip that he did not want to take. It was the first time his wife had voiced her fears with such clarity. It made him feel like shit.

He wanted to fall into her arms, pull his fingers through her hair and feel the weight of her against his chest. He wanted her to grant him forgiveness.

Martin wished that he had explained it better, told her that it was too late for him to fix things, he had to go. He wanted to shout out that he didn't want to go to Afbloodyghanistan. He didn't want to go anywhere. He was thinking of what to do or say next when she folded her arms around her waist and crept into the bathroom. Martin walked into the dark lounge and lowered himself onto the sofa. He rubbed his flat palms over his two day stubble, giving his wife a few minutes to get into her nightie and under the covers before creeping into bed beside her. He lay far out of reach without touching or speaking; he felt the opportunity for repair diminishing and was swept by a new wave of despair.

They spent their last night together on a cold mattress with a large space between them. Despite his exhaustion Martin didn't sleep; he listened to Poppy moving and breathing, knowing that he wouldn't be hearing the telltale noises of her presence for some time, missing her before he had even left. The atmosphere was so strained it was as if the air had physical weight, bearing down on them as they each struggled to escape through slumber.

This was the sad reality of their last night together. The bottle of wine remained in the fridge, its screw top firmly in place. Poppy's clean hair absorbed the tears that ran over her nose and towards her pillow. The pain at his leaving was so great; both wanted it to be over. It couldn't have been any further from what Martin had imagined their last night together might be.

Now, in this dingy room, he wished with his whole being that he could go back to that room, that night and make things right. He would have found the courage to reach across the mattress; he would have found her hand under the covers and held it tight.

Five

Poppy hardly slept. The morning taunted her through a gap in the bedroom curtains. She considered the cruel trick Father Time played on insomniacs, making each restless minute in the wee small hours feel like an hour, yet when the day arrived, it sprang from the dark with alarming speed, hours passed in minutes and minutes became seconds... She was tempted to stay in bed, to pull the duvet over her head and let the world turn without joining in. Almost instantly she saw an image of Martin, tied up and dirty. She knew that while he was in that state, in that place, wherever that place was, she would not allow herself the luxury of wallowing in bed and reflecting on her own sorrow. She would stay strong for him, for both of them.

Poppy tried to shake off the fug of futility. Deep down she knew it wasn't her fault, but something bad had happened to someone she loved and she could do nothing to fix it. She felt useless and responsible all at the same time. As for guilt, she had the monopoly. Guilty for having a hot bath, imagining this wasn't possible for Mart. Drinking tea made her consider his thirst; every small, common activity left her full of remorse.

It was to be a horrible day spent in limbo. Coincidentally, it was Poppy's day off. Welcoming the diversion, she cleared up the kitchen; scrubbing at the fish finger pan until it shone, disposing of the burnt offering and mopping the sticky floor. Her attempt to gain mental solace through the restoration of her physical space failed.

Since her husband had been deployed, Poppy missed him at quite a basic level; aware of the space on the sofa next to her, the preparing, cooking and eating of a meal for one, or having to take the rubbish out to the communal bins on her own in the dark. That was always Mart's job; she hated doing it, partly through a dislike of rats, but mainly a fear of the drug addicts, tarts and gangs that hung around the bins. Despite her anxiety, it made her smile with an ironic lack of comprehension, of all the places that you could congregate and make your patch, why pick behind the stinking bins?

Poppy developed a coping strategy, by NOT thinking about him too much. She found that by keeping herself busy and in a fairly tight routine, it didn't leave too many thinking gaps. There were times when this wasn't possible, if something funny or interesting happened, she would instantly want to tell Martin, to share the joke or get his opinion. When she couldn't, the fact that he was not close to her would have to sink in all over again.

Poppy ran her finger over the wedding photo on the mantelpiece, taken only three years ago, and yet right now it was like looking at a snapshot of another lifetime. She studied her reflection in the edge of the picture; her image suggesting she had aged considerably more than the thirty-six months that had passed since that moment in the pub.

Their wedding was a quiet, informal affair at the local registry office. They were getting hitched at two-thirty pm and with ceremonies at two pm and three pm, were nervous passengers astride a nuptial conveyor belt.

Poppy and Martin were sandwiched between Courtney and Darren, and Carmel and Lloyd. Carmel and Lloyd sounded to Poppy like an expensive department store.

She could picture one of the women from the big houses on the other side of the High Street with the expensive hairdo, four by four, nanny and en suite, saying to her husband as she looked for the car keys on the scrubbed pine dresser, 'Darling, just nipping off to Carmel and Lloyds for some foie gras. We're running a bit low and I couldn't bear the idea of not being able to offer any to Charles and Felicity tonight.' Her husband, irritated by her nasal tone, would barely register her comments as he shook invisible creases from his *Telegraph*. Courtney and Darren turned out to be chavs.

All attending guests had been muddled up by a useless security attendant. Poppy had since wondered if maybe he wasn't useless, but instead found his job so monotonously soul destroying that he did this kind of thing occasionally on purpose to relieve the boredom. They began reciting their vows when someone shouted, 'That's not our Courtney!' Poppy looked up to see Dorothea crying onto the suited shoulder of a very dapper black man, who was meant to be attending either the wedding that had finished early or the one that had not yet started. Most girls would have been angry about such a monumental mix-up on their wedding day, but not Poppy. The whole thing struck her as extremely funny, the idea of her nan, blissfully unaware that she was sharing her granddaughter's special event with so many complete strangers.

The upshot was that Martin and Poppy sniggered and tittered through the short, matter-of-fact ceremony with none of the presupposed emotion that you might assume accompanies a girl's big day. There wasn't much big about any of it, if you disregarded Courtney's arse, which was huge and clad in peach sateen. Poppy had glimpsed her in the garden with a cigarette clamped between her carmine-painted mouth, taking care not to set fire to the over-sprayed curls that sat on her heavily rouged cheeks. She reminded Poppy of a big, fat dolly, although no dolly she had ever seen or played with uttered the phrases that left Courtney's mouth on that day.

Poppy watched, fascinated, as the trembling photographer

tried to coerce the reluctant wedding party onto the steps for a group shot. Courtney removed her fag and held it aloft as her numerous children bunched around her legs. She drew breath and bellowed towards the car park, 'Darren get over 'ere you fucking idiot!'

It made Poppy cringe, it made her sad. The diminutive Darren with his shaved head and twinkling diamond earring, ambled over at his future wife's behest. His hands thrust deep into too shallow pockets; shoulders hunched forward accentuating the tight fit of his jacket and a thin, hand-rolled cigarette dangling unlit from his bottom lip. He looked beaten. She couldn't see a happy ending for Courtney and Darren who, even on this their 'Special Day', appeared steeped in abject misery. They looked utterly disappointed and angry, as though they had hoped for a small reprieve from their wretched lives for twenty-four hours. They had probably assumed that as this was their 'Special Day' they would feel special, but, the fact was, their lives were still crap. The only difference was that today they were crap in a hired suit and a second-hand frock.

For Poppy Day, there was no church, choir or vicar, no flash dress, bridesmaids or flowers, no real reception, wedding cake or confetti, no floating down the aisle with piped music among bunched lilies and trailing ivy, no veil, no dad to give her away, no dad full stop. No honeymoon somewhere hot with terribly good food, no photos capturing the 'essence of their nuptials', none of those things. Oh and no mum, but that's a story in itself. Instead, it was twenty minutes of laughter, a pint in the pub with their mates who sang 'ta da da da...' repeatedly to the tune of *Here Comes the Bride* as they arrived, then home to bed.

Poppy phoned her mum a few weeks before the wedding. The handset that reunited them across the miles was slippery in her sweating palm.

"'ello love.'

Poppy could tell that she was lighting a cigarette as she was speaking. It was that particular talking out of the side of the mouth voice with teeth clenched as she sparked the flint into action.

'How are you Mum?'

'Oh, you know.'

Poppy did know. It was for Cheryl another disappointing venture that had promised gold dust and delivered saw dust. Another bloke that had promised her paradise and for the first few weeks had seemed like a prince as he wined, dined and snogged the face off her, but what do you know? Shock! Horror! Gasp! He turned out to be a fat, balding cretin, once she stayed sober long enough to realise. Yet again she found herself shackled to a loser cast from the same mould as all the others, in a downmarket beach resort. After a few drinks, her new home looked like the Caribbean, but on a rainy Tuesday with no money or friends, it might as well have been Blackpool. At least in Blackpool, Cheryl could have got a decent cup of tea and chatted to the locals.

'I've got some news Mum.'

'Yeah?'

Whether Poppy was about to announce a terminal illness or a big lottery win, her mum couldn't have cared less. Actually that isn't true; a big lottery win would probably be the one thing to grab her interest, 'Mart and I are getting married!'

'When?'

'In about four weeks' time.'

'Not when's the wedding. When are you due?'

'Due for what?'

'The baby! You silly cow!'

It took Poppy a while to follow her train of thought or lack of it. Luckily, her life with Dorothea meant she was well practised in drawing threads from incoherent rubbish and turning it into something recognisable. 'There is no baby,' Poppy bit down on her bottom lip and avoided the temptation to add, 'you silly cow.'

'No baby?'

'No baby.'

'Well thank Christ for that! I can just see Terry's face when I told him he was shagging a granny!'

'Nice.'

'Why are you getting married then?'

'Why?'

'Yeah, well I mean if there is no baby...'

'Because we love each other Mum and that's what people in love do. Well, it's what we want to do.'

'But Martin Cricket...'

Poppy felt her hackles rise, putting her instantly in defensive mode, 'What about Martin Cricket?'

'Oh I don't know babes. He's not exactly going to set the world on fire is he?'

Poppy didn't answer. She knew that if she started on how he loved her, looked after her and always had, it might escalate into how her mum didn't and hadn't. Poppy avoided those conversations at all costs; it was better for everyone like that.

Cheryl squealed suddenly, 'Ooh Poppy! I bought a lovely turquoise, chiffon frock with a matching coat that will be perfect with the right jewellery!'

Poppy smiled at the first hint of enthusiasm in her mum's voice, deciding to ignore the fact that this energy had been reserved for discussing clothes and not her forthcoming marriage. She was going to be there and that was something,

'So you'll come then?' she tried not to sound too surprised or hopeful.

'It's my little girl's wedding, my baby's big day! Of course I'll come. I wouldn't miss it for the world.'

Poppy beamed down the phone, inexplicably delighted. It would be nice for her nan to have her there.

'I'd like to help out moneywise but...'

'Don't worry Mum; it's all been taken care of.'

It wasn't until the day after the wedding that Poppy remembered her mum, realising at the same time that she hadn't been there. Jenna, en route to the registry office, had spotted her outside a pub off the precinct. It had been some years since she'd seen her and she was shocked by Cheryl's reed-thin figure, indicative of a body sustained by alcoholic fumes and liquid calories. A turquoise coat hung on her depleted frame. Emaciated ankles teetered and slid inside white patent leather heels. A gold handbag with an ornate clasp, the kind that made a satisfying audible snap when closed, banged against her bony hip. She was with a couple of blokes from the market. All three were paralytic, unable to talk or apparently stand as they slid down the wall, ending up as a heap of entwined limbs. Cheryl's frothy, pale blue creation covered them all and one of her drunken chums sported a feathered hat of similar colour, sitting askew his lolling head.

At the time, Poppy didn't know whether to find it sad or funny that her mum managed to get all the way from Lanzabloodygrotty to London, but was then so distracted by a bottle of Vodka that she couldn't make the last five hundred yards to the service or reception. She now thought it was sad, not funny. Not funny at all.

As she arranged the cushions on the sofa, the doorbell rang. Poppy could hear Jenna's loud, off-key singing before she saw her. She slid the chain. Her friend didn't wait for an invite; they were years beyond that. Jenna pushed past her, casually planting a kiss on her face between lyrics. She skipped into the kitchen and proceeded to fill the kettle. Poppy stood in the hallway, unmoving. *SOS*, the Abba song of choice, was being belted from the kitchen.

'When you're gone, though I try, how can I carry on? When you're gone, how can I even try to go on...?' Jenna danced back down the hallway until she stood in front of her friend. She sang into a wooden spoon that usually sat in a ceramic storage jar shaped like a chicken, next to the back of the cooker. She was singing, laughing and waiting for Poppy to join in, but she didn't. Jenna stopped abruptly. Poppy's expression and lack of enthusiasm for the performance told her that something was not quite right, 'What's wrong babes? Wha'samatter?'

Poppy shook her head; once again her tears pooled. Jenna's anxiety levels rose almost instantly. It wasn't like Poppy to behave in this way, especially when there was the opportunity to indulge in a spot of hairbrush karaoke. She would usually lead the singing and then jump into an impromptu dance routine, but not today. The longer she was silent, the more panic set in. It became tangible, swirling around, cocooning the girls in a mist of impatience and anxiety that prompted Jenna to start guessing,

'Is it Dorothea?'

'No, no.'

'Your mum?'

Poppy smiled as if to say, what on earth could have happened to her that would bother me? 'No.'

There was a moment of hesitation while Jenna considered the other, more obvious option. She placed her hand on her best friend's arm, 'Poppy, is it Mart?'

Poppy looked at her mate's faces, etched with the worry of someone that loved her and was hurting to see her hurt. She nodded.

Jenna swooped forward, enveloping Poppy in her arms; her tears were instant and sincere,

'Oh my God Poppy no! Oh Poppy, is he dead?'

Poppy's words were muffled against her friend's shoulder. She answered as truthfully as she could, 'I don't know.' It made her tears fall harder and quicker. The two stood in the hallway, unmoving; each trying to decide what to do next.

'Come and sit down baby,' Jenna somehow corralled her mate into the lounge, depositing her on the newly plumped cushions. She sat on the floor at her feet. In fact, Jenna was *on* her feet, firmly anchoring her; Poppy didn't have the heart to tell her.

'Tell me everything Poppy. You know that I'm here for you right?' Jenna used her mummy voice, the one she had soothed Poppy with countless times over the years, even when they were both too young to recognise the role that she was adopting.

'I had a visit yesterday from two soldiers. They told me that Mart was missing.'

'Why didn't you call me? I'd have come straight over; I hate to think of you on your own...'

Poppy looked at Jen. Why hadn't she called? It was hard to phrase her need for isolation.

Jenna didn't wait for a response before launching her next question, 'What does that mean 'missing'? They can't have lost him.'

Poppy smiled at her, 'Actually they have lost him, kind of. When they first told me, I thought that they meant he was dead and that they hadn't found his body or identified him, or something.'

She was again interrupted by Jenna's tears, loud and messy, 'Oh Poppy, poor you, poor Mart!'

Poppy patted the back of her hand, 'Then when I was at work…'

'Oh my God, I can't believe she made you go into work, after what you had been through! I'm going to sort that Christine out, she is such a cow!'

'It's alright Jen, I didn't tell her, she doesn't know.' Jenna's loyalty was fierce, her indignation no matter how misplaced, touching. 'Anyway, I was doing Mrs Newton's hair and I suddenly got this really strong image in my head of Mart. I know how crazy it sounds, but it was like I was watching it on a film, only I could hear and 'feel' what he was going through. I knew that he had been taken.'

'What do you mean taken? Taken where?' Jenna tried to make sense of it.

'Taken as in captured. Taken hostage.'

'Oh my God!' Jenna placed both hands over her open mouth. Jenna had no verbal braking system, no means of censoring what was floating around in her head, 'Oh Poppy! That's terrible, it's just like that Terry Waite bloke from Blackheath. They chained him to a radiator for years and wouldn't let him look at a Bible even though he was a vicar. His teeth went bad and when he got rescued he had to get full dentures. That bloke that was with him, John someone, his girlfriend chucked him when he came home, which was really shit. Not that you'd chuck Mart just because he got all beardy and scabby and he wouldn't want to look at a Bible, but it'll kill him not to know how Spurs are doing.'

Poppy smiled at Jenna, rambling through her tears. She tried to think of Martin tied to a radiator like Terry Waite, who she knew was not a vicar, but a special envoy from the Archbishop of Canterbury, but decided against trying to explain this to Jen. Poppy tried to apply reason, 'Mart's a different kettle of fish, Jen. He's not a vicar and he won't be gone for years.'

Jenna looked at her, 'Oh God, did I say the wrong thing? Truth is, mate, I don't know what to say...'

'This is a weird situation Jen; it's ok to say whatever you want. We don't know how we should act do we? It's all new, strange and bloody awful.'

'It is bloody awful, really bloody awful,' Jenna concurred. They were silent for some seconds, 'What happens next?'

'I don't really know. They have assigned me a liaison officer, a bloke called Rob who is coming to see me later, hopefully with more information. They seem good at keeping me up to date, so I guess we will just have to wait and see.' Poppy decided against telling her that they knew who had Martin and that one of his colleagues had been killed, it wouldn't have served any purpose other than upset her more; give her more to think about.

Jenna looked at her mate, 'Have you got dental insurance Pop?'

'What?'

'For Mart's dentures, they can be really expensive.'

Poppy laughed because the alternative was to cry some more. She knew there were going to be a lot more tears to come.

Jenna's tone was one of concern, 'What are you going to do?'

Poppy didn't know how to answer her. What *could* she do? It was during these early chats that ideas started to germinate. Poppy tried to order her thoughts, attempting to take more mental control which, even if it achieved nothing, made her feel much better.

'Are they going to rescue him?'

It was a simple enough question, but one to which Poppy didn't know the answer, 'I assume so Jen. I mean they wouldn't just leave him there would they?'

The two looked blankly at each other. Would they? She reminded herself to ask Rob exactly what the plan was for getting Martin out of there.

Jenna chewed her bottom lip as she did when she was thinking, before shrieking, 'Oh my God! I think it's on the news Poppy.'

'What is?'

'About Mart.'

'What about Mart?' Poppy recalled Rob's words; twenty-four hour news blackout, but the media were already on it.

'Well, not exactly about Mart, because I didn't know that it was Mart, but I heard something on Sky this morning. I didn't pay it much attention.' Jenna, like most of the population, was emotionally saturated when it came to soldier deaths, which were too numerous to mentally invest in. It would only be the immediate family that felt their world torn apart. For many, it was simply the third headline after celebrity misdemeanour and the showbiz of politics.

Poppy jumped up and switched on the TV. She punched the digits into the remote control and waited for the screen to flicker to life. There was an item about falling house prices, a celebrity's frock had fallen off during an award ceremony, followed by a piece about the Bank of England's decision to cut interest rates. The girls watched in silence, waiting.

Then POW! It came on the screen. Poppy felt her heartbeat quicken. The girls edged closer to the screen, keen to note each small detail, hear every word. Ordinarily, sitting ten feet away from the telly with the volume turned up, was enough to glean all you needed, but not today. There was a small photograph on the top right-hand of the screen; a young, smiling soldier in his uniform. It was Aaron Sotherby, the same Aaron Sotherby that had his breakfast, shaved and dressed with Poppy's husband only a day or so before.

The news wasn't that detailed. It gave his age and stated that he'd been with the Princess of Wales's Royal Regiment for eighteen months; this was his first tour, he left behind a wife and a little boy of two. The way that they said 'left behind' made it sound as if he had gone by choice; Poppy didn't like it. She pictured Aaron's wife sitting on a sofa, probably with her family around, her little boy close, wondering why she had been left behind.

Poppy couldn't decide whether it was better or worse to have a little boy in the world with no daddy. She thought of having a little boy sat by her side right now, and decided that it was definitely better.

She was considering this when the voice on the TV seemed to boom, 'During the incident in which Private Sotherby was killed, another soldier from the same unit is believed to have been taken hostage by an, as yet, unnamed group. There have been no demands made for his release. His family have been informed. We will give you any details as and when they come in...' The newsreader turned his frown into a smile and it was off to a film set in Elstree and an item on the latest 007 Movie.

It felt bizarre, knowing it was Martin they were speaking about, and even weirder that she was 'the family' to which they referred. She knew they said that to stop the thousands of other army families worrying. By the time it hit the TV, you would already have been informed. Poppy felt a combination of distress and excitement. She didn't want to be in this awful situation, but at the same time it was a bit like, 'Wahey! We are on the telly!'

'Shit Poppy!' Jenna's succinct appraisal accurately summed up the situation.

The two continued to gaze at the box, waiting for it to be played again, desperate to see if they'd missed anything. It was shown once more before the doorbell rang. Poppy was relieved by Rob's arrival. She and Jenna had talked themselves around in circles, fuelled by caffeine. Poppy felt shaky and sick. Whilst it was lovely to have company, she also wanted her friend to leave so that she could figure out what needed to be done. The reality was, however, that there was nothing to be done; only more waiting.

Jenna scowled at Rob as their paths crossed in the hallway; she too wanted someone to blame. Poppy thought it funny that her environment was subject to such extremes, silent and morgue-like when she was alone or bustling with activity. She tried to remember what it felt like when it was her and Martin; normal.

'How are you today Poppy?'

'Ok I think. Cup of tea?'

'Ooh yes, lovely,' Rob removed his cap and leant against the kitchen cabinet.

Poppy was grateful he didn't feel the need to fill the silence with small talk, happy that they both had thinking time. It made her relax. 'I've seen the news Rob,' she decided to pre-empt his question.

'I guessed you might have. What d' you think?'

'It's really weird to think that they are talking about Mart, very surreal. His capture is obviously smaller news than the fact that Aaron has been killed, so it's masking it for the moment.'

'Why do you say for the moment?' Rob placed his index finger over his mouth and moustache, he looked thoughtful.

'...because I think when people really start to listen and register another death, that's when they'll turn their attention to the fact that a soldier has been taken hostage. I think some people will find it a bit exciting. It will become more important.'

'I think that you are exactly right Poppy.'

'I noticed that they didn't say who'd taken him, even though we know.'

'That's quite standard. These groups want media coverage and we don't want to give them any more publicity than we absolutely have to. We're hoping that they get in touch with some demands, which will force an announcement about who they are and give us a way forward. By announcing it now, we'd be playing into their hands.'

'I see. It's strange for me Rob, talking about publicity and acting as though it's something invented; a game. Yet, my husband is in the middle of it, being held somewhere and going through God knows what.'

'I can only imagine how difficult this must be for you Poppy.'

'It's not so much that it's difficult, it's more frustrating. I feel useless. I'm not used to sitting back and letting someone else fix my problems. But I don't know how to fix this and that's what's driving me nuts.'

'You have to believe Poppy that the right people are doing the very best thing for Martin.'

There was something in his tone that made her abort the tea making. She placed the box of tea bags on the counter next to the empty mugs and folded her arms. It was something as innocuous as a small catch in his voice. Poppy didn't know where the question came from, but she asked it anyway,

'Rob, do you believe that the right people are doing the very best thing for Martin?'

He hesitated, his mouth went to form a response, but he remained silent until his lips formed a different shape as though his mind had changed direction, rejecting 'yes', 'Maybe. I don't fully understand the negotiation process Poppy so I'm not the best person to ask.'

Poppy stared at him, 'That means no.'

He was quick to answer, 'No, it doesn't. It means that there are probably things going on behind the scenes that I don't know about, things to secure his release that if I did know could endanger him or others. Our intelligence on the ground will be talking to intermediaries, and as soon as they have anything concrete to go on we will act.'

'I get that Rob, but I am still unsure of what the actual plan is. How are they going to get him back? What are they doing right now to get my husband back?' Poppy was aware that she had raised her voice.

'I don't know Poppy, but we have to believe that they are doing something.'

'You mean that there is a chance they are doing nothing? Is that what you think Rob?'

'No!' he was emphatic, but Poppy saw the look in his eyes. She had learnt enough about Rob over the last couple of days to see a very real fear in his face. This was precisely what he was thinking. That's the thing about being smart, sometimes you can be a bit too clever for your own good. This was definitely one of those times.

The tinny transistor on the shelf belted out 'the golden oldies' as Poppy washed setting lotion from plastic rollers in the back sink. Her foot tapped involuntarily along to

Build Me Up Buttercup. She considered the previous day, taking great solace from the fact that Jenna knew. It wasn't that she could do anything to make the problem go away, but it helped, knowing her friend was thinking about her, sharing her burden and sending love and support. Poppy also thought that it was better for Martin; her theory being that the more people willed him to be OK, sent him love across the miles, that he might somehow feel it.

Poppy had never been overly concerned with the existence of God. Religion was a background idea that she hadn't properly analysed, an undercurrent of which she was aware, but avoided its pull. Yet now, in this time of need and reflection, she not only explored the idea of an omnipotent being that could help her, but welcomed it. She prayed for her husband, open to the possibility that her words might reach a force able to respond. Her requests were both small and large, ranging from 'let him be comfortable tonight', to 'send him home to me'.

Poppy smiled to see the tongues of the blue rinse brigade wagging as they tried to figure out why she was being met from work by a soldier that wasn't her husband. Rob hovered on the pavement, waiting for Poppy to finish. He could hold his own on the battle field, was trained in jungle warfare and knew how to handle attack from bullets and artillery. But he was reluctant to enter the realm of the middle-aged and elderly, where the weapons of choice were perm curlers, gossip and scalding tea.

Poppy shrugged her arms into her cardigan and left without saying a word. She decided to keep them guessing for a bit longer. The nosey old cows.

'How are you today Poppy?'

'You always ask me that Rob; it's the first thing you say.'

'Do I? Yes I guess I do, and do you know why?'

Poppy shook her head, 'No.'

'Because I'm worried about you Poppy and when I go to bed at night, I wonder if you are OK.'

'Do you and Moira talk about me?' it intrigued her to think that these people, who knew so little about her, would chat about her life and situation. She found it strangely interfering, yet also quite comforting.

'Yes we do.'

'What does she think about all of this?'

'Moira thinks that you are very brave and strong to be coping in the way that you are. She's sad that someone of your age has to go through this at all. Things like this were always her worst nightmare when I was on tour and she is very grateful that it was just a horrible idea. She never had to live through it like you.'

'What do you think Rob?'

'I think I agree with her Poppy.'

'That's because she is your wife. Legally you have to agree with her!'

Rob laughed, 'You know it.'

'I'm off to see my nan. You can walk me there if you like, or do you want to go and get a coffee?'

'I'm OK walking and talking if you are?'

'I think I can manage that. So, what's happening Rob?'

'Well, no real change I'm afraid Poppy. Major Helm would like to come and see you tomorrow. I said I would arrange a time, if that's alright.'

'Why does he want to see me? Does he have news?' Poppy couldn't keep the excitement from her voice.

'Not so much news as an update and, before you ask, no, I don't know what he wants to discuss.'

'I didn't warm to him when I met him last time.'

'You don't say?' Rob's smile was wide.

'Was it obvious?'

'Not to him I don't think, so don't worry.'

'I don't know what it is about him, the way he spoke to me, as though he was really superior. I hate that.'

Rob was silent, but she could tell by his expression that he wanted to agree with her, even if it was just a little bit.

'Tomorrow will be fine Rob. I'll be at the flat at lunchtime if that's any good.'

'Yup, that's great. If there is anything to tell you before then, I'll give you a shout.'

It was only a short walk; they quickly arrived outside 'The Unpopulars'.

'Here we are.'

'Right then Poppy, I'll say goodnight. Will you be alright getting back on your own?'

This made Poppy laugh, he was referring to the streets where she had lived her whole life, where she had wandered solo since the age of six, 'I think I'll be fine.'

He nodded and strode off towards the tube.

Poppy walked up the path and knocked on the front door. Mr Akwal met her in the hallway, 'Ah good evening Poppy!'

'Good evening Mr Akwal. How are you?'

'Very good Poppy, very good. Miss Dorothy will be pleased to see you as usual! I have some small news; Mrs Akwal and I are going overseas next week, so we won't be around for a while.'

'Ooh how lovely! Are you going somewhere nice? Not another one of your cruises?'

'No! No such luck, but yes, somewhere very nice. We are going home to Pakistan to bring back my daughter's husband. He is living in Peshawar and when we come back there will be the biggest wedding a father can give his daughter, she will bankrupt me for sure!' Mr Akwal threw his hands above his head; it was his favourite joke, to talk about his impending poverty while jangling the keys to his enormous Mercedes, as his Rolex glinted on his wrist, 'I am sure it is the same with your daddy, Poppy! I bet he spoils you rotten!'

Poppy didn't have the heart or the desire to tell him that she had never met her daddy, much less be spoilt by him, 'Yes Mr Akwal, that's me, a right little daddy's girl!'

'I knew it Poppy! I knew it. I can tell.'

Poppy thought about his trip. She pictured the globe on the shelf in the geography room at school and could visualise the region of Pakistan he would be visiting. The Akwals would be a mere mountain range away from Afghanistan. Her heart lurched inside her ribcage. Why did everyone travel apart from her? It was that luck thing again.

As a child, Poppy knew that it didn't matter how strongly you yearned to be like the posh girls whose mums were never fat, were rarely tattooed and whose dads dropped them off in flash cars. The girls with shiny, blonde hair and straight white teeth, who would go to university to become all the things that Poppy could only dream of. Why? Because that is just the way it is. Think of it as luck, or lack of luck, or bad luck or unlucky. It was luck who you were born to and the place you were born in.

The shiny blonde girls at school were lucky. They would marry the super smart or really gorgeous boys because they all belonged to the same secret club. It's a club that Poppy could never join because she had been brought up in the flats. She had never been abroad, said 'me nan' instead of 'my granny,' 'afters' instead of 'pudding,' 'lounge' instead of 'sitting room' and 'settee' instead of 'sofa.' There were a million other examples, she watched QVC not the BBC.

She went 'up the dogs' instead of 'to the races'. None of her class mates had been called Phoebe and she wouldn't think twice about wearing her slippers up the Spar. Her dream home consisted of a picture she had seen in a catalogue of a shiny faux leather, brown sofa with two fluffy cushions, a cream rug on a laminate floor and a large vase with twigs artfully poking out of the top. She never ate sushi, preferring a nice Chinese takeaway which she and Martin would eat on their laps whilst watching soaps. It was like having working-class Tourette's, a reflex she couldn't escape, hide from or even disguise. She gave herself away every time she opened her mouth and Poppy opened her mouth a lot.

These are just a few of the many reasons that would deny Poppy entry. Her teeth weren't that straight or white. She didn't look or sound right, and her family were representative of those you found on cheaply produced TV shows. The ones where the impoverished go to not only wash their dirty laundry in public, but to iron, fold and put it away as well. That meant no entry, barred for life. Did she mind? Only sometimes.

Poppy remembered one of the wealthy girls in her class, Harriet, who sent a postcard to her class from the South of France. Their teacher read the card out. It was full of the usual uninteresting facts; the villa was nice, the weather hot and Harriet had tried frogs' legs. Poppy and her classmates had been indifferent; Harriet's experiences were so remote from their lives and concerns that they may as well have been snippets from a story book.

Poppy cared less than most about the random bits of information that were being shared, or the fact that Harriet and her family jetted off to places that she could only locate on a globe with no hope of ever visiting. What she could do, however, and what she wanted to do was hold that post card. Towards the end of the lesson, tiptoeing up to Miss West's desk, she asked in a small voice if she could hold the card; it took all of her courage. Miss West understood; she smiled as she reached into the drawer. Handing over the rectangular card, she spoke in an equally small voice, 'You can keep it Poppy.' It was their secret. Poppy suspected that she was just as disinterested in Harriet's antics as they were; she was a lovely teacher and knew that life was pretty tough for most of her class. She was kind and never patronising. Poppy liked her a lot. Miss West was one of the few people in her life that told her she was smart, that she could do and be whatever she wanted to, and that the only thing that would hold her back was her lack of confidence. Ha! That and the fact that she was tethered to her family by an invisible thread woven from guilt and duty.

Poppy kept that card for years. In fact, it's probably still lurking in a drawer somewhere. She would often hold it, looking at the picture on the front of a very straight avenue lined with tall trees and vineyards on either side. The post mark read 'SAINTES.' She looked it up in the geography book in school and learnt that it was near Cognac, where the drink came from. This was all fairly interesting to her, but the biggest fascination was that this actual piece of paper had travelled from that far away city and ended up in her hands; amazing! When she was a little girl and her whole world comprised of three streets, it was truly incredible.

Poppy wanted to ask Mr Akwal to go over the mountain, to get close to Martin and give him a message. Could he please tell her husband she loved and missed him, that she wasn't complete without him and she wanted him to come home? Poppy swallowed to flush the hard ball of tears that had gathered at the back of her throat. She stared at

Mr Akwal's shiny shoes, blinking hard; she counted the tiny perforated holes that formed a pattern around the toes. It was a diversionary technique that she used to distract her emotions, 'Have a lovely trip Mr Akwal.'

'I will Poppy Day. See you when I get back,' he nodded to indicate conversation over.

Poppy trod the corridor until she reached Dorothea, sitting silently in her room. The telly was off which was most unusual.

'Hello there. You alright Nan?'

She looked up quickly. It took a fraction of a second to recognise her granddaughter, the biggest indicator that she was tired. It intrigued Poppy, the things that bothered her nan, the moments when she was completely lucid and the things that slipped through her ever-widening net of reality. There seemed to be little justification for her various fixations.

Standing proudly on the bedside table, was a picture of her and Wally on their wedding day. Poppy could see by the set of Wally's face and measured stance that his nature did not creep up on him over the years. He was a misery guts at twenty-three and a misery guts at seventy-three, just older. It was a black and white photo, but her nan's mouth and eyes had been crudely painted in crimson and turquoise, making it look more Andy Warhol than Uncle Harold's Kodak. Sometimes Poppy pointed to it, 'Who's this Nan?'

'Oh that's a very pretty lady!'

This made Poppy smile because she was right, it was a very pretty lady and one that bore no resemblance to the woman slumped in front of her, whose features hung, having slipped from their anchor points. It made Poppy sad that Dorothea didn't remember, but worse still was when she did remember and Poppy glimpsed that sadness.

On these occasions, she clutched her granddaughter's hand in desperation, 'How did I end up here Poppy Day? Where did everyone go?'

Poppy would blot the tears that ran unchecked down her face, and stroke the crêpe like skin on the back of her hand, 'I don't know Nan. I don't know what happened.' That was the truth. Poppy never lied to her, never would.

Dorothea's face was crumpled in agitation, 'Yes Poppy Day, I'm fine, just having a bit of a think.'

'Oh right. What are you thinking about?'

'I'm sitting here thinking about that other baby.'

'What other baby Nan?'

'The baby that our Joan had before she had you, the one she put up for adoption. I've been thinking that if she hadn't, then I would have two grandchildren wouldn't I? I'd still have my Poppy Day, but there would be one a year older an' all.'

Poppy was stunned. It was the first time she had heard the idea of another baby. It might have been one of her nan's stories; the fusion of an articulate tongue and a slippery grip on reality, meant this baby could be dismissed as easily as her claim on Joan Collins' parentage. No doubt that is what most would think, but Poppy knew differently. Dorothea's eyes were the biggest clue to her state of mind, often appearing glazed or unfocussed when she was uttering fancies. Tonight however, they were sharp and clear; her mind, despite her fatigue, was not only present but ordered.

Dorothea continued, 'I guess he is out there somewhere isn't he? I wonder what he is doing right now. Do you think he could be close by?'

'I guess so Nan.'

'I mean just because your mother didn't want him, doesn't mean that I didn't. He went to a good family.

I know she made sure of that. I've got a funny feeling he's not far away Poppy Day. Imagine that, he might be living right around the corner. You might see him every day and you wouldn't even know it!'

'What was his name Nan?'

'Who's name?'

'The other baby.'

'What other baby Poppy Day?'

'The baby Mum gave away for adoption? The baby we were talking about.'

'Poppy Day you do talk some rot. Our Joan only ever had you. You were the apple of her eye! She worshipped you.'

This made Poppy smile; the lie, the deceit, the pureeing of the truth to make it a bit more palatable. She imagined the conversation that her nan and Mr Akwal might have about her, 'She's the apple of her mother's eye, how she worships her!' He would chip in with, 'Yes but still a daddy's girl!' They would laugh at the cherished existence that was the life of Poppy Day. The much-loved daughter adored by her doting mother and spoilt by her attentive father, what a lucky, lucky girl.

Poppy's tiredness hit her like a wave. It was a new feeling to be mentally tired. Her body had hours of life left in it, but her mind was fuzzy, confused and switching off after too much thinking.

'As long as you are OK Nan, I'm going to get off. I've had a really long day. I'll see you tomorrow. Shall I bring you something nice to eat; is there anything that you fancy?'

Dorothea shook her head, her bottom lip protruding, arms folded tightly across her chest. She was clearly miffed by the brevity of her granddaughter's visit. She reminded

Poppy of an overgrown toddler. Poppy bent forward and kissed her forehead, 'Goodnight Nan. Sweet dreams.'

Her nan's voice boomed against her back, urgent and deliberate, 'Simon. His name was Simon.'

Simon. Simon. It didn't matter how many times Poppy repeated the name in her head; it didn't help to make him into a person, a brother that she could picture. She tried to calculate the year of his birth, how old would Cheryl have been fourteen, fifteen? It was with a mixture of excitement and suspicion that she contemplated her nan's revelation. It might be true; she could have a sibling named Simon, a big brother that could help her find Martin, offer support with Dorothea. On the other hand, he could be a complete tosser if his dad was one of the blokes her mum had always managed to attach herself to. They were a particular type, with perma-tans and a fondness for chunky gold. They were usually called Terry or Trevor and were interchangeable, always rough and reckoned they were a bit of a hit with the ladies. These tracksuit wearing Terry/Trevor hybrids would call Poppy 'Sweedart,' be on a first-name basis with both the local bookie and pub landlord, drive old, slow, dented Fords and had never read a book or paid income tax in their lives.

A picture swam into her mind of a boy at school, two years above her and Martin. His name was Simon, his hair was darker than hers, but the freckles were similar. She shook her head, 'Get a grip Pop.' She had enough to think about without throwing her mysterious, potentially non-existent brother into the mix.

Six

Incarceration threw up unexpected challenges for Martin. He learnt to live with discomfort, the acute fear he had felt upon capture subsided and his humiliation diluted with the passing of time. Incredibly, it was the interminable boredom and isolation that proved to be the biggest threats to his sanity.

Night and day were indistinguishable. Without any concept of time, every hour was the same. He existed in a purgatorial cycle, lying in a rat-infested square with no idea when the next punishment was going to be delivered.

He slept as much as he could and relished the escape it offered. He would often dream that he was at home and could feel the soft pillow cradling his head, could sense the slow rhythm of Poppy's chest as it rose and fell, could hear the milkman rattling bottles at some ungodly hour in the morning. When he woke, for the first split-second of consciousness, he wouldn't know which was dream and which the reality.

In his darker moments, despair gave way to anger. Frustration would bubble away until a guttural shout of 'Bastards!' would leap from his throat, a small protest against his incarceration. It served to remind his jailors that he was human, a man who had a life and a future, before they replaced his optimism with fear. It angered him that this predicament had not happened by chance, but by design; someone had chosen to take his freedom.

It was a strange dichotomy. Martin had never experienced such isolation, yet was never alone, not for any discernible length of time. It nearly sent him mad; the constant scrutiny of at least one pair of eyes. Unspeaking, silent eyes set in different faces, yet all betraying the same hatred, the same fervour. The level of supervision amused him. What did they think he was going to do? Nibble his way through the brickwork? Even if he had been able to reach the window, he had no hope of removing the planks and even less chance of surviving alone outside of these four walls. To put it in terms that his army buddies would understand, he was up shit creek...

There was the odd second during the 'changing of the guard' as Martin called it, when he would be alone and those odd seconds were to be relished. He could still hear the men outside, the mutterings of handover, the slap of leather-soled sandals against the floor and the click of metal gun against walls, but he was out of sight and that meant privacy of sorts. Not that Martin needed physical privacy; his body wasn't responsive or functioning in any normal way. This fact alone made him feel sad, emphasising just how broken he was.

These precious seconds gave him the chance to think about Poppy in peace, without the grunting and breathing of some hairy bloke in the corner, cleaning his gun or praying. He would talk to her out loud and not just in his head, 'Hang in there baby. I miss you, but I'm always with you. Be strong for me, my beautiful Poppy. I love you so much.'

A couple of the guards were peasants, rough looking and poorly dressed. They were the worst. Taunting Martin, shouting at him in a language he had no hope of understanding, punching him, or worse, if they got the chance. They found it amusing when he wet himself, but he had no choice, he was often tied up and couldn't move. The combination of ammonia on raw skin and the intense heat meant his legs were quickly covered in sores. It was horrific for him, the stench unbearable and it was his own smell. He could only imagine how bad it must have been for someone else.

A new guard arrived after a few days, laughing loudly as he entered the room. Martin turned his head towards the door, his heart racing; this ebullient display was unusual and unnerving. The guard walked over to where he lay, peering into his face. He was a lad in his late teens, with good white teeth and a ready smile.

'Manchester United!' he over-pronounced the 'r', turning into a roll, a long almost French sound.

Martin nodded.

His guard continued, 'David Beckham, Ryan Giggs, Wayne Rooney!'

In spite of the absolutely dire circumstances, Martin laughed, 'Yes, Manchester United!' Although as a Spurs fan it nearly choked him. Martin bloody hated Manchester United.

The lad laughed and patted Martin's shoulder. His touch, this one small display of empathy when he was used to being prodded like a dog, caused a lump to rise in his throat. He swallowed and sniffed to abate the tears. It was also the first time since his capture that anyone had said anything he could understand. It sounded like poetry, his language from his country, his beautiful England.

Whether coincidence or not, with the arrival of 'Man U' as Martin called him, his life seemed to get a little better. The morning he was told to take his clothes off was a significant milestone. Martin was petrified. After stripping, his uniform was bundled up and taken out of the room. Another guard came in, holding a large, metal bucket of tepid water. There was a small, dirty rag floating on the top of it. Martin didn't notice the rust on the receptacle or the holes in the wash cloth; to him, it was the luxury bathroom of a fancy hotel.

It was wonderful for him to feel water on his skin, to run it over his legs, down his back. When he'd finished, he was given a traditional Afghan outfit of long pyjama-style trousers and a cotton caftan with slits up the sides. Martin was grateful to have fresh clothes, even more so to be clean. He was allowed to keep the bucket to use as a loo and that alone made his life bearable.

It was a strange thing that happened to Martin in captivity. He quickly became dehumanised by the humiliation, the squalor. Then, when things picked up slightly, got a little bit better – like being given a dirty bucket to go to the loo in, or the fact that he could lift up his hands, which were untied, to touch his own face – these small things became huge; they meant everything. The cotton fabric of his new clothes made it much easier to live in the intense heat.

With the removal of his uniform and the growth of his beard, Martin's treatment changed. He concluded that his desert combats were a constant and fresh reminder of what he represented. Without them, he blended in, noticing that abuse from a couple of the guards stopped. His beard was a symbol that his Muslim captors welcomed, although for Martin, it was a daily reminder of a shave that wouldn't happen, a day that he couldn't strike off in his quest to get back to Poppy. Whether the guards had been told to stop his ill treatment or because they were more used to him, confident that he wasn't going to try and escape, didn't matter. Either way, it was a welcome development. He was given greater freedom, able to sit or lay on the bed, and it was wonderful to have the choice. For this too, he was thankful.

Escape had been playing on Martin's mind. The many and varied methods of his sprint to freedom had been imagined and dismissed. Too many unknowns blighted every idea. He knew his best opportunity to get away had been at the point of capture. What had he been taught? To use the confusion, the panic, create a diversion, make a noise and fight back. He mentally flipped through the training manual, trying to locate the page that detailed what to do when holed up in a darkened room under the constant scrutiny of an armed fanatic. Despite the dire odds of success, he was still determined to try.

A bout of diarrhoea had left him in a weakened state. His skin bore the filmy sheen of a fevered sweat. He lay on the mattress, straining to hear any activity outside of the room. It was one of those rare minutes when the guards were changing and he was alone. He had decided that this would be the moment, a small window that would prove the best chance of escape. He swung unsteady legs around until he was in a sitting position. A fresh cramp tore at his stomach as his bowels spasmed, fortunately they were empty. Swaying and upright, he stepped forward with his hand outstretched; the door handle was now only inches from his grasp.

It was simultaneous; as he placed his trembling palm against the frame for support, the person on the other side turned the handle. Both started, neither expecting to come face to face with the enemy. Whether it was good luck or bad it's hard to decide, a different captor might have not been so keen to arrive and could have given him a few more precious minutes in which to escape. Similarly, he may have drawn a weapon and put his charge out of his misery.

It was the startled face of Man U that mirrored his own. The young Afghan glanced nervously over his shoulder before entering the room; had there been other witnesses, the matter would have been taken out of his hands. Martin wobbled, threatening to fall. Man U took him by the elbow and guided him back to the bed. He sat his charge down and crouched in front of him, like a tired parent addressing a taxing child. His manner was calm, his tone inflected with kindness. He shook his head while holding Martin's gaze. It was an impasse. Man U delivered his words slowly, gone were his trademark exuberance and grin. He drew his index finger across his throat with great deliberation, 'Georgie Best.'

Martin received the message loud and clear. He nodded, strangely touched by Man U's stance. It wasn't characteristic of the oppressor, but was more in the nature of protection and friendship. Martin considered it a lucky thing that Man U had been his interceptor. God forbid he had been metered out a dose of Georgie Best...

In Martin's darker moments he would think about Aaron. He tried to wipe the images from his mind but couldn't. In the same way the tip of a tongue seeks out a decaying tooth, so he would mentally jab at his pain, replaying his friend's final moments in slow-motion detail. It would make him feel sick, angry and, shamefully, a little bit relieved. They had killed Aaron and spared him, but it could so easily have been the other way around. While he was alive there was hope, no matter how small, that he would get to see Poppy again. He wanted nothing more than to hold her in his arms, hear her wonderful voice and to tell her that he loved her. No matter how bad his circumstances, that glimmer of hope was the most precious thing and he clung to it.

Even the thought made him feel guilty. What wouldn't Aaron have given to hold his missus one more time, to see his little boy, mark one more birthday, celebrate one more Christmas, enjoy one more walk in the park, read one more bedtime story..?

Martin's wish, no, his prayer during those dark times was that his friend's body had been repatriated and that he had been given the burial he deserved. Martin couldn't bear the idea that Aaron's body had been left somewhere, taken or still missing. He took comfort from the image of the soldier's coffin, flag-draped and saluted, back home where he belonged in the country that he loved.

Martin woke with a start in the middle of the night. He had dreamt that he was woken by Poppy. He could tell it was his wife by her touch and smell. She was stroking the hair away from his forehead. Her voice a gentle whisper, 'Mart... Mart... It's OK baby I'm here.' Her words and the touch of her fingers against his skin gave him a jolt of elation. It felt real. He could sense her. It made him miss her so much, he wanted to cry. Martin didn't want to open his eyes because he knew that he would lose her all over again. Clamping his lids, he tried to keep on dreaming, tried to remain focussed, to keep her with him.

When he woke and sat up on the dirty mattress, in his grim prison, it felt even more like hell because he had remembered that there was a better place, a place that he wanted to be, with the woman that he loved. It was at times like these that he missed her the most.

He drifted back into a light sleep, with the memory of her voice and the sound of her laugh playing in his head. It was beautiful and painful all at the same time.

Martin's quiet reflection inspired him. He woke with the new idea that maybe he wasn't the only person that had been taken captive; perhaps someone else was being held in the same building. As the suggestion grew, so did the possibility of who else they had taken. Not only could there be someone else like him, held in another room, but it might even be someone that he knew, someone from the same patrol or, at the very least, another soldier.

The prospect of this was wonderful, giving him a strong feeling of hope and excitement. Martin decided to ask Man U the next time he saw him. He wasn't sure how he was going to make him understand, but he was determined to try. He had purposely avoided making conversation or trying to engage with the guards, figuring out quite quickly that if he was invisible, it made life easier for everyone. Those that didn't want to guard him weren't reminded of his presence, and those that felt hostile he didn't antagonise. His childhood had given him all the training he needed for this, don't breathe too loudly and don't be obvious. Quietly disappear.

Man U walked in the very next day with his arms held aloft as though he had just scored a goal. His smile fixed. He stepped closer to the bed before announcing, 'Manchester United!'

'Yes! Yes! Manchester United!'

Martin knew what was coming next, 'David Beckham!'

'Yes!' again he nodded, 'David Beckham!'

The whole charade was a whole lot easier than you might imagine. It wasn't too different from dealing with Dorothea, although Martin never visited her without Poppy, finding their interactions when he was alone, if not frustrating, then certainly embarrassing.

They exhausted the few common words that they shared when Martin decided to take the bull by the horns. He pointed at his chest in a Tarzanesque manner, 'Me, David Beckham.'

Whether he understood or not, Man U laughed and nodded, repeating the words, 'David Beckham!'

Martin then pointed towards the door, trying to

indicate the wider building, 'Ryan Giggs? Wayne Rooney? Other David Beckham?' he tried to make his tone sound as much like a question as he could.

The guard nodded, 'Manchester United!'

Martin tried again, pointing at his own chest, 'Me David Beckham, soldier.' Martin then pointed at his captor, 'You Ryan Giggs.'

Still the grin didn't falter.

Martin pointed at the wall, 'More David Beckham soldiers? Here or here?' he used his finger to indicate different parts of the building.

The lad smiled at Martin, 'Ah!' as though a penny had dropped. He nodded furiously.

Martin felt a surge of anticipation.

Man U bent low towards his face and paused, concentrating on his next words, which were almost a whisper, 'Alex Ferguson!'

Martin's frustration and disappointment were so acute that he wanted to punch him. He smiled and whispered back, 'No you dickhead, not Alex Ferguson or anyone else in your sodding team. You are a moron; I hate you.'

The young guard smiled and patted Martin's shoulder.

It was to be a long day; he was left feeling low by the whole encounter.

He hoped that things were going on in the background to get him back, of course he did. He had to believe that there would be some sort of diplomatic activity or, at the very least, that the army big wigs were wading in, using local intelligence to find him and negotiate his hand over. He knew it was a race against time. Would the army get him back before his captors decided to kill him? That had been the recognised pattern with all other hostages. Hostage. It was difficult to think of himself in that way.

It never occurred to Martin that he might be newsworthy or that anyone at home might know what had happened.

He knew by that stage Poppy would have been informed by the family liaison team. They had been briefed on the process before being deployed. He had digested it at some level before putting it to the back of his mind. He and all others deployed had to believe that the chances of you, or your family, needing this service were very, very slim. The sort of occurrences that would require their intervention were the very things that only happened to other people, or so he thought.

Martin hated the fact Poppy would be worried sick, but he never thought for one minute that his mates in the pub would have the chance to read about his capture, fellow Spurs fans, people in his city, in his country. He couldn't picture his story pinned up in the garage where he used to work, or a banner up on his old school gates, but this was exactly what was about to happen.

Martin, like every other human, could only see himself as the ordinary person that he was. Someone's husband, someone's son and someone's neighbour; he never considered that he, or anything about him, might be of interest to anyone outside of a small group. It was a strange and unnatural situation; he was an ordinary bloke, living an ordinary life, who found himself caught up in something extraordinary. Martin reasoned logically, that if it could happen to anyone and his selection had been random, then he hadn't done anything to deserve it. Had he?

He, like Poppy, hadn't given much thought to God and heaven, but his situation forced him to reflect on things outside of the normal. He considered the reasons why he was fighting there at all and it came full circle back to religion. Martin marvelled at the fact that, in the name of God and faith, man would happily blow each other up, maim and kill; he concluded that it was a funny kind of religion that endorsed this.

He tried to understand what the people who lived in this harsh terrain were willing to sacrifice in the name of their belief. They had so little and without the poppy crop and support of a terrorist organisation, they had absolutely nothing. For them to fight and potentially die, meant they were risking their families' livelihoods and futures.

Martin thought about his own death. He wondered where he would go next, if anywhere and began to ask for help. He confided his fears. Martin's ideas of God were sketchy, but he reasoned that if he was praying, he must have believed that there was someone or something to pray to. He couldn't say with any certainty that his prayers were answered, but it certainly made him feel better. It could have been self-soothing, but equally it might have been an all-powerful being, sending him messages of peace and hope. Who knows, maybe they were.

Martin used to imagine talking to Poppy. Her voice would be clear, as was the image of her flicking the fringe from her eyes, rubbing away her tears with the back of her hand...

If that's not prayers being answered, communicating with his wife thousands of miles and a whole lifetime away, then what is?

Seven

Poppy paced the flat, eager for Rob and the Major to arrive. It was important to her that the place looked nice, she wanted them to see her calm and in control. She couldn't shake the feeling that Major Helm felt superior to her. He wasn't and she wanted to show him that. He'd been successful in his chosen career, so what? It was that luck thing again. Rob smiled at her when she opened the front door. Anthony Helm stood slightly behind him, hovering, as if trying to delay his entry.

Rob walked through into the lounge, leaving her to face the Major, 'Hello Poppy. It's good to see you.'

Poppy knew it was mean, but the instant he opened his gob with his falsely rounded vowels and overfamiliar expression, she wanted to sock him one. She tried to overlook the way he shook her hand, whilst trying not to survey the poverty in which she lived. Poppy held a fascination for beautiful voices; with Major Helm it was different. He sounded arrogant, condescending, especially since this was the voice that he had cultivated. Poppy didn't like it one bit.

The trouble was, the more he spoke the more irritated she felt, the less she warmed to him and the colder she became. Meaning the more uncomfortable he became and the more he spoke. The two were locked in a downward spiral of awkwardness that left her wanting to shout at him, 'For God's sake shut your trap!'

'Come through,' she managed, holding the door wide for him to pass.

He removed his hat and trotted into the lounge, sitting where he had before. Poppy recognised him as a human that sought out the comfort of the familiar.

'Can I get anyone a cup of tea?'

'Not for me thanks.'

Poppy suspected that Major Helm didn't want to risk drinking from her catalogue-bought, budget cups with possible hairline cracks and the abomination of cheap, supermarket own-label tea bags. It didn't occur to her that he might not want to put her to any trouble. He had set the tone; Rob shook his head in decline. Poppy could tell by the set of his mouth that, whether he wanted one or not, he wasn't about to buck the trend. This made her smile. She took up her seat on the sofa, all present and correct.

Poppy noted how, before they could get down to anything interesting, Major Helm needed to go through his set piece. God forbid he might actually go off script. He feared spontaneity like any good soldier should. Ask Martin; spontaneous meant without a plan and that meant all kinds of trouble.

'So Poppy, how are you bearing up?'

She bit the inside of her cheek, reminding herself to be nice. He had come all this way and might have something of interest to tell her. 'I'm fine. It's difficult obviously...'

He nodded and simultaneously interrupted, 'Obviously.'

'...the most difficult thing is that I feel so useless. I wish that there was something that I could do to help, instead of sitting here watching the clock go around.'

'Absolutely Poppy. I understand, but you must realise that you are doing a fantastic job, waiting for Martin and staying strong for Martin. It's exactly what the chaps on the frontline need, to know that they are supported, that they have something to come home to, someone waiting...'

She looked to Rob for guidance; he had conveniently averted his gaze towards the ceiling, unable to look at her. Under different circumstances she was sure that there would have been the suggestion of a smile playing around his lips. She was still hearing the words in her head. Had he really said 'fantastic job' and 'chaps'? His language was more Jeeves and Wooster than MoD speak.

'I am sure that you are right, Anthony, the trouble is that my chap isn't on the front line or performing a fantastic job is he? He's banged up in some Godforsaken place that I can almost guarantee doesn't have room service and what I really want to talk about is what you are doing to get him back.'

'Of course, of course.'

Poppy noticed the stain of scarlet that started at his neck and swept up to his forehead. She misconstrued it as embarrassment. Anthony Helm, however, was not embarrassed, he was angry. Did this girl have no manners?

'There have been measures taken Poppy to ensure Martin's safe return.'

'I'm very glad to hear that Anthony. What measures?'

'I'm sorry?'

She knew that he had heard and was going to use the repeated question as thinking time. She answered slowly, giving him a chance to formulate his response, 'What measures? What exact measures have been taken to ensure Martin's safe return?' An earlier question sat at the front of her mind ...they wouldn't just leave him there would they?

'Right, yes,' he touched his fingers into a pyramid at chest height, only separating them to emphasise a point, after which they would go back to their anchor position. 'We have people within the unit who are trained in negotiation and are using local intelligence. These people are working tirelessly to gather information which will allow us to formulate a plan.'

'That's wonderful. So you are saying that there are

people within the unit who are able to talk to the locals to gather information about who took him and where he might be held?'

'Correct.'

'And at what point will they all stop talking and start 'going and getting' because, by my reckoning, he has been held for nearly four days now and I should imagine that each hour is a lifetime for Martin. Do we have a timescale?'

'A timescale?'

'For the 'going and getting?'

'Not exactly a timescale no. I'm afraid it's not that simple,' he laughed with this tongue poking out, stuck to the centre of his top lip. Silly girl.

'Forgive me Anthony, but I need it in simple terms, treat me as if I'm a bit thick. Talk me through EXACTLY what is being done to get my husband back to a place of safety, because I think we both know that the first seventy-two hours are absolutely crucial with the percentage of live hostage retrievals slipping by five per cent after each day in captivity. This doesn't make Mart's odds very good and we don't want a 'pass it on' case on our hands do we? Where he is sold on and on until the chain of capture is so weakened, the demands so vague, that it's almost not worth bothering to go and get him back.'

Rob put his hand over his mouth; this time she knew it was to suppress a smile. Poppy was aware that her confident stance was almost certainly in part to impress him. The three were silent for some seconds.

Anthony Helm, in the face of Poppy's questioning, decided to cut the crap. He pinched the top of his nose and pushed an invisible point on his forehead, 'Right Poppy. I am going to be blunt with you.'

It was her turn to interrupt, 'Please do Anthony. I just

want to know what's going on.'

'They know where he is being held, or at least they did. There was an operation, covert of course, in the early hours of yesterday morning. But I am sorry to have to tell you that it wasn't successful.'

Poppy's heart swelled in her ribcage, her poise collapsed. Despair sat on her chest, a physical block to stem the rising panic. Mart... Mart... Mart... The Major's words swirled inside her head, jumbled like a foreign language; words she recognised but whose meaning refused to sink in. Her vision blurred, a breath caught in her throat as a fresh bout of grief sucked at her ability to function, 'Was Mart hurt? Is he alright? Did anyone see him?'

'No. No one saw him, it was the wrong building. We were misinformed, or there's a chance that the information was correct but that he's been moved.'

'When are they going to go again? Now that they know where he isn't, does that mean that they are closer to finding out where he is?' her voice was tainted by the creep of hysteria.

The Major exhaled loudly, 'Poppy, It is not that easy.' He considered his next choice of phrase, his tone now more direct, for which Poppy was grateful, 'We're pretty sure that he is being held in the Garmsir area. We are confident of this because we have the whole area patrolled and our sources on the ground say that he hasn't been moved out. We also have a fair idea of who has taken him...'

Poppy looked at Rob. There was an almost imperceptible shake of his head. She received the message loud and clear.

'The trouble is that it's a tightknit community and these people are intimidated by, and indebted to, the tribal warlords that run the province. Getting them to give us the information that we need is very tricky, especially after one failure. It's made everyone more than a little edgy.'

She thought about what he'd said. The whole problem suddenly felt enormous and insolvable. 'I don't know what to do next,' the admission of her weakness and confusion slipped out.

Rob held her gaze, 'You don't have to do anything Poppy, it's not your job to fix things; it's ours.'

Poppy realised how much she had come to like Rob, he was a kind man.

'Thank you for that, Sergeant,' the Major emphasised his rank.

Poppy fought the desire to tell him not to talk to her friend in that way. Instead, she found another way to break the tension, 'How about that cup of tea?'

Major Helm flashed a tight smile, 'Not for me. In fact I'll be off.' He barely registered the fact that Rob had stood. 'See you soon Poppy,' his mouth once again twitched in a reluctant smirk.

Poppy and Rob faced each other, each feeling the gap that the Major's exit had left.

'Was that 'yes' or 'no' for a cuppa?'

'Well, as you're making...' he smiled. The two breathed easily for the first time since he had entered the flat. They filled the tiny kitchen. Rob leant on the work surface while she filled the kettle and wiped up the cups.

Poppy wondered what Martin would say if he could see her, making tea and chatting to the Sergeant as though he was one of their mates, 'How could they have messed it up Rob?'

He shook his head and swallowed his biscuit, 'We don't know that they did mess it up Poppy. The Major was right, it could have been false intelligence or just that their intelligence was better than ours. It is far more complicated out there than we realise, every move is a delicate balancing act.'

She liked the way he used the words, 'Than *we* realise'; it made her feel for the first time like she and he were a team.

'When will they try again?' Poppy needed the comfort of knowledge.

'I honestly don't know. There are so many factors, reliability of information, availability of specialists, cost.'

'Cost?' she was dumbstruck, nearly. 'What about cost? This is Martin's life we are talking about, how much is that worth to the British Army? To the bloody MoD? It's not like I'm asking them to pay a contractor's salary or order a new bloody plane. It's a life! It's my husband's life!' Poppy snapped the lid of the kettle into place. Countless newspaper headlines slipped into her focus;

'Desert soldiers forced to buy their own boots'; 'Not enough helicopters contributed to our son's death'; 'Lack of radios killed soldier in Iraqi police station siege.'

Her stomach flipped as two things occurred to her. The first was that if maybe Martin's life wasn't considered valuable enough, how much would they spend on trying to get him back? Secondly, newspapers, publicity, that was what she needed. Jenna, bless her, even Jenna knew a bit about Terry Waite; OK the facts were slightly skewed but she had the gist and why? Because of newspapers! Poppy decided to keep this revelation to herself.

'They have to consider cost Poppy. I know it sounds cold and distant but every conflict has its cost.'

'Oh I know that Rob. I'm just not prepared for the price to be my husband's life.'

The two stood in silence and listened to the hiss

of the kettle.

'Do your parents live nearby?' Rob obviously hadn't read the background on Poppy Day file.

'No. My mum and I aren't really in contact. She's living with some bloke in Lanzarote or Tenerife, and, as for my dad, he might live next door or he might live in Timbuktu. I've never met him. I have my nan though, Dorothea, who has always been a bit bonkers, but is now suffering with dementia, bless her. Apart from Mart, she is all I've got. I kind of look after myself Rob, I always have.'

Rob contemplated the information while the kettle hurtled towards its goal, 'It sounds quite lonely Poppy.'

'What does?'

'I don't know, looking after yourself, having the responsibility of your nan, Martin being away...'

She resisted the temptation to say, 'Oh Rob, it's just peachy!'

'Do you take sugar?' Sometimes it was easier not to have those conversations.

After another restless night, Poppy stood bleary eyed in the middle of the lift; someone had recently taken a black marker pen to the floor level buttons, successfully making them identical. A nightmare for novice lift users, but for Poppy and most of its occupants, their fingers instinctively went to the button that meant home or bread, milk and fags. The lift shuddered the eight floors down. It was a weird coincidence, auspicious some might say. As she stepped gingerly to avoid the discarded Chinese takeaway that spewed from its container across the floor, a man rushed over to her. He wasn't threatening or running, but, with his tan brogues clip clopping on the pavement, his walk was brisk.

He was tall. Poppy noted that he was wearing too many layers, either to try and bulk out his wiry frame or because he felt the cold, possibly both. His jeans were dark, almost the same colour as his short waxed jacket, under which a green v-necked jersey, checked shirt and grey scarf were visible. His hair was collar length, curly and needed a wash. He wore black framed glasses that she suspected were designer and pricey but looked identical to the free NHS goggles that in another era would have invited *Thunderbird*-related ridicule. A large satchel was slung over his shoulder, making him look even more like head boy. She stood still, holding her coat closed at the neck.

'Mrs Cricket?'

'What?'

'It's Mrs Cricket isn't it?'

'Why do you want to know?'

'I'm sorry to bother you,' this was the first and last time that he would lie to her. 'My name is Miles Varrasso. I'm a journalist and I would like to talk to you about your husband, about Martin.'

She stared at him, unsure how to react. She had been told that it was inevitable, they would find out Martin's name and they would come looking for her. It was just sooner than she had anticipated. As far as Poppy was concerned it was a good thing. She'd thought about it all night, the more publicity the better. If people prayed for Martin, asked questions and thought about Martin, willing him to be free, the less the MoD could 'ignore' him. She had decided not to let that happen. He would not be used as currency, not her husband.

'Yes, I'm Mrs Cricket.'

'Can I buy you a coffee?' he pushed his glasses up onto his nose even though they were already in position, one of his many nervous habits that would become endearing.

'I'm on my way to work, but I guess half an hour isn't going to make much difference; sure. There's a cafe around the corner.'

They walked in silence to the cafe where Martin and Poppy had eaten a thousand breakfasts; where she and the girls had laboured over a thousand cups of tea and coffee. Poppy considered the stranger that strode along beside her; well spoken, posher than she was comfortable mixing with. He was expensively dressed, with very kind eyes that crinkled into more lines than you would expect to see on someone of his age, which she couldn't easily determine.

Sonny saw her enter. Having been to school with her mum, he had known Poppy her whole life. He was enormously fat and was, as usual, resplendent in his food and drink spattered apron, holding court from behind the counter, "ello my darlin! Long time no see. How's my gel?'

'I'm fine thanks Sonny.'

'That's good to hear Poppy Day and what about that bloke of yours, keeping his chin up and his head down I 'ope?'

She smiled at Miles Varrasso and then at Sonny, 'Yeah, something like that.'

They sat at the wipe-clean table, nursing hot cappuccinos. Poppy didn't know where to start but she didn't need to, Miles was a consummate professional.

'Why did he call you Poppy Day?'

'Err... because it's my name?'

'Really? Poppy Day? That's fantastic!'

'Why is that fantastic, Miles Varrasso?'

'I don't know; it's just memorable. It's good to have a name that people will remember. How many John Smiths are ever immortalised?'

'Well, there was the Labour leader, the beer brand and wasn't it a John Smith that helped colonise North America? I remember reading something about him and Pocahontas...'

'OK, bad example, but Poppy Day is a great name,' Miles smiled, creating those wrinkles and emphasising the word 'grrrreaat'.

Poppy had once asked her mum why she had called her Poppy, knowing full well that her surname was Day. Cheryl looked at her daughter with a quizzical expression, took a deep drag on her cigarette and ran her tongue over her front teeth, a habit she had of checking for lipstick that might have adhered itself to the stained enamel. A confused crease appeared at the top of her nose, the one that she got whenever she had to make a decision or answer any question that wasn't, 'What you 'avin?' The answer to that was always instant and unchanging, 'Voddie and Coke', as though calling it 'voddie' made it more of a cocktail. It was, however she referred to it, the first resort of the alcoholic. She stared at Poppy as though she didn't have the foggiest idea what she was talking about. Poppy realised then that she didn't, bless her. Poppy Day had a name that amused other people, the quips were endless. Poppy paid it little heed. It's who she was, who she would always be.

She could have changed it when she got married, but decided against becoming a 'Cricket'. She thought Poppy Cricket sounded worse than Poppy Day. Maybe that's part of the reason why the two were drawn to each other. They both knew what it felt like to have a name that other people found hilarious or fascinating. The kind of name that when it was asked for and you gave, people would repeat, at least once,

'Poppy Day?'

'Martin Cricket?'

The bemused listener would stare with one eyebrow cocked as though they had made them up. Why would they? Poppy used to wonder what it would be like to live as one of the girls in her class who never had their name repeated either in disbelief or amusement. She thought that must be nice. Martin and Poppy knew that no matter what anyone thought of their names, when you were little and when you were them it was unfortunate, but there was naff all that you could do about it.

Poppy looked at the journalist, but said nothing. She wasn't in the mood for the name conversation, not today. Unbeknown to the two, they were establishing the foundations of their friendship. She liked his enthusiasm and he her knowledge.

'How old are you Poppy?'

'I'm twenty-two and you?'

'And me?'

'Yes, how old are you Miles? It's just that you have one of those faces that could be a young forty or you an old thirty that's had a really tough paper round.'

Miles laughed then, 'You are right. It's the latter by the way. I am thirty-three but live off rubbish food, late nights, way too much caffeine and the odd cigarette, in fact, lots of odd cigarettes.' He sipped his coffee greedily, as though there was no connection between the beverage in his hands and the previous statement.

'You won't make old bones like that Miles.'

'Who says I want to make old bones?'

'Mmmn... I guess maybe you don't. I just assumed that no one wants to die before their time is up, before they have finished. I think that would be the worst thing, time suddenly running out for you without warning.'

'Before they have finished what?'

'Everything! Learning, teaching their kids, making the things that are important to them safe and secure. Seeing the world, making a difference.'

'Goodness, I wasn't banking on such a heavy conversation before breakfast!'

'Miles, I think we both know that that's not true,' she smiled at him then, to let him know that she probably knew what he knew and that it was alright to mention it.

'You know why I want to talk to you about Martin?'

'Yes.'

'Right. Good,' he exhaled with relief before continuing, 'Can I ask you some questions Poppy? I promise you that whatever I write, you can approve first if you want. Is that OK?'

'Yes, I think so; this is all a bit new to me.'

'I'm sure it is. I can't imagine how difficult this must all be for you, Poppy.'

'Yeah, everyone keeps saying that.'

'What's he like, Martin?'

'What does he look like? It's difficult to describe someone that you know really well, isn't it? There are so many expressions and different faces that I've lodged in my memory, that when I think of Mart, it's difficult to think of just one. I can picture him in a zillion different ways, and places. They're like tiny snapshots of an expression or a glance. He is five foot seven; just tall enough is how I describe him. He had very blonde hair when he was small, almost white. In his early teens it was just blonde, now in his twenties it's dirty blonde. I can see him ending up sandy with a little bit of grey. It makes me smile to think of him like that. I'll know then that we have come full circle, beginning, middle and end. He is solid. You know one of those men that are square and firm to touch. My mum used to say if Mart got hit by the number 97 bus she wouldn't take bets on who would come off worst, the silly cow. His nose got broken when he was small. Noses don't just break do they? More specifically someone broke his nose when he was small. He won't tell me how it happened, but I suspect it had something to do with his dad. He never got it fixed, so he looks like a bit of a bruiser. This makes me smile because he could not be more unlike that. He's sweet, gentle and kind. He wouldn't hurt anyone, well unless he had to, like for work and stuff, obviously.'

Miles cleared his throat, searching for the right words to politely ask for less detail, he didn't have all day.

Poppy took the hint, his fidgeting leg and cough put her on track, 'I tell you what, why don't you tell me what you know about Mart's current situation and I'll see if I can fill any gaps, then we can go from there?' She sounded confident.

Miles was surprised, but happy, to let this girl take the lead; so much for the kid gloves that he had assumed he'd be wearing. He unlatched his satchel and was thoughtful; trying to decide if she was naive and hadn't fully appreciated the situation in which her husband had been placed, or whether she was cold, hard. The dilemma drew his brows into an upward 'v'. If she was naive, then she would have little idea of what this level of publicity might mean and if she was a hardnosed opportunist then her motive was probably money.

It was as if she read his thoughts, 'I think I know roughly how this works Miles. I know what I want from our meeting. I've been thinking over the last few days that unless I take control and make things happen, it's all going to continue moving too slowly for my liking. I know it's going to get a lot worse before it gets better, but at least now I feel like I'm doing something.'

Miles nodded. She had answered his questions. He had underestimated this girl, she was smart and aware, 'Right then, shall I kick off?'

Poppy nodded. He pulled out a cheap spiral-bound notebook and flipped over the cardboard cover. Poppy noticed the doodles that adorned the cover; random shapes and patterns, reminding her of an ornate Maori tattoo. He held his pen like a cigarette, whether consciously or not, he was telling the world that he wanted a fag; maybe that was why he spoke so quickly. He read without censorship. It made Poppy's stomach clench and her insides flip over. He knew more than she did, more than she wanted to. It was awful and fascinating at the same time. She wanted to hear it, wanted to know what he knew, but at the same time, she didn't.

He blew out from inflated cheeks, mimicking the exhaling of smoke, 'Right, what have we got, a sortie in support of an American patrol code-named 'Kryptonite'. They were intercepted in the Garmsir area of Helmand Province and that was... four days ago. Two were taken, both Brits, one Aaron Sotherby, they decapitated and shoved his body, complete with severed head, at the gates of the barracks. Eye witnesses confirm that one other, namely Martin, was taken hostage certainly beaten upon capture, but probably not dead. Bundled into the boot of a car and taken further into the residential area of the province. We know it's the ZMO and there has been one failed rescue attempt, with no further rescue attempts currently planned. So far negotiations have failed and it's all gone a bit Pete Tong.'

He exhaled again and looked at Poppy. She could tell by his expression that he had forgotten who he was talking to, delivering the facts as though he were briefing a fellow hack and not the wife of 'the other, namely Martin who was beaten, but probably not dead... bundled into the boot of a car.'

'Are you OK Poppy? I thought that you would know that stuff, I'm sorry if I...'

'It's OK Miles,' she tried to focus on what to say next, but all she could see was Aaron Sotherby and his decapitated body, his smiling photograph at the top of her TV screen, but without the head. If they had done that to Aaron, what would they do to Martin? Her legs shook under the table; tiny tremors that made the plastic, ketchup-filled tomato jiggle. Her earlier feelings of confidence and control had disappeared, replaced with fear and shock. *Beaten... bundled into the boot of a car...* that was her husband they were talking about; this had happened to Mart, her Mart. She pictured him in the park in his teens, swigging from a can, laughing loudly and suddenly until beer foamed from his nose. How had he ended up like this?

'Poppy are you alright? You look really pale.'

She refrained from uttering, 'No shit.' 'I'm really tired. It's just the last few days taking their toll.'

'So, is that about the gist of it or have I missed anything out? Is there anything that you can add to that?'

It was Poppy's turn to laugh out loud, snorting pig-like into her cappuccino, most unladylike.

'What's so funny?'

'I'm sorry Miles; it's just that I don't have anything to add to that. You have more than got the gist of it.'

'I want to run the story tomorrow Poppy. What do you think of that?'

'I think that would be fine.' It didn't occur to her to check or get permission. Why would it?

'Can I have a photograph of you Poppy?'

'Oh God, I guess so. I hate having my photograph taken and I haven't got any of me on my own...'

Miles was prepared, 'That's OK. I can take one now. You can see it first.' He pulled out a small digital camera and started to click. He turned the small screen to face her, 'What do you think?'

Poppy looked at the image of a girl that looked a bit like her, but was thinner in the face, with dark circles under her eyes and an expression combining abject terror with exhaustion. She was a girl with the weight of the world on her shoulders. 'Fine,' she muttered, neither caring nor understanding where this picture would go and what it would mean.

'Can I ask you something Poppy?'

'Sure.'

'What would you say to the people that are holding Martin if you could get a message to them right now?'

She considered her response. It was her turn to speak honestly and without censorship, 'I would say, please let him go. What's going on out there is nothing to do with him, nothing to do with us. I want him to come home where he belongs. He shouldn't be mixed up in this whole thing. He didn't even know where Afghanistan was. He just wanted a better life for us, that's why he joined the army. I always knew it was a mistake.'

Miles looked at her for a second, 'Thanks for that Poppy Day.'

'You are welcome Miles Varrasso.'

'Here's my card. I want you to trust me, Poppy.'

'I trust you.'

He smiled, 'Call me if you need anything or want to discuss anything, anything at all.'

'Will do, thanks Miles.'

As they stood to leave, he turned to Poppy, 'They would have killed him by now Poppy if they were going to, so don't you worry, you will get him back safe and sound.'

She smiled at his superior knowledge; really, really wanting to believe him and, at that point, she probably did.

Eight

Poppy thought she was dreaming of the loud thuds that filled her head, she wasn't. It was the sound of fists hammering on the front door. Jenna shouted through the letter box, 'Oh my God Poppy! Open the door! It's me!'

Her heart pounded as she ran up the hallway in her pyjamas, shaking off the last fog of sleep, whilst trying to negotiate the moving armholes of her dressing gown. She unlocked the bolt and twisted the lock, 'Jesus Jen! What's the matter?'

'Oh my God, Poppy!' Jenna didn't say anything else, but instead unfurled the red-topped newspaper, holding it three inches from her friend's face before doubling over with hands on hips, trying to regain her breath.

Poppy was looking at her own face, almost actual size, on the front page!

'POPPY DAY PLEADS FOR HUSBAND'S SAFE RETURN.'

Then the print got smaller.

'The human face of our futile struggle in the Middle East is represented here by the wife of Private Martin Cricket (22) of The Princess of Wales Royal Regiment, who is being held by terrorist faction, the Zelgai Mahmood Organisation (ZMO) in Afghanistan. Mrs Cricket, or Poppy Day as she is known, confirmed that her husband did not know where Afghanistan was prior to being deployed. Yet another fine example of British Army training, sending our boys out to a place they couldn't pinpoint on a map. Poppy Day (22) a hairdresser from Walthamstow, East London, said, "Please let him go, what's going on out there

is nothing to do with him, nothing to do with us. I just want him home where he belongs; he shouldn't be mixed up in this whole thing. He just wanted a better life for us, that's why he joined the army. I always knew it was a mistake".

The MoD has declined to comment on her statement. But we can only agree with you Poppy Day, when you say, 'What's going on out there is nothing to do with us..."

On it went, detailing what had happened to Martin, how he had been taken and revealing the full horror of Aaron's death. It made her think of his wife, his little boy. They didn't need to know this stuff.

She looked at Jenna's shocked face.

'Oh my God, Poppy!'

'Yes, you've already said that Jen.'

'Now everyone will know and you won't get a moment's peace! I'm worried about you, more than I was before, and let me tell you, that was a lot.'

Poppy smiled, 'I'm sure no one will pay any attention to it Jen, people are too busy with their own lives.'

They were interrupted by the broken bell. Poppy pulled the dressing gown taut around her body. It was Rob, 'Morning Rob.'

'Poppy!' His tone was sharp.

'What?'

He looked at her with an expression of disappointment. She knew in that split-second what it was like to be a daughter with a dad, and what it felt like to let that dad down. She considered singing her pre-prepared hymn, but decided that it probably wouldn't help the situation.

'I take it you've seen the article?' his tone was clipped.

'Some of it yes, just now.'

'When did you speak to him?'

'Yesterday, yesterday morning.'

'Without speaking to me first?'

'I... I didn't...'

He shook his head.

Poppy felt terrible, like a naughty child that has been caught crayoning on the wall.

'No Poppy, you're right, you didn't.' He scanned the article, hoping to find something that he had missed, something misconstrued, 'Is this accurate Poppy? Is this what you said to him?'

She looked away briefly, 'Yes, pretty much. I mean it's what I said, but not necessarily *how* I said it, if that makes any sense.'

Rob didn't speak.

'I thought it was a good idea Rob.'

'You thought what was a good idea?'

'To get publicity. I was thinking about Terry Waite and that other one who came out with the big beard, whose girlfriend chucked him.' She repeated Jenna's dire summing up of the event.

Rob shook his head again.

She wished he would stop doing it; it made her feel foolish, like she'd missed the point, or was going outside of the plan.

He closed his eyes and raked at his moustache with his fingers, 'Poppy, promise me that you will not talk to anyone or do anything like this again without checking with me, with us first, OK?'

She nodded without speaking, without looking at him, because she didn't want to lie to him and couldn't be one hundred per cent sure that she could keep that promise.

Jenna shrieked, jolting Poppy into reality with both her volume and message, 'Oh shit Poppy! You can't let

Dorothea see this!'

'Shit! You are right Jen!'

Poppy ran into the bathroom to scoop up jeans and a sweatshirt that were waiting to be hurled into the washing machine and shoved them on. She was still wearing slippers but it was going to have to do, 'I'm sorry Rob. I need to go and make sure that my nan doesn't see this. You can wait here if you like, I won't be long.'

'I'll wait here for you,' he shook his head in a 'you-have-really-let-me-down' kind of way.

Once again, he sounded and felt like her dad, or how she imagined her dad to sound, when he wasn't very happy with her. For some reason this made her smile; it felt quite nice.

She ran to 'The Unpopulars', arriving in a matter of minutes. Poppy knew there was little chance of her nan seeing anything about Martin's situation on the telly. Unless Zelgai Mahmood was making a guest appearance on *Ready Steady Cook* or helping Jamie with a pasta creation, it would be outside of her viewing spectrum. But she knew for a fact that every morning Dorothea devoured the tabloids along with her cornflakes.

The balls of her feet ached, having been slapped against the pavement without the support of a proper sole. Poppy marched up the path as one of Mr Akwal's daughters opened the front door. Poppy wasn't sure how many daughters he had, but she had met at least four. It fascinated her that they were all stunningly beautiful, clear skin, shiny hair and great teeth, yet Mr Akwal and his wife were not similarly blessed. Maybe Mrs Akwal was a real lithe looker before she started popping out little Akwals by the bucket load, and spending all day sat in her husband's shiny Mercedes on her fat arse, munching cashews, while he drove all over East London pulling together various business deals. Who knows?

'Good morning Poppy Day!'

'Good Morning, Barika, Binish, Bisma or Batool!'

The girl roared with laughter as she swished her long, shiny curtain of hair over her shoulder. Poppy knew all their names and could place them in order of age; she couldn't, however, remember which name belonged to which girl. She started to walk down the hall, 'It's Bisma!'

Poppy laughed back at her, 'I knew that!' Of course it was, beautiful, blessed Bisma, with the looks of a supermodel and a dad that worshipped her... what good luck.

It was nice for Poppy to see her nan in her finery so early in the morning. By finery, don't think of mink and cashmere, accessorised with strings of pearls. A better word would be, clean. A clean blouse and cardigan teamed with elastic-waisted pants, she was pristine! Poppy usually saw her at the end of the day. Her clothes and hair by that late hour would resemble an artist's palette. It was as if Dorothea herself and the clothes she wore were food and mess magnets; before retiring for the night, she would be clad in everything from scrambled egg and gravy to jam and hot chocolate.

Poppy was sorely tempted to sneak her nan's clothes into a bag and enter them for the Turner Prize. She would call it, 'Everything on the Menu'. Art critics for miles around would come and marvel at the originality, wondering how she managed to come up with the alternative genre. They would ask what her preferred materials were, she would tell them, 'My inspiration is Dorothea Day, who spends the time either pissing herself or trying to convince people that she is the mother of Joan Collins, and, as for materials, I favour whatever Mr Akwal has managed to get a good deal on at the cash and carry and is currently trying to poison her with.'

It was nice to see her looking so neat, more like her lovely nan and less like a crazy old lady that's lost her hair brush and spent the day chasing pigeons around the park.

'Morning Nan!'

'Ah! Poppy Day! How lovely to see you.'

'It's lovely to see you too. You seem jolly today, any special reason?'

'Oh Poppy Day, it's good to be happy because life is just too bloody short!'

'You are right Nan,' she hovered then, waiting and thinking what to do next, not entirely sure how she was going to shield her from the papers.

Nathan appeared from nowhere with a tray full of breakfast. The day's paper was secured under his arm. It was Dorothea's cue, 'Ah, now Poppy Day, there is someone that I would like you to meet...'

The usual rigmarole ensued. Nathan smiled at Poppy with a fixed grin, while trying to figure out what her wild semaphore and rolling eyes were trying to tell him about the rolled-up daily which thankfully never got delivered.

When Poppy got back to the flat, Jenna and Rob were chatting like old friends. It made her laugh, two more dissimilar characters with different life experiences you would be hard pushed to find, yet, with her as their common connection, they were drinking tea and setting the world straight. She managed to catch the tail-end of their conversation.

'So, have you ever killed anyone?' Jenna was wide-eyed with anticipation.

There was a pause while Rob considered his response, 'Put it this way, I've never killed anyone that didn't totally deserve it...' He let the fact trail.

Jenna bit, of course, taking the bait whole, 'What did they do to deserve it?'

Poppy could sense her friend's desire to know more, mingled with the fear of what she would hear.

'Oh you know, just what you would expect really, stirring my tea the wrong way, giving me the plain biscuits instead of the chocolate ones.'

Jenna's laugh was loud, unrestrained, 'Oh My God! You're winding me up! I totally believed you. I thought you were going to tell me some terrible war story or something.'

Rob smiled as Poppy walked out through the door, 'Disaster averted?' His timbre indicating he had calmed slightly over the article.

'Yep, thank goodness. I got to Nathan before he gave Nan the paper.'

Jenna piped up, 'That's good mate, Ooh! Some bloke called for you and wants you to call him straight back. He said it was very important.'

'Oh right. Who was it Jen?'

She looked at Rob, 'Who was it Rob?' This was typical Jenna; she could remember that it was important, but not who it was.

He filled in the gaps that she had left, 'It was Tom Chambers, your local MP, no less.'

'What did he want?'

Rob continued, 'It seems he saw the article and, as your local MP, wants to know if he can help you in any way.'

'Oh, well that's a good thing isn't it?' Poppy was still trying to turn her actions into a positive.

'Maybe Poppy, just don't go agreeing to anything without speaking to me first OK?'

'I'm sorry Rob, about the article and everything.'

He shook his head slightly, smoothing his moustache

with his thumb and forefinger, 'It's not your fault Poppy. If I hadn't made our position clear to you then it's my fault, but I also suspect that you were probably duped slightly. Some of these journalists are master manipulators; they know their trade a lot better than you. They have ways of getting you to tell them what they want to hear.'

She could only nod in agreement, unable to tell him that Miles Varrasso had more than met his match.

Poppy went into the hallway and dialled the number that had been left, thinking that it would go through to an answer phone, switchboard or, at the very least, his P.A. Instead a man's voice was loud and clear on the other end. He answered quickly, giving Poppy no time to practice what she was going to say or even think about it. She reminded herself not to sound like an idiot.

'Hello, yes?' he sounded a little impatient.

'It's Poppy, sorry, Poppy Day. I missed your call earlier?' She cringed. How many Poppy's would he have tried to call in the last half an hour?

'Ah yes! Poppy Day! Thank you so much for calling me back.'

The word that he gave the most emphasis to in his sentence was 'so'. This told her all she needed to know. He sounded really, really posh and really, really loud; a combination that always made her feel awkward. It's another character trait of the secret club, the one that Poppy had no hope of belonging to, ever. He sounded like the type of bloke a girl like Harriet would marry.

'That's OK,' she cringed again, recognising 'that's OK' was as moronic a response as 'fine.'

'Reason for my call Poppy is that I wanted to first offer my thoughts and prayers to you at this dreadful time. How are you bearing up?'

How was she bearing up? Barely, she was barely bearing up, but thought it might be inappropriate to say so.

'Fine,' she screwed her eyes shut and bit her bottom lip.

'Well that's good, excellent. Secondly, I wondered if you would like to meet up, to see where things stand and make sure you are confident that all that can be done is being done to try and get your husband home?'

His words were wonderful and exciting in her ears. He sounded so posh and confident. How could he possibly fail to get anything done? He had also said the magic words, 'husband' and 'home'; a beautiful combination.

Poppy didn't care that she sounded horribly eager, 'Yes! Yes meeting you would be great, thank you. I need all the help I can get at the moment.' She hoped that Rob was out of earshot, not wanting to sound disloyal.

'Excellent. Excellent. Well, I have a surgery this afternoon and could schedule you in for an hour or so after that. How would that be for you?'

Poppy had to think on the spot. How would that be for her? That would be bloody marvellous! 'That would be great. Thank you Mr Chambers. I really appreciate this.' Her cringing continued. What should she call him? Your Excellency? Sir?

'Righto. Excellent. I will see you at my rooms which are on the High Street; at shall we say four pm?'

'Four pm would be fine.'

'Excellent. Oh, and Poppy please do call me Tom.'

'Right, OK. Thank you, Tom.'

One click and he was gone. Tom, her new mate, who was very posh, who said 'excellent' a lot, even if it didn't really fit the question or what was being discussed, and who wanted to help her. Poppy didn't care about the finer detail, he could have spoken any language, used any word, if he was the key to getting Martin back home where he belonged then nothing else mattered.

Four pm came around quickly. She hadn't given much thought to what she should wear until she was outside his office, and then wished she had worn something smarter. The front door was painted dark green, she wondered if this was a cleverly chosen neutral, to spare the council having to repaint after elections. A highly polished brass plaque read 'Tom Chambers, Conservative MP, Walthamstow East'. Poppy rang the bell. The door almost instantly buzzed, opening slightly.

In front of her were some steep wooden stairs with a shiny brass handrail that had been recently polished. She could smell the Brasso. She reached the top where there were two rooms, one off to the left and one to the right. Poppy peeped into the one on the left when a voice boomed from the room on the right, almost behind her because of how she was positioned. She was shocked by both its volume and proximity.

'Ah you must be Poppy! Do come in, do come in!' He seemed happy to see her, like they were old friends, which made her feel comfortable and nervous all at the same time. If he had treated her like a stranger, she would have known how to behave, but his super-friendliness without having met her before, confused her.

He stood back in the doorway, holding his arm out straight for her to pass by into his office. It was an interesting room, a cross between a doctor's surgery and a library. Poppy admired the way rich people could collect stuff and pile it up on expensive tables, making it look artfully poised, as if everything was a precious artefact, handed down from generations past. Whereas, do the same in any council flat and it looked like piles of clutter; more car boot than shabby chic. There was a large wooden desk in front of the window, with bookshelves all around the room holding leather bound textbooks that looked academic and weighty. Large paintings hung on the walls and the gaps between the bigger paintings were filled with smaller ones. The overall effect reminded Poppy of the inside of a stately home, but on a tiny scale.

Tom Chambers himself was just as he had sounded on the phone. He was wearing a navy blue pinstriped suit with a pale pink shirt and a blue tie. He was going bald; his remaining hair was a bit too long and gelled back on his expanding forehead. He had very large teeth, which his lips struggled to close over; giving his mouth equine overtones. There was a large gold signet ring on the little finger of his left hand with a crest of some sort stamped into it. She put his age at somewhere between mid to late forties.

'So, Poppy...' he looked at her earnestly. She wasn't sure if it was a question or a statement, so she remained silent. She was used to people saying her name as a question the first time they met her, 'Poppy Day'? Confirming they hadn't misheard. But a question when asked usually makes the person's voice go up at the end and that's how you know it's a question, unless you are from Bristol where your sentences go up at the end anyway. Poppy knew that if she ever went to Bristol, she would constantly be trying to answer everything that was said to her until she got the hang of it. While she was thinking about this, specifically how Tom's voice had *not* gone up and yet the way he had said 'Poppy Day,' had felt like a question, he carried on talking, 'How are you bearing up?'

This was definitely a question. She resisted the temptation to say, 'You already asked me that on the phone.'

I'm actually OK as long as I'm busy, as long as I feel

that things are being done to get my husband back,' Poppy figured that her words would prompt him, give him the opportunity to come out with a strategy or, at the very least, his ideas on how to take things forward.

'Excellent, yes. Excellent.'

More inappropriate 'excellents'. Poppy stared at him, suddenly feeling that her confidence in him to help her deliver Martin home simply because of how he spoke might have been a bit premature, if not completely misplaced.

'I thought the article was very well written. I liked your candour, the fact that you weren't afraid to state the situation how it is; that was refreshing, excellent in fact.'

Poppy thought that maybe he thought she had written it, 'Well, I only spoke to Miles Varrasso, the journalist, he pulled it all together. It wasn't down to me at all.'

'Quite, quite, but still, a really compelling article. Well done, well done you.'

Poppy didn't know why, but she said, 'Thank you,' as though she could take some of the credit.

There was a second of awkward silence before Tom broke the deadlock, 'When was the last time you had any actual contact with Aaron, Poppy?'

'I'm sorry?' she needed him to repeat the question and it was nothing to do with thinking time, but more the hope that she had misheard the MP for Walthamstow East.

'When was the last time that you had any actual contact with Aaron?' he asked.

She was slow in forming her response, 'I have never had actual contact, or, in fact, any contact with Aaron.'

'No contact at all? What, not since he was sent on tour?' he looked totally confused. Poppy was later to realise that was because he was.

'No... None at all.'

'Surely you don't mean that you haven't been in contact since you were married?'

'No. What I mean is I have never been married to Aaron. My husband is Martin. Martin Cricket?'

Tom scanned the article which he had unfolded on the ink blotter in front of him. He scratched his scalp, his expression blank, 'Oh... right... yes, Martin of course, excellent. So, who is Aaron?'

Poppy bit down on her lip, thinking of how to respond. The words of Miles Varrasso came into her head, uncensored, brutal and exactly what she was looking for, 'The situation, Tom, is this; two soldiers, both Brits, were taken in a carefully planned ambush in the Helmand Province of Afghanistan. One Aaron Sotherby, they decapitated and shoved his body, complete with severed head at the gates of the barracks. One other, namely Martin Cricket, my husband, was taken hostage. Eye witnesses confirm that he was certainly beaten upon capture, but probably not dead. He is currently being held captive by the ZMO, somewhere in Garmsir...'

Poppy didn't intend to be rude or offend. He stared at her without speaking. She felt angry, furious, in fact, that he had asked her there with the offer of help and didn't even know who her husband was, much less the situation. She decided he was a dickhead.

When he did speak, it all became perfectly clear. Tom Chambers was a petty opportunist who could probably do very little to help her cause, 'Well that's excellent...'

'What is?'

He looked perplexed again, 'What is what?'

'What exactly is excellent, Tom, about what I have just told you?'

'What?' he screwed his eyes shut. His top lip curled up over his large teeth as he tried to make more sense of the conversation.

She decided to try and cut him a bit of slack, not exactly feeling sorry for him, but seeing that he didn't have the brain capacity to effectively mentally joust with her, more's the pity, 'OK. Let's start again shall we Tom?'

He nodded, almost grateful for the guidance.

'I need all the help that I can to bring my husband home. I will do whatever it takes. Whether that means publicity, or the right word in the right ear, I don't know, but what I do know, is that I will try any avenue, including liaising with you and your party, if that means that I get Martin home. OK Tom?'

He nodded.

Poppy took for understanding and continued, 'So, what is it that you want from me? You seemed very keen for us to meet up?'

'Yes, well I was...'

'Not so sure now you have actually met me though, right?'

He grimaced lightly, not laughing in case that, too, might be the wrong thing to do. Poor Tom, 'Not at all Poppy, although you are certainly not what I was expecting.'

'What were you expecting?' he had her interest.

'I don't really know, but I guess someone a bit less, spirited!'

'Ah Tom, when you grow up around here, 'spirited' is definitely a good thing. In fact, 'spirited' is highly desirable, if survival is a high priority for you.'

'I don't know anyone that grew up around here.'

This made Poppy chuckle loudly at her MP, 'Of course you don't. Why would you?'

He stared at her with a look of absolute confusion.

'So, as I was saying, Tom, what exactly is it you wanted

from our meeting?'

He reddened slightly, an indicator that what was coming was the truth, 'I figured Poppy that with you being anti the deployment, and stating how unprepared your husband was by the army, that maybe you might say a few words in support of what we are trying to achieve, politically. I mean, it's the other lot that sent our boys there in the first place and a bloody mess it is too, and getting worse if this unfortunate episode is anything to go by...'

Poppy smiled at this. Why was it always 'our boys' when trying to garner support, yet 'misfits who lived on the edge of society' when out of the army and living off benefit? Yes, an unfortunate episode indeed, 'OK. Supposing I agree to say a few words in support of you and what you are trying to achieve, politically, what will you do in return to help me?'

He leant forward, chuckling awkwardly, 'Goodness Poppy, these things are jolly high-profile. I should think that the Prime Minister would be your best bet. That I can't organise, but I do have the ear of the Foreign Secretary, a fellow old Etonian, year above me, but a good friend. We played in the first fifteen together. He would be able to advise you up the chain, as it were.'

'Fine.'

Again that look of confusion, 'What's fine?'

'It's a deal Tom. You get me in front of the Foreign Secretary and I will say or do whatever you want me to. I'll even walk the length of Hoe Street with a sandwich board bearing a slogan of your choice!'

'Excellent. That is excellent. I'll get right on to it Poppy.'

'Great, that's great Tom. You have my number, so give me a shout.'

'Will do Poppy.'

She stood then to leave.

'Poppy?'

'Yes Tom?'

'Just one question...'

'Fire away!' she felt confident, more in control than this man she had judged so wrongly.

'Where is Hoe Street?'

What you looking so smug about missus?'

'What d'you mean smug?'

There was the odd evening when Dorothea was spoiling for a fight the moment her granddaughter arrived. This was clearly one of those nights.

'You know perfectly well what I mean Poppy Day. I'm not stupid you know.'

'I know you are not stupid Nan.'

'Good, because I'm not.'

There was silence as both mentally reloaded, considering how to continue. Sometimes when she was in this sort of mood, Poppy could distract her with a carefully chosen subject, or divert her with some snippet of information.

Her nan spoke first, denying her the opportunity to deflect her mood with trivia, 'Mrs Hardwick told me, so you don't have to.'

'Mrs Hardwick told you what?' Poppy tried to sound aloof, as if there was no news...

'About you in the paper.'

'What about me in the paper?' her tone was surprised, indifferent. Inside, however, she was thinking, 'Oh shit!' It hadn't occurred to her to try and stop everyone at 'The Unpopulars' seeing the newspapers. She kept calm, trying not to show her agitation. Until she knew how informed Dorothea was, there was no point in panicking.

Poppy hated the thought of her nan being given distressing news that might confuse or upset her.

'Mrs Hardwick told me that her son had told her that he'd seen you in the paper Poppy Day and I believe her. He went to grammar school her boy; he is very clever.'

'Obviously.'

'Anyway, it doesn't matter what you say. I know what you are up to.'

'You do?'

'Yes. You are trying to follow in your mother's footsteps and get into films aren't you? Aren't you?'

Poppy didn't know what to say to her lovely nan, whose greatest fear was that she had courted publicity trying to follow in the career path of her imaginary mother, Joan Collins. She wanted to laugh, as much with relief as anything. She felt the giggle bubbling in her throat, 'You got me! Well, it does sound quite nice Nan, making films on a warm beach somewhere, with people doing my hair and makeup every day, or being driven around in a limo. I could have a worse life.'

Dorothea leant forward, pulling her hand-knitted cardigan closer around her body with one hand and the finger of the other pointing at her granddaughter's chest, 'Now, you listen to me Poppy Day and you listen good; you have a decent job with Christine, she will always look after you. If Joan had wanted you to be an actress then she would have written to you and told you wouldn't she?'

Poppy thought about receiving a letter from Joan Collins saying;

Dear Poppy Day, I want you to be an actress. Best wishes, Joan Collins'.

This too made her smile, 'You are probably right Nan.'

'No probably about it my girl. I don't want to hear another word on the subject.'

'OK Nan,' Poppy reached out, patting her hand.

'That's my girl.'

'That's right, I am your girl.'

'He works at the council.'

'Who does?' Poppy had lost the thread.

'Who does what?' Dorothea countered.

'Who works at the council?' Poppy tried to maintain a placid tone.

'Who works at the council?'

'Yes!' Poppy was tired. She struggled not to sound impatient, suppressing the instinct to snap.

'I don't bloody know, Poppy Day, lots of people I expect. Although, judging by the state of the flats, not enough of them!'

Poppy stood, knowing that in her state of fatigue she was in no shape for a verbal game of chess with half the pieces missing. She kissed Dorothea on the forehead, 'I'll see you tomorrow Nan. Have sweet dreams.'

'Will do darlin'. Night night.'

'Night night Nan.'

'Mrs Hardwick's son,' Dorothea caught up.

'Mrs Hardwick's son what?'

'He's the one that works at the council. He does all the typing.'

'Well, good to know that grammar school education wasn't wasted.'

Dorothea turned towards the telly, whilst reaching for the remote control, her constant companion.

Poppy wandered home, smiling. Her nan in her often confused state seemed more 'with it' to her than Tom

Chambers had. She couldn't understand how he had got to where he had without any nous, presence, or anything about him that would encourage Christine to employ him to sweep up the hair cuttings every day. He had come across as vacuous. Poppy considered this further and had to admit that she knew exactly how he attained his position; his ticket into the first round would have been an education at Eton, the rest would have been easy. The second statement was untrue, as well, of course. Christine would have employed him. He wore trousers didn't he?

Co-incidentally, when she got home there was a message on the answer phone from him, along with three others. His loud voice was instantly recognisable, 'Poppy, hi, it's Tom. Yup, all sorted for Tristram. He's completely on board and has suggested day after tomorrow about three-ish, at number eleven. He's had a cancellation. You've probably got half an hour so plan it a bit. So, well excellent. Will be in touch. Very good then. Cheerio!'

Poppy replayed it a couple of times. He was really unbelievable, 'All sorted for Tristram.' Luckily she knew who he was referring to, 'He's had a cancellation' ah! So that was why he was seeing her. No burning desire to help with her cause, but a spare half an hour that she could occupy. 'Plan a bit!' This made Poppy smile, 'Thanks for that Tom. What, like you did you mean? Not even knowing who my husband was, or whether he was alive or dead! Bloody brilliant. Excellent, in fact. Don't you worry, Tommy boy, I'll be prepared.' She spoke to the machine which was still blinking.

Pressing 'play' again, she heard Rob's voice, 'Hello Poppy. It's Rob. Major Helm and I are hoping to come and see you tomorrow morning at ten. Remember Poppy, that Anthony Helm is the media liaison officer for Martin's deployment. He can really help you Poppy, so... well, you know... You have my number if you need me at any time just call. Good night Poppy.'

She could hear the vague sounds of a TV in the background, could picture him in his slippers with Moira sat beside him on the sofa, it was a nice image. She replayed his message and considered the pauses, '...can really help you Poppy, so...' She mentally filled the gaps, 'so be nice and don't rub him up the wrong way.'

Once again it sounded like dad advice and once again she liked it. Her diary was filling up thick and fast. Luckily Christine was paying her, letting her take whatever time that she needed. Poppy was grateful.

The third message was from Miles, 'Hi Poppy, Miles here, give us a shout, just trying to find out what's being done to get the boy home. Call me.'

The best, however, was the final message, drum roll please...

'Oh my Gawd, my baby, my poor baby. I seen you in the papers today, we get them a bit late and I said to Terry, that's my baby! That's my girl and her poor bloke is about to get 'is 'ead chopped off by them bloody Iranians. It's just so awful, you are so young to be widowed, but you listen to me my girl, you listen to me because I know. Don't let it get you down, you get your lippy on and you get out there, because you are still young and there will be more fish in the sea for you Poppy Day, you keep your chin up. If you want to come out for a bit of a holiday, me and Terry would love to see you. I'm a bit of a celebrity now my little girl is plastered all over the papers; don't think we've paid for a drink all night! Oh, it's me, Mum by the way, I was....' The lack of tape cut her off mid flow, thank God.

Poppy hadn't heard from her for a couple of months.

She sounded older and slightly pissed, of course. Poppy started to laugh; quite unexpectedly it turned to crying. She sat for a while, long enough for her legs to go numb on the carpet and the light of day to give way to darkness.

It was an odd thing for Poppy; she knew that Cheryl was a crap mum, yet, no matter how much time passed or how much older she got, it was always the same. As soon as she heard from or saw Cheryl, in fact, any contact at all that confirmed how totally useless she was... It was like she was six again.

Poppy didn't love her mum. It's difficult to love someone who doesn't love you back. It could be a wife, husband, boyfriend, girlfriend, a mum or a dad; you can do it for a while, but not forever.

Poppy did it for about eight years until realisation dawned that she was alone in her strength of feeling. It then started to feel pointless and embarrassing, even at that tender age. The energy she had wasted on this one-sided love made her slightly resentful. The process of unloving her mum began without conscious design or pre-planning, but by the time it was under way, she realised that it was fine not to love her. Poppy would still be who she was, she would be OK.

The standard gift for her daughter for both birthday and Christmas was make-up from the Avon lady, when all she really wanted was books, any books. There was no overt abuse like you see in the papers. It was more as if Cheryl didn't realise what she had to do with a child, as if it never occurred to her that Poppy couldn't look after herself, that she had to *do* something for her, or to her. She treated Poppy like a neighbour's child or someone that she didn't know very well. That last part is true actually; she didn't know her very well.

When Poppy spoke to her mum, no matter what Cheryl

was doing, watching TV, smoking or putting her mascara on, she would look at Poppy and say, 'What?' as though she hadn't realised her daughter was in the room until she had spoken. Poppy would then have to repeat what she'd said. Her mum never listened. It was a bit like she wasn't interested, in fact, exactly like she wasn't interested.

It's not that Poppy expected anything different, yet it was still somehow disappointing. Poppy would have been more shocked if she HAD asked after her ageing mother, who, for all she knew, might be dead and buried. Or if she'd said that she was jumping on the next available flight to come and be by her side at this terrible time. Of course, she never would and Poppy knew this. She knew the best she could expect is exactly what she got, a suggestion to go and see if she could pull while her "usband was gettin' 'is 'ead chopped off by them Iranians!'. Poppy's disappointment turned to anger, she felt that her nan deserved more, deserved better.

The message left her feeling empty and let down. It was as if there was a physical cut on her heart that, despite being healed and hidden, at the very second that she heard her mother's terrible, misunderstood, stupid suppositions and rantings, opened the scar up instantly and painfully. Poppy would then bleed inside until she could figure out how to put it to the back of her mind.

She gathered her thoughts and emotions, tidying them up the best that she could, and called Miles Varrasso. She got his answer phone, 'Hey Miles, in response to your question, 'What is being done to get the boy home?' The answer is 'absolutely nothing' as far as I can tell. It's shocking Miles really, a bloody disgrace. Anyway, call me back and we can catch up, thanks.'

Poppy didn't know how Miles did it. She left her message for him at about six o'clock and the headline that stared up at her from the newsagent's rack the very next morning was;

'Poppy Day disgusted as army do absolutely nothing to bring one of our boys home!'

Poppy couldn't believe it. The rest of the story was a re-hash of what had already been printed, along with several 'quotes' from Poppy and that same crappy picture.

She started to lose her nerve, wondering if the maximum publicity strategy was the right one. She bought the paper, as well as the milk that she had gone into the shop for. Pulling her collar up, she scurried home, feeling slightly embarrassed, exposed and desperate to put a call into Nathan. She couldn't face another mid-morning sprint in her slippers.

Her guests arrived at ten o'clock, sharp. They couldn't manage to get her husband back to safety, but if they said ten o'clock, then ten o'clock it was! Rob walked into the lounge and removed his beret, as was now the custom.

She noticed that the Major had a folded copy of the paper in his gloved hand. He followed Rob into the lounge. The three sat in a triangle arrangement around the room. Poppy decided to take the lead, 'Can I get anyone a cup of tea?'

'No thank you,' Major Helm had again apparently spoken for both of them. He removed his hat and placed it on his lap, next he peeled off his gloves and laid them in the upturned hat, preparing to begin; ready and action! 'How are you bearing up Poppy?'

Why did people keep asking her that? Was there not some more appropriate phrase that they could use? Bearing up? What did that mean exactly? She reminded herself to look it up, 'Well, I'm OK I guess. As I said to someone yesterday, I'm fine as long as I know that things are being done to actively get Mart back. It's the idea that efforts have stopped, or that nothing is happening that worries me the most. That is the one thing that keeps me awake at three in the morning, that idea that he is just, gone and no one is doing anything to get him home safely.'

'Well, let me reassure you on that point. Lots of things are being done to ensure his safe return. Even if the efforts aren't obvious, there's masses going on behind the scenes and on the ground, but I totally understand your frustration that it doesn't appear to be happening fast enough, it must feel like that. I can only imagine what it must be like for you.'

It was her turn to nod, 'Well that's good to hear Anthony. What things are going on behind the scenes and on the ground?'

He cast his eyes towards Rob, 'It is complicated Poppy.'

'Yes of course,' she concurred. Rob coughed to clear his throat, but to Poppy, it was a 'remember my phone message and don't be rude or wind him up' cough. Thanks for that dad.

'It's not as easy as just storming in and getting him out.'

'Well no, we tried that last week didn't we, and it was the wrong house. What a cock up!' Inside her head Poppy was reprimanding herself, for God's sake shut up! He is on your side. He didn't seem to take offence, but rather felt that it confirmed his stance.

'That's exactly right Poppy. That's a good example of how difficult it can be to get the right intelligence and act on it, but it doesn't mean that we have stopped trying.' Touché Major Anthony. He wasn't done, 'I did want to talk to you about the interview that you gave to Miles Varrasso, if that's OK?'

'Sure,' she felt confident, cocky almost.

'Miles Varrasso is a subversive. He and plenty others like him are anti the whole campaign. If they can use someone like you at this difficult time to further their cause, and get their message across, they will. You seem very together Poppy, but believe me when I tell you, that at this time you are vulnerable and people like him will take advantage of you if they can. He has no regard for your wellbeing, and will do whatever he can to convince whoever he can that we shouldn't be out there, and that our servicemen and women are acting in futility. Can you imagine how demotivating that is for the troops that are deployed believing that they are doing a vital job? Or how insulting it is to families that have lost loved ones in the line of duty, families like Aaron's?'

Although she couldn't warm to him, Poppy realised Anthony was cleverer than she had first thought. His words resonated. She thought about Aaron's family.

'I wanted to give the interview because I figured that the more people know about Mart, the more he'll be spoken about. He won't be forgotten will he, if everyone is talking about him? Then they are more likely to let him go.' It didn't sound quite as convincing as she had hoped.

'I can see that sounds logical Poppy, but have you considered the whole reason these groups revert to taking hostages is that they get publicity for their cause? It, therefore, makes it beneficial to take people like Martin, and the more you publicise their activities, the more you are encouraging them, supporting them.'

'I hadn't thought about it like that, no.'

'Well luckily you have a great team in Rob and me to help and advise you at every step. I'm here Poppy to make sure that you are being kept informed and to do everything that I can to ensure that, from your perspective, we are handling this in the best way possible.'

His words offered Poppy little comfort; they sounded scripted and insincere, spoken through an unsmiling mouth as his knee danced in restless anticipation. He wanted to leave. He didn't care about Martin and he didn't care about her, 'Actually I do have a question.'

'Fire away. Anything.'

'I'm meeting the Foreign Secretary tomorrow and I'm not sure how best to get into Downing Street. It's usually closed off at the end isn't it? Do you think they will have a note of my appointment and just let me in?'

The room was silent. Anthony Helm looked angry, whereas Rob looked proud. Eventually Anthony found his voice, 'Let me get this straight, you are seeing the Foreign Secretary tomorrow?'

'Yes.'

He looked at Rob, 'Is this the first you've heard of this?'

'Yes sir.'

'Poppy, I don't know what you are trying to prove, but I will not condone or authorise a dedicated team to be at your beck and call if you are insisting on playing the maverick, pulling stunts like this. You seem intent on doing the very opposite of what we recommend, but if you want to go it alone, then so be it...' He wasn't shouting, but was concentrating on controlling his tone and pitch. '...although I would have thought that to be kept fully up-to-date with any development concerning your husband would have been foremost in your thoughts.'

'That's just it Anthony, what developments? What news? We are no closer to getting Mart back than we were when he was first taken and I need to do something, just like you would if it was your wife or partner. You wouldn't sit back and wait for something, anything to happen, you know you wouldn't.'

'Actually Poppy that is where you are wrong. I would sit back and wait, because I have great faith in the British Army to act in the right way and do the right thing.'

'Then you have more faith than me because they have given me no reason to.'

'Where did this lack of faith, this hostility come from Poppy? Why are you so cynical?'

She laughed then, loudly, 'I think my lack of faith, my hostility and cynicism probably started on the day that my husband was failed by you and your army. Taken hostage while trying to do his bloody job! That has been further compounded by the fact that some weeks later we have no idea where he is and are no closer to getting him back! Try looking at it from my point of view; night after night I climb into our bed and I don't know where my husband is, or how he is, or even if he's alive. If he is alive, I know that he will be desperate and I don't feel like anyone cares...'

Again no one spoke. Poppy didn't know how she kept getting herself into these situations. It felt like she was the only one that could see the reality of the situation and no one was listening.

Anthony stood and jammed his hat on to his head. He walked towards the door, 'Good bye Poppy.' His voice was clipped, curt.

Rob stood in the lounge with his hands on his hips; he rolled his eyes skyward and shook his head, 'Well, that went well.'

Poppy bit her lip to stop herself saying anything else inappropriate, in fact, to stop her saying anything at all.

The following day Poppy smartened up. She scraped her hair back into a ponytail and checked her face in the hallway mirror. She thought she looked like an idiot, but it would only be for a few hours. She considered ignoring the telephone that rang as she was about to make her exit.

'Poppy?'

Yes.'

'It's Miles. Did you see the paper?'

'Ah Mr Subversive! Yes I did.'

'Okaaay. You don't sound as happy as I thought you would. I had to fight for that front page slot.'

'In that case, thank you.'

'I accept your thanks even if it's not graciously given!'

Poppy snorted her laughter.

'Thought I would give you a shout Poppy, as I won't be around for a while.'

'Oh right, off on holiday, lucky thing?'

'I wish. No, I'm off to Afghanistan,'

Poppy felt a surge of jealousy, first Mr Akwal and now Miles; it felt like everyone could get within a few feet of her husband except her.

'I'm leaving from Brize Norton tomorrow, but I promise to give you a ring as soon as I get back and, obviously, if I hear anything while I am out there...' He didn't need to say anymore.

'Take care of yourself Miles.'

'Fear not, care is my middle name! Actually it's Alessandro after my great uncle, but that's another story.'

Just as Poppy predicted, she walked to the end of Downing Street where a policeman stood in a little booth with an armed colleague a few feet away. He looked well past retirement age, and had one of those big, fat, bulbous noses that you only get with old age and the consumption of too much port.

Poppy consciously tried to avoid looking at his huge proboscis; wondering why it was, that when she met anyone with even the slightest affliction or deformity, it was so fascinating to her, that she was the one that was acutely embarrassed.

It had always been a problem for Poppy, with her 'mouth in gear but brain not engaged' habit. It meant that she often said what was in her head before fully censoring it. She wasn't in the same league as Jenna, there was no verbal diarrhoea, it was more of a 'why *did* you say that Poppy?' thing. If she met a nun or a priest she would say 'Jesus Christ' in every sentence, and respond with, 'Oh my God' to everything they said. If there was a lull in conversation, she would have to physically stop herself from saying, 'So, immaculate conception, no one really believes that do they? Surely Mary just got caught out and had to think fast before her dad got home and found her standing there with the Clearblue in hand registering positive!' That would be her icebreaker, her starter for ten. It wasn't always easy being her.

'Hello,' Poppy spoke to the nose.

'Hello there. What can I do for you?'

It felt embarrassing, incredible and unreal; not only the schnozzle thing, but the very fact that she was standing there saying to this bloke, who expected her to ask for directions to the nearest Pizza Hut, 'I have an appointment with the Foreign Secretary at three o'clock.' It was a quarter to; Poppy thought this was just about the right amount of early.

To his credit, he didn't raise an eyebrow, 'Your name?'

'Poppy Day.'

For a split second he hesitated, swallowing the desire to

repeat it. He lifted the receiver of a clumsy looking black telephone, which looked more like a prop than a working phone, and spoke into it, 'I have a Miss Poppy Day here for Mr Munroe at three pm?' It was a statement, but, as mentioned before, he went up at the end so it was, in fact, a question as well. He nodded a couple of times as though the person on the other end could see him, maybe they could.

He then replaced the receiver and looked at Poppy, 'Thank you Miss Day, someone will meet you at the door.' That was it. Through the gate and off she trotted, walking up Downing Street to go and meet with the Right Honourable Tristram Munroe, Foreign Secretary. As you do.

Poppy didn't know what she imagined it to be like behind the famous front door. If she had to guess, she would have gone with a beautiful lounge-like hallway, with a large fireplace and grand portraits hanging on the walls, one of those little tables shaped like a half moon with a decanter on it and crystal glasses sparkling on a silver tray, in case someone in a dinner jacket fancied a brandy after supper. She also imagined uniformed staff to be floating around silently, but busily, a bit like *Downton Abbey* or the original *Upstairs Downstairs* with that bloke in it from *The Professionals* or 'The Professnials' as her nan used to call it. It was nothing like that, more like posh offices than a house and huge, really big! Lots of staircases, rooms, corridors and walkways leading to goodness knows where. Poppy was sure there were more places to live, work and hide in this building than anyone would ever need.

She was met by a middle-aged lady, smartly dressed in a navy suit, but with the kind of grey curly perm and face without make up that made her look more dinner lady than important-working-for-the-Foreign-Secretary type. Dorothea would have christened her 'a right old chatterbox.' She opened the door without checking to see if she was 'Poppy Day, expected visitor of Tristram Munroe' or, in fact, someone down on her luck selling household goods, dusters and the like.

'Do come in.'

Poppy stood like a lemon in the big hallway, feeling so much like a fish out of water, she had to gasp for breath before she suffocated on the air.

Poppy was thinking about his name, 'Tristram'. It's such an obvious class thing isn't it? The instant you hear someone's name, particularly a name like that, you place them in a class. If any boy had been called Tristram and lived on Poppy's estate, he would have had a good kicking on a daily basis, as would Miles Alessandro Varrasso. Where Tristram lived, he was probably one of several, in the same way that Dean's and Darren's had to be slightly renamed in her world, so that she and her mates knew who they were talking about. For example, there was 'Gingerdarren', obvious as to why; 'Veggiedarren', who born with an intolerance to protein, couldn't eat meat; 'Upandoverdean', who could make the swing in the park go right over the bar; and 'Deanthepoof'. Poppy wondered how his peer group would differentiate between Tristrams: Tristramfiftyacres? TristramwiththeThaiaupair? Tristramtherighthonorourable?

Her mind was wandering, she was suddenly nervous, feeling out of her depth. She thought of Tom's words 'plan it a bit'. Poppy thought she had planned it a bit, certainly on the bus on the way up. She had rehearsed her piece, sounding smart and credible, but now as she stood in that vast hallway, she didn't think she would have known her name if someone had asked it. She felt like shite.

Dinner lady woman had disappeared, so Poppy stood alone and adrift, until eventually a man in a flash suit appeared from around a corner, 'Is it Poppy?'

She nodded and smiled, that was it! She was Poppy, Poppy Day, on a crazy mission to save her husband!

'Follow me Poppy. I will take you up to Tristram's office.'

'Thank you.'

He stopped walking and turned to face her as if she had given him a big compliment, 'Why you are most welcome!' He sounded to Poppy like a character from *Gone with the Wind*; one of the southern ladies, not Rhett Butler. He was incredibly smart and smelt like fresh laundry, walking quickly and neatly, and taking up no more space in the corridor than was absolutely necessary. He reminded Poppy of a little bird, a sparrow man. They wandered along corridors and through rooms until they came to the end of a hallway. He knocked on the door.

'Yep!' called the voice from within.

'Don't look so nervous Poppy. You will be absolutely fine!' he whispered. His words of encouragement gave her confidence. She remembered her speech and all the points that she needed to make, in the words of Tommy Cooper, 'just like that.'

Her little sparrow man escort, pushed open the door and there he was, Tristram Munroe, stood behind a big desk. A desk that was much bigger than Tom Chambers', proving that the more success you had, the bigger desk you got. Poppy figured that the Prime Minister's desk must be vast; acres of polished wood, probably with the telephone in the corner, so far out of his reach that he would have to jog around to pick it up every time it rang. No wonder he looked so trim.

Tristram Munroe looked slightly different from how he did on the telly. He was taller, slimmer, but still with an ample stomach, pushing the buttons adrift on his striped shirt. He had one hand on his waist, as though he was about to launch into *I'm a Little Teapot*; the other held a phone to his ear. He cupped his teapot hand over the receiver, 'Sorry! Shan't be a mo! Sit down! Sit down!'

She sat. After all, who was she to refuse a direct instruction from the Foreign bloody Secretary? Poppy tried not to eavesdrop on his conversation, but it was difficult. She tried to concentrate on a picture above his head, trying to give him a bit of privacy.

'Patrick, it's a real honour, really is. Only difficulty is the timing. Pretty sure we have a state visit going on. Can't remember which lot it is. Want to say China, but possibly not. Doesn't matter. Point is, I think I am tied up so it's a no can do. Simply because I can't physically make it, not because I don't want to.' He spoke in shorthand, a man so busy that he couldn't waste time linking his thoughts with needless words. He paused while whoever Patrick was answered him. 'Yup, yup, absolutely. OK buddy, will do. Love to Charity and the little man. Yup, excellent. Cheerio.'

He ended the call with a touch of a button as he simultaneously jogged around the desk with, not one but, two hands outstretched. This was an entirely new handshake tactic to the ones that Poppy had been used to. Thankfully he took the lead, sparing her the dilemma, holding her left hand between both of his, 'Poppy, thank you so much for coming to see me today. I'm sorry to have kept you waiting.'

She smiled. This was great, any remaining trace of nerves evaporated. He sounded pleased to see her, it was wonderful! He continued talking before she had a chance to answer him.

'That was my nephew on the phone, Patrick. He and his good lady Charity have bestowed upon me the honour of asking me to be the godfather to their little boy. Sadly, I don't think I can tie in the christening dates–wise. More's the pity; the poor little chap may not be with us much longer...'

'Who your nephew?'

He let go of her hand, which she was glad about, 'No, no, not Patrick, his son, Teddy. He has lots of difficulties, bless him.'

'Oh God. That's a shame,' Poppy didn't know what else to say, what he wanted or expected her to say.

'Yes, it is damn bloody shame. It's a weird one; they couldn't have any kids so they adopted her sister's boy. She apparently took one look at him, heard about all his issues and potential problems and promptly decided to give him away to the highest bidder. Then she hot-footed it to Spain to start a new life with some Spanish lover! What do you make of that?'

'She sounds awful, selfish. I don't know how any mother could abandon her baby, it's not normal is it?' She thought about adding that she knew how his nephew's son felt. Her own mum having also hot-footed it to Spain and, yes, it was shit, really shit. That little boy was lucky in some ways, not with his difficulties obviously, but he did have a mum and dad that would love him. At least he wasn't left with his loopy nan in a stinking flat.

'Exactly right, awful and selfish. No Poppy, not normal at all. It's hard to fathom some people isn't it? Still she will have to live with herself and thank God she had Charity and Patrick, who are a couple of soft touches really, to pick up the problem. Appalling woman. Never met her, don't particularly want to.'

Poppy was aware that they only had half an hour and, interesting though it was, didn't want to waste her precious minutes talking about Tristram's dysfunctional relatives and their problems. She had enough of that in her own family thank you very much. It was as if he read her thoughts.

'Right Poppy, time being of the essence and all that. Let's get down to business shall we?' he sat in his chair and leant forward onto the desk. His expression and tone were now completely different, as if he had switched into work mode, 'I cannot begin to imagine what you are going through, it's a horrendous situation. I want to give you and your family all of my sympathy and best wishes...'

She nodded, not sure of how else to respond.

'How are you bearing up?'

Poppy had looked up the term that very morning, the dictionary definition had read; *To withstand stress, difficulty, or attrition; to hold up, support, raise one's spirit, not despair...* So how was she bearing up? Not too well actually, but what did she say? 'Fine.' (But you knew that right?)

'When exactly was Martin taken, Poppy?'

She was impressed. Without referring to notes, he had correctly assumed that she had never been married to Aaron, and managed to recall her husband's name; so far so good, 'It's nearly a couple of weeks now.'

'A couple of weeks? That must feel like an eternity.'

'It does.'

'I can imagine. Are the army supporting you Poppy, keeping you up to date?'

'Yes, yes they are, not that there is much to report...'

'I heard about the attempt to recapture him, bit of a disaster by all accounts.'

'You could say that and what is worrying me sir...'

'Tristram, please,' he interrupted.

'Thanks. What is worrying me Tristram, is that no one can give me any concrete proof or any information that makes me believe that he is ever going to come home,' Poppy felt the tears gathering at the back of her throat.

He placed his hand over his mouth, splaying his fingers and holding the bottom of his face. He nodded, deep in thought.

Poppy carried on, liking the feeling that he was interested in her and what she had to say. Inside she was thinking, 'You are right Poppy, this rallying of support for Mart is the right thing to do, you go girl!'

'I don't want to sound ungrateful for what the army is doing Tristram, and I don't want to put anyone at risk, or demotivate anyone.' Anthony Helm's words flashed into her mind, 'I just want to get my husband home and I would be grateful for any suggestions as to how I can do that.'

He spoke through his fingers after a pause, 'The first thing to say is that you can't do that. It is up to other people to get him home, I know how tough that must sound. It's not an easy situation Poppy as I am sure you can appreciate. Being completely honest with you, whilst I can give you a sympathetic ear, the best I can do is put you in touch with someone that might be able to help you better.'

'That's what Tom Chambers said, that's how I ended up here,' Poppy was beginning to find the lack of progress frustrating; she wanted an answer, a solution, a way to get Martin home.

'I can imagine what it feels like Poppy; that you are being passed around or fobbed off, but that is not the case. One thing you have to realise is that, whilst this is your absolute priority, it might not be for others and that will prove to be your biggest frustration.'

She liked his honesty, he was right of course, 'It is my biggest frustration, but how do I make Mart's return their priority Tristram? I am genuinely worried that no one cares apart from me, almost as if he is expendable, currency that can be spent for the cause.'

He stood up and looked out of the window with both of his hands on his waist, his elbows stuck out at right angles, more pre-highland jig than little teapot. He spoke to her without turning around, 'Maybe you can't Poppy. Maybe you will have to accept that the wheels turn slowly, but you must accept that they ARE turning. Does that help at all?' he turned to face her again.

'Truthfully?'

'Yes.'

'No, not even a little bit.'

'Thought not. You are a determined girl Poppy. I admire your tenacity. Don't give up on me. I will give it some serious thought and I will get back to you.'

'Thanks for seeing me today, I know you are busy and...'

'Not at all, I have really enjoyed meeting you,' he sounded sincere.

'I'll wait to hear from you Tristram.'

'You are an extraordinary person Poppy Day. Martin is very lucky to have you on his side.'

This made her smile, not because of the compliment, but because she doubted that Martin felt very lucky about anything at that point in time.

He carried on, 'You are a real tour de force. Maybe it *is* down to you, maybe you should go and get him back yourself!'

He laughed and she laughed, but unbeknown to both, a tiny seed had been sown. A small kernel of a solution that over the next few hours would be fed, watered and would grow until it had legs. Then Poppy would have no choice but to run with it.

Poppy headed straight to 'The Unpopulars', still in her finery.

'What's the matter Poppy Day?'

'Nothing Nan, I'm fine.'

'I know you are not fine, so don't say that to me if it isn't true.'

Her voice was slightly sterner than usual. She hated Poppy not being straight with her, knowing her well enough to sense when she was not.

'I am a bit worried about Mart, Nan. You know Mart? Mart, my husband,' she added the little memory jogger in case his was one of the names and faces that was lost. Poppy pictured Dorothea's memory like a big fishing net, with the holes getting bigger and bigger, wider and wider apart, so more and more stuff fell through. What was left sitting on top were the biggest, most important fish that wouldn't disappear until the net had almost gone. Poppy figured she must be like one of those enormous tuna fish that took three Japanese men to haul over the side. When they do it's amid a tidal wave of blood and guts as the filleting begins. That was Poppy; a giant flapping tuna fish, caught in her nan's net, not going anywhere, not just yet.

'I know who Mart is for Gawd's sake,' it was the stern voice once again.

Poppy thought carefully about how to phrase what came next, searched for the right tone and level of detail, avoiding at all times the full-blown horror. She mentally edited her response, 'You know that he went to visit Afghanistan?'

'Fighting wasn't he?"

'Yes Nan, fighting, well, he has only gone and got himself

lost!' she tried a small giggle to show Dorothea that there
was nothing to worry about, that she was fine, that it was
all fine.

'Lost?'

'Yes Nan, lost.'

'What on earth do you mean girl? Do you mean he
needs a map or do you mean lost in action, killed, dead.'

'No! No, not killed and not dead. He's...' Poppy
struggled again to find the right tone and wording.

She pictured him them, his frightened eyes, the blow to
the stomach. She bowed her head until her chin was on her
chest. She always thought of him tethered, with a rope or a
sheet and always in a makeshift blindfold. She pictured him
dirty, ingrained with filth and needing a wash. She couldn't
stop the steady flow of tears that slid down her face and
snaked unbidden into her mouth, 'Oh Nan!'

Exhaustion and worry caught up with her; Poppy
dropped to the floor. She knelt on the lino at her nan's feet,
where the scrub marks of a thousand little accidents were
etched on its surface. She placed her head on Dorothea's
lap as the old lady stroked her hair. It was exactly what she
needed, to be six again, to have her nan pet her hair and
tell her in between 'shhhhh's' that everything was going to
be alright. The skin of her knees stung against the cold
hard floor, but Poppy didn't care. She could have stayed
there for hours. She wanted to stay there for hours. It felt
wonderful for a minute, not to be the person that held it all
together, but instead to be taken care of, even if it was just
for a minute.

Her nan's knobbled, bent fingers stroked her hair and
face as she cried into the crimplene trousers with their
elasticated waist. It made Poppy smile to think that she
would leave a damp patch that later might be misconstrued.

Nathan would tut as he changed her for bed. At least he had the joy of knowing that all his hard work and effort would be rewarded when he got his hands on those million pounds.

'Now Poppy Day, sit up straight and tell me what this is all about? Why the tears? This isn't like you at all,' she cupped her granddaughters face in her crooked hands and made her look up. Poppy sidled off the floor and took her place on the creaky plastic chair. Dorothea took Poppy's hand into her cold, smooth palms and, for the second time that night, the girl was grateful for her nan's contact, 'Come on Poppy Day, whasamatter darlin'?'

Poppy drew a sharp breath and shared her burden with the only person in the world other than Martin who might care about what she was going through, 'Mart is missing Nan. Well, that's what they say officially, but the truth is they know where he is. He is being held by a religious fundamentalist group...'

'Baddies?'

Poppy smiled, 'Yes, baddies. The worrying thing Nan is that I don't think that anyone is trying very hard to get him back, almost like they are going to let him be lost and hope that he just, disappears.' The horror of these words spoken aloud caused her tears to spring again.

'Is he still alive darlin'? '

'Yes.' It was as definitive as she could make it. Poppy had to believe that he was. She still thought that she would 'feel' if anything else were true; her husband, her love.

'Are people helping you? You know, his work people?'

'Yes. In fact I had a meeting at Downing Street today; imagine that, Nan, me at Downing Street! I met with the Foreign Secretary; fat lot of good it did me.'

Dorothea ignored this inconsequential piece of

information. Loopy or not, she had little regard for title, money or status. What would she say, in her more lucid years? 'I couldn't give a rat's arse if he was the Queen of Sheba, Poppy Day. People is people. We all come into the world the same way, we all leave it the same way and that makes us all equal.'

'And you think you know where he is?'

'Yes Nan, not exactly, but roughly whereabouts.'

She bent towards her granddaughter as though they were co-conspirators, speaking slowly after a few seconds pause, she whispered, 'You need to go and get him Poppy Day. You need to go and find him and bring him home. He is your husband and he loves you. When I'm gone he is all that you'll have left,' she was direct, she was lucid and she was far, far from crazy.

Poppy stared at her. The tears stopped falling. She laughed and her nan laughed back. She was right, he was her husband, he loved her and when her nan was gone, he would be all that she would have left. It struck her as more than a coincidence that two people had said the very same thing to her in as many hours. A quirky twist of fate? To some maybe, but not to Poppy, to her it was a sign.

Poppy's future without Martin was unthinkable. If you asked any of their friends about the Cricket/Day duo, they'd say that it was hard to think of one without the other, like an old couple that have been together for so long they are viewed as a single unit. So much so, that when you said one of their names, your lips automatically form the shape to say the other, like fish 'n' chips or Fred 'n' Ginger.

They had been a proper couple from the age of fourteen as opposed to best mates since they were six. Was this sweet or a little bit sad? How did they know if they were with the right person if they haven't looked anywhere else, or tried loving other people? Did they simply settle for what was on offer? These would be fair questions, but it would be wrong to assign them any credence. Very wrong.

As with the Jackie Sinclair in the playground episode, any sense of danger, embarrassment or harm that could possibly come to Poppy and ping! Martin would be there like a genie from a magic lamp, to soften the blow, make sure she wasn't hurt and comfort her when and wherever she needed it. They may have known each other since they were six years old, but what they shared was deep, dedicated love. She would die for him and him, her. That's just how it is. To the ears of the cynical this might sound clichéd, but for Poppy and Martin it was the foundation of their love, a deep, unspoken commitment to be there when they were needed, wherever they were needed.

Poppy considered the idea of going out to Afghanistan and the possibility that she might be able to bring him back. Strangely it didn't feel stupid or implausible; in fact, quite the opposite, it felt possible and necessary. It was the solution that she'd been searching for. Poppy knew, without any shadow of doubt, that there was no one in the whole wide world who would have the same vested interest in bringing Martin home as her. No one else would lose sleep or the will to live because he was missing. It was down to her, she had to be the one to bring him home. Her, Poppy Day, she would go and get her husband back! Practicality started to creep into the idea, blurring the edges of the plan, 'I won't be able to see you every day Nan if I have to go and get Mart. I might be gone for a little while and I don't know how long.'

Dorothea shrugged her shoulders. These words were of little interest, as if not seeing her for a while was a sacrifice that they would both have to be make. She was right.

'Oh 'ello Nathan!' He stood in the doorway, 'I'm so glad you are here. There is someone that I would like you to meet...'

Nathan stepped forward and shook Poppy's hand, 'Pleased to meet you Poppy Day.' Nathan realized as soon as he had spoken that they had not yet been 'introduced.'

They paused, mid-handshake, both staring at Dorothea, waiting for her reaction. She looked down at the wet patch on her trousers and looked back up at Nathan, 'I appear to have pissed myself.' Nathan and Poppy laughed long and hard as Dorothea sat stony faced, unmoved by their hysterics.

Later, when she was ready for bed, resplendent in her flannelette pyjamas and bed jacket, Poppy stood and kissed her on the forehead, 'Goodnight Nan, I'll see you tomorrow. Have sweet dreams.'

'You have sweet dreams too my Poppy Day.'

Poppy stood to walk out of the room.

Her nan's voice halted her progress, 'Poppy Day?'

'Yes Nan?'

'Don't waste a single second my girl. I don't want to see you here tomorrow. You go tomorrow; you go and get him back. I'll be right here waiting and I'll see you when you come home.' She looked away from her then, fixated by the TV remote control; there had to be a cookery programme on somewhere.

Poppy leant her head on the frame and captured the image inside her head. She whispered across the air, the atmosphere now full of the canned laughter and recorded clapping from the crap on TV, 'Thank you, I will Nan. I will bring him home. I love you.'

Nine

Once again Martin dreamt that he was woken by Poppy. He could tell it was Poppy by her touch and smell. Again she stroked the hair away from his forehead. Her voice was gentle, 'Mart... Mart... It's OK baby, I am here...'

This particular dream was the worst form of torture. He would have preferred a short physical shock than the dreadful slow realisation that her presence was a vision and he was still so very far away from her.

When Martin reluctantly opened his eyes, he spied a tiny white feather that had danced through a small gap and found a resting place on his arm. He pinched it between his thumb and forefinger, raising it to his lips, feeling the sweet tickle against his skin. To most, it would be seen as a little white feather that had drifted into the room, shaken from a far-off eiderdown or fallen from a scrawny chicken, but for Martin it was a gift from his Poppy; a signal of hope, a token of love. He held it tight and he kept it.

The day, that started with such an offering, continued to be a memorable one. 'Man U' entered the room, beaming and clearly excited about something. He had an agitation that Martin recognised in someone who has a secret, usually either a practical joke or surprise present, but something so exciting that the information is literally waiting to burst out of them. Man U could hardly contain himself. After hopping from one foot to the other, he pulled his hand from behind his back to reveal two folded pieces of newspaper. He held them out to Martin. He had bought him a gift and was very pleased with himself.

'What is it?' Martin was curious, as eager as a child for the diversion.

'Manchester United!'

Martin took the newspaper into his hands. It was one complete page and a cutting of about eight square inches. He hadn't read or seen written English in what felt like a very long time. His eyes took a little while to focus on the black print that was slightly smudged in places. The whole time he studied it, Man U stood nodding and smiling, like an eager puppy wanting praise and recognition. Martin laughed loudly and put his hand on the man's arm. There was never much physical contact; his captor could read a lot by the gesture. He was absolutely delighted.

Martin, in recent years, had tried to make up for his lack of academic achievement by reading. To say he was a big reader wouldn't cut it; he was an avid, addicted reader, devouring books on any topic as though making up for lost time. He remembered what he read, which gave him an incredible vocabulary and a wide knowledge. He felt a certain embarrassment about learning that was typical of his peer group, reading secretly and never confessing to his mates that he deliberated over Le Carre as well as watching the football. Poppy would tease him, 'No one cares that you are a book-obsessed nerd Mart! The bigger boys aren't going to pick on you now, you are a grown-up and you can do what you like!' He would usually throw whatever he was reading at her. To be able to study words, no matter how random the reading material, was a wonderful gift.

The smaller piece was an advertisement, a complete advert taken from a paper. It was fascinating. '*Dyson*' it read across the top, Martin learnt it word for word;

Ball technology: The idea for Ball™ technology came about from an engineer studying new ways to steer. It started crudely - an old wand handle attached to a wheel. Eventually the wheel became a ball and an ideal home for the motor. We've done

away with wheels. The new Dyson upright machines ride on a ball
so you can steer with ease, no more push/pull around corners and
obstacles. Inside the ball is the motor, giving the machine a lower
centre of gravity and improving manoeuvrability even further.

It wasn't that Martin was particularly interested in housework, but it was a link to another world, his world. In that place that was strange and unfamiliar, here was a little square of paper that enabled him to picture the carpet at home, their furniture and the two of them sitting on it. He could envisage his Poppy doing the housework and it gave him comfort.

It was a scrappy piece of paper that was so much greater than the sum of its parts. Martin figured that it had probably been touched by hands like his, belonging to someone who would live in a house, in England. Possibly someone like him, imagine! After days of having very little to do, other than reflect on his predicament, this gave him something to concentrate on; the idea for the product, how it might work. Martin spent hours trying to understand the technology.

As if the advert wasn't amazing enough, the other page was completely bloody brilliant! It wasn't news of the campaign or information about the world in general, it was much, much better than that. It was a TV listing page, a whole page of telly programmes. It detailed shows from a weekday. The top of the page had been ripped off, so it was impossible to know what the day or date was, but it didn't matter. Martin could tell that it was a weekday by the lack of a 'big Saturday night' programme or film.

He went through each programme, reading the content synopsis. He then lay back and imagined the particular show, picturing it and joining it together with episodes that he had seen or could remember. He got so good at this;

it was just like watching the telly inside his head. There was an episode of *Only Fools and Horses* billed as 'Yuppie Love'. It was the one where Del Boy and Trigger end up in a wine bar with a bunch of yuppies. Martin considered it the best bit of television in the whole world. He and all his mates loved it; it's the episode where he falls through the bar. Martin lay on the mattress, hearing the words, picturing Del Boy with his elbow out, drink in hand and bang! Whenever he watched the clip, it made no difference that he knew what was going to happen, and when he waited for it, it was still hilarious as Del Boy fell from view, smack onto the floor. Martin laughed until he cried. It was brilliant.

Every programme on that sheet got the same treatment, even the kids' shows, most of which he'd never heard of. Martin had never considered himself to have a good imagination, but this disproved the belief. He took bits of information and turned them into shows inside his head. It was magnificent.

Physically, Martin was in bad shape. The severe beating he had received upon capture had left him sore, bruised and aching. Having existed for a few days with his hands above his head, his shoulders had been left with an acute pain that peaked every time he moved. One of his fingers had been broken and started to heal without any attention. It throbbed when left alone, but if snagged against the mattress or his clothing, sent a searing pain shooting up his wrist. It was a constant reminder of what he had been through, made him think how lucky he was to have survived. It made him think of Aaron.

His face had suffered after its incarceration in the filthy sack. His eyes continued to ooze, clotting his eyelashes upon waking and impairing his vision; it was as if he viewed the world through gauze. His teeth felt loose in their gums, he would regularly spit large globules of blood, flecked with gum and fragments of tooth.

When he had been taken he had been very fit and muscly, which helped. His deterioration would have taken a worse toll on someone less able. He would run his hand over his torso, feeling his battered ribs, fondling the scabs of coagulated blood with his fingertips; nature's salve for the man-made digs and scratches.

He was given a meal once a day; the guards would eat when he ate and what he ate. He wasn't deprived of food; the meagre rations were not confined to him. It was always rice with some vegetables and sometimes a splash of yoghurt. Once or twice there was meat, small pieces of chicken and another brown meat, possibly lamb. Martin definitely wasn't getting enough protein, none of them were. The guards looked thin, like they too needed iron and more calories. Martin felt that he was morphing into them, especially with his two-week beard growth. He was as unkempt and battered as an old mule, and he smelt about the same.

He had a terrible upset stomach. It was the worst thing imaginable, with only a dirty bucket to use for the loo and no water for hand washing, but he knew the importance of eating, to keep his strength up and to survive. He quickly got used to the food. He was so hungry, he didn't think too much about what he was getting, happy to be getting something. The guards shared a large plate at meal times, eating with their fingers. Martin was served in a separate smaller bowl; they didn't want him to contaminate their food.

He lay on the bed and considered how he had deteriorated in such a short space of time; remembering the soldier that arrived in Afghanistan, full of energy, with a longing to get the job done and get back to his wife. Returning to Poppy had remained his primary focus.

He tried to calculate how much closer he would be to getting home had he not been captured. He could only guess, but he reckoned it would be approximately ninety shaves...

Ten

Poppy didn't prepare. She wasn't thinking straight; functioning on auto pilot, without packing or saying goodbye, she left. Anyone watching her lock the front door, with the familiar double push to check it was secure, or encountering her in the lift, would think that she was off to the shops, or to visit her nan. There were no outward clues, nothing that would indicate what she was planning.

Sliding down on the nicotine-scented, velour seat, Poppy watched the concrete of the capital give way to industrial estates. The rhythmic sway of the car encouraged her to doze; one minute grey factories and warehouses, and the next, houses, all squished together with identikit white, plastic conservatories bolted on the back. Hundreds of families carrying out their lives, shopping, sleeping, eating and loving, cocooned within those red brick walls and draughty lean-tos. Postage stamp-sized gardens were littered with trampolines, rusted swing sets, abandoned ride-on tractors and deflated paddling pools. Food-encrusted barbeques and grubby gazebos sat amongst miles of clean clothing that shifted gently in the breeze. It all belonged to people, people in families. Poppy envied each and every one of them.

Finally, the backdrop was countryside and cows replaced people. She knew she must be getting close. Houses and, then, fields as the world sped by through the taxi window. Almost three hours after leaving E17, the boxy Nissan dropped her off at the entrance to the base. She handed over the contents of her savings jar and stood alone in front of the high-wire fence, feeling instantly self-conscious and slightly illegal.

RAF Brize Norton was like a large airport without

any of the advertising hoardings, shopping malls, car parks or shuttle buses. The surrounding perimeter fence was ominously topped with barbed wire. It made Poppy think of prison and concentration camps.

There were military signs everywhere, telling Poppy that she was entering a Ministry of Defence Facility, where only authorised access was permitted, along with other deterrent messaging. She felt as if those signs were written especially for her, they might as well have said, 'PS: Go Home Poppy Day, Leave Right Now!' But Poppy was determined, she had come this far and wasn't about to give up, not yet.

She walked through the gates, past low-level huts with corrugated iron roofs, until she arrived at the security building. There was a queue of people. It reminded her of the snaking lines that you see in Argos, as though they had all taken little tickets and were waiting for their number to come up, 'Number forty-three!'. But no one there was waiting to get their hands on irons, sandwich toasters or pieces of flimsy gym equipment that you might use for a month before shoving under the bed for a further six months and then disposing of.

Instead, they were clutching passports and pieces of paper saying goodness knows what. What did Poppy have in her bag? A change of pants; her striped notebook with matching pencil; a photo of her and Mart, opportunely snapped in a photo booth at Kings Cross before jumping on the tube; a pot of cherry lip balm; a packet of Polo's; a bottle of perfume, 'Angel' by Thierry Mugler, which she loved because it smelled like chocolate; a bunch of keys; her fake Gucci sunglasses and her iPod – sadly no passport.

Not that Poppy had expected to find a passport, she didn't own one. They were for other people, people like Harriet and her family who jetted off to the South of

France and sent postcards from towns just outside of Cognac. The queue was moving quickly, Poppy didn't have any time to think, which was probably a good thing.

The large gap in front of her meant it was her turn to approach the counter. Poppy stood in front of the burly female security guard, or RAF person, she couldn't decide which. With the RAF wearing that particular grey/blue colour, they looked the same as the security guards that patrolled the floors at Bluewater, or the man in Poppy's local precinct that chased all the fourteen-year-old shop lifters until he ran out of puff, which was usually just past WH Smith. The woman wore her hair in a tightly scraped bun, her florid complexion devoid of makeup.

'Yes?' the woman waited, knowing what Poppy's response should be, but sadly Poppy didn't.

'Hello,' it bought her a couple of seconds.

The woman had the twitchy mouth of someone that was starting to lose patience, 'HellowhatcanIdoforyou?' She tried to make up the time that Poppy was losing by speaking extra quickly.

'I've come to say goodbye to my husband, he is flying out today.'

The woman nodded, 'Where to?'

'Afghanistan.'

'Passport please.'

Poppy bit her bottom lip, 'I haven't got my passport.' She could feel genuine tears gathering; not the fake this-would-be-a-good-time-to-cry variety, but genuine tears as she thought to herself, 'What the bloody hell are you doing Poppy? Why are you here? You are a hairdresser from Walthamstow, what did you possibly think that you could achieve?'

'I need to see your passport,' the woman's eyes darted

above Poppy's head as she assessed the numbers waiting, trying to emphasise the need for haste.

Poppy's tears fell unchecked; she did nothing to stop them, 'I didn't know I would need my passport. I just wanted to surprise Martin.' Poppy felt it was alright to say that because it wasn't a lie. She was telling her the absolute truth; she wanted to surprise her husband...

The woman breathed out, speaking more slowly this time, 'Do you have any other form of ID on you, your driving licence, anything with a photograph?'

Poppy fumbled in her bag, lip balm, notebook... she spied her purse, was there anything in there of use? Bank card, library card (no photo), eighteen pounds in cash and some coins. She shook her head.

'I'm sorry. I can't let you through without your passport or other photographic ID. I'm very sorry.'

Poppy looked her in the eye. Her mind raced with two main themes. Firstly, how was she going to get back to London from wherever the hell she was? Secondly, was this it? Was this as far as she was going to get in the great, 'I'm off to rescue Martin plan'? She felt pathetic. Her voice sounded small and defeated even to her own ears, 'I don't have a passport. I've never had one because I have never been anywhere, and I never will go anywhere. I'm not like bloody Harriet or one of those girls that nips off to Europe with her girlfriends on her gap year. I am going nowhere, not ever. I only came all this way in a stinking bloody taxi because I wanted to surprise my husband. I didn't know about the passport thing.'

The woman sighed again, casting her eyes over Poppy, checking her out and making a judgement call, 'Have you got anything else useful on you, anything at all?'

Poppy could see that she was giving her a chance, trying

to help, wanting her to succeed, 'I don't have any proper ID, but I've got my library card and my bank card.' Poppy held out the small plastic rectangles.

The woman hesitated before taking them, 'Look at the camera please.' Poppy looked up into the little white square and tried not to cry some more.

The woman disappeared for what felt like hours and returned with a two-page form, 'Can you fill this out please?'

Poppy picked up the plastic Bic pen with the chewed end from the counter, and filled out her name, address, date of birth and, bizarrely, her national insurance number. Her hand was shaking; tears and a runny nose were smeared at regular intervals across her cheeks with the back of her hand.

Poppy handed over the form, not sure what was going to happen next, still expecting to be turned around and escorted from the base. The woman left the desk again and came back with a laminated blue square. Poppy's picture was in the top left corner, her tearstained face looked back at her. The details she had given were captured behind the sheet of plastic, all accurate, right down to her national insurance number. It hadn't occurred to her to lie.

'Do you know where you are going?'

Poppy shook her head, still unsure if she was being told to leave or whether she was going to where the planes took off.

The woman gave Poppy a paper map and drew a cross on it with a red felt-tip pen, 'You are here. When you get outside, turn left, then right and then straight on. You'll eventually see the car park for the terminal.'

Was that it? Surely it couldn't be that simple? Surely this woman was not going to let her go through? But she did.

Poppy allowed herself a small smile, 'Thank you.'

'Remember your photo ID next time, OK?' she gave Poppy a small smile in return.

'OK, thank you,' Poppy knew that there would not be a next time. She didn't know why the woman let her through. Maybe she, too, knew what it felt like not to be Harriet. Maybe she had hoped for more from life than scrutinising passports at the security desk. Whatever the reason, Poppy would always be grateful.

She walked out into the blue day with its clear sky and clean air; it was crisp and pretty, typically English. Poppy looked out of the base to the fields and green spaces that surrounded it. She thought how lovely it must be to live in the countryside, to be able to breathe this air every day without the stench of drains, cars and people at every turn. She decided that when she had her baby, she would want to bring it up somewhere like this, in a house big enough for Dorothea as well. One big, happy, crazy family, living in the countryside; it would be like *The Darling Buds of May* meets *EastEnders*. She was already worrying about Dorothea. It was hard to believe that it was only last night she had told her to go and get Martin. Poppy had travelled millions of miles in her mind since then.

'Do you need the minibus?'

Poppy looked at the man as though she knew what he was talking about.

'Are you press?'

Poppy nodded.

'Right then, luggage in the back and hop in, we'll be off in five. There are a couple of others to wait for.'

She didn't trust herself to speak. She wandered towards the minibus parked at an angle a few feet away. There were already people sitting inside; three men, all in casual clothes, not uniform, not army, not RAF.

Poppy walked to the open door, ignoring the double doors at the back; she didn't have any luggage to deposit there. She considered undoing her handbag and laying her single pair of pants in the back, but decided against it.

She trod the steps up into the vehicle. All eyes turned towards her, she received a 'Hi', 'Hello' and a nod. They were all very polite. Poppy was relieved not to hear the cry of outrage that she had half expected, 'Who are you? Get off our very important bus for very important people, which you are not!' There was, instead, silence as they surveyed her; not to critically scrutinise, but more as though they were appraising an equal, which she didn't mind at all. The three men were in their thirties. All wore cargo pants, walking boots, fleeces and waterproof coats which meant they were either mountain climbers, outdoorsy types or tossers.

They looked harmless enough, well groomed, soft and educated; not the sort of people she usually mixed with. Poppy plugged her iPod into her ears, but didn't turn it on, she wanted to listen. Everyone turned their heads towards the door as a man's voice started singing loudly, 'Whoa I'm goin' to Barbados! Diddle iddle do do! Whoa! Palm tree, palm tree!' The three started laughing. One of them looked at Poppy, 'Guess who?' She smiled a little, but tried not to join in, wanting to fade into the background. She didn't want to guess who.

The voice that had been singing clambered onto the bus. He was black, in his late twenties with a camera around his neck, 'Hey lovely people! Here we all are aboard the love bus! Let the adventures begin!' He was frightfully posh.

He made his way down the aisle, shaking hands with or hugging his colleagues. He looked quizzically at Poppy.

She felt awkward, fearing that it was obvious to him that she shouldn't have been there. He sat two seats behind her. He spoke to the blonde man sitting opposite him, 'Who's Freckles?' Poppy concentrated on looking out of the window, trying not to listen or give herself away. She could sense the blonde guy shrugging, hear the crumpling of his acrylic jacket; he didn't know, none of them did. The strange thing was that Poppy wasn't sure that she knew, who had she become?

The black guy got out of his seat to stand in front of her, 'Hello!' he stuck out his hand. Poppy took it; he shook hers up and down vigorously with pantomime-like exaggeration for what felt like a bit too long. 'I am Jason Mullen. How do you do? I'm *Sunday Times* and this is Max Holman, freelance,' he pointed to one of the blokes, 'Michael Newman, *Telegraph*, Jack Hail, *Sunday Times*.'

Poppy nodded nervously at each one. She couldn't find her voice; couldn't find any voice, what would come next? Were they going to throw her off the bus? Were they going to ask for her passport? Did they want proof that she was allowed to travel with them? No they didn't, none of those things.

Jason carried on, obviously intrigued, 'So, you are..?'

Poppy chewed her lip; she was thinking and didn't answer instantly.

He filled the gap, 'It's customary in our country if someone gives you their name by way of introduction to return the same information; we call it 'getting acquainted,' or 'saying hello!''

Poppy couldn't decide if he was rude or impatient. She couldn't think fast enough.

Jason spoke again, making his own suppositions, 'Aaah, do you not speak English? Is that it? Français?

Deutsch? Español?'

She smiled at him; he was funny.

'Well, that's me done; I only know those four languages. Well, five including the language of lurve, which I am very happy to converse in with you Freckles, any time...'

'Leave her alone Jase,' it was Max Holman, Freelance, that had come to her rescue.

Jason sat down and the group commenced discussing a prestigious award that one Miles Varrasso had been given only a month before. Jason, especially, seemed more than a little impressed by the accolade, saying very loudly how Miles was 'the man.' Poppy was curious to know what her Mr Subversive had done, having never heard of the particular award or the 'scoop' that had earned him the prize.

The bus engine roared as the chassis shuddered into life. Once again Jason burst into song, 'I'm on my way from misery to happiness today...' Poppy liked his energy; at least she knew her adventure wasn't going to be dull with Jason around. Little did she know...

The bus slowed as the barrier was manually raised by an armed airman; it then hurtled along a straight road flanked by large aircraft hangers on either side, before negotiating several mini roundabouts. A few minutes later, the bus started to brake and halt. It would have been quicker to walk to the terminal than to sit and wait; the security aspect wasn't something she considered. Poppy got off the bus and loitered next to the guys; wanting to feel like part of their group, wanting to feel like part of anything, other than face the reality that she was completely alone and didn't know what came next. The 'press' guys seemed to have a huge amount of bags and equipment; for this she was grateful and could pretend that at least one of those black zipped-up holdalls was hers.

The terminal inside was one huge room, about two thirds of it filled with plastic chairs that were screwed into the floor. What did the MoD think? That a daring soldier in transit may try and sneak a couple onto the plane or into their hand luggage? There was a small cafe which looked far too tiny to cope with the throng of soldiers, service men and women that stood around in their desert combats, looking alternately nervous and excited.

Three young girls with buggies and babies stood together just inside the door. They were wearing tracksuit bottoms and sweatshirts. Their blonde striped hair was pulled back into ponytails; they sported the obligatory graduating gold hoops and necklaces. Poppy wondered if they knew each other before they had arrived, or whether they had all bunched together for support, happy to have found someone like them. They looked like the sort of girls that she would have been friends with, reminding her of Jenna. They looked like her. She stopped herself going over to them, to try and join in, to seek out kindred spirits.

One of the girls was red eyed and inconsolable. She held a soggy, disintegrating paper tissue against her blotchy face. Her body convulsed every time she tried to breathe in, every time she cried. With her free hand she scooted a small, sleeping baby back and forth in its buggy, whilst waving occasionally to a soldier who looked younger than the rest. The young Private stared mostly at his feet, as the queue in which he stood wound its way into another room. He laughed at the inaudible things the bloke behind him was saying, but chewed his bottom lip in between the laughing, his shoulders hung down. He wasn't fooling anyone, for the want of an ounce of confidence or another year of maturity, he would have run to his woman, taken her in his arms and told her that it was all going to be OK.

One final kiss, one final hug.

Poppy wanted to shout at him, 'You are right to feel like that, don't go! They have taken my Mart! My husband is missing! Stay here with your baby, please don't leave them, whatever you are thinking, this is not worth it!' She kept quiet. She thought about Martin then, flying out from that exact spot. Had he stood there? Had he thought about her as he had disappeared through those double doors that lead to who knows where? She knew the answer was yes, yes he had thought about her, of course he had. Oh Mart, where were you?

Poppy noted the way the men and women in uniform reacted to the orders being barked; it was almost instinctive, 'Weapons to be checked in! Make sure you have no prohibited items in pockets and hand luggage! Bags in the crate! Helmets to be properly labelled and kept on your person at all times!' All military personnel appeared comfortable with the instructions. It was nothing that they hadn't done a million times before, but this wasn't a drill, it was the real thing. They were shipping out, off to the action; Afghanistan.

There seemed to be lots of banter, jostling and childish humour. Poppy suspected these were the tactics deployed to hide how they were really feeling. It wasn't the 'done thing' to admit to anxiety, nerves or even the underlying excitement, particularly the excitement. It probably induced guilt to be finding any joy in their situation, but Poppy could see that there was joy. It was actually happening, it was real. They were going to work, to do the job that they had been trained for. The thrill must have been tempered, if not cancelled out, by self-reproach. It must have been hard to feel happiness, knowing that the people you were leaving behind would worry and miss you. Poppy knew for a fact that the last thing those left behind would be feeling was excited or happy, she knew they would be feeling desolate.

An RAF bloke with a clipboard stood in front of the group and coughed loudly. It made Poppy laugh. Was that how he thought he could get everyone's attention, a jolly good cough? 'Righto, ladies and gentleman of the press. I am Flight Lieutenant Ward and I am your press liaison officer for the duration of your trip. I know you are all seasoned hands, but any questions please do shout.' There was the rumbling of gentle laughter at the very idea of having any questions.

He shouted out a name, and a chap that she had not seen before put his hand up and walked forward. He was given something; it looked to be a folder of some description. This went on for some minutes. Poppy watched with fascination as men, all similar types, were called and marched up like little children at a school prize giving; all eager to be seen and collect their scrolls.

She was concentrating on what was happening, trying to think of her next move, when he said it again. And it was only because he repeated it that she became aware that he had said it once before, 'Nina Folkstok?' Only the second time he went up at the end.

Poppy glanced around and no one was responding. Every other name that he had called had caused a hand to shoot up immediately and claim the identity. This one, however, seemed to be going spare. Poppy didn't know why or how, but she put her hand in the air. Not half-heartedly, or in a way that anyone watching might suspect that she was not Nina Folkstok; it was, instead, a full confident raised arm, like the one she used in school. 'Capital of Peru?' 'Lima'! Up her arm would shoot! 'Oberon's Queen?' 'Titania!' ...up it would go again. Poppy couldn't help it, when she knew the answer, she wanted everyone to see that she knew the answer; it was important to her.

This was like that, a straight up instant reflex, in no way bashful or apologetic, an 'It's-the-God's-honest-truth-look-how-straight-my-arm-is' response, 'Yup'. No one laughed or challenged her. No one questioned or even looked at her. She walked forward and the crowd seemed to part slightly. Flight Lieutenant cough-a-lot, handed her the plastic A4 wallet, without looking at her face. He nodded in general acknowledgment as he searched his list for the next name, using his Montblanc as a pointer. Poppy walked back to the space that she had previously occupied. She opened the package and studied the contents; not because she was particularly interested, but it was the only way she could guarantee not to catch anyone's eye. She could deny herself the chance to smile and say, 'I'm not really Nina Folkestone or whatever her bloody name is, not really. I don't even know why I put my hand up! I am actually Poppy Day and I live in Walthamstow. I'm a hairdresser you know.'

There was a pass in the envelope, laminated plastic on a yellow thread with the name 'Nina Folkstok' on it and then the word, 'Denmark'. Shit! Of all the countries that Nina could have hailed from! Had it been France, Spain, or Germany, Poppy could have picked a city, faked some history, dropped in some plausible facts and even had a stab at the language, but Denmark? Thanks a bunch Nina. Poppy had to think fast. What was the capital city? Oslo? No, that was Norway... Denmark's capital city was... Copenhagen! Of course! Wonderful, wonderful, Copenhagen.

Poppy was smiling, happy to have this fact in her head, when a man sauntered over. She missed what he said the first time because she was thinking about Copenhagen

and not how she should react if someone spoke to her.
She heard him clearly the second time, 'Hi Nina, would
you like to accompany me outside for a cigarette? We are
going to be a long time up.' He then pointed with his
index finger towards the sky. Poppy looked at the familiar
animated palm of the smoker and recognised the owner of
that hand. It was her Mr Subversive, Miles Varrasso.

She shook her head, 'No thanks.' Poppy felt the creep of
embarrassment over her neck and face. She spoke quietly
so as not to alert anyone in close proximity to the fact that
she was actually from Walthamstow and not West Jutland.

Miles Varrasso stood by her side, 'Are you sure?' his
emphasis was on the last word 'sure'.

'I… Yes,' she almost stammered, but not quite; managing
to sound quite normal for a very scared Danish journalist
that had never been to Denmark or flown on a plane before.
She had been identified by the one person that she had
hoped she would not bump into. Her heart thudded inside
her ribcage.

Miles leant closer towards Poppy, bending his head
until their fringes were nearly touching; he was too close
for her to feel comfortable. She could see dust on the
inside of his glasses, and tiny pinpricks where blackheads
used to lurk on the side of his nose. She wanted to take
a step backwards, but she couldn't move. She was stuck.
He seemed to hesitate before speaking. He breathed out;
she could smell his aftershave, minty chewing gum and the
tang of cigarette smoke. He put one arm across his stomach
and his other hand up onto his chin, the elbow of that arm
resting on the one across his stomach, making a little frame.
He had two of his fingers raised, almost hiding his mouth, as
if someone might be trying to lip read and this would stop
them. Poppy looked up from under her fringe and waited

for him to speak.

He ran the point of his tongue over his top lip, 'What are you doing here Poppy? Are the MoD shipping you out? Has something happened? Is there anyone 'in coming' I should know about?'

Her mouth had gone dry; her lips were somehow stuck to her teeth. She smiled at Miles' interest, keen to secure the scoop. If only. She closed her eyes, thinking for a glorious second that if she couldn't see anyone or anything then they couldn't see her, like an Ostrich or baby playing peek-a-boo.

She opened her eyes slowly; he was still there with his long curly hair and his fixed expression, 'No Miles, nothing like that. I'm here on my own.'

'It's OK Poppy; you don't have to look so scared.'

'I look scared because I am,' she had to concentrate on not crying because the truth of the matter was, she was really frightened. Afraid of so many things, like crying in front of all those people and making an idiot of herself, of being thrown off the base, not being allowed to fly, being made to fly; but primarily she was scared of not getting to the place she needed to, so that she could find her husband and bring him home.

'Miles, what am I doing?'

He pushed the glasses up on his nose, 'Come outside, we haven't got long.'

Poppy didn't know where she was going or what he meant, but she followed him anyway. Sometimes in life you just have to go with your instinct and listen to that little voice that tells you to trust, to follow. It is usually right.

They turned left out of the automatic doors and, once outside, stood against the wall of the terminal building. Poppy looked at the red bricks that firmly placed its construction in the nineteen seventies. She was trying to think of anything other than what he might be about to say to her. She had been asking herself a question; how far do you honestly think that you will get Poppy? Now she was only seconds away from the answer, she had made it to the flight terminal, and that was that, only to be busted by Miles.

He held her arm as though this was the best way to get her attention. She noticed that his fringe was far too long and thought about offering to snip it for him, she was fully qualified after all. Gone was the jovial banter of their coffee shop encounter, he looked deadly serious; no trace of anything in his expression other than urgent.

He spoke quickly. Poppy understood that time really was of the essence, 'Poppy, what are you doing here?'

'Truthfully? I'm not too sure. I've got half a plan…'

'Christ, I shouldn't have told you I was flying out today. Is it my fault that you're here?'

Poppy shrugged, unsure how to answer, it was partly his fault. She wouldn't have known there was a flight today if he hadn't told her, but she hadn't expected to bump into him directly, figuring there must be several flights a day and if you missed one, you could hop onto the next, like the circle line but with fewer stops and better air conditioning.

Miles ran one hand through his hair and with the other he held his chin, 'Shit.'

'Is that good or bad shit Miles?'

'Honestly?'

Poppy nodded.

'I don't know,' he paced to the left and right before stepping closer. Once again Poppy felt he was too close to her. He spoke quickly and sounded even posher than he had before, 'How did you get to this point? Did you use a false name?'

'A false name?' she laughed out loud, accompanied by one of her unattractive nose snorts that she had a habit of producing. Who the bloody hell did he think she was? She was Poppy Day not James Bond! 'No, I didn't use a false name. I used my own name and I didn't have my passport, so I showed them my bank card and my library card.'

It was Miles' turn to laugh, 'You are kidding me right? You waltzed into the security check point with no passport, you filled out the relevant documentation with your real name and details (that being the wife of the most highly publicized British soldier at this point in time), and they allowed you to breeze through; and you have now taken the identity of a Danish journalist who is probably stuck on the A40 right now, hoping that she doesn't miss her flight?'

'Yes, that's about it.'

Miles shook his head as though it was unbelievable, but believe her he did, 'Poppy, we haven't much time. I need to understand the situation, because if you are trying to do what I think you are trying to do, I just might be able to help you and if you are not, then you just might be in a whole heap of trouble, so speak to me and do it very quickly.' He looked at his watch, making Poppy feel as if she was being timed, which only made her gabble and rush. She wasn't sure that she made any sense.

Poppy swallowed, knowing that she had to trust him, and that she had to talk, 'I have decided to go and get Mart. I am going to find him. I know that sounds crazy, but no one is looking for him Miles. I know this for a fact because I trust Rob and he's already told me way more than he should have done. I said to him, what if it was Moira? I think that made him understand a bit of what I was going through. I feel that if I don't go and look for him then he will be 'lost,' possibly gone for good. The idea that you and Mr Akwal can jump on planes and be minutes away from him while I'm stuck at home is horrible. The Foreign Secretary told me that I should go and get Mart as a kind of joke and then my nan, Dorothea, said that I should bring him home. It wasn't just one her turns, like the whole Joan Collins thing or leaving Nathan a million pounds. She had that look in her eye like she does when she talks about things that she remembers, like Wally. It felt real and it felt like the only solution that I had been offered. I can't stand looking at the walls of the flat for one more day, knowing that he is being held and possibly hurt and I wasn't doing anything to help him. It's like I have no choice. I have to find him and bring him home because he is my husband. And I know, for a fact, that if it was the other way around, that he would be on his way to get me, without even thinking about it, without blinking, because he loves me.'

Miles shook his head slightly. He took off his glasses, pinched his nose and closed his eyes. He opened them again. Poppy wondered if he too was hoping that when he opened them, she might be gone. This she understood, having herself only recently played a similar game. But she wasn't gone; she was standing in front of him and wasn't going anywhere, like one of those enormous tuna fish stuck in Dorothea's net. 'What?' his confusion was evident.

'What do you mean 'what'? You've said that twice to me now Miles and it makes me really flustered,' Poppy genuinely didn't understand the question.

'What do I mean what? I mean, what do *you* mean? I still don't get the plan. What is it you are planning to do and why?'

'I am going to go and find Mart! I know that sounds crazy, but no one is looking for him and I think that if

I don't there is a danger that he won't ever come home…'

'OK, stop there. I don't need to hear about Joan Collins or whatever the hell that other stuff was,' Miles was confused, words were his craft and it was very unusual for him to be hearing and using words that did not make perfect sense to him. 'Does anyone else know that you are trying to get over there, Poppy?'

'Yes.'

'Who?'

'I've already told you, my nan.'

'Your nan?'

'Yes, as I said, my nan Dorothea. She's in a home and she's a bit bonkers some of the time. In fact, most of the time.'

'Are you sure no one else? Poppy this is very, very important.'

'No. No one else.'

'No one?'

Poppy looked him in the eye and repeated what she had already told him, 'Absolutely no one.'

'Right OK, think, think,' he pinched his nose again. Poppy wasn't sure if he was talking to her or himself, 'Are you sure that you want to do this?'

She nodded.

'Do you have any concept of how dangerous this could be for you Poppy? For others? Even for your husband?'

'Yes,' she lied. It was obviously convincing.

'If you are absolutely determined Poppy, then I am going to have to ask you to trust me and do exactly what I tell you. Do you understand?'

Poppy's thoughts were whirring. What did he want from her? What was in it for him? Could she trust him? The answer to all three was that she didn't know. Once again she had that feeling of being backed into a corner.

By her reckoning she had two choices; she could sink down onto the floor and give up the game; or she could come out fighting and face the challenge that was ahead of her, 'I understand.' A deal had been struck, he was to lead and she was to follow.

Poppy felt relief at handing over the reins to someone that might have a better idea of what was going on than she did. It gave her a feeling that wasn't dissimilar to when Dorothea had stroked her hair the previous night. Was that only the previous night? It could have been a lifetime ago.

'Stay close to me Poppy. Do not speak unless you absolutely have to, OK?'

'OK,' she smiled at him, feeling far from OK. She, in fact, felt terrified and sick with fear.

Poppy ambled behind Miles back into the terminal, where they joined the press group. The three girls once again caught Poppy's eye. They had formed a triangular hugging monster, reminding Poppy of those Siamese stuck-together-for-life twins that feature on freak shows masquerading as documentaries. The ones where the reporter asks the question that the whole world is willing him to; namely, how one of them managed to get married and have S-E-X whilst joined to the other one. Random arms sticking out from the mess clutched at used tissues. They had collapsed; each dependant on the other to remain upright.

There was no one left for them to wave to. The soldiers were no longer in sight; having passed through the double doors, they were now out of reach. Poppy decided this must be the hardest part; their men were gone, yet still close. They were the furthest point in time they would be from seeing their loved ones again, but were, in reality, only a few feet away from them on the other side of a swing door.

Flight Lieutenant Ward was coughing again. The media teams looked in his general direction, 'Righto chaps, and chapesses,' this was the cue for titters from those who found his particular brand of humour amusing, 'your body armour and helmets are ready for collection before you pass through. No need to put it on until you're boarding the final flight to your transit destination, the usual drill.'

Poppy didn't have a clue what he was talking about. Body armour? Second flight? Transit destination? What was the usual bloody drill? She bit her thumb nail, feeling so out of her depth that she was fearful this whole thing could only end in disaster.

Poppy had been so preoccupied with her identity and worrying about getting discovered that she hadn't thought about getting on a plane. She had never flown before, hating the idea, the very thought of it, yet knowing she was going to have to do it and soon. Her stomach manufactured another layer of butterflies to add to the ones that were already fluttering around in there. It must have been like the insect house at London Zoo.

The press group formed a line and made their way through the double doors to the departure area. Each was holding a navy blue vest of body armour and a helmet with matching blue cover. Poppy collected hers from a pile as did Miles and they joined the queue.

'Are you alright Nina?' he accentuated the word Nina; his way of reminding her of her new name. She was no longer Poppy Day, not for a while.

Poppy nodded, unable to speak.

There was a further security check. Miles handed the man his passport, and responded to the usual questions. Had he packed the bag himself? Did he have any of the following items in his luggage? Knives? Gels? Liquids? To each point raised, Miles answered with a definitive, 'No.'

Poppy found the line of questioning interesting, having earlier witnessed soldiers checking in weapons and ammunition. God forbid Miles might inadvertently smuggle on a bottle of hand cream whilst sat next to the gun toting warriors. Poppy remembered her perfume and lip gloss, 'Shit!' She rummaged around until she located the two offending items and held them over the plastic bin, placed for oversights just as this. Her grip tightened as her hand hovered; it was her only bottle of scent, a birthday present from Martin and she didn't want to throw it away. There was no option. She closed her eyes as the glass bottle clattered against tins and jars similarly disposed of. 'I'm sorry Mart,' Poppy sighed at the thought of her fifty quid bottle of contraband, so easily discarded.

The man tried to wave Miles through but he stayed put. Turning to Poppy, Miles gestured with his hand for her to come forward. She took three faltering steps until she was by his side. Miles addressed the man, 'This is my colleague Nina Folkstok.' He turned to Poppy, 'Pass?' This he uttered with a vaguely Nordic slant to his phrase.

Poppy pulled out the laminated plastic square stating, if not confirming, that she was Nina Folkstok from Denmark, fellow journalist of Miles Varrasso, freelance.

'Miss Folkstok had her passport and her documentation stolen this morning from her car. We have already cleared it with Flight Lieutenant Ward, but he said that I should just have a word with you. Nina's English isn't too great.' He spoke the last bit of the sentence out of the side of his mouth as though Poppy wasn't meant to hear, yet making sure she could.

Poppy stared blankly at the man; trying to look Danish

and like her English wasn't too great.

'That's a nightmare. Makes you proud to be British doesn't it?' his sarcasm was well meant.

Miles smiled at him, 'Absolutely. It was a really horrid experience for her.'

'Well, I guess if it's already been covered and she is with you, sir, then it should be fine. I will just check the manifest if that's OK.'

'Yes, yes of course,' Miles smiled at Poppy and then at the guard, who disappeared to check the flight manifest and was reassured to see the name Nina Folkstok on the list, nestled between Mike Fisher and Nick Foster.

He returned satisfied, 'Tell her she is clear to go through as long as she can get me Peter Schmeichel's autograph. I'm Man U through and through!' He smiled then, happy to show that he was far from ignorant, he knew someone from Denmark, even if he couldn't have told you where it was on a map.

Miles turned to Poppy, 'Você gosta de microplaquetas ou de salada, Peter Schmeichel?'

Poppy smiled and laughed, nodding her head at the security guard. Miles laughed as well a little too loudly. It was some time before she learnt that he had asked her if she wanted chips or salad, in Portuguese.

The partners in crime went through and sat on more plastic chairs bolted to the ground. There had been little problem for Poppy, the impostor, gaining entry into this secure and sensitive environment amongst hundreds of servicemen and their weapons unchecked and uncleared, but God forbid they might try to move a chair.

Jason approached them before they had a chance to confer, 'Aha! Aren't you the award-winning journalist Miles Varrasso? Confidante of some of the world's baddest baddies and expert at writing foolproof copy while a sniper is trained on your arse?'

'You are a funny guy Jase, leave us alone.'

'Ah! It all becomes horribly clear – leave US alone! Miles, you dark horse, and there was me thinking that you batted for the other side.'

'Jesus, you are incredible. Just because some of us prefer our sleep to going out wherever we are in the world and scoring, does not make me gay.'

'You are right, that was a bad thing for me to have said, especially in front of Freckles, but you really don't have to call me Jesus, 'sir' is fine.'

'Piss off Jason, please.'

'OK. I am pissing off but bagsy sit next to you on the plane!' Jason skipped away from them.

Poppy was unsure what to make of the whole encounter.

'He is an acquired taste, like anchovies.'

'I've never had anchovies.'

Miles looked at Poppy as though it was the most shocking thing that he had heard. Forget the fact that she was illegally schlepping out to Afghanistan under a false identity to try and bring her captive husband home. Never had anchovies? My God! They were from different worlds.

Poppy decided to give him another shock, 'I've never flown on a plane before either.'

He continued to stare at her, but his expression didn't look quite as critical as it had at her anchovy revelation, 'There is nothing to it, you just sit back and someone else does all the work. Before you know it, you are right where you expected to be and how you got there is forgotten. Besides, I will be with you and there is nothing to worry about.' He pushed his glasses up further onto his nose and smiled at her. He reminded Poppy of a calm and interested teacher, a bit like Nicholas Nickleby, a righter of wrongs, the voice of the underdog. Was that what she was; the underdog? A cause? She smiled, knowing that she was both.

When they finally boarded, Poppy felt a flutter of excitement, she had almost done it! She was going to get Martin; she would bring her husband home. The first plane was a regular civilian passenger jet, like any that she had seen on TV, and Miles was right, the actual flying wasn't too bad. The noise of take-off unnerved her but everyone else's calm demeanour was infectious.

Within minutes of the plane lifting from the tarmac, Poppy fell into a deep sleep. It was a combination of exhaustion, nerves and an instinctive sense that this was to be one of the last sound sleeps that she would have for a while. She slept through both the food and movie. Miles gently shook her as the plane approached Kuwait, where they were to get their connecting flight. There would be no food, movie or sleeping on this one.

Kuwait was hot and smelt foreign, different. Despite having seen hundreds of men dressed in every type of regional costume from all over the world within five feet of her own front door, Poppy found the men in Arabic garb fascinating. It was the first time that she had been the foreigner.

Miles checked regularly on his charge, assuming a brotherly role that both were comfortable with. It made her feel safe. This was a feeling that was not to last much past the next twenty-four hours. They boarded the Hercules in full body armour and helmets, which for Poppy felt bizarre, uncomfortable and restrictive; as though she was dressing up or playing a part, which is funny because, of course, that was exactly what she was doing. She may have looked like

Nina Folkstok, hardened war journalist on the outside, but on the inside she was most definitely Poppy Day, shit-scared hairdresser from Walthamstow.

Eleven

It suddenly went dark, not pitch black, but the light was minimal, just enough to make out shadow and form. Poppy felt a new level of scared, she was terrified. She had a scale for fear that was: concerned, alarmed, scared, frightened, terrified and petrified. She thought she was as scared as she possibly could be, but within a few days of her arrival, would discover a whole new level of fear, where you almost wished for death because the escape would be better than what you were experiencing.

They were packed like lambs in transit, only they weren't standing on the slippery floor of a moving truck, but were instead strapped into seats. The seatbelts were woven canvas, harness-like; the sort of thing Poppy could imagine wearing if she were parachuting. Poppy and Miles were clad in body armour and helmets as per their instructions. Those that carried weapons had them clamped between their knees or placed in the racks behind the seating that lined the walls. Poppy hated seeing the guns, being so close to them.

She closed her eyes and once again had the vision of when Martin was taken. She saw it quite clearly, his tanned face, his desperate tone, 'Over here! Jonesy! I'm over here!' His eyes wide, with the whites around his iris exposed. He looked petrified. Again she saw the blow to the stomach, and then nothing but darkness and quiet. Poppy was jolted back to the present. She didn't want to picture his capture, not then.

At the back of the plane were two large metal pallets on rails, with bags and equipment strapped under taut cargo nets. They looked like captured beasts; irregular shapes straining under their ropes, two giant bundles waiting to be launched. The plane suddenly jerked to the right, then immediately to the left and then back to the right, zigzagging in the air in a jumpy, uncontrolled way. It was, of course, neither of these things, not jumpy or random in any way, but carefully planned in its execution. It took a huge amount of skill to fly the cumbersome behemoth in that way.

Miles reached across and took her hand. Despite her dislike of physical contact from strangers, she was very glad to know that there was someone else there in the dark. There were nearly a hundred or so occupants being thrown this way and that but, despite being in a large group, Poppy felt alone. She felt lonely as well as scared.

He squeezed her hand slightly in a very reassuring way and she smiled in the darkness. The plane was silent, apart from the obvious engine noise and the creaks and groans of the metal. There were no human noises, no talking, no moving and hardly any breathing. The atmosphere was electric. It was better that Poppy was unaware that the darkness and manoeuvring were to avoid any insurgent's tracking device that may be watching and waiting for their arrival.

Poppy considered the silence and how it felt. It's easy to be silent when you are alone, but she had never been in a situation before where there was a communal silence; it made it more eerie, more special. She suspected that mass worship must be similar, but the only sombre service she had ever attended was on Remembrance Day and her experience was very different. It was never solemn, meaningful or an opportunity to 'remember'. It was always, always more about avoiding the comments about her name, waiting for the next joker to say something that she had heard a million times before. It was always far from special and was completely crap for her actually.

The mass hush was for a number of reasons. It was certainly the first time that the situation became real, dropping and swerving in a dark plane over a war zone. For those that had never been on tour before, it was a sobering moment, realisation that there was no going back, they. They had arrived, but were they ready?

For those that had experienced it before, the banter and excitement of the travelling was over as realisation dawned that it would be a very long time before they were on a plane heading in the opposite direction, back towards their family and loved ones. This was the primary reason for the noiseless reflection; the collective visualising of those that had been left behind. The wives, husbands, children and parents, the girlfriends and boyfriends; all were being missed. The longing had started. It was a dull ache that no amount of mail, email or phone call could cure. This was quickly followed by the 'what if?' thoughts: 'What if I don't get home alive? What if I am home soon but injured? What if something happens while I am away? What if no one misses me or, worse still, fills the gap that I have left? What if I am replaced or forgotten?'

When they disembarked from the Hercules, Poppy was overwhelmed by strong emotions. She was euphoric, wide awake, excited, nervous and full of energy. She had to stop herself from running forward and shouting at the top of her voice, 'I am coming Mart! Hang in there baby, I am on my way!' She felt so close that he would be able to hear her. She had done it; she had managed to get to Afbloodyghanistan!

She put her hand in her mouth to stop the shouts and whoops from escaping; such was her joy and excitement. She wanted to run up to every soldier and say, 'Do you know Martin Cricket? Do you know where he is? It's alright, you can tell me what you know, I'm his wife!'

It was still a few hours before she realised that she didn't have a plan and that she was in danger, but in those first few hours of arrival, it was really incredible.

When Poppy had sat in 'The Unpopulars' with her nan, thinking that she should go and get her husband back, she didn't think beyond getting to the country in which he was being held. If she was being totally honest, she didn't think that she'd get that far. How would she? No passport, no money, no transport, no friends and no legitimate reason to be there. It was such a huge and impossible task that she daren't believe that she would arrive. Yet there she was, only eighteen hours after closing her front door.

She shook her head and thought about her achievement, she had got through passport control and security with an assumed identity, been given food, drink and protection, had flown there on a military plane and made a friend who would help her in ways that she couldn't even begin to imagine. As for a legitimate reason, what better reason could there be other than to bring her husband home?

Poppy wanted to see everything; wanted to ask a million questions. She was abroad, she was in a war zone, but, most critically, she was in the place where her husband had lived and worked up until a couple of weeks before. It was all consuming; amazing and scary all at the same time. She desperately wanted to see where Martin had slept. She would have liked to touch his things, place her head on his pillow, or against his clothing, to see if she could smell him, but of course she could do none of these things because she was Nina Folkstok, impartial journalist from Denmark.

Minutes after leaving the plane, things happened very quickly. It felt like organised chaos. Poppy's nostrils filled with the smell of jet wash and the baked clay of the earth. Despite the hour of the night, it was still uncomfortably hot. Hundreds of people milled around, yet the groupings were not indiscriminate, there were queues of sorts. Poppy and her party were whisked into the terminal. Large groups of soldiers were taken off into side rooms, briefed then shipped from the airport to the base in buses, like the ultimate school trip. Civilians were being met by minibus or private cars. Some of them were contractors, working for security companies, or engineers off to help with the infrastructure, logistics or military support. Poppy stared after them, truly unable to understand why they would go out to a place like that unless they absolutely had to. The money was good, agreed, but the possibility that they too might be forced to go through what she and Martin were going through was a price that was too high. What amount of money was worth losing your life or liberty for?

Poppy shadowed Miles like a child nervous of being separated from its mum.

He turned to her, 'Are you alright Nina?'

She nodded, knowing that he was checking she was OK, but also reminding her to stay in character.

The journalists were taken into a room for a briefing; the soldier that delivered the session seemed tired, fed up at having to repeat the same information on a daily basis. His voice was flat, he sounded bored and disinterested. He informed them if the siren sounded, when it sounded, they should respond by getting as flat as they could on the ground as quickly as possible. Body armour and helmets if not being worn, were to be kept to hand at all times. Poppy listened intently to the fact that they would receive daily briefings and military personnel would be made available, who would act as their media buddies, guides and protectors. Poppy prayed that none of them would be Danish nationals; she knew she couldn't get by for long by repeating West Jutland and nodding.

The journalists were a group to which Poppy started to mentally align, believing her assumed role, although her mission was slightly different to everyone else's. The group were herded on to a separate bus and taken into the camp. The 'Media Centre' was where they would live and work for the duration of their trip.

Miles sat next to her on the bus, 'How are you doing?'

'I'm alright actually. A bit nervous, but I'm fine.'

He smiled his lovely open smile that crinkled up his eyes and changed his whole face from serious to happy, 'That's good to hear. There are a couple of things that I wanted to say. Firstly, don't talk to too many people, far better they think you are serious and aloof than blow your cover.'

Poppy laughed out loud because he had said 'blow your cover'. It sounded so hilarious and, once again, she felt as if she was in some crappy spy movie.

'Poppy, this is not a joke, you will be in serious danger if you do not do and say exactly what I tell you. Do you understand?'

His reprimand made her tears gather. Her emotions were extreme, strong feelings at either ends of the spectrum hovered near the surface, one minute laughter, the next crying tears. Poppy was unaware of how much danger she was in and didn't fully appreciate how much danger she was placing others in. It still felt like a spontaneous adventure, making her sound naive, juvenile and, with the glorious gift of hindsight, she would admit she was a bit of both. OK, a lot of both.

'I'm sorry Miles. I promise I will do what you tell me. I'm grateful for all your help.'

'As I've said, don't talk to too many people and, secondly, when you encounter anyone new, tell them you were a student in London and that's where your accent comes from, OK?'

Poppy nodded, 'OK.'

'Good. Finally keep close to me and keep in regular contact because that's how you will keep safe and that is how we will get you close to your husband. I'll be the catalyst Poppy, but if anyone, anyone at all gets a sniff that all is not as it should be, we are both on the first plane out of here and my career is in the shredder. Do you understand?'

'Yes,' although she wasn't sure that she did fully understand, not at that point.

She was waiting for him to tell her more; having hinted that he had the semblance of a plan, she was intrigued, when Max Holman and Jason Mullen appeared in the aisle.

'Hey aren't you that award-winning journalist that I read about? Can I have your autograph?' Max delivered this with a slight American twang.

'Are you never going to let it drop Max?'

'Sure I am big shot, in about twenty years' time...'

'Oh, when you get recognised you mean?' Jason quipped in defence of his friend; Max clearly needled him as much as he did Miles.

Jason addressed them both, 'Well young lovers, here we are back in theatre. Ah the smell of the greasepaint! The roar of the crowd! Wouldn't you simply die without Marlow?' He collapsed onto the empty chair to the other side of the aisle in a mock faint.

Miles laughed, 'He's nuts.'

Poppy had turned her attentions to the other side of the window. It was dark, but she could make out rows of tents and makeshift buildings all the colour of dung. Then, beyond the perimeter fence; nothing. Not just a little bit of nothing either, but nothing as far as you could see;

they were in the middle of nowhere.

The journos were shepherded off the bus and taken to their accommodation. Poppy's gait was lumbered; she was still unused to the body armour and helmet that would be her constant companions. The 'Media Centre' was actually just a group of tents. Poppy was freezing; she hadn't known that as the sun went down and the day slipped into night it would be so cold. She had always pictured this landscape with camels, hot sun and sand. Her teeth chattered in her gums, you would think being born and raised in Denmark she would have been more accustomed to the sub-zero temperatures...

There were approximately ten tents grouped together; each one slept up to five people, although they weren't full. Poppy was shown to her accommodation. Inside, the tent was divided by what looked like thick mosquito netting, more to give each occupant some private space than to offer any protection. Within each netted area was a cot; a rickety camp bed with a sleeping bag and a pillow folded neatly on the end. To the left of the bed was a hanging canvas rectangle, which unzipped to reveal shelves and a small mirror; Poppy's own personal space for her meagre belongings. Had she thought about it with any level of sense, she would have packed very differently. It was another subconscious gesture, illustrating the doubt that she wouldn't get further than the North Circular.

The other beds in the tent were bare and unoccupied; this she registered with a mixture of relief and disappointment. Poppy didn't want to have to talk to anyone, remembering Miles' instructions; similarly she hated the idea of sleeping alone, especially in such a strange environment. Miles, Jason and a couple of the others were in the tent opposite. She was glad of their physical proximity, figuring they were only a shout away from coming to the rescue, should the need arise.

Bastion wasn't like any campsite that she had seen or imagined. It was more like a city whose buildings were made of corrugated iron and canvas. It was huge. Crude signs were everywhere so you wouldn't get lost. The pavements were made up of pallets; the walkways covered with a plastic duckboard made up of little hexagonal shapes where the sand lodged in the corners. Poppy ate with the other journalists in one of the large canteens; the food was part way between motorway service station and school. It was served on disposable white plastic trays with dents in for different foodstuffs. They were a standard prison issue, quite disgusting really, but the food was warm and plentiful and she was hungrier than she had realised. Eighteen hours of travelling and the constant rush of adrenalin had given her an appetite.

Poppy didn't speak to many people; following Miles' instructions, appearing 'serious and aloof' turned her into quite a novelty. She didn't really care.

That first night she climbed into the sleeping bag fully clothed and pulled the spongy cover up over her shoulders. She placed her hand on her flat stomach. Poppy had secretly hoped to conceive before Martin had gone on tour, thinking being apart might be easier if she carried their baby while he was away. To have part of him growing inside her would certainly ease her sense of abandonment and would be the beginning of the family that she craved.

In moments of daydream she saw how it would happen. Martin would come home from tour and she would hand him his son or daughter, 'Thank you Poppy! Thanks for doing all that hard work while I was away. You have grown a beautiful baby while I was sat in the desert building sand castles.' But there was no baby for Poppy, not that night.

Her empty womb pulsed with longing for both the presence of her husband and the stretch against muscle of her baby's limbs. It was a craving that she couldn't satisfy, an ache that no amount of stroking or words of consolation could allay. In the same way she pictured Martin lost and waiting for her to claim him, so she pictured her unborn babies, Peggy for a girl, Charlie for a boy, swimming in limbo until she could give birth to them. Her palm rested on the cool skin, 'Hang in there baby, I'm coming.'

Poppy could hear the dull echo of people moving and the muted tones of speech all around her. She felt strangely close to Martin, willing him to feel her getting closer, 'I love you Mart. Sweet dreams darlin'.'

She also sent a message to Dorothea, telling her that she loved her and hoped she wasn't wondering where she had got to. Poppy had never thought of their little flat as luxurious, but as she lay her head down on the sagging cot, she pictured her lovely IKEA bed and realised that there were worse places to lay your head every night, much worse.

Twelve

Martin thought a lot about their bed at home. He longed to feel the soft mattress under his skin. He wanted to lay his head on the floral pillowcases that Poppy had chosen, the ones he had mocked as girly, whilst secretly applauding her taste. He wanted to feel her chest rise and fall as she slept close to him. He knew that when he lay on that mattress, with his beautiful wife nestled in his arms, that he would truly be home. That was Martin's definition of home; he and Poppy in bed together, her snuggling up to him for warmth.

Once again he dreamt that he was woken by Poppy, again she stroked the hair away from his forehead. Her voice gentle, 'Mart... Mart... I am here.' It made him miss her so much his gut ached with longing. He didn't want to open his eyes, knowing that he would lose her all over again, but she was fading...

The door banged against the wall, Poppy was gone in an instant. It was unusual for it to be opened in such a way; there was never any need to startle him, his captors could be certain that he was always in the same spot, exactly as they had left him. Their entrance sounded aggressive and urgent; Martin instinctively knew that something was wrong. Life in captivity had become mundane and this had led him into an almost false sense of security. He had forgotten the horror he felt when first taken; not that it had gone completely, there was always a lingering, subdued anxiety in the pit of his stomach, but the raw terror, that life or death feeling, he had almost erased it. It returned in an instant, an energy zapping fear that fuelled his anger, but also rendered him weak.

Martin sat up on the bed, shaking his head and rubbing

his eyes, trying to go from asleep to alert as quickly as he could. He snagged his broken finger against his face, but there was no time to consider the throb of pain which would become insignificant soon enough. Two men stood in front of him, with shemaghs tightly wrapped around their heads, covering most of their faces, apart from a small gap around their mouths that was exposed. They wore sunglasses and more worryingly for Martin, were carrying Kalashnikov assault rifles. One of them shouted an instruction in his native tongue. The words meant nothing, but Martin could tell by the man's tone and speed of speech that he wanted him to act quickly.

He leapt from the mattress. This was apparently the wrong thing to do. The second man ran forward and smashed the butt of his gun into Martin's face, the force of which knocked him back down onto the bed. His teeth, already a little loose in their gums proved no resistance to the hard wooden stock as it collided with the soft pulp of his face. Fragments of tooth mixed with the warm swell of plasma, filled his mouth. His swollen tongue snaked over the crumbly remnants of at least two of his teeth. He was shocked and in pain, but his overriding emotions were panic and fear. Fear of what came next.

Martin thought a lot about Aaron's demise and had only recently considered how strange it was that people gave so little thought to their own death. It occurred to him that it was the only certainty, highly unconsidered. Hours could be spent mentally frittering lottery wins, romancing the unattainable or celebrating a victory goal in the shirt of your nation, yet very little thought was applied to how your life might end.

He guessed that most people outside of this war zone, if pushed, would envisage a warm bed in old age, eiderdown tucked under chin, a clutch of grandchildren whimpering into hankies on the floor below, and slipping into a blissful dream that lasts for eternity. Yet at every minute of every day, all around him, people young and old came face to face with the grim reaper after encountering pain, shock and confusion. Not so much a happy release, but more often a grapple with crushing, asphyxiation or the agonising shutting down of organs that meant vitality. Death could of course be peaceful, calm and poetic, but, in as many cases, brutal, violent and disturbing. Martin felt confident in that moment that he could predict which category his own end would fall into. His final wish, however, was not for himself, but that Poppy should, when her time came, experience the exact opposite.

The shouter came over to the bed and pushed him downwards, rolling Martin onto his stomach. He pulled at his arms until they were behind his back. Martin felt the familiar bite of plastic ties as they cut into the skin of his wrists. He could almost predict what came next; it was his old friend, the lice-ridden sack. Martin felt sick and frightened; his brain tried to process the answers to the many questions that were firing inside his skull, 'Are they going to rape me? Am I being set free? Am I being moved? Where would they move me to? Are they going to kill me? Where will they kill me? Will they kill me how they killed Aaron? Will anyone know that I have been killed? Help me. Help me someone. Hear me God. Please, help me, please help me God.'

His captors hauled him up onto unsteady, bare feet. He walked with the faltering steps of a new calf; his head swooning with the exhilaration. Unable to see, and with his hands tied, he felt a new level of vulnerability. The muzzle of the Kalashnikov jabbed at his lower back; his captors wanted him to walk. He felt a strong yearning to stay in that shitty room, the rat-infested hovel that he had longed to escape from, the home of his beatings, his prison for an indeterminate number of days and nights. He could not be certain that where he was heading wasn't going to be that much worse and, if he was being taken on his final walk, he wanted to delay it.

With his guards walking behind him, Martin very quickly found himself outside. This told him that he had been in a small building or at least on the edge of a larger one, closer than he had imagined to the outside world. He could hear voices in the distance, it sounded like children, chatting and playing. How could that be? Martin found it hard to understand that everyday life was going on right outside those walls where his own world had fallen apart.

He stumbled forward as jagged stones, chunks of brick and shards of glass bit the soles of his feet. The guards didn't want him to walk any slower just because he couldn't see and had no idea of what was in front of him. Martin could have been at the top of some stairs, the side of a road or the edge of a cliff, the butt of the rifle now prodded his back, making sure he kept the pace up.

He tripped and almost lost his footing. His captors found this most comical; his legs were out of practice. He wobbled and wavered like a drunk. Then he nearly fell, floundering and stumbling, threatening to fall down, but not quite. The reward for keeping his balance was a swift kick in the stomach, which caused him to stagger then sprawl onto the floor. He lay, trying to catch his breath.

Falling without being able to put out his hands was both horrendous and painful. Instinct caused his elbows to jolt upwards as nature tried to apply brakes, but with his hands so tightly secured, it was futile. Martin felt his face receive even more collateral damage. He breathed slowly, trying to recover. The men drew pleasure from their brutality, there was no need to kick the man that was already down, but kick him they did. Martin yelped as the leather sandal carrying a man of weight, crushed against his spine.

His breathing returned to a natural rhythm and, as it did so, Martin felt awash with a strange calmness, inner warmth that could do little to soothe his body, but certainly helped focus his mind. He thought about Poppy and was so, so glad that he had dreamt about her. It made him feel close to her. He thought about how he wanted to be seen, if these were going to be his last few minutes on the planet. Did he want to shrivel and bend like someone apologising? No. No he did not. He was a British citizen; he had fought for his Queen and his country. Martin decided to hold his head up. He thought of Aaron and he thought of Poppy. He wanted to make her proud. He thought of his dad, he would show him, the bastard. He would show him what courage was. He would be defiant, he would make a stand. He would be a man.

Martin stood slowly with difficulty, until he was rigid and tall, holding his head high. Sucking in his stomach, pushing out his chest and ignoring the pain, he practically marched. One of his captors held his arm, 'Don't touch me, you bastard!'

The guard didn't understand the words, but Martin's tone was sufficient to reveal the sentiment. The guard removed his hand immediately.

Martin laughed as blood dripped in large globules from his macerated mouth, soaking the hessian sack. Once again he swooned with the exertion. One of his eyes was swollen shut; his head felt heavy, too heavy for his neck, his words were slurred, 'I am Martin Cricket, Infantryman with the Princess of Wales Royal Regiment. I am a soldier with the British Army, the best. I am your prisoner, but I am also a man, a man who is loved.'

He felt powerful, in this desperate situation, bound, hooded and without a weapon. He felt invincible. It was a strange sensation, almost of time standing still. Martin wanted it to be over, half thinking, 'Just shoot me you bastards, shoot me and get it over with,' but there was another part of him that wanted one last gulp of air, one more image of Poppy, one more prayer. It was an adrenalin-fuelled combination of anticipation and suspense, nerves and excitement, but strangely Martin wasn't afraid. He had no fear at all, quite the opposite.

He felt a hand on his chest and held the position, standing still. Waiting. The blood pulsed in his temples, his heart beat was steady. He thought about his wedding vows, Poppy had looked so beautiful and he was honoured to be her husband. He envisaged the moment he placed the small gold band on her finger...

He heard the dry drawing of metal inside metal, followed by the tell-tale click as a weapon was made ready for firing, or it could have been the smooth slice of a sharp edge against leather as the blade was drawn from its sheath. He couldn't be sure which. It didn't really matter, not now.

Thirteen

The next morning Poppy showered in the communal block, careful to avoid eye contact and conversation with the two female soldiers that passed through. She waited until they had both left before washing out her pants in the sink. With only one other pair, she was going to have to rotate their use. She smiled, contemplating the fact that only she would travel to the other side of the world in a daring rescue attempt, to liberate her husband from a band of religious fundamentalists, with a packet of Polo Mints and sunglasses as her weapons of choice.

Miles met her outside the block, 'Morning'.

'Gud Morrnink Miles,' Poppy laughed, her accent was an intriguing mix of Polish and Muppet Swedish Chef.

'Did you sleep OK? These cots take a bit of getting used to.'

Poppy was ashamed to admit that actually she had slept brilliantly, having fallen into a deep and exhausted slumber, not stirring until there was activity outside the tent that very morning.

'Let's go somewhere and chat,' he guided her off the path.

They ducked into an empty Portakabin that inside looked like a makeshift internet cafe. Four high-spec computers with tired keyboards blinked on separate tables, each with a payphone to the side and a plastic chair; no comfort, no privacy. She ran her fingers over one of the grubby keyboards, knowing instinctively that Martin had been there, this was where he had emailed from on the odd occasion, 'Hang on baby. I'm coming.' This was her silent mantra.

Miles jolted her into the present with his words, his urgency and inability to look at her face, 'Poppy...'

'Yep?'

'Poppy...'

'For God's sake Miles, you've already said that! What is it? What's going on?'

Miles ran his fingers through his hair and finished by pushing his specs over the bridge of his nose, 'Oh Poppy. I need to talk to you...'

She knew he was playing for time, trying to phrase the words correctly in his head and it scared her. It scared her a lot. 'Well you are talking to me, so spit it out,' she smiled, half joking.

'I have made a few enquiries, I had an idea. I didn't want to promise anything, but I was pretty sure that I could get us in front of the ZMO.'

'Really? How?' she was absolutely captivated; this was wonderful news, the first real glimmer of hope.

'The award that I got last month...'

'The one that Max is so sore about?'

'Oh you noticed that too? Yes, that one. Well, basically I got it for an interview that I did with a well-known Taliban leader in the mountains in Pakistan. It was an amazing experience, blindfolded in and out to preserve their location, and an opportunity to sit face-to-face with one of the most politically influential men in the world at the moment. It was a once in a lifetime opportunity and I got lucky. These groups like my anti-invasion standpoint; the widely held view is that because I am so against this war, I'm in some way sympathetic to their cause...' Miles was verbose and edgy.

'That's bloody brilliant! Yes do it! Get us in front of them Miles and we can negotiate something, this is great!' Poppy drew her clenched fists up under her chin, the anticipation was overwhelming.

He drew a deep breath, 'I'm afraid that something has come to light and it's something that has thrown me rather, and this is what I need to tell you.'

She nodded, silently anticipating what might come next.

'I heard a rumour from a fairly reliable source, they had some news. It concerned Martin.'

'What news?' her voice was a tiny whisper. She wasn't sure if he had heard.

'Sit down Poppy.'

She sat. Miles bent low in front of the office swivel chair on which she perched and looked up into her face, 'I started to make my enquiries about a possible meeting and was told that there was no point because things had developed Poppy and not in a good way...'

'In what way then?' This was worse than the knock on the door moment, far worse.

'The rumour is Poppy, that Martin may have been hurt,' he bit his bottom lip.

'Hurt badly?' this time she knew her voice was too small to be heard.

'Poppy, it is unsubstantiated, but I've been told that he may have been killed.'

Her breath came in huge gulps, too big for her aching lungs to cope with.

'I'm sorry Poppy, I really am.'

'Who told you that? How would they know? They are lying to you Miles. They are bloody liars!'

'They could be, but there is no value in them lying Poppy, it's what they believe and we have to consider the possibility that they might be telling the truth.'

'No. No. No. No. That's not it, that's not what has happened. No. I'm sorry, but no.' She shook her head.

'I understand, Poppy, that this is the worst thing for you

to hear, but you are not alone, I will help you get home, we can make arrangements...'

'I don't want arrangements. I want Martin! I've come all this way to get my husband Miles. I've come to take him home and, whether I walk back with him holding my hand or I carry him in a box, this is what I am going to do. Do you understand? Do you bloody understand?' Her voice was hoarse. Tears gathered around the corners of her mouth and nostrils. 'I won't leave this horrible place until I have him with me. I will not. It's as simple as that,' she leapt from the chair and made for the door.

'Pop... Nina, please don't run out, we need to talk about this!' Miles called to her back as she ran from the building.

She found solace inside her sleeping bag, welcoming the dark that enveloped her. Hours slowly ticked by. There were no more tears just a dark, cold stain of grief that spread until it filled her. She dozed in and out of sleep. Poppy remembered a time when they were about nine, sitting on the swings in the dark, 'You're my best friend in the whole world Martin...' It was dark, but Poppy knew that he was smiling, 'And I would be very sad if ever you moved away or couldn't play with me anymore.'

'That's never going to happen, Poppy. Where would I go?'

She had shrugged in response, unable to picture where he might disappear to.

'I promise you Poppy that I will always be your best friend. It's like we are joined together by invisible strings that join your heart to mine and if you need me, you just have to pull them and I'll come to you...'

Poppy had laughed out loud, loving the idea of their invisible heart strings, '...and if you pull yours, I will come to you Martin. That way, I'll always know if you need me.'

He reached out a hand in the dark until he found Poppy's small fingers and he placed them inside his own.

Poppy sat up in her sleeping bag. Her heart strained inside her chest. She was grinning. Donning her shoes, she ran from the tent. Sod being low key and elusive, this was important! She spotted Miles in the canteen at a far table and raced through the tray wielding masses before crashing down into the chair opposite him, 'Do it Miles, organise your meeting if you can, get us in front of the ZMO. Martin is alive.'

'Poppy, you don't know that for sure...'

She interrupted him and raised her palm to stem any negative comments, 'Oh, but I do. I do know it Miles!' She beamed at her friend and co-conspirator.

'Who told you...how?' his investigative brain wanted facts.

'He did Miles; Martin pulled on my heart strings!'

'He what?'

'It doesn't matter mate and you wouldn't understand even if I did try and explain. It would be like the whole Joan Collins thing, but I have never lied to you Miles, and I am telling you that he is alive. I can *feel* it.'

'Maybe Poppy, that's just what you want to feel...'

Again she raised her palm, there was no room for his doubt or hesitation, 'Trust me Miles, he is alive!' She swiped at the tears that splashed onto the table.

And for no other reason other than the conviction with which this extraordinary girl spoke, Miles believed her. He removed his specs and rubbed at his face.

'How are you going to do it? Is there someone here that can help?' her energy was infectious.

'Not exactly, but the point is, Poppy, that I am trusted and I'm current. If anyone can get in front of the ZMO it's me. I have a contact that I was planning on seeing later today to try and organise a meeting, an audience if you like with the head honcho, Zelgai Mahmood himself.'

'Oh my God! Oh my God Miles. That is absolutely brilliant! Do it Miles, meet him, make it happen!' Poppy put her head forward and pushed the heels of her hands into her eyes, the tears sprang regardless. This was real, it was actually feasible.

'Poppy, this is still only a possibility; it is not set in stone and it's a bit of a long shot. We still don't know for sure that Martin is with them or if he's...'

'Don't say it,' she placed her fingers over his lips. He resisted the temptation to kiss the soft pads of her hand, the exertion made him dizzy.

'I just want you to understand that there are no guarantees, there are never any guarantees. These negotiations and plans can fall over at any point, at any time, so until we, you or I, get in front of the person that we need to, it is not a done deal. It is so important that you realise that, I don't want you to be disappointed.'

'I do understand Miles, I do!' she lied through her tears.

'I don't believe you Poppy, but that's OK. I will do my best. I'm not doing it for completely altruistic reasons, if I can pull this off then I will officially be THE western voice of the terrorist. It will keep me in business for years! I'll come and find you when I get back.'

'Can I come with you?'

'No. No you can't. This is very risky and very dangerous...'

'Miles I don't care! Let me come with you, please.'

'No. One hundred per cent no. I will go alone and I'll come and find you when I get back. Jesus Poppy, does nothing scare you?'

She thought for a moment, 'Yes, the idea of not seeing

my husband alive again.'

That shut him up.

Poppy spent the day laying on her cot, waiting. The hours passed unbearably slowly. She listened to the daily bustle of the camp around her, catching snippets of conversation, the odd cough and at least three different songs being hummed. She looked at her watch every few minutes and was convinced that at one point time went backwards. Her mind started to wander down doom-filled alleyways and into booby trapped corridors, imagining all sorts of frightening things. Supposing they kept Miles too? What if they hit a roadside bomb? She realised for the first time how much she had come to rely on Miles in a very short space of time. He wasn't only her protector and advisor, but also the only person that actually had a plan, the only person who was giving her concrete hope.

To everyone else she was Nina Folkstok, but he knew who and what she was. Poppy realised that she drew enormous comfort from having one person that she could be herself with. She started to think about what would happen to her if he didn't come back. She couldn't visualise it, the prospect was too scary, doubt started to creep in. What was she doing? She was supposed to be in her flat in Walthamstow, cutting hair in Christine's salon and visiting her nan. Instead she was in a tent, on an army base in Afghanistan, masquerading as a Danish journalist. It was so bizarre, it was almost funny.

Poppy would have sworn that she was awake for the whole day, but apparently she had fallen asleep because she was being woken up. Miles shook her shoulder. She sat upright, instantly alert, 'Oh my God! Well?'

'It's nice to see you too Poppy.'

'Sorry Miles. It's just that I've been waiting for you all day! It's been awful; I was really worried. I've imagined all sorts of terrible things. I thought you were never coming back.'

'Well here I am. It's been quite a journey in a slow and unreliable car, and then there was the wait for transport back. It's been a very long day, I'm shattered.'

'How did you get on Miles? Are they going to see us?'

'I don't know yet. I met with a representative from the ZMO. He was there with an armed guard; luckily for him I hadn't sharpened my pencil. He asked lots of questions about the other interview. They are interested in my credentials and my views on America.'

'What did you tell him?'

'What he wanted to hear Poppy and it seemed to work. He has taken away my request for contact. He'll get word to me whether it is possible or not.'

'When? When will he get word to you?'

'Goodness Poppy, have you ever thought of becoming an editor? You are so demanding!'

'I know I am. I'm sorry; it's just that I am really impatient.'

'I hadn't noticed.'

'You're a funny guy!'

Poppy felt a surge of hope. Miles had made contact with someone that would know where her husband was and whether he was alive or... He had to be alive. No one would allow her to come that far only to discover that she had arrived too late. All they could do now was wait, wait and hope. Exactly as she had for the last couple of weeks, only now she had to wait in a sandier environment and without the means to make a decent cup of tea.

Three days later, Poppy's whole world was turned upside down. Three days that felt like weeks. The worst thing about waiting was the interminable boredom. Her iPod had long since run out of charge and trying to pass time when there was absolutely nothing to do was torturous. She hid away during the day, unable to wander freely. The real journalists were conducting interviews, typing up copy, tip tapping and sending it around the world on their laptops. Not Poppy, she was without lap top; instead she had her notebook and pencil for company. It was bloody boring and bloody hot.

She wished that she could have a gossip and a coffee with Jenna; she missed her mate and her nan for that matter. Poppy was desperate to know that she was OK and couldn't bear the idea that Dorothea might think she had abandoned her.

It was a cold night in the desert. Poppy was initially thankful for the respite from the heat, but quickly became uncomfortable. She closed her eyes and envisaged their big, fat duvet on the bed at home. She wanted an extra blanket or thicker pyjamas, or ideally, her husband to snuggle up to. She hated being cold, it reminded her of her childhood.

Poppy never had a coat. When she'd asked for one, the response from Wally dozing in the chair of power had been, 'Stop moaning, you're waterproof. If you get wet, you'll dry off soon enough.' You know what? He was right! Clever old Wally, the sleeping, moaning dickhead.

What he didn't understand was what it felt like for a little girl to get so wet on the way to school that she remained so for most of the day, shivering as her hair dripped onto her artwork, turning every poster paint creation into a smudged rainbow river. At the exact moment her wool and polyester jersey finished steaming, it would be time to go outside for break, where she would get wet again, remaining so until just before lunch when she would get rained on all over again.

Poppy spent hours shaking so hard that she couldn't concentrate on what the teacher was saying. She could only hear the word 'C... c... c... cold' repeated over and over in her head, chattering through clenched teeth. In her mind, there were whole days, if not weeks, when she was permanently soggy. A small puddle would form under and around her chair. Her socks remained moist and her toes pruney skinned inside them until she could get home and put the damp grey strips on the heater. This would fill her grotty bedroom with a damp, cheese-like smell. Her wet hair clung in thin, brown stripes across her pale face, which, for Poppy, seemed like prison bars. She felt isolated, trapped and bloody uncomfortable.

Poppy decided that when she had a little girl she'd buy her a big furry winter coat with a hood, a set of matching hat, scarf and gloves and a little cagoule folded up into a bag that she could carry around her waist for 'just in case'.

It was the early hours of the morning in her desert home when she stopped shivering. It was maybe four or five am, someone was standing by her cot. Poppy gasped and jumped up, still inside the sleeping bag. She stood like a large green, padded slug, unable to run or move; a stationary target, trying to focus on the shadowy figure that loomed ahead of her.

'It's alright Poppy; it's me, its Miles,' he put his hand on her shoulder.

She flinched, 'Blimey, you scared me!'

'I'm sorry. I didn't want to call out and risk waking anyone else. Get dressed Poppy, we are off.'

'What do you mean? Off where? When?'

'Now! We are off now. I've just had word from my contact and it's on, but we have to go right now, to meet our lift. This isn't unusual Poppy; they often do it this way, not giving anyone a chance to plan, tell anyone or predict the outcome. Listen to me Poppy, and listen carefully, you are Nina Folkstok don't forget. Do not speak Poppy, I am telling you this because it is really important that you understand. Don't speak until I tell you that you can and let me handle everything. Do you understand?'

Poppy nodded, not trusting herself to speak. This was it; she was being taken to the people that had her husband. She was going to get Martin. It was unbelievable, exciting and scary all at the same time. She didn't know why she was scared, didn't know why she should be scared. She would find out soon enough.

She had only once before felt this level of anticipation and that had been a long time ago for a very different trip; she prayed that the outcome of this adventure would be better. Poppy was eight when she went on a school outing to London Zoo. Boy was she excited, the anticipation was almost unbearable! The night before she couldn't sleep and spent the hours jumping around the bed, her head full of all the possibilities of what the day might bring. It was to be an epic adventure; Poppy never went anywhere or did anything. She desperately wanted to study a seahorse, having only recently learnt they were not mythical creatures as she had believed. She pondered this fact every night leading up to the big day, promising herself to similarly investigate mermaids. She glued the typed out, photocopied note about it on the wall above her bed, reading it over and over;

'The coach will leave from main school gates at approximately 9am. Children should bring a packed lunch and come equipped for rain...'

Poppy could still recall it word for word. When the day of the big trip dawned, Poppy got up early to make her packed lunch. The distraction and excitement meant she didn't notice the freezing air inside her bedroom, or the cold plastic of the bath against her skin, which, despite the warm water, did nothing to relieve her chills. In the tiny kitchen, she clambered onto the Formica work surface, rooting around in the cupboard to find something to take. The contents of that packed lunch would stay with her forever. Jam sandwiches – the standard two slices buttered, strawberry smeared then stuck together – were cut in half. The butter, too hard to spread, pulled the soft white dough into large holes, but she didn't mind. There was a piece of cheese wrapped in foil and three cubes of uncooked jelly, lime flavoured.

Poppy put the whole lot inside an empty bread bag and set off. She was happy to be going to the zoo and just as excited to be in possession of a packed lunch. There were kids in school who enjoyed a packed lunch daily, but she couldn't possibly have prepared food every morning as well as get her uniform ready and Dorothea up and into the bathroom. Besides, she was entitled to free school meals, buying supplies for a packed lunch every day would have been out of the question for her.

Poppy skipped, bread bag in hand, along the pavement, circumnavigating the dog poo and hopping over the cracks. Jenna was already sitting halfway up the coach with her brother. Poppy didn't mind a bit, she was, at that tender age, already assured of her place in Jenna's affections. Poppy placed the plastic bag on her lap. She ran her fingertips over the shiny seat next to her, feeling the smoothed surface where a million excited bottoms had wiggled away the nap of the once plush fabric. Harriet sidled into the space and sat next to her. The catchment area of Poppy's school included the council estates and flats where she grew up, but also the big houses near the tube where the money brokers and city traders raised their families in seven bed-roomed Edwardian splendour. They were two completely different worlds, each equally fascinating to the other.

'Good morning Poppy,' the way she spoke made Poppy feel ordinary. Harriet was the sort of girl that always had Tipp-Ex, a spare pen and a sharpener in her pencil case, while Poppy and her mates scrabbled around in the disused ice-cream cartons to find something to write with. No matter what topic was being discussed, from Victorian railways to the Egyptians, Harriet always had a relevant book, relic or objet d'art to bring from home. In later years, Poppy wondered if she had an 'in' at the British Museum.

Harriet was very clean and very pretty, but the most amazing thing about her on that particular day, was her lunch box. It was a pink plastic suitcase, the perfect size for sandwiches and a couple of treats. Poppy was desperate to look inside. Ten minutes into the journey she was rewarded when Harriet casually flipped the lid to reveal the most wonderful sight. Tiny triangle sandwiches made from brown bread were filled with ham, the crusts of which were missing. It made Poppy think of her nan, who would have said, 'No crusts? She'll never 'ave curly hair!' This was one of her many sayings, turned into belief based on nothing more than repetition. The sandwiches were on one side, making space for a carton of orange juice with its own little plastic straw. An individual pot of yoghurt with a teaspoon sat neatly in one corner and there were, not one but, two chocolate biscuits. Most intriguing of all, was the plastic twist of cling film with four washed, sugared strawberries in it. It was a glimpse into another world, a fantastic sugary, crusts-deliberately-missing-on-your-sandwiches, world.

Poppy was transfixed.

Harriet saw her staring. Lifting the box, she held it towards Poppy's face, 'Would you like something Poppy?'

Again, with that way of speaking that made Poppy think she should definitely do Harriet's bidding, whatever it might be. Poppy wanted all of it, but how could she say that? Instead, she shook her head, too shy to be honest, trying to ignore the rumble in her tummy. Poppy dug deep, plucked up the courage and found her voice, 'I like your lunch in its little box Harriet.'

'Thank you Poppy.'

'Did you make it yourself?'

'Did *I* make it?' Harriet's eyes widened, her eyebrows shot upwards towards her blonde fringe. It was as if she had heard something outrageous, unfathomable. She laughed, revealing flossed and polished teeth, 'Of course not silly! Mummy made it for me, but I chose what I wanted from the fridge and she said I could have treats even though it isn't Thursday, which is sweetie day in our house!'

Poppy was enthralled. There were two things about Harriet's fabulous insight that gripped her completely. Firstly, she couldn't imagine living in a house where these sorts of goodies were hanging around in a fridge waiting to be picked. Secondly, in Harriet's house they had a sweetie day, which Poppy now knew was Thursday. This information left her with a large void in the base of her stomach, an acute ache that she carried with her until she fell properly in love with Martin Cricket some years later. These facts filled her throat with the bitterest of bile, making her feel utterly hopeless.

Cheryl would not know if her daughter had eaten much less *what* she had eaten. If Poppy didn't get supper for her and Dorothea they would both go to bed without food. Cheryl would be too busy putting on her face or watching something on the telly. Harriet's mum not only had a fridge bursting with treats, but crucially cared enough about Harriet's health, teeth and well-being to only allow her sweets once a week! Poppy felt bloody sick and bloody jealous. She realised at that precise moment, looking at her squashed jelly cubes and the jam sandwiches with big holes in them that had gone hot on her lap, that her mum was really quite crap.

She scrunched up the bread bag with its sordid contents and pushed it down the side of the coach seat. It was a crappy packed lunch that reminded her of her crappy life. She wasn't sure if the empty aching feeling in her tummy was hunger or something else entirely. Sadly, this was Poppy's overriding memory of that day. She couldn't remember if she got to study a seahorse and didn't recall the elephant that sprayed its trunk on cue. Instead, her strongest recollection was of her packed lunch and the fact that she grew up a bit more; lost even more of the magic...

Back in the real world, Poppy tried not to think about the man with the gun in the front seat. It wasn't a little pistol that she might have been able to ignore, but was one of those great big machine guns, the ones you see in films, where the owner also has a large row of bullets over his shoulder accompanied by a big droopy Mexican moustache and a fat cigar clamped between his teeth. Miles and Poppy sat in the back seat; they'd handed over their bags and their pockets had been emptied. They looked out of the windows, purposely not looking at each other. Poppy felt sick. She had always had a tendency to feel sick in a car, but this was different. There was an element of her ailment, but she was also frightened sick, it was horrible.

She looked at the empty dusty roads as they bumped along; wondering if this was where he had been captured. The image of Martin on his knees, winded, with his head covered came into focus again. It was still relatively dark outside; the car headlights threw two beams out to light the way ahead. The landscape was that of her vision, it could have occurred anywhere, the image of him on his knees was, in fact, everywhere she looked.

The driver had his face wrapped in a scarf and was wearing sunglasses. He reminded Poppy of *The Invisible Man*; she considered the possibility of unwrapping the man's head gear and finding nothing.

As the journey continued, the day cast its light over the sand until it was bright. The creamy terrain caught the early sunlight, giving the whole landscape a pink hue. As the morning progressed and the light changed, the dunes went from yellow to gold until the large red sun shone high in the sky and the earth positively glowed the colour of burnt cinnamon. It was beautiful. The scene, however, did little to relieve her anxiety. Supposing Martin wasn't there? Supposing he was hurt or worse? She had wanted this for a long time; it had been her dream since the day that he'd been taken, to get him back and to make a difference. Yet, now she was getting close to achieving some or all of that, she felt nothing but fear. She whispered under her breath, 'I am coming baby. You hang in there, I am coming.'

After some hours she spied a small settlement ahead of them; a selection of houses, a larger building and what looked like a derelict mosque. It had to be where they were heading. Poppy's heart rate increased and she was sweating. Miles turned towards her and placed his finger on his closed mouth, reminding her that she was Nina Folkstok and that she mustn't speak, as if she could have forgotten. She smiled at him with her mouth, but her eyes were frozen with an expression of trepidation.

The car began to slow and then stopped. The man with the gun opened the back door; apparently they were going to walk the rest of the way. She wasn't prepared for what happened next. He went to Miles and placed a black scarf over his eyes and tied it tight. Miles spoke loudly, 'That's right, we are now blindfolded and will be until we are inside, all quite normal and it won't be for long.'

Miles, bless him, was telling her not to be scared, that it would soon be over. It went against all her instincts to stand still, allowing the man to cover her eyes. She wanted to pull it off and shout in protest.

The scarf man then took her hand and placed it on Miles shoulder. Poppy could tell it was Miles shoulder by the fabric of his shirt beneath her fingertips, thin corduroy. This was how they walked the rest of the way, in a blind conga without the music or leg kicks. This would have made Poppy laugh under any other circumstances, but she was too scared to find anything funny.

It was a further twenty minutes before they were inside and their blindfolds removed. Poppy found herself in a large hallway, with a wide staircase and a wrought iron banister that wound around in a circle. It reminded her of an entrance to one of those posh hotels that you saw in the West End. There were several doors leading from the hallway, each had a guard with a gun. There were more men with weapons on the stairs and one or two hanging down over the ornate balcony; they were surrounded. Poppy couldn't have spoken if she'd wanted to, her tongue was stuck to the roof of her mouth and there was no spare spit to loosen it.

One of the doors opened and a tall man in traditional

Afghan dress came out. His beard was really long, almost down to the middle of his chest and on his head was one of the scarves that all the men seemed to own, but it was wound around into a turban. He stepped forward, 'Hello and welcome. I hope that your journey was a good one.' With palms upturned and hands splayed, he looked and sounded like the perfect host, not the fearful warlord that she had been expecting. It was surreal; he seemed oblivious to the guns and the tension.

Poppy stared at him.

Miles took a step forward, 'Thank you for your welcome. The journey was fine, although we are glad to arrive.'

'Glad to arrive, yes I am sure,' he laughed in acknowledgement of the shitty roads and the whole blindfold incident. It was bizarre, the whole thing. Poppy had pictured him as a monster, but he was chatting to Miles like an old friend of the family, someone you might meet in the supermarket that you only know a little bit. So you talk about traffic and the parking, enquire after their health... Then hope that you don't bump into them again in the fruit and veg because you have exhausted everything you might possibly have to say to them. It was like that, they stood making small talk. It was the weirdest moment for Poppy. He shook Miles' hand, 'I am Zelgai Mahmood.'

'I am Miles Varrasso.'

Zelgai bowed his head slightly. Poppy knew he was coming to her next. She knew it, anticipated it, yet Miles hadn't told her that she could speak, but. But it was too late; he was there, in front of her, with his hand outstretched, 'You must be Nina.'

She placed her shaking hand into his, 'Yes, I am Nina Folkstok.'

Again he bowed slightly, 'I have never been to Denmark.

It can be very cold I understand.'

She drew breath and spoke quietly, not wanting to give away too much of her accent, 'Yes it can be very cold but beautiful.'

'Your homeland is always the most beautiful place in the world is it not? No matter where it is.'

Poppy nodded and glanced at Miles, who winked at her quickly. It told her all that she needed to know, so far, she had done well.

Zelgai put his arm out to indicate the rest of the house, 'Shall we go into my office?'

'Thank you, yes.' Miles was happy to speak on their behalf. Poppy was happy to let him.

Zelgai walked slowly, the two followed at an almost reverential pace. The man from the car with the gun walked behind them, another conga-like procession. They approached some double doors made of dark wood with elaborate carvings. The armed guard who had been blocking them turned the handle and pushed them open. The room was vast and could have been Tristram Munroe's office, if you replaced the rugs with pictures and the tiled floor for carpet.

There were two Arab men already seated at either side of the desk. Zelgai took the vacant leather seat in the middle, Miles and Poppy sat on smaller chairs in front of the trio. Poppy crossed and uncrossed her legs before clasping and unclasping her hands. Zelgai laid out the rules of the interview, 'You may make notes with a pen and paper, but not use any electronic equipment.' The two were still without their bags and their pockets were empty; where he thought they might be hiding electronic equipment, God only knew.

'We will tell you what questions to ask and we will

refuse to discuss anything that we do not wish to discuss. The interview will be over when we say it is and you will be taken back to the base in the same way that you arrived. Is that all straight forward?'

Miles again leant forward, the official spokesman, 'Yes that is all understood. May I please take this opportunity to thank you for speaking to us today Mr Mahmood?'

Zelgai nodded. The man in the chair to the left of the desk spoke in a low whisper. Zelgai turned around and listened. They spoke in the throaty Arabic that excluded Miles and Poppy. The conversation was brief. Zelgai suddenly stood as did the man sat to his right; this man now addressed them, as he and Zelgai did a form of do-si-do and swapped seats. Poppy glanced at Miles who kept his eyes facing forward.

'I must apologise for the subterfuge. I am Zelgai Mahmood.'

Miles seemed totally unfazed, whereas Poppy was thinking, what the shitting ada is going on here?

Miles bent forward slightly, with the hint of a bow, 'I am most grateful for the opportunity to meet with you, sir.'

The real Zelgai just nodded as if to say, 'Yes, you should be'. He was fastidiously groomed, his beard close and neat, his brows trimmed, his nails had the perfect almond shape and lustre of a recent manicure. His eyes were like tiny chips of grey flint, cold and blank. Whether it was because Poppy knew who he was and what he was capable of, or whether it was the truth she would never know, she was certain that she had never seen such malevolence in any eyes. It was as if she could see into his soul and the colour was black. A shudder ran along her spine, causing her shoulders to jerk.

He turned to Miles and said, 'I am familiar with your writing Mr Varrasso. I like your work.' His voice was accent-

…ess, with the clear-cut precise vowels of a BBC announcer. His perfect English placed him firmly on the playing fields of a good public school; he might even have been in the first fifteen with Tom and Tristram...

Miles piped up, 'Thank you, sir.'

'I think that your view is balanced, which is not something I can always say of your colleagues,' Zelgai and his associates laughed. Miles chortled softly so that he wasn't left out; although Poppy bet that he didn't find it that funny.

'Tell me, are you a rugby man Miles?'

'Err... not overly. I'll watch if it's on, six nations that sort of thing,' it was diplomatic, concessionary.

Zelgai nodded, noting there was little point in asking Miles for an update on The Harlequins' progress. It was the thing he missed most.

Without warning, he sat back in his chair, resting his chin on his hand. He turned to Poppy, 'Who are you?'

She lowered her head slightly; when she spoke her voice was again quiet, 'I am Nina Folkstok.'

He stared at her for some seconds, before exhaling loudly with a low, irritated hum. When he spoke again, it was as if time stopped; her stomach shrunk around her intestines, which had turned to liquid. She clenched her buttocks to prevent an accident. Her heart had moved into her throat, which she could not only hear beating, but which prevented her from breathing. He smiled at her, now sitting upright with his long fingers forming a pyramid over his lap, 'No. No you are not. I asked you a question and I would like an answer. Who are you?' He was still smiling, but it was the sadistic smile of a mad man, not the friendly smile of someone trying to put you at ease.

'I... I... am...'

Miles started to speak, 'She is a journalist, she...'

'You shut up!' Zelgai's voice boomed around the room. He stood as he shouted, pointing at Miles. He conversed with the guards in his native tongue, the double doors opened; the gun toting, blindfold man came in. He marched over to Miles as Zelgai fired off short bursts of instruction. The guard yanked Miles from his chair and spun him around until he was facing the door; with his gun in Miles back, the man began to push him from the room.

Miles stammered over his shoulder as he was forcibly removed, his sentences fragmented as the pleas stuttered in his mind, 'Please, she... I, let me, it's not... please...'

Poppy didn't move, couldn't move. She sat repeating in her head, 'Please don't kill Miles. This is my fault, it's nothing to do with him, please don't kill him!'

'What are you going to do with him?' Poppy hadn't realised that she'd spoken aloud until Zelgai answered.

'That depends on how honest you are. If you lie to me, I will kill him.' She could tell by his tone that he meant it. Poppy was terrified. Zelgai sat down, all the while looking her squarely in the face, 'I ask you for one final time, who are you?'

Poppy could hear Miles's words in her head, 'Don't speak! You are Nina, don't say a word, you are Nina Folkstok.' She didn't have the strength to lie; too frightened to think straight, let alone concentrate on an elaborate story. She took a deep breath, 'My name is Poppy Day. I am English. I'm a hairdresser. No one knows that I'm here, no one has sent me. I came here because I believe that you have taken my husband and I want him back, please.'

No one spoke for what seemed to Poppy like an age. She felt as if her legs did not belong to her body. She was shaking. Zelgai spoke to his compatriots without averting his gaze. They stood and left the room. Poppy thought that without the scrutiny of the audience it might be less scary, but it was quite the opposite. She did not want to be alone with him. He stroked his beard, 'Tell me one more time, exactly who you are and what it is you want.'

Poppy held his gaze and told him the truth, 'My name is Poppy Day. I am married to Martin Cricket, a British soldier. I am English, I'm a hairdresser. No one has sent me or knows that I am here. I have come because I believe that you are holding my husband hostage. I felt that nothing was being done to get him released and I want him to come home. I really want him to come home.'

He waited until Poppy had finished before starting to laugh, a real belly laugh as though she had told him the funniest joke in the world. He thumped his thigh, trying to regain composure and then wiped at his eyes.

Poppy felt small and helpless. She was six again, there was no one to look after her and no one cared. She missed Martin more than ever; she wanted to be at home. She wanted them both to be home as though none of this had ever happened, as if he had never been away.

'Why do you think that I will listen to you? Why do you think that I will do anything to help someone like you? Why do you think that you can come before me in my own country and make any demand at all?' he spoke quietly, with menace. Poppy had always associated anger and aggression with loud, violent speech. She now knew that this was not always the case.

She shook her head in an attempt to clear her thoughts, 'I don't know how to answer you. I hadn't thought about why or how you should help me. I just knew that I couldn't sit at home and do nothing. I am not one of these girls that can sit by the phone and hope the problem will sort itself out. I am smarter than that, I wanted to take control and

I wanted to fix it. I thought if I could get in front of you and tell you that I miss my husband and that I want him to come home, that this mess is nothing to do with us...'

He interrupted her, 'You are right Poppy Day, it is a mess. But don't be so ignorant as to believe that it is nothing to do with you. It is you that have voted in your government in your democratic society. It is your husband that chose to join an army whose weapons are trained on Afghan families every minute of every day, killing innocent women and children, destroying communities. It is you that live in a society that is sliding into moral decay without looking over its shoulder or pausing for breath. So do not sit there and try to tell me that it is nothing to do with you. It is everything to do with you!'

For the first time in her whole life, she didn't feel very clever at all. Poppy didn't know what to say or do next. She didn't have to; he was in control, calling all the shots.

'Do you love your husband?'

The question took her by surprise, 'Do I love him? Yes of course I love him! I love him more than anything.'

'More than anything?'

'Yes, more than anything.'

'More than you love yourself?'

Poppy paused for a moment, Martin was her whole world, the only person who had made her crappy life bearable and without him she had no life, 'Yes. I love him more than I love myself. I have since I was a little girl.'

'I like that,' he nodded his approval.

He stood then and walked around to the front of the desk, as though in deep contemplation. He was wearing a pale blue, long cotton kaftan and black leather slippers. He leant on the desk and folded his arms across his chest, 'OK. You can take your husband home. You are both free to go.'

Poppy daren't trust what she had heard. She sought confirmation, 'Really?' She didn't want to give him the chance to change his mind, but similarly had to be sure that she had understood correctly.

'Yes, really. You are both free to go. I will arrange for a car to take you both to the base that you came from.'

'Is he here then? Is Mart in this building?'

'Yes, he is in here in this building. Only a few walls and a couple of guards separate you right now.'

'Oh my God! I can't believe it. Can I see him? Can I see him now? Where is he? Can you take me to him?' Poppy felt her tears pooling. She placed her shaking hand over her mouth, unable to hide her absolute joy, relief and happiness. She was overwhelmed, simultaneously beaming and crying. She felt the weight lift from her shoulders, her spirit as light as a feather. Martin was here! She had done it, she was taking him home!

Poppy dashed away the tears with the sleeve of her sweatshirt, she wanted to be composed, 'I want to say thank you to you, sir. Thank you so much. This means everything to me, to us. He's my whole world and he has always looked after me. You have no idea what this means. None at all. I am so grateful to you. Thank you. You have made all my dreams and wishes come true.'

He spoke slowly, 'I accept your thanks. You may both go in the morning.'

'In the morning? OK, thank you. Thank you so much.'

It didn't strike Poppy as a particularly odd request; she assumed it was a transport issue. She didn't care; if they were together she could happily spend the night anywhere. My Mart, my love, I'm coming.

'There is one condition. Tonight you spend the night with me and in the morning I return you to your husband

and you are both free to go.'

'Spend the night with you?' Poppy smiled as she spoke, the reality of what he was asking hadn't sunk in. It wouldn't sink in; it was too awful to comprehend.

'Yes. You will spend the night with me as my whore and in the morning you will both be free to go. If you refuse, I will rape you and then I will kill you. Then I shall give the order for your husband to be killed. We will show him your body before we cut off his head.' He was smiling now.

What Poppy was hearing was so offensive to her senses, so shocking to her ears that her brain refused to accept it. She had to replay his words to try and get them to make sense. He was speaking English, perfect English, but it was as if it were a foreign tongue that she couldn't grasp. She studied his face, hoping for some sign of reprieve, a hint of flexibility; there was none. He was made of stone; he was indeed the monster she had thought he was.

She nodded. Fear rendered her unable to speak, or move.

'Good,' he turned away, preoccupied with some paperwork on his desk.

That was his final comment, 'Good', this one small, mediocre word that sent Poppy's world spiralling out of control.

She was taken up to a bedroom, told to wash and wait for Zelgai. She spent the next few hours in the guise of an automaton. Poppy knew that if she thought too much about what was about to happen, she would go mad; not in a metaphorical sense, but she felt quite literally that she could lose her mind.

She bathed and put on the white nightdress that she had been issued with. The room was sparsely furnished, the bed being the most dominant piece. It was lavishly dressed with a grey silk counterpane and white linen cushions piled high.

Poppy tried to lie down, but the pillows smelt greasy, with the tang of male sweat and unwashed hair. It was disgusting. She sat on the mattress with her knees up under her chin and she waited. Poppy didn't cry or make noise, she didn't do anything.

She thought about Martin, whom she had been told was under the same roof. She thought about her nan. She even thought about her crappy mum. She tried to fill her mind with anything other than what was about to happen. She pictured her body, naked beneath the white linen, deciding to think herself away, mentally escape...

Poppy was thirteen when she got her first period, it wasn't the Victorian shock it was for her nan's generation. She didn't sit crying in the bathroom with the door locked because she thought she was going to die. She knew exactly what was going on thanks to a small cardboard-bound book handed out by the school nurse. Although frankly, the cartoon shapes with oversized coloured-in organs in *This is Your Body* looked nothing like anything on or near her body!

When Poppy first saw the diagrams at the age of eight, she took a few minutes to look for the large black arrow pointing downwards from her belly button after reading, 'below is a picture of you.' She then spent the evening in a state of high agitation, wondering how to broach the subject with her mum that she was in fact one, if not two, large arrows short of being normal.

Poppy confided in her nan, not so much for guidance, or because she needed the obvious supplies, but rather she wanted to share the news with someone, to mark the rite of passage. Well, she did and she didn't. It felt embarrassing and important all at the same time.

Poppy slithered up to her chair. The curtains were

drawn, telly on, 'Nan? I've… err…'

'You've… err… what?' Dorothea looked away from the TV as she stubbed the little rolled-up cigarette into the square pewter ashtray that was permanently on the arm of the chair. It defied science, often teetered, but never actually fell. It was also never washed, the best it could hope for was a quick bang against the inside of the kitchen bin to release the ash, sticky filters, bits of paper and flecks of tobacco that were stuck to its sides with spit. 'For Gawd's sake Poppy Day, whasamatterwivyou?'

'I think I've started,' she mumbled the phrase that she'd heard the girls on the estate use, hoping this would be enough to convey her latest state to her nan. No such luck. Poppy, tinged puce to her very tips and sucked her cheeks into her back teeth to stem the tears.

'You think you've started what?'

'You know…'

'No love, I don't bloody know!' Dorothea moved her head away from Poppy's body. The chef on the TV began to reclaim her attention; pulling her into the pixelated vortex in the corner.

Poppy had to act quickly or lose her to the vacuous rubbish being transmitted, 'My period, I think I've started my period.' Poppy cringed as she tested out the alien word, a grown up word heavy with connotation and expectancy.

Dorothea sprayed laughter over her granddaughter, 'Jesus Poppy Day! By the look on your mush, I thought something terrible had happened!'

'It is terrible!' Poppy wailed, finally unable to curb the hot tears. She wasn't entirely sure why it was so terrible or why she was crying, but she struggled to find anything positive about it.

'Oh Poppy Day! What you crying for? If you think

that's bad girl, wait till you have to give birth. It's like pushing a watermelon through a straw, now that *is* terrible. Or when you get your heart broken. Or both. These will cause you real pain. You don't know you're born love. It's just life, it's just normal!'

Well great. That made it a whole lot better, knowing that there was far, far worse to come. Poppy still carried the mental image of a watermelon going through a straw; it made her clench every muscle she had. It was easy for her nan to say the words, but it didn't feel just like life, or just like normal; in fact, it made everything feel different and not good different either.

'Don't tell Mum, don't tell anyone,' it was Poppy's parting shot and her undoing.

'Why 'Don't tell Mum?"'

'Just because!'

'Just because!' Dorothea mimicked Poppy's voice.

'I mean it Nan.'

Dorothea squeezed her granddaughter's hand, 'What do you think I'm going to do Poppy Day? Put an advert in *The Walthamstow Gazette*?'

It made the little girl laugh; it made her smile. Big event over. Or so she thought. Poppy came home from school five days later to find her nan sitting at the little table under the window, doodling her finger on the floral oilcloth and chuckling over a cup of tea.

'What you laughing at?' Poppy waited for her reply, knowing that it could be a million things; nearly all of them not considered funny by anyone else.

'You know the other day when you said not to tell people about 'you know what?'

Poppy reddened, 'Yes.'

'Well, I got a bit confused. Did you say *do* put an advert

in the *Walthamstow Gazette* or don't?'

Poppy's mind span, 'You didn't!' Dorothea didn't answer immediately, 'Nan! Nan please tell me you didn't!'

Producing the folded paper from under the table, she held it out of her granddaughter's reach.

'Oh no Nan! Please no. Oh my God!' Poppy ran around the table, grabbing at her nan's arm until she managed to hold it fast and pulled the paper from her grip. A two-inch square had been red ringed with a felt-tip pen. Her heart beat too fast. Her eyes, sticky with tears, squinted, concentrating on the wording;

Your Nan loves you
Poppy Day and she
always will! XXX

She smiled, knowing that she loved her nan right back and that she always would.

Poppy swallowed, whispering a missive to Dorothea, 'Nanny, my nanny, please help me, please...' It was similar to grieving, her heart felt like it would break, this. This was mixed with the most terrible fear. Her limbs shook and spasmed involuntarily. She couldn't breathe properly. It was during that period of waiting that Poppy thought that death might be preferable; she was petrified. Had it been only her death, she might have considered it, but it wasn't, and she couldn't begin to imagine being responsible for the execution of her beloved husband, her Mart, who was under the same roof as her, just as she had wished, as she had dreamt of.

As she sat waiting, her blood turned to ice in her veins,; her heart slowed to an almost near-death state and she started to count, one... two... three... Poppy counted the seconds that she had remaining. She counted the last seconds of her old life before it was changed forever. She spent the last few moments of being her, the proper her, counting.

Zelgai entered the room some hours later and initially ignored her. He turned the main light off. The only remaining glow was that which came from under the door and a lamp that shone brightly through the window. The room was bathed with honey-coloured radiance. She watched him move around the room, realising that she had lost a bit of her fear of him. She knew the worst that there could be, or thought she did; there was nothing else for him to threaten her with.

'How do I know that I can trust you? How do I even know that Mart is here?'

He didn't respond.

She spoke quickly, nerves fuelling her speed, 'I said; how do I know that you will keep your word, because you might not? You might... do what you plan to do, do what we have agreed...' Poppy couldn't say the words 'sleep with' or 'have sex with'; it would have made it real and, right up until the moment where she couldn't deny it anymore, it wasn't real. It was nothing more than a horrible thought. '...and then you might kill me, you might kill us both, and so I want you to tell me: how do I know that I can trust you?'

He stroked his neat beard before his mouth twisted open into a smile of sorts. She noticed for the first time that the gap between his front teeth was wide, almost wide enough for a small spare tooth. He pushed the tip of his tongue through the gap until it rested on his top lip; his mouth was wet and open. It made her shudder with revulsion. He scratched at his chin a few more times, as though it was a neglected pet. Then he stopped and popped his tongue back into his mouth, 'It is simple, Poppy, you cannot.'

'What does that mean?' Poppy knew what it meant but needed to hear the clarification.

He rubbed his palms together and walked towards the bed. His fingernails were beautiful and longer than most women's that she knew. He leant back, tilting his head to one side as he breathed out deeply, 'I think you heard me Poppy. It's simple really, you cannot trust me, but you are not stupid are you? You have told me that already. So I'm sure that you do not trust me; thus proving you are smart, because only the stupid are dumb enough to trust me and most of them are now deceased.'

Poppy understood loud and clear. For the first time in her life she felt far from smart. How clever had she been to get into this nightmare situation? She prayed then. She prayed to God and to Martin, asking one of them, or both of them, to help her, 'Please help me, please, please help me.' Neither of them appeared to be listening at that particular moment.

'Are you scared of me?'

Poppy nodded, 'Yes.'

This made him smile, 'That is a good thing.'

Poppy shivered as he walked closer to the bed. She tried to make herself very small. He sat on the edge of the mattress which sagged under his weight, raising his dress slightly to sit down. Poppy could see that he had cotton pyjama-type bottoms on underneath. He leant towards her, as he spoke, she could smell the mint of mouthwash and toothpaste on his breath. It was the way Martin smelt when he got into bed. Her mouth filled with water, she swallowed it quickly. This was no time to be sick.

'I like your name, Poppy. Poppies are my business.'

She bit her lip to prevent the words 'and raping, kidnap

and killing' from tumbling out.

'It suits you much better than Nina Folkstok,' he laughed.

'How did you know?' Poppy didn't know where she found the courage to talk to him. She was shaking with fright.

'My organisation is in touch with Ms Folkstok and that was why she was travelling out here. She is known to us and you are clearly not she,' the way he emphasised the word 'clearly' told Poppy that Nina was superior, better and smarter.

She stared at him. How could she have known? How could Miles have known? They couldn't, they didn't. It was that luck thing again, only this time it was a bad luck thing.

Without warning, he put his hand out, gently pushing the cotton sleeve up over her wrist. He touched his fingertips against her inner arm, softly he stroked the pale area where the tiny purple rivers of blood forked and meandered under her skin. It was as if he had cut her. She physically jumped backwards, gasping loudly. He withdrew his hand, and she settled slightly. Then he slowly reached forward, putting both of his hands around the tops of her arms.

Poppy could feel his hands on her, and his beard centimetres from her face. She knew that it would possibly be the last chance that she had to speak,; she searched for the words and even though they came out jumbled and confused, she was glad that she spoke, glad that she tried, 'Is my Mart close by? Is... Is he near me now? I have only ever... only ever Mart, no other man, ever. I... I... can't... I... My husband... He's my husband...'

He spoke so quietly that his words were barely audible; she had to really concentrate to hear, 'If you say his name, speak again, cry or flinch, I will cut you.' He then reached into the top of his pyjama bottoms and pulled out a very shiny, silver-coloured knife with an ivory handle. He placed it on the pillow and told her to lie down.

Poppy couldn't breathe properly. She could only breathe in shallow pants; unable to get a lung full of air. It was as if he was lying heavily on her chest, crushing the air from her, but he wasn't, not at that point. It was her very own, personal, made-to-measure torture. Poppy wondered whether he could read her mind, see her fear.

He kissed her neck and stroked her face with his elegant fingernails. He kissed her for what felt like an eternity. It made her feel nauseous. She had to fight back the tears and concentrate on breathing. She didn't want to be cut. Then she prayed again, inside her head of course, 'Please, please help me'. But nothing happened. She pictured her heart strings and she mentally pulled them as hard as she could...

Zelgai reached over for his knife, with one hand he held Poppy's wrists over her head, and with the other he used the blade to cut away the thin fabric of the nightdress. The material fell against her naked skin in ribbons. She was trembling. It was worse than Poppy could have imagined. Her nudity, the feel of his hands and face against her skin was more of an ordeal than what came next, much worse. The worst of it was the combination of intimacy and close contact, her greatest fears brought to fruition, her nakedness, his hands on her skin and his mouth against her neck...

Poppy didn't sleep at all that night. Not once did she close her eyes, the pull of the moon could not lull her into slumber. She was wide awake, alert and yet strangely vacant. Zelgai left at some point. He crept from the darkness, furtive, rat-like, but Poppy couldn't have told you when.

She thought he might have set a trap and was waiting for her to fall into it. She was paralysed and lay unmoving, expecting him to come back, dreading him coming back; yet if he was coming back, wanting it to be soon to get it over and done with, anything to take her closer to the morning.

Fourteen

Poppy had watched the purple bruise of night fade to the softer, pinky hue of daylight. The door opened, indicating morning. A flunky came in carrying a silver tray with a drink and bread roll on it. Poppy didn't want anything, only the chance to leave and to take Martin with her. It was a strange reversal for Poppy. She had wanted nothing more than to see her husband for so long, yet, at that point in time, the idea of Martin seeing her was horrific. She felt sure that she was changed, physically marked in some way. The man also carried her clothes which had been washed and dried. Poppy looked at the pile of her possessions, the jeans and sweatshirt, items that reminded her of her life, clothes that had felt the touch of her nan's hand, soaked up the spills and splashes of food cooked in their home and bore the sweat of every mile she had walked in pursuit of her husband. They were now tainted. She knew that as soon as she was able, she would throw them away; the very sight of them offended her. Where they had been, and who had handled them, was ingrained in the fabric and would always be enough to transport her back to that room.

He placed everything on the table without acknowledging Poppy. She swung her leaden limbs from the bed and slipped into the bathroom. She ran the shower, watching the water cascade, listening to the sound of it hitting the tiled floor. She looked down at her body and knew that she was altered. It was as if part of her had been taken, a vital piece that made her the shape she was, that made her Poppy Day. It was gone forever. This made her so sad. She was broken. Poppy knew that no matter what happened from then on, those hands and that face against her skin would always be but a blink away in her thoughts. Without warning she threw up, her vomit splattered into the shower tray. At that moment, Poppy truly would not have cared if he had come back and killed her. She felt like she had died inside.

Standing under the shower, her shock subsided somewhat and she cried. She had been spoiled for Martin. She had done it for him, without option or consent, but these facts seemed irrelevant, she had the most awful feeling that the cost had been too high.

It occurred to Poppy as she scrubbed at the stain of Zelgai's violation, that she had often spoken and thought about the cost of getting Martin safely back. In the most bitter and ironic of twists, she had become the currency. She was the price that had been paid.

Poppy sat on the bed in her freshly laundered jeans, trying to gather her thoughts, trying to hold it all together. Her tears stopped eventually. The tray man came back, gesturing with a flick of his head that she should follow him.

Poppy was shown along a corridor to a wooden door that looked like all the others apart from the two guards outside, both armed. One of the men she recognised as the fake Zelgai from yesterday. She bit the inside of her mouth to stop from quizzing him about Miles, still unaware of his fate. She couldn't look at him directly, figuring he would know where and how she had spent the night; yet, he seemed totally disinterested in her.

Tray man stopped outside the door. Fake Zelgai nodded to him before turning to Poppy, 'Your husband is in here. Be ready to go in half an hour.' He delivered his words above her head into the middle distance, as if she was dirty, contaminated. She wanted to say to him, 'You are right, I am both!'

Poppy stared at the door handle. Could this really be it?

Was it possible that there was only four or five centimetres of wood, separating her and her husband? She felt a swell of excitement in her stomach, despite the tempest that raged inside her. The fake Zelgai said something to the guard; he opened the door, stepping aside to let her pass. Poppy flattened her fringe against her head and pulled her sweatshirt down; she wanted to look as nice as she possibly could for Martin.

The room was dim and smelt fusty, as if men had slept in it for a while with all the windows shut. Poppy fought the desire to gag. There was another armed guard on the other side of the door, which made her smile; the situation was absurd. Martin had never been a scrapper; even she could wrestle all five foot seven of him to the floor and get him to submit with some strategic tickling. What did they think he was going to do against at least two armed guards? Poppy looked around the room. It was sparse but clean enough; not quite the bug-infested hellhole that she had pictured, and for that she was relieved and grateful.

Her eyes were drawn to a man asleep on a bare mattress. Poppy studied him in the shadowy light. She didn't recognise him. He was skinnier than Martin, had the beard growth of a man that hadn't shaved for a month, and when she got closer his stench was overwhelming. It was a combination of sweat, faeces and the acrid nasal sting of ammonia. She was now inches from the face, a face that was smashed, covered with blood, crusted sores and pus. It was disgusting, but it was at close range, unmistakably the face of her beloved husband.

His mouth was swollen, bloody and open slightly. His breath was a rattly snore. Poppy could see that some of his teeth were missing, this made Jenna flash into her mind, 'See Pop, should have gone for that insurance. I told you that his teeth would be buggered.'

Dried blood filled his nostrils, his eyes were a mess. Her heart jumped in her chest, he was hurt, injured. Her poor man, her baby. What had they done to him?

Poppy hadn't planned what she would say or how she would say it. Thoughts rushed into her mind at that point. Had he been drugged? Would he recognise her? How badly was he hurt? Had he broken anything? Would it be too much of a shock? She had no option other than to trust her instinct. She sat gently on the edge of the bed. His mouth closed slightly; his profile, while battered, was that of the face that she'd loved since she was a little girl.

She put her hand out and stroked his hair away from his forehead. It was hard and sticky, a combination of blood and sweat. Her voice was almost a whisper, 'It's OK baby. I am here, Mart, and I have come to take you home.'

As he slept, his mouth twitched into the beginnings of a smile. Still he didn't move. Poppy spoke a little louder, aware that they had to leave in half an hour, 'Mart, it's me, it's Poppy. We are going home baby.'

Poppy hoped her words would filter through and be real to him. She touched his beard, which seemed to be full of scabs; it hurt him slightly, causing him to flinch.

Martin had slept quite soundly, which was unusual. The guards, which they doubled up at night, had thankfully been quiet. Some evenings they would gabble away, or take it in turns to sleep, which was even worse; a couple of them were real snorers that kept him awake with their wheezing and snorting. To get lumbered with that at night when you were tired was bloody awful.

Martin had his favourite dream. He dreamt that he was woken by Poppy. He could tell it was Poppy by her touch and smell. She was stroking the hair away from his forehead and saying his name. He could hear her gentle voice, 'Mart... Mart... It's OK, I'm here, I'm right here.'

The sound of her voice and the touch of her fingers against his skin made him so happy. It felt so real, he could feel her, sense her. It made him miss her so much that he wanted to cry. He didn't want to open his eyes and lose the image. It usually ended there, but today it was different, 'Open your eyes baby. It's all over, I am here and I have come to take you home.'

Martin didn't open his eyes because he didn't want to lose her. The words, the very idea was so wonderful that he wanted to hang on to her for as long as possible. He would then spend the whole day remembering every little aspect of the dream. He felt her hand on his face; his beard was pulling on his skin where she was stroking. It hurt. Martin thought it was odd, he didn't usually feel this irritation in his dream. It made it feel even more real.

Martin opened his eyes slowly and it was as if she was right there! He could see her so clearly perched on the edge of the bed, her beautiful freckles and her toffee-coloured hair. She was in her sweatshirt and jeans, 'I've come to get you baby; it's all over.'

Martin thought he was mad. He considered his hallucination and the realisation scared him. He thought that he'd finally lost the plot. He could see and feel her, but it wasn't possible, he knew it wasn't possible, so the only other possibility was that he had finally lost his mind. He looked at the guard who raised his hand and then stepped outside of the door, leaving them alone.

The vision spoke to him again, 'It's alright baby... It is all over, I have come to take you home.'

He looked at Poppy, but didn't see her; he was in fact looking through her. Poppy was unnerved by his expression, it was a look of madness and the look of someone that was unsure of what was reality. A person that had seen too much.

The two sat for a couple of minutes; he staring in disbelief and she cooing and stroking his skin, coaxing and reassuring. Martin tentatively reached out, like a small child, enraptured by the thrill of bubbles blown for their amusement. He blinked and it was as if something clicked. He sat up, and with trembling fingertips ran them over the curve of her jaw, her lips.

'Aaaaaaagh!' His release was a guttural, primal wail.

He allowed himself to believe that she was real. He continued to howl in a loud cry that seemed to go on forever; he couldn't help it. He sat looking at her with tears running down his face and into his mouth. He made the most awful sobbing noise, a cross between a scream and a gurgle. He was a drowning man; he couldn't stop it.

He pulled her into his chest and held her as tightly as his unconditioned arms would allow. Poppy lay her head in the curve of his shoulder, it felt like Martin, it felt like her husband. He crushed her to him and the two sat locked together. He cried into her hair. Martin knew that he would never fully be able to describe exactly what it felt like to feel her body against his, to smell her, to hear her voice, it was... magic.

Martin couldn't stop the tears that soaked into her hair and clothes. She too cried with unrestrained emotion. They sat like that for some minutes, trying to fully comprehend that they were together, that it was all nearly over.

Poppy drew away and looked into his face.

'Help me Poppy, help me,' his voice was cracked, his tone beaten.

Poppy knew there and then that she had done the right thing. She knew that, in spite of everything, in spite of *everything*, she had been right to go and get her husband.

Martin could hardly speak. He kept repeating her name, 'Poppy... Poppy...' and then, 'Help me... help me Poppy.'

She could only respond with, 'It's OK baby, I have come to take you home.' He believed her, without question, he believed her. She was real and he knew that she had come to take him away from this prison.

Poppy was desperate to be out of that house and heading back to safety. She was conscious of not hurrying Martin too much, but also didn't want there to be hitches. She had been told that there was transport leaving in half an hour and, no matter what, they were going to be in it, on it, or riding it, whatever it was.

She helped Martin walk into the bathroom adjacent to the room. He was wobbly on his legs, as weak as a lamb. She hated seeing him like that, but was glad that she was the one there to help him. She thought about the vows that they had giggled through, 'in sickness and in health'. Martin shook his head at her, they laughed at the ludicrous situation and it was good to see him smile. His breath, however, was disgusting, reminding her of rotting meat, but with a sickly sweet undertone; it was repellent. Poppy did her best not to show him.

She hated the fact that he was wearing traditional Afghan clothing. It made him look like them. She knew that it was a small point, not one to be discussed; her priority was to get him to safety, to medical care and then home. When they got home, he could tell the army what they could do with their job and they would start over. She had it figured out, a plan for their future.

She thought about the green spaces that she had seen

around Brize Norton; it was another world and one that she wanted them to explore. It was just what they needed, a new start in the countryside where they could have babies and keep them all safe, a good place to make their little family.

Martin was still amused by the novelty of a bathroom. Poppy had no idea that he had only been moved there recently and couldn't understand how excited he was to see that room. There was a proper loo, which Martin found painful to sit on. He had been kicked and smacked across the buttocks and lower back, his bones still ached. He'd lost a lot of weight and sitting on the porcelain, with his weight pushing down on his bony bottom, felt quite painful. He smiled, after spending so long dreaming about sitting on a proper loo it hurt so much that he almost longed for his trusty bucket.

Ordinarily, this small disappointment would have further broken his spirit, but not today, today was one of joy. Martin walked over to the little sink in the corner. There was a small rectangular mirror screwed to the wall. He glanced into it and physically jumped backwards. He looked behind him to see who had come into the bathroom, but there was no other man there. He looked back slowly, it took a second or two for him to realise that it was his own face that he was looking at. He could never have imagined looking into a mirror and not recognising his own face, the idea and the reality, were both shocking.

He had a thick beard. Having only ever had a weekend's worth of stubble at most, he looked unkempt. His long whiskers held both sores and food. His mouth was a swollen mess, bloody and misshapen, thanks to the butt of the Kalashnikov and the hard floor. The teeth that hadn't fallen, or been knocked out, were stained and vile.

His left eye drooped slightly. Martin was unaware that the infection he had contracted would permanently damage his sight. He ran his fingertips over the eyes that were red and oozing; one was bruised black and yellow, another memento from his recent fall. His hair was longer than he had ever worn it and stood on end like tiny rats tails; it, like the rest of him needed a good wash.

Poppy watched him survey the damage as she leaned against the wall; there was nothing that she could say, no words of solace. Martin could see the reality before him, any condolence would only have served to patronise.

'Look at the bloody state of me Pop,' his voice was still a hoarse mumble. His tears fell again unchecked. He ran his hand over his face and head, his tears abated as anger took over. He was mad that his wife had to witness him like this. It was no accident, someone had made him look this way, someone had so changed his life and his luck that he looked into the mirror and didn't know who he was.

'What have they done to me Pop?' there were other, endless questions. What right did someone have to do this to a human being? What right did anyone have to bend a human being to their will, to deny them freedom and play with their mind? Why had it happened to him? To them?

Martin knew that as far as his captors were concerned, he wasn't a person and if he wasn't a person, then what was he? What was less than a person? When he thought about the answer to that question, he wasn't just angry, but filled with frustration and rage.

'Baby, I don't want to rush you, but we have to get going, we have to get out of here,' her tone was urgent, despite her attempt to soothe.

Martin was embarrassed to be so weak; he stumbled and teetered like a toddler. Poppy had to prop him up.

He found it hard to accept that she was there. He had a fear that at any moment he might open his eyes from a drug-induced state and she would be gone, and he would be back on that mattress. He shook his head as though this would help clear the fog, help him find the reality.

Martin's eyes darted around, trying to take in every small detail; it was the novelty of not having his eyes covered as he moved. He tried to memorise the layout, any detail that might help identify where he had been held and by whom; his training kicked in.

Poppy thought about the last time she had trod the stairs, she had been different. It had been before... before... There was no time to think about it, to mourn or reflect; they weren't safe yet.

The two ventured out into the hallway, fake Zelgai and one of the guards from the previous day were waiting with blindfolds. Once again they were marched conga-style, with Martin leaning heavily on Poppy's frame, until they were guided into a car, which, by the echo of their footsteps, sounded as though it was parked in a garage. Poppy couldn't be sure, but it felt like the same car that had delivered her and Miles the previous day. She couldn't believe that it was only the day before, it felt like a lifetime ago. Poppy thought about Miles then, praying that he was OK. She said a lot of prayers over that twenty-four hour period, not all of them were answered.

Martin and his wife sat close together on the back seat. Poppy was comforted by the fact that she could feel his thigh against hers. She thought about the times they had sat on their sofa watching the telly with their legs touching, at home, safe and sound. Twenty minutes passed and their blindfolds were removed. It was the first proper opportunity they had to look at each other in the light. Poppy was newly shocked by her husband's deterioration; he looked like an old man or a tramp, someone that you wouldn't chose to sit in close proximity to. He kept shaking his head, as though he couldn't believe that she was there. Every time he did this, she gripped his hand as if to confirm that she was real, by his side and that she always would be. His eyes screwed shut every time she squeezed. She thought it was high emotion, unaware that his finger was broken and every time she applied pressure he was in agony.

Despite having so many unanswered questions, the two were strangely quiet, both acutely aware that they were in the custody of his captors, more specifically, 'their captors', with their big guns. Although unspoken, both shared the fear that they would not be delivered safely to the base, anything could still happen.

Poppy didn't fear death at that moment. If those were to be her last minutes, then she was glad to have had the chance to see Martin and feel his arms around her one last time. She figured that if her one last act had been to show her husband how much she loved him by attempting his rescue, then that would be no bad thing.

Martin, although outwardly calm, was gripped by a new terror. What if they didn't take them back? What if they were driving them into the desert to kill them? He thought of Aaron, he pictured what they did to his friend and he pictured them doing it to Poppy. Aaron's last moments were vivid in his mind, but it was Poppy's face that stared back at him, her expression pleading with him to do something, anything to help her... His stomach lurched. He knew it would be his own private hell on earth. He couldn't stand the thought of it. He would have pleaded, begged, he would have done anything. Courage and dignity in death would not have entered his head; it would all have been about saving his Poppy. They could do what they liked to him, but he couldn't let anyone lay a finger on Poppy.

The silence was a welcome balm.

The road started to look familiar and, sure enough, as Poppy squinted into the daylight, she could see the edge of the camp. It was tiny and high up in the distance, reminding her of mud-coloured Lego. It looked wonderful. She felt a surge of hope and relief that they were going to make it. They were going home.

When Martin saw the camp in the distance he knew that it was nearly over. He felt himself breathe for the first time. His muscles started to unclench.

The car slowed and stopped some way outside of the base. The guards were almost polite, opening the doors and standing aside, before driving off without a word. Martin thought it strange, after all that they had done to him, all he had been through, they simply got into the car and left. Naively, he would have liked some reconciliation or explanation. There they stood, husband and wife, not speaking, not moving. It was a mixture of shock and relief. It was surreal.

They stood for a minute or two, until Poppy put her arms around Martin's waist and held him tight. They enjoyed being able to touch without being watched.

'How did they do it Poppy? How did the army get you to me? Why did they risk using you? It doesn't make any sense to me.'

'They didn't Mart. They don't even know that I'm here.'

'What d' you mean?'

'I mean, Mart, that I came by myself. The only people that know I am here are a journalist that helped me and my nan.'

Martin was thoroughly confused, 'How? How Poppy?'

He wobbled again and nearly fell.

'Don't worry about it now baby. We have all the time in the world for questions; let's just concentrate on getting you to a doctor.'

'Poppy?'

'Yes baby?'

He held his hand out towards her. Pinched between his thumb and forefinger was a tiny white feather, 'I got your feather; it gave me so much hope. Can you look after it for me?'

'Of course I will,' she popped it inside the fabric of her jeans pocket. Poppy didn't fully understand the significance of the talisman, but it had been important enough for Martin to keep and that made it special to her too. Martin's relief was evident, he could now relax knowing that his feather was in safe hands, her little calling card that she had sent to him when he needed her the most.

The duo was spotted by one of the cameras placed around the edge of the base. A soldier in the observation station alerted his superior. It was an extraordinary conversation that would be traded over a cup of coffee more than once.

'I think you should take a look at this sir.'

'Take a look at what?' the officer snapped at the young soldier, who seemed intent on disturbing his reading.

'It appears to be a young white male, in Afghan dress, supported by a young white female, in jeans and sweatshirt. They look like they might be dancing or swaying, but certainly laughing...'

The officer abandoned his flask and reluctantly swung his boots off the desk and onto the floor, 'Swaying and laughing in the middle of the desert, dressed in jeans and a sweatshirt?'

'Y...Yes sir, I think...' the officer's tone sufficiently

filled his subordinate with enough fear to doubt his own judgement.

'I think you need a better pair of binoculars soldier!'

'Yes sir.'

The officer grabbed the glasses and trained them in the middle distance, 'What the...?' It wasn't often that he was lost for words. 'Get the quick reaction force out there immediately.'

The first Land Rover approached them at high speed, slowing as it got closer. Two men, with SA-80 rifles trained on them, jumped out of the vehicle and another four took up positions behind them. As they got closer, one of them shouted out, 'Stop! Stand still and show us your hands! Do not run! Do not move!'

Adrenalin coursed through Poppy's veins. The soldiers had come out of nowhere, British soldiers, which she assumed meant a friendly welcome. She couldn't believe that she was at the wrong end of yet another gun.

The soldier shouted again, 'Do not move! Show your hands!'

Martin fainted. Poppy felt it was her time to respond, 'Don't move? You're having a laugh! Where the bloody hell do you think I am going to go? I'm stood in the middle of the sodding desert, my husband has fainted and I am trying to hold him up!'

The two soldiers at the front of the group looked at each other, 'Who are you?'

'I am Poppy Day. This is my husband Martin Cricket. I've just gone and got him from the ZMO and he is getting very heavy.'

There was a pause while they spoke into their radios. Poppy listened to the crackle and response of distorted voices as she lost her grip on Martin; he started to slip to the ground. One of the soldiers ran forward. The others remained stationary with guns trained over their colleagues' back. 'Martin Cricket?' he looked alternately between Poppy and Martin, his expression one of sheer disbelief.

'Yes, Martin Cricket. I think he's fainted; he's not in good shape. Can we get him to a doctor please?'

The soldier signalled over his shoulder, two of his colleagues ran forward. The pair lifted Martin from her arms and carried him to their vehicle, 'Did you say you are his wife?'

'Yep'

'His wife?' he repeated

Poppy placed her hands on her hips, 'Yes I am Poppy, his wife. I came to get him and bring him home because you lot sure as hell can't be trusted to look after him, look at the state of him!'

'Are you hurt?'

Was she hurt? She didn't know what to say, her heart was ripped in two at the sight of her husband. Her spirit had been rendered numb by what she had endured. The state of extreme fear that she had been forced to live in over the last few hours had taken its toll. With the adrenalin subsiding, she was mentally exhausted, thirsty and confused.

'I'm fine.'

'Stay close to me.'

Poppy walked very close to her armed soldier and smiled. She had been alone and unarmed with a murderer for a number of hours, while his knife smiled at her from the pillow. She had travelled in cars with gun men capable of killing in remote deserts and he was worried about her walking four feet into an armoured car, whilst surrounded by armed British soldiers.

The two men carrying Martin placed him on the back

seat; he was slumped, still unconscious. They were squashed into the first vehicle. One of the soldiers smiled at Poppy, 'I am a mate of Martin's; it's brilliant to have him back. I can't believe it.'

'Did you know Aaron too?' Poppy didn't know why she asked. She wasn't thinking straight.

He nodded.

The vehicle trundled over the sand in silence, all occupants lost in memories, apart from Martin, who hadn't yet woken up. Poppy almost envied him.

As soon as the vehicle had cleared security, they were driven further into the compound. Martin was rushed off to the medical centre. Poppy ambled from the car to find herself surrounded by people. It was hard to assess the numbers in such a confined space, but it felt to her as if hundreds of people were approaching her, all with questions or some just wanting to have a look. She spied Jason Mullen among the crowd, 'Jason! Is Miles here? Is he OK?'

'He is OK Freckles; worried about you but fine!'

Poppy wanted to cry, but couldn't, not with all those people around her. She was relieved and so happy, Miles was safe, 'Will you tell him I'm fine Jason? And tell him thank you!'

'I will Nina!' he winked at her, any subterfuge clearly forgiven.

This was the point at which Poppy felt most like she had succeeded, mission accomplished. Martin was safe, she was back and Miles was OK. It was wonderful news, the best.

Someone placed their arm on her back and seemed to be pushing her in a particular direction, a soldier leant toward her, 'Come with me, we will get you checked over and then there are a few people that would like a chat with you.'

'Sure'.

They entered a large building that still had the air of Portakabin, but was clearly some sort of high-tech communication headquarters. There was a bank of computers and large screens on the wall showing Sky news, below them sat rows of telephones. Seven people sat at various desks. One of them she recognised instantly,

Major Anthony Helm was angry. Poppy could tell by the way his face was red and blotchy. She noted how he bit into his lip to stop himself from saying something that he would regret. She did that too and recognised the trick, 'Mrs Cricket.'

'I've already told you to call me Poppy.'

He ignored her, 'Are you hurt or injured in any way? Do you need medical attention?'

His clipped tone told her that he didn't care whether she was hurt or not.

'No, I am fine. How is Mart?' as usual she couldn't give a stuff if she'd offended the Major; her only concern was for her husband and his wellbeing.

'He is dehydrated, his ribs are badly bruised, he's broken a finger and cheekbone, but he will live.'

Poppy knew that he meant this literally and not in the way that a civilian might use it. Once again she was relieved, 'Can I go and see him?'

'Can you go and see him?' he narrowed his eyes, anger finally getting the better of him, 'What do you think this is Poppy, a cottage hospital? We don't have visiting times as such; there isn't a nurse's station for you to drop off flowers and chocolates! This is an operational theatre where people are engaged in combat. This is bloody a war zone!'

'So does that mean I can see him or I can't?'

Anthony balled his fingers into fists and took a deep

breath, 'How did you get over here Poppy?'

Poppy had already decided that her best option was to tell the truth, the whole truth and nothing but the truth. Lying had got her into too much trouble already, 'I came over on an army flight from Brize Norton, a few days ago, maybe a week ago now, I'm not entirely sure, time seems to have gone a bit fuzzy.'

'You came over on an army flight from Brize Norton?' She nodded.

He looked at the others in the room, who looked at him and then looked away, 'So, let me get this straight, you just pitched up and said, 'Hi, I'm Poppy Day, here is my passport and I would like to get on this flight to Afghanistan please'?'

'Not exactly.'

'Not exactly?'

Poppy wondered if he was going to repeat everything that she said, 'No.'

'Enlighten me Poppy; tell me why 'not exactly'?'

'Well, I didn't have a passport.'

'You didn't have a passport?'

She shook her head and thought about saying, 'Anthony Helm is a dickhead', to see if he would repeat it. 'No I didn't have a passport because I don't own one.'

'What ID did you have then if not a passport?'

Poppy knew before she spoke that he wasn't going to like her response, 'I had my library card and my bank card.'

He almost spat the words, 'Your library card?' She nodded.

'You used your real name, your real details, you showed your library card and they let you get on the flight?'

'Well, yes kind of, I was crying. I was very upset. I think the guard at the first security desk felt sorry for me...'

'Jesus H Christ!' once again he looked at the others,

scanning their faces, wanting someone to blame; again they averted their gaze.

'I didn't get straight on the plane though, I made out that I was a Danish journalist whose passport had been stolen and the other guard at the second check let me through.'

'Did you cry for him as well?'

'No.'

He was visibly twitching at having to control his anger, 'And then Poppy, once you had arrived, how did you get into the camp and where did you stay?'

'I got on the army bus and I have been staying in the media tents.'

'In the media tents?'

Here we go again... 'Yes, the media tents.'

'But that's where I stay.'

'Hey, we're neighbours!'

Someone in the room laughed; this sent him over the edge. As he spoke, spit flew from the corner of his mouth. His accent was the strongest that she'd heard it, as if he couldn't do angry and voice control at the same time, 'You seem to find this whole episode extremely amusing. Let me assure you Mrs Cricket that there is nothing vaguely funny about what you have done. If you had been killed, can you imagine the conversation that we would be having now?'

Poppy couldn't help it, she knew she shouldn't have said it, but she did, '...well we wouldn't be having one would we, if I had been killed?' Her inner monologue was screaming 'Oh my God shut up Poppy!' This was Martin's boss after all.

'I can see that there is no point trying to engage you with any kind of logic, but just what did you hope to achieve? Why could you not sit back like every other army wife that I have ever met and let us handle the situation?'

'I am not 'every other army wife'. I couldn't give a shit about coffee mornings and convention! I told you why once before, my exact words were that I had a lack of faith in you and your army, which started on the day that my husband was failed by you and taken hostage while doing his bloody job! That was further compounded by the fact that some weeks later we had no idea where he was and you were no closer to getting him back. With that in mind, I decided to go and get him myself. I didn't believe that you could do it and I was right. As for the question, what did I hope to achieve? I hoped to get in front of Zelgai Mahmood and to negotiate the release of my husband.' Poppy swallowed as a picture of the 'negotiations' swam into her head, 'I am happy to report, Anthony, that I achieved both.'

This time everyone looked at her, 'You met with Zelgai Mahmood?'

'Yes.'

'And you negotiated Martin's release?'

'Yes.'

The Major walked backwards and sat on a swivel chair. He placed his head in his hands as though this final piece of information was too much, 'Jesus H Christ.'

Poppy noticed that this was the second time that he had said this. What was he asking for? Help? Divine inspiration? She almost felt sorry for him, having been looking for both herself only recently.

Everyone was looking from him to Poppy and back again. The tension in the air was tangible. He closed his eyes and breathed deeply, seeming to reach a conclusion in his head, 'OK. OK. Enough. I don't know how you managed to achieve what you did Poppy, and I can see that what you have done could be interpreted by some as a great success, but it was reckless, dangerous and could have meant loss of life for a lot of innocent people had it all gone wrong. That aside, what we are left with is potentially a public relations disaster on a monumental scale, and I am left in the unenviable position of having to ask you for your help.'

He had her interest now, 'Of course I will help you. I will help you in any way that I can. I didn't want to cause trouble for you, Anthony, or anyone else, I only wanted my husband back.' Poppy meant it, she really meant it. His smile looked genuine; it was his turn to be relieved.

When Martin awoke he was lying on a trolley in the Medical centre.

'Hi there,' the medic was staring at him, as if she had been waiting for him to wake up.

'Hello.'

'How are you feeling?'

'Fine,' Martin lied. He felt weak and more than a little bit confused.

She bent over and shone a light into Martin's eyes, 'You've got badly bruised ribs, a knackered finger and your cheekbone is cracked. You have other severe bruising and a nasty case of conjunctivitis, but other than that you are doing alright. You fainted with dehydration, that's why we have you on a drip. We will leave you hooked up to the IV for a little while longer and then we can move you somewhere more comfortable. If you need anything just shout.'

Martin nodded, 'Where is my wife? Where's Poppy?' As the question left his lips, he felt fearful that he might have imagined the whole thing, that the medic might say, 'Your wife? Oh mate, you've had a bump on the head...'

She didn't, 'Ah yes, or Lara Croft, we haven't seen

her down here. I expect she is being de-briefed, we can probably get a message to her if you like.'

'Yes, can you tell her..? Can you tell her..?' Martin couldn't speak through his tears, she was real; he hadn't imagined it. What did he want to tell her? There were no words that he could say to his amazing girl, nothing to begin to describe his gratitude. He would try to tell her in his own time, when they were alone, when they were home.

All personnel had been asked to go, leaving Anthony, Poppy and a Colonel Blakemore. Someone had given Poppy a cup of tea; it was the sweetest nectar, reminding her that she hadn't eaten, drank or slept in a very long time. It also reminded her of home. She thought about her nan, sitting in her little room with the telly turned up too loudly.

Anthony took control. Poppy hated the way he spoke to her as if she were stupid. She hated that from anyone, more than anything, 'We find ourselves in a very delicate situation Poppy. It is, of course, wonderful that Martin is back safe and relatively unharmed, that was always our sole objective...'

Poppy bit her tongue, said nothing.

'...however, the British Army is so much more than its daily activity and its soldiers. Do you understand what I mean by that?'

She shook her head, thinking, 'Sorry, dickhead; once again you've lost me'.

'We have a reputation and it is our reputation that precedes us in every campaign that we enter into, every deployment we undertake. Our reputation is everything.'

Poppy nodded to show understanding; gotcha so far Tony.

'This war against terrorism and terrorists is different to

any other war that we have been engaged in. On 9/11 our world changed, your world changed and what we have now is rarely a physical battle, but much more a battle of wits, if you will. It is a matter of intelligence and counter intelligence, covert activity and high-tech endeavours, specialisms if you like. Gone are the days when brute force and who has the biggest guns equalled success. Above all, Poppy, it is about perceptions and belief...'

She was still listening.

'...it's not only about what our soldiers in theatre, and what the public at home perceive and believe, but also what our enemies perceive and believe. I cannot begin to describe the damage that your foray could do to our reputation and peoples' perceptions if it were to become public information,' Anthony was quiet, awaiting her response.

'I can see that it would put you in a difficult position. If it was known that the Special Forces operation to rescue Mart failed because you got the wrong house, yet me, a twenty-two year old hairdresser, managed to breach every aspect of your security and meet with the head of the ZMO to bring my husband back, I guess it wouldn't do much for your fearsome reputation and the perception that your force is a force of excellence.'

'Quite,' she noticed that a nerve twitched below his right eye.

'So, what are you suggesting?' Poppy wasn't being clever; she was genuinely struggling to see where he was heading with his argument.

'When we get back to the UK, there will be a press conference to announce that Martin is back and safe. We would like to confirm that it was a Special Forces operation after weeks of negotiation that made it possible. How do you feel about that?' He looked at Colonel Blakemore.

Poppy watched them nervously awaiting her response. She was quiet for a while, thinking it through. She was tired and this made thinking about anything difficult. She closed her eyes and rubbed them with her fingertips, 'I don't really care how you say he was brought home. I don't care because to me it isn't important. I was only ever interested in getting him home, not in showing up your army, or for any personal glory.'

They both sighed, visibly relieved to hear this, 'That's good Poppy. It would have been terrible for Martin to get home, only to have you imprisoned for the many violations that you have committed. The breaching of two countries' immigration laws alone carries a custodial sentence, without even looking at the penalties for trespassing on a MoD airfield and stowing away on a military aircraft...' Anthony finished on the threat, letting it hang in the air. The bastard.

It was some hours later before Martin was well enough to scan the out-of-date newspapers that someone placed in his hands. He couldn't believe what Poppy had achieved. She was on the front page, asking for his release! He read every word over and over, wanting all the detail. It felt very strange to be reading about a situation that felt like a story, an awful, sad story, but just that. When he stopped to think about the fact that it was his story, their story, with Poppy's picture staring back at him, it was surreal.

Poppy made her way to her tent. The little cot was there, just as she had left it. She ran her hand over its surface; it was a different person that had laid her head there so many hours before. She had been so preoccupied that she had managed to push what had happened out of her head, but as she sat on the end of the little bed all alone, she broke her heart. She thought about what Zelgai had done to her and she sobbed. Her skin prickled in revulsion and shame. What had she done? What on earth had she done?

A figure entered the tent. She sat up and tried to stop crying. It was Miles. Poppy was delighted to see him, delighted to see anyone at that point. She needed the comfort and reassuring presence of another human and she was so glad that it was him. Jumping up, she threw her arms around his neck and carried on crying. He held her close against him. She felt safe, protected and was so glad to see him alive and unharmed.

'Oh Miles, I am so glad to see you! I had imagined all sorts. Jason told me that you were safe, but I knew that I wouldn't be happy until I had seen you!' Poppy looked up to see that he was crying too, 'What's the matter with you, you silly sod?'

Miles removed his glasses and pinched his nose as was his habit, trying to pull himself together, 'You have been worried? Jesus Poppy, you have no idea! I begged them to let me stay with you. I had no clue as to what they were going to do with you and it was entirely my fault. I took you there; I put you in that danger; I didn't think it through. I was arrogant and selfish. I am so, so sorry...'

'Don't be daft! I insisted on you taking me with you; you gave me the solution! You have protected and helped me all the way along, Miles. I couldn't have achieved anything without you. None of it would have been possible. I'd still be stood like a silly cow, trying to hitch a lift back to London from Brize bloody Norton, wherever that is. It has all been possible because of you, all of it, and I will never ever forget what you have done for me, what you have done for us!'

'I could never have forgiven myself Poppy if anything

bad had happened to you...'

Poppy shook her head and lied to her friend, her dear friend, 'Well Miles, nothing bad did happen to me so you are in the clear mate, off the hook!'

He rubbed his palm over his stomach, trying to settle the swirl of emotion, a hurricane at his very core; it was relief and something else too. Miles recognised the stirring of a deep and unrequited love. He knew that the object of his desire was forever bound to Martin. Their future and their history had been scripted and sealed, long before he arrived.

Martin's visitors were restricted; he didn't get the chance to catch up with many of his mates which he would always regret. He was informed that Aaron's body had been recovered and had, indeed, been given the burial that he deserved. Martin took great comfort from this, and hoped that Aaron's family did too.

He was told the story that they were to stick to at the press conference. He agreed, but was suspicious of how something that everyone was talking about at Bastion was going to be contained, and how exactly they were going to prevent the truth from leaking out. He figured that they knew more about it than he did, so kept quiet. He was so proud of his wife and that was all that mattered to him at that point.

By the time he got on the plane to travel to Brize Norton, Martin had been given a much needed haircut, a shave and generally cleaned up. He still looked rough and haunted, but a million times better than when Poppy had found him.

Martin couldn't believe that he was actually travelling back to England, going home! It was the most wonderful feeling. There had been times in the previous weeks when he had felt sure that he was never going to get back there or, even if he would live to see another day, and there he was, in a clean uniform, with his beautiful wife by his side and he was going home.

It felt wonderful.

So many people in the camp wanted to shake his hand and wish him well. For some it was relief, glad that it hadn't happened to them. You know; the whole statistic thing? If a soldier was taken hostage, let's say once every three years, then they were safe.

Poppy and Martin were told there would be a press conference when they got back, that the media would probably be there, but they had no idea of the scale or the level of interest. The army had no clue either, no idea of exactly what they were dealing with, none at all. It was completely overwhelming.

Fifteen

Poppy barely registered the fact that she was flying; her fourth plane journey had quickly become the 'usual drill'. She felt nothing but relief to be leaving the arid planes of Afghanistan. The touchdown on British soil was bumpy, nervous titters were audible as the plain skittered for a split second on the wet tarmac. Martin marvelled at the grey drizzle that greeted them, he had never seen weather so beautiful. The party were led off by Colonel Blakemore with Major Helm kowtowing behind him. The Crickets gripped each other's hands as they walked down the steps to face a sea of people in the distance. Poppy wondered what they were waiting for. It didn't occur to her that the reception might be for her and Martin.

A car met them on the tarmac. Their destination: a room in the main block that had been set up for the press conference. As the car drove along, flashes from cameras fired through the window, people were waving flags, hands, scarves, anything they had. Some were crying, others cheering. Hand painted banners and posters read 'Welcome home!' and 'Martin our Hero!'; it was complete madness. Martin was excited and overwhelmed by the reception. He closed his eyes; it smelt like England, felt like England. People cheered and clapped, they were going crazy. Children were hoisted up by the armpits to see and be seen. They were waving homemade placards as if greeting pop stars. It was incredible, ordinary people had turned out to say hello and wish them well. Martin was humbled by the outpouring; he wanted to thank them all. They were brilliant, every single one of them. The faces in the crowd were mainly service families, whose loved ones were on tour and who watched with heavy hearts from the same positions as the coffins returned home, flanked by comrades. For them, Martin was a symbol of hope, something to be thankful for and a reprieve from the burden of worry.

The car snaked its way through the masses. Anthony Helm seemed not to notice the celebration or the sheer numbers; he was distracted, fractious. The party eventually pulled up at the back door of a low building and were led through a narrow corridor. Even Brize Norton personnel craned their heads around office doors to catch a glimpse of the man that got away. They too were seemingly not immune to the furore surrounding the Crickets. Poppy wondered if a certain female security guard was around so she could get a glimpse of the girl that had travelled somewhere after all... At the end of the passageway, a door was held open and the two were led up the steps to a podium.

Martin, resplendent in freshly laundered desert fatigues, was next to Poppy, with Anthony and the Colonel on either side; like the top table they never had at a wedding beyond their means. There were at least eight microphones set up in front of them. Poppy was anxious, but this wasn't about her; she was there to support her hero, her Martin, who looked pale. He reached for her hand under the table. They knew what was going to happen; Anthony the dickhead was going to read out a prepared statement, Martin would then answer questions about it. He couldn't imagine what he was going to say that would be of interest. He also felt like a fake. It was Aaron who was the real hero and Poppy too; what she had achieved was unbelievable. He needn't have worried.

It took a while to attain order in the room and for it to fall quiet. The small space was packed with people at different levels. Some stood at the back, the lucky few were on chairs, and even more were crouched down on the floor in front of the podium. All were holding microphones, mobile phones, tiny tape recorders or PDAs, some clutched old-fashioned spiral note pads and pens.

Anthony pulled his tunic taut and shot his cuffs before speaking. Poppy noticed that he was using a strange posher than usual voice, his telephone voice probably, 'Ladies and gentlemen of the press, I thank you for coming here today on the wonderful occasion of welcoming Private Martin Cricket back home...' He paused while there was an impromptu round of clapping and cheering. Martin squeezed his wife's hand tighter, squashing her fingers.

'...we are, of course, entirely grateful for the interest and immense support that the British public and media have shown for this story, and we are delighted that Martin is safe and well, here with us today. We would like to confirm that after weeks of negotiation, it was a Special Forces operation on the ground that made this remarkable rescue possible...'

Major Helm was part way through his statement. Martin was aware of a cheer every time his name was mentioned. He was busy thinking about the questions he might get asked, when utter chaos broke out.

It was as if someone had thrown an invisible switch. A hundred different voices were screaming and shouting at Poppy. Martin found it quite funny at first but this quickly turned to anxiety. The noise was deafening and Martin knew too well what an aggressive crowd was capable of. He couldn't make out too much of what they were saying, but could clearly hear his wife's name, 'Poppy! Poppy!' They were shouting it in every direction he looked.

Poppy wasn't sure who yelled first, but it was as if someone had shouted 'GO!' There were screams and shouts from all corners of the room. The noise was thunderous. They surged forward, a seething mass, mouths opening and closing in an uproar of words and questions. It was impossible to decipher which words came from which person. Through the cacophony, she could distinctly make out the following,

'Is it true Poppy that you went and got your husband back?'

'Is it true Poppy that you masqueraded as a journalist to get into the country?'

'Poppy! Poppy! Over here! What was Zelgai Mahmood like?'

'Were you armed Poppy?'

'Do you like the nickname Lara Croft?'

'Were you scared Poppy?'

'Do you think you will go back to hairdressing, or will that be too boring?'

'Poppy, your mother has said that you were always adventurous. What are you planning on next? Tackling Hamas maybe?'

'Martin did you expect your wife to come and get you out?'

'Poppy, what did you know that the British Army did not? How did you do it?'

The two were dumbfounded and shocked. Poppy couldn't speak, couldn't answer. The flash bulbs blinded her and the noise made it hard to think straight. She felt a hand on her shoulder, it was Major Helm. He was trying to make her stand, but was looking at Martin. His voice had lost its haughty tone, 'Get her the fuck out of here. Now!'

Poppy wanted to say to him, don't you talk to my husband like that! But it was pointless, no one would have heard, and she could see that Martin wanted to get out of the place, quickly.

Major Helm stood with his shoulders back, as if on parade. He looked ready to explode. Martin resisted the temptation to say 'I told you so.' He'd known they wouldn't be able to contain the news that his wife had been instrumental in his release; too many people at Bastion knew and it was too incredible. It was the sort of story that people would phone home to tell their families, who would then tell their mates, who would tell their families, who would then tell their mates... What Poppy did was a victory for everyone that has ever felt that the world was too big a place for them to make a difference in. She proved that it isn't. It was the sort of story that newspapers would find irresistible, at least, that was what he thought and it turned out he was right.

They were ushered off the stage. Martin, Anthony and Poppy found themselves in a narrow corridor between the makeshift press conference room and some offices. The din next door had quietened. Martin turned to his wife and started laughing. She laughed back as he fell into her. The two slumped, weak-kneed against the wall, giggling into each other's hair under the full glare of the fluorescent strip lights. It was partly nerves and partly because it was hilarious.

Poppy looked over Martin's shoulder into Anthony's face. He was staring at her with hatred in his eyes. She hadn't done anything wrong and didn't think she deserved to be looked at like that. 'What?' she asked him. It stopped her laughter.

'What? What?' his nostrils flared with each 't'.

Oh God, he was back to repeating everything. Poppy stared at him, 'Tony, do you think that you were a parrot in a former life?' She didn't know why she said it, possibly to make Martin laugh more. It worked, he was near collapse, but this only made Anthony even more furious. Poppy, however, didn't expect the tirade that followed, didn't expect him to be so nasty.

'I expect you think you are very clever. Did you have a word with your journalist friends Poppy? Do you think this all some kind of fucking game?' he was spitting at her, small gobs that hit her face and the wall behind her.

She shrank backwards, feeling frightened, unsure of what to do next. She hated the way that he spoke to her as if she was nothing, but was confused because they were on the same side; he was one of the goodies, supposedly.

'Do you recall nothing about the conversation we had in Bastion? Do I need to spell it out to you? You want to be very careful Poppy Day, because you do not know who you are messing with...'

Martin was shaken sober from his laughing fit. He caught the Major by the lapel, 'What do you mean she doesn't know who she is messing with? If you're threatening my wife, sir, it will be you that needs to be careful!'

'Remove your hand from me soldier!' he shouted loudly. Martin stood rigid. He was caught between wanting to sort the bloke out and the fact that the Major was his superior officer. He had to act in accordance with that. It was unbelievable to him that this man threatened Poppy. Martin wasn't going to let him talk to his wife like that; he wouldn't let anyone talk to his wife like that. Mindful of Helm's position, he faced a horrible dilemma; any other bloke on any other day and he would have socked him one.

It was as if someone had held a touch paper to them. One minute they had been euphoric with a feeling of real excitement, then suddenly, the anger and venom. Major Helm continued to stare at Poppy as if she was responsible, but it wasn't her fault; she had only done what she needed to do to get her husband home. Poppy considered the smiling, waving faces of the people outside. Why couldn't he be like them? Why did he treat her as if she was in some way deceitful, guilty?

Colonel Blakemore popped his head into the corridor having heard the kerfuffle. He addressed the Major, 'All OK?' and then continued without waiting for a response, 'They are not going to settle or be satisfied until they have asked her some questions, or she has at least given a statement.' He spoke directly to Major Helm, as though the 'she' in question was not present.

With his hands on his hips, the Major turned to Poppy, 'Well, it looks like you get your fifteen minutes anyway.' This made Martin furious all over again, as if Poppy had done it for the fame and the attention.

She looked at her husband, 'What shall I say Mart?'

'The truth baby, tell them the truth.'

The Major jumped in, 'The truth?'

Martin was glad Poppy didn't start with the parrot thing again.

'She can't just go out there and tell the truth! We will be a laughing stock!' He was quiet then, cupping his chin, contemplating the best angle for damage limitation, 'Right, you get out there and you tell them the watered–down truth. You say that there was a wider Special Forces operation that you were part of, and success was down to detailed local intelligence gained on the ground after a covert operation. OK?'

He spoke to her as if she were one of his soldiers. She squeezed past him, still holding her husband's hand. They made their way back up onto the podium.

It seemed more ordered the second time, as though the collective media had been reprimanded and were on their best behaviour. Poppy could tell by the eyes trained on her, fingers and pens poised, that it was her that they wanted to talk to. She hoped Martin didn't notice.

The Colonel spoke, 'Questions from the floor please'.

It seemed like a million hands went up in the air and about a dozen shouts of, 'Poppy! Over here! Poppy!'

The Colonel pointed at a reporter in the front row, 'Martin, what did you think when the rescue party turned out to be your wife?' It was strange for him to hear someone that he had never met using his name like he was an old mate. It was weird that so many people seemed to know all about his life, or, at least, about a bit of his life and he didn't know anything at all about them.

Martin was more nervous that he realised. His tongue stuck to the roof of his mouth, he mumbled his response, 'She's amazing and nothing surprises me when it comes to Poppy.'

Instantly another voice shouted out and Martin's response was all but swallowed in the fray, 'Poppy, Poppy! Did you see any evidence of anyone else that had been taken? Did they discuss or acknowledge that they had murdered Aaron Sotherby?'

She bit her lip, 'I didn't see very much at all. I only discussed what the army had told me to...' She had been coached well and did Major Helm proud.

Martin got the feeling that no one had any real interest in what had happened to him or to Aaron, it was all about Poppy. After one quick question, it was whoosh! Straight on to the matter in hand, he felt like the support act.

The crowd were baying to get at her, although now quieter, their collective stance was still one of impatient confrontation. She was the one with the story, the one that would sell their papers. Martin didn't mind that he was surplus to requirements, but he was bothered that a good man, a father, had been murdered, yet it didn't seem to be that important. He was also worried about the level of attention that Poppy was getting, as usual putting her welfare first. There was no jealousy on his part; he was, instead, proud and very glad to be safe, home.

Poppy didn't want to talk about Aaron, and by the way Anthony glared at her across the podium, she figured that he didn't want her to either. She answered the question in the way that she had been told.

Max Holman stood out from the crowd. He wasn't doing anything to stand out particularly, but because Poppy knew him, recognised his face among the sea of strangers, he seemed to be bigger and clearer to her than anyone else in the room. His eyes were wide and bright, his expression, one of real excitement. Poppy thought it was because he knew her, that maybe he was pleased that with so much competition in the room, he had a route in. He was clearly confident that he was going to get his question answered over and above every other journalist because he knew Miles, he had shared a bus with her and he knew what she had been through. Poppy didn't know just how much he knew about what she had been through.

'Yes Max?' she felt assertive in asking the question.

'Hi Poppy,' he smiled as if greeting an old friend.

Poppy was pleased to see him, 'Hi Max.'

He continued to smile as he spoke, 'Your story is a remarkable one...'

'Thank you!' she interrupted him, some of the assembled crowd laughed.

'...but it wasn't without a price, was it Poppy?'

Her voice faltered slightly as she started to lose the thread of what he was saying, 'Sorry, I..?'

'What did you have to do to get Martin back Poppy?

It is incredible and unbelievable in its truest sense that you simply waltzed into the house of a ruthless warlord and demanded that he give you your husband back. And he did, just like that, because you asked him to? Do you expect us to believe that he rolled over like a puppy and gave you what you asked for without compromise or bargain? It doesn't wash Poppy. So I ask you again, what really happened? What did you do? What did you have to do to get your husband released?'

Zelgai's form swam before her eyes. She heard his words with absolute clarity just as he had spoken them, 'Why do you think that I will listen to you? Why do you think that I will do anything to help someone like you? Why do you think that you can come before me in my own country and make any demand at all?'

Max had spat the words from his mouth, almost a snigger. Of course, it wasn't Poppy he was having a go at. He was trying to get at Miles, Miles the award-winning journalist, the superior journalist, superior man. Did he think there was more to their relationship than there was? Did he not know that she loved her husband? Had her actions not proved that point?

Poppy felt as if the room had lost its air. She couldn't breathe properly, feeling every pair of eyes in the room on her; the collective breath of all present was held, awaiting her answer. She felt her skin blush crimson. Despite being hot, the sweat was cold against her skin. She could feel the brush of a beard against her neck, the rake of manicured nails against her arm, the whisper of unfamiliar breath as it tainted the air around her mouth. She thought she was going to pass out.

The next thing she heard was her husband's voice; which echoed slightly, 'Enough!'

When she awoke, she was in the back of a car.

Martin had listened to the stuck-up prick taunting his wife, 'What he..? He just let your husband go did he? Just like that?' It was like listening to the Major all over again, as if she had been lying. He felt his fists bunching in readiness when he looked at Poppy and could see that she was going to faint.

The Colonel and he more or less carried her to the car that had been organised to take them to the hotel in London. Martin sat in the back with Poppy next to him. His ribs throbbed in pain, but it was a discomfort he could happily tolerate, he was glad to finally be heading back to his home town. Home, finally.

When Poppy came round in the car; she found herself in a big, flash motor with leather seats and a chauffeur. Her head was on Mart's shoulder, he was stroking her hair. It was one of the first times they had been alone since his release. The driver was preoccupied with the M4, meaning they could talk without being overheard by Anthony Dickhead Parrot Helm, Colonel Blakemore, a guard, a chaperone, one of a million journalists, or someone wanting to wish them well. It felt lovely to be with her man, but she was agitated, nervous.

Her mind was racing. She didn't know how Max Holman knew, she wasn't sure what he knew, but he sure as hell knew something. Maybe he, too, was in contact with the real Nina Folkstok. The way he had looked at her, his mouth set in a sneer; it made her feel sick, afraid and dirty all over again, 'I love you Mart.' She wanted to reassure him that she did and that no matter what she had done, it had all been because she loved him.

There was something in her tone that got Martin thinking. It was reminiscent of the old bad news sandwiched between two bits of good to soften the blow. More relevant, it was the tactic employed by someone who wants to finish a relationship with you, 'It's me, not you, I will always love you, but I can't do this anymore...' As if the fact that they love you and the fact that it's not your fault makes it easier; it doesn't. It would still make you feel really shit, not any less shit.

Martin knew Poppy so well, knew her every mood and expression, that he caught the same tremor in her voice that he would expect to hear in those exact circumstances. His heart constricted when she said it, 'I love you Mart.' He almost expected, 'but...' to be her next word. It ripped his heart open, the thought; the very idea of her saying those words to him was enough to induce panic, especially now when his head was such a mess, when he needed her more than ever. He knew that to hear rejection from her lips would be, in its truest sense, (to quote that other dickhead from the press conference), unbearable.

For Martin, the love of Poppy Day was like fuel, the thing that allowed him to wake up with a smile on his face and go to bed happy for nearly his whole life. No matter what the day threw at him, he had the love of Poppy to make everything better. It was a safety blanket that warmed and protected him; it was all he had and the one thing, the only thing, that made him special, made him someone.

Poppy never had a secret from Martin, never, not one. Having always known each other, there had never been anything to hide. He knew her back to front and inside out, as she did him. All the crappy things that had happened to Poppy as she was growing up, all the things that she carried around in her head, he knew it all because all those experiences are what made her into the person she was. He never laughed at her many foibles, like her obsession with sticking tiny scraps of soap together to get one more use out of them, rather than throwing them away. He knew she remembered not having soap and the idea of being unclean horrified her. That's how they existed, without one single secret. Until now. She hated him not knowing what had happened to her. The facts sat in her stomach like heavy rocks that she hauled around all day, the facts that made eating and sleeping impossible. She hadn't told him because she didn't know if she had the courage to say those words to him, or to anyone; even the idea of it would send her to the loo to be sick. The idea of having to phrase it, say it out loud, to admit to it, would then make it true somehow.

She tried not to think about it, tried not to remember; it was easier that way and she hoped that one day she would forget enough to be able to move forward. The worst thing now was the idea that someone else knew and that 'someone' could easily tell Martin. He would find out those dreadful details from someone else and not her.

The car was driving along the embankment in no time. It was lovely to be back in London, really lovely in the way that being in a familiar place after any time away is. Poppy looked at Martin, who was staring at the river and the buildings; he looked like a kid taking in the sights for the first time, wide-eyed and excited. She wanted to talk to him, really talk to him, but couldn't find the right moment.

Poppy continued to rest, her head on his shoulder. He stroked her scalp, feeling her silky hair slip through his fingers. He always felt the most love for her when she was sleepy or asleep, leaning on him. He loved the feeling that he was protecting her and that she trusted him enough to fall into a deep sleep, knowing that he would be there, keeping watch. He thought that she looked small and vulnerable; he quite liked it.

They were getting closer to the hotel. Martin was looking forward to seeing their room and to having a kip, he was exhausted. Poppy looked up at him and she did it again. She wrinkled her nose and brow as though she had something to tell him, hesitating for the briefest second before she spoke, 'I really love you.'

Martin knew then. He didn't know what, but he knew that she had something to tell him. He also knew that it was something he really didn't want to hear.

They walked into the hotel reception, both feeling horribly out of place, it was so posh. There was a red velvet board up behind the reception, 'Tariff' was written across the top. Poppy couldn't believe it; she had to squint to confirm the numbers. A double room was nearly five hundred quid a night! A night! There was a junior suite for six hundred quid. That was more or less their monthly outgoings including rent, for one night.

'Why would anyone pay that?'

Martin shrugged in response.

Yes, it was nice but six hundred quid a night nice? Poppy couldn't get her head around it.

They were shown up to their room along a tiny striped corridor with striped paper on the walls and striped carpets. Poppy supposed it was chic, but she could only think that it was like walking through a barcode. They were shown into a suite, not a junior suite mind, but your full on, with own sitting room and bath big enough for two, suite. When the porter left the room, they ran around, laughing and mucking about, opening the doors, looking in cupboards, examining the biscuits and the little soaps. They flushed the loo, ran the gold taps and then collapsed on the enormous bed to admire the view of Hyde Park.

Poppy lay with her head on Martin's shoulder. He put

his arms around her. It felt lovely to have her man back, to feel him so close and lovely because it was intimate, without either of them wanting anything more. Neither was ready for that, for very different reasons.

They must have drifted off because it was about an hour later when they were being woken by the telephone...

Martin woke with a start and felt instantly ill-at-ease. The opulence was the polar opposite of what he had experienced in recent months and the step change was almost unbearable. It was like giving a starving man a cream gateau, when all his body desired was a simple broth, slowly, slowly... The initial novelty of their environment had worn off, he felt out of his depth. He had never been in, let alone stayed, anywhere like it and, if he was being truthful, he didn't like it that much. It was amazing, flash and smart, but Martin felt like an intruder. He was tense as though at any time someone was going to come in and say, 'Who the bloody hell let you in Cricket? Get out!'

He would much rather have gone straight home to his own bed. It was exciting for about two minutes to have a good nose around the room, but all he really wanted was to go home, he wanted to go home.

They lay on the bed. Poppy still had her head on his chest. It felt how he had imagined it would on so many nights away from her, waking with his wife in his arms, it was wonderful... The bloody phone continued ringing and couldn't be ignored any longer.

It was Rob Gisby. Poppy was disappointed that the moment was over, but was so pleased to hear his voice.

'I've been having difficulty getting hold of you Poppy. Have you been away?'

Poppy laughed; funny old Rob, 'I couldn't have told you Rob, I couldn't have told anyone.'

'Poppy you are an enigma. An exasperating enigma, but an enigma nonetheless.'

'Is that a good thing?'

'It depends who you are asking. I would say yes, a very good thing, off the record of course!'

'Of course!'

'But, if you said the same thing to Major Anthony Helm, you would get a different response.'

'I bet I would,' Poppy recalled the Major's twisted mouth as spittle flew past her head.

'Don't make me say another word Poppy; you have got me into enough trouble as it is. Listen, I need to come and see you both and talk you through the next few days if that's alright?'

'Yes of course, it will be great to see you Rob.'

'In about an hour?'

'See you then!'

Poppy wanted Martin to be excited, to look forward to meeting him, but he wasn't. Martin couldn't get enthusiastic about it. In fact, if anything, he didn't want to meet him at all. Poppy had mentioned him frequently in the most glowing terms. It made Martin feel ill at ease that there this was this bloke, senior to him, who he had never met, who appeared to have got very close to his wife while he was away. She seemed impressed with him and, no matter how obvious the platonic nature of their encounters, Martin was jealous nonetheless.

Martin also resented the fact that Rob was coming over to tell him how he was to spend the next few days of his life. He wanted to be in control of his own destiny, eat when and what he wanted, sleep in his own bed, wear his own clothes and shut his own front door on the world. He also wanted time alone with Poppy, unwilling to share her with anyone, no matter how nice or well-meaning they were.

An hour later it was too late to voice this opinion. Rob walked in and shook his head. For Poppy it was another dad moment; he was pleased to see her, yet mockingly disapproving.

'Come in, come in! What do you think of this?' she swept her arm around the room.

'I think it's very you'.

'It is isn't it? I reckon we could get used to it!'

She pulled him over to the corner where Martin was sitting in a small chair behind a table, surveying the view. He looked distant. Poppy couldn't tell by his expression what he was thinking, which bothered her. Prior to his capture, she could always gauge his mood, guess at his thoughts, but there was a new place in Martin's mind in which he would wander and Poppy had no access.

'Mart?' he jumped slightly at the sound of her voice, 'This is Rob who I've told you about...'

He stood and pushed his chest out as though standing to attention, 'Sir.'

Poppy didn't like hearing Martin talk to Rob like that. Not Rob who had drank from their cheap cups and sat on the sofa that Martin had paid for monthly in their little flat. It made her feel awkward.

Rob ignored the comment almost. He stepped forward and shook Martin's hand, 'It is good to meet you at last Martin.'

Martin blushed.

'Good to be home I expect?'

'I don't know. I haven't been home yet.' It sounded slightly aggressive, his resentment simmering.

Poppy realised at that moment that she hadn't thought things through from his perspective; he had been dragged all over the place, following instructions. She could see at that point that he probably just wanted to go home, have a pint and put his feet up.

Rob understood this. He ignored Martin's tone, 'I'm sure it won't be too much longer now until you can. Is this all a bit much for you?'

Martin nodded and looked down at the floor; yes, it was all a bit too much for him. It made Poppy feel a big surge of love for her man, who was only ever an expression and a gesture away from being her little friend in the playground.

Martin looked up at Rob, 'I'm sorry sir.'

Rob placed his hand on his arm, 'You don't need to say sorry son. You've been through a lot; and it's Rob.'

Mart sniffed his tears back up and nodded at the carpet.

Poppy felt strange then; it was lovely to see her husband taking comfort from someone like Rob, but the way that he had called Martin 'son' sent a small quiver of jealousy through her. Maybe she wasn't so special to him; maybe he was everyone's dad.

Poppy made them strong tea in dainty little cups with a band of gold painted around the top. They sat like three old ladies, perched on the edge of the overstuffed cushions, sipping tea from the bone china as they admired the view of the park, it was very *The Importance of Being Earnest;* it made Poppy laugh. They talked about nothing much, ordinary things, Tottenham Hotspur, the weather, the price of their room per night. They didn't talk about Martin's capture, Poppy's adventure, the mental anguish, the future... keeping it light and trivial. They spent a lovely hour; it was like having an old friend to visit.

'Right then, the next few days,' Rob drew them into the present. 'Tomorrow there will be a press conference in Whitehall. Are you both up to that?'

They nodded.

'Then straight after, the Foreign Secretary has invited you and Colonel Blakemore to attend a lunch hosted by him.'

Again they nodded, they were MoD pawns.

Rob took a deep breath and continued, 'There have been several requests for interviews from just about every newspaper and news agency on the planet. The danger is that if we don't give them a story, they have a tendency to create their own, which makes it very hard for us to control what gets published, factually. You have a number of options open to you; we will help and guide you through every one of them. For example, you could prepare a statement that we can distribute and someone from our end can fill in the blanks, or we can organise for someone from the press office to come over and interview you both and then we can distribute that interview accordingly...'

Poppy didn't wait for more options; she was already preoccupied with her own idea, 'Can Miles do it?'

Martin looked at her, 'Can Miles do what?'

'Interview us! I don't think I want to talk to a stranger, but I'd be happy to talk to him and I know that you would be OK talking to him, Mart, because, in a way, it is his story too, or at least part of it.'

'Would he want to do it?' Rob asked.

'I don't know. I'll ask him.'

Martin once again felt as if he was being swept along, but had to admit that after speaking to Rob, he did feel better. Poppy was right, he was a nice bloke. Even though it was relaxed, he kept thinking in the back of his mind about what he had been doing that time last week; strangely he could only picture himself as if he was a character in a book, or that he was watching himself in a film. It looked like someone else, unshaven, incarcerated and wearing traditional Afghan clothing. It wasn't him, it was someone else.

The next day or so seemed to have been mapped out. Martin nodded in all the right places, agreeing to go with the flow. Words like 'Whitehall' tripped off their tongues as though it was an everyday occurrence. They had been through so much that was bizarre and unimaginable, that having lunch with the Foreign Secretary was no stranger than anything else they had experienced.

That evening the two fell into a deep sleep. They slept through the night, which was unusual for them both of late, but they were completely exhausted. It certainly wasn't down to an ordered mind and clear conscience.

The next morning Martin woke with a start, feeling confused; his breathing irregular. He didn't know where he was. It was a foggy few minutes until he understood that he was safe, in London, with Poppy by his side. He decided to watch some football, wanting to see if doing something mundane and every day, something that he always used to do, might make him feel more normal, but it didn't. He had been desperate to watch a match while he was away, but found that he couldn't care less about what he was seeing and hearing. It felt unimportant, irrelevant. How could he raise enthusiasm about a little ball being kicked around a patch of grass when Aaron had been killed and his life had turned to rat shit? His experiences had changed his perspective on what was important, on what mattered in the world and it wasn't bloody football. These thoughts confused him because it used to be a big part of his life.

Poppy watched his agitated awakening and his thoughtful expression; she could tell that things weren't right. That's when everything began to unravel. She saw how he avoided the news and didn't want to know what was happening anywhere in the world, especially anywhere that he had been recently. He could only cope with things that were neutral and safe, things that wouldn't remind him. Poppy sat next to him on the bed as he watched the match.

'What's going to happen to us Poppy?' he continued to stare at the television as though the answer to his question might jump out of the screen.

She stroked his arm, which he pulled out of her reach. Poppy didn't know if he did this was a deliberate or subconscious act; her gut twisted just the same, 'What do you mean?'

'I mean. What will happen to us? What will happen to me when we go back out into the real world?'

Poppy didn't know how to respond, 'We will go home and we'll gradually get back to normal. We will *learn* to get back to normal Mart, but I don't know how long it'll take. The one thing that you can be sure of is that I will be right by your side and we will do it together.'

He turned his face towards her and stared for a little while before he spoke, 'I can't remember what back to normal is Poppy.'

She cried then, instantly and noisily, his words were so very sad. She understood that he had been through too much for her to understand, and knew that it couldn't be fixed with a liberal application of tea and a few good jokes for distraction. She knew because it was the same for her.

'Why are *you* crying?' his words were threaded with hostile overtones. She read between the lines, 'Why are you crying? Because you have no right to cry – it was me that was taken, me that was beaten, me that watched my friend killed and me that is having the nightmares'.

Poppy was trying to think of how to answer him when

he started firing more words at her, 'For God's sake shut up Poppy Day. Stop crying! You have dragged me here into this bloody pantomime. This fancy hotel where I'm too nervous to leave the bloody room, with my head totally messed up. And you sit there crying as though it's you that have been through all the shit, but it's not Poppy, it wasn't you, it was ME! I feel like I am the only one that remembers that, it was ME!' He was shouting, 'I have given press conferences and sat there like a spare bloody part. I've played tea parties with you and your mate while my head's spinning, and I have had enough! I saw them cut his head off Poppy; they cut his fucking head off! It fell on the floor. I swear to God, before they made that first cut, before they put that blade to his throat, he was looking at me! He was looking right at me as if to say, help me. But I couldn't help him, I couldn't do anything and they killed him Poppy. They fucking killed him!'

Poppy held him as they both shed tears of frustration and sadness for what they had lost. Poppy thought the time had arrived for her to tell him, because she *did* have the right to cry; Mart was wrong. She had been through shit too. She babbled, crying so hard that most of it was unclear. Poppy should have planned what she was going to say but didn't. She just started talking, 'Mart, it's not only you! You have to help me Mart, you have to help me and we have to help each other. I can't do this on my own. Please Mart make it all go away, make that picture go away! Don't let anyone touch me, don't let anyone near me. Please Mart!'

She verbally jumped all over the place. Her nerves were infectious, making his panic rise; tension seeped from his pores. He held her by the tops of her arms and, despite his anger, his anxiety, his hands felt weak around her muscles; the strength had gone from his arms. He wanted to hurt her because she was hurting him by not talking, by not giving it to him straight. He wanted to hurt her because he was angry and confused. His heart was racing, his breathing was out of sync, but of course he didn't hurt her, not because he wasn't capable of it, but because he would never and could never hurt her. He loved her.

Her babbling was unnatural, it scared him. He looked her in the eyes, 'Tell me Poppy and tell me now.' He said it through gritted teeth. He looked and sounded aggressive. She had never seen him like that.

He felt her shrink inside his grip; she visibly deflated as her head hung forward. It was as though her neck had gone floppy; her hair fell over her face. She couldn't see him; didn't want to see him. Maybe it made it easier to talk without having to see the look on his face. He could understand that.

'Tell me Poppy, please,' his tone was softer now. He knew that frightening her wouldn't help and hated the idea of making her feel like that. They were both quiet for a minute; she was getting ready to give him the information, mentally preparing, and he was getting ready to receive it, or so he thought.

When she eventually spoke, her voice was small. Martin held his breath so that no other sound got in the way of his hearing. She sat, slumped forward, reminding him of a rag doll, 'I didn't have a plan Mart. I didn't think things through, so I didn't know what to expect. I didn't know what would happen. I wanted to get you back. I was so frightened that no one was looking for you and I know that you would have come and got me...' Her tears muffled her voice, dripping down her nose. She did nothing to stop them, or mop them, as she wept.

He held her close to him then, her head was still

hanging down, but he held her tight, 'Yes baby, that's right. I would have come and got you too.'

He held her tightly to him, squashing her face, but she didn't care. She wanted to feel him that close, wanted his arms around her to make her feel safe. She knew that she had to keep talking because if she stopped she probably wouldn't be able to start again, 'I know I tell people how clever I am Mart.'

'That's because you are clever darlin'.'

This made her cry even harder, she shook her head, 'No, no I'm not. I won't ever think that I am clever again, because I should have thought, I should have thought things through. How many people would jump on a plane and go to Afghanistan with only a notebook and a packet of bloody Polo Mints? That was really stupid.'

'That wasn't really stupid, that was just you were desperate to get to me and doing it in a hurry without thinking. The fact that you managed to get there and survive with a notebook and a packet of mints makes you very clever indeed Poppy Day. There are grown men, trained soldiers that could not have got as far as you did and managed to survive in the way that you did.'

Martin felt relieved. He thought she was telling him that she shouldn't have gone. He thought that maybe Major Helm's words and criticism were finally getting to her, but he felt overwhelming relief because he knew how to cope with that. It wasn't the big bad thing that he had been half expecting, it was just his lovely Poppy wobbling, overanalysing, probably with a bit of shock thrown in for good measure. He could cope with all of that; he could make it better...

Poppy hated him being so nice to her, not when she was trying to tell him something so terrible, 'I also didn't think about how I was actually going to get you home, how I was going to get you released. They could have killed me Mart. They could have taken Miles and I deep into the desert, killed us, and no one would have been to blame but me. I put me and I put you in terrible danger and that was stupid.'

'...but they didn't kill you Poppy Day. You are here and you are safe, we can carry on just as we were before. In fact, not just as we were before, but better because you did something amazing and brave for me. I knew that you loved me before, but now! Bloody hell Poppy, how many husbands can say that their wives have ever done anything so incredible for them? Eh? How many?'

'...I let you down.'

'No, no you didn't Poppy, you could never let me down, never...'

'I did. I let you down Mart.'

'...don't talk like that, please Poppy, you didn't let me down, you couldn't. You are wonderful and I love you, I love you so much...'

'I am not wonderful; you don't know what I did.'

For Martin it was as if the world stopped. Time stood still while he held his breath. He could feel the blood rushing in his temples, waiting, waiting for her to speak, waiting to hear the big bad thing that for a moment he thought he had escaped from, evaded, dodged. He hadn't, it was only a reprieve and it had been there all along, hiding, waiting to jump out at him. Martin stared at the tears rolling down her lovely face, which magnified her freckles. His fingers twitched with the temptation to stroke them away from her skin. Neither of them spoke for a while, each hoping for a change of direction, but neither knew the co-ordinates. When Poppy finally spoke, it was with a quiet voice that he had to concentrate to hear. She looked just like Poppy Day in the playground when they were little, the Poppy Day he used to have to look out for and protect from the whole world, including Jackie Sinclair.

The next voice that he heard wasn't Poppy's; it was his own, 'What did you do?'

Poppy lifted her head and looked into her husband's eyes. She tried to find the words to tell him that another man had touched her skin, kissed her neck and seen her naked. Her heart felt like it would break in two, at the damage that she was about to inflict, 'Mart... Mart...'

Martin heard his name, it sounded as though she was begging him to understand, but he couldn't understand because she hadn't told him anything. He went back to the words he had used earlier. The dictionary in his head had dried up, he couldn't think of how to phrase want he wanted to say, so he repeated, 'Tell me Poppy and tell me now.'

Poppy knew that she had to; she knew she had to tell him the secret that was destroying them both. She exhaled slowly and stopped crying instantly as though someone had figured out how to turn the tap off. She sounded calm, in control, 'I didn't want to do it Mart. I want you to know that I didn't have any choice, no choice at all. I also want to tell you that I love you very much, I always have and I always will. It has always been you Mart, always you and only you, you know that don't you?'

Martin tried to guess what was going to come next, 'but I have changed my mind and I want my freedom' or 'having had the chance to travel and have an adventure by myself, I want to do some more, I am leaving you...' His heart leapt in anticipation of all the terrible possibilities. He was absolutely transfixed by her mouth, watching it quiver with emotion, listening to the syllables that would tear him in half.

What came next did tear him in half, but it wasn't what he was expecting to hear. He stared at her though his eyes were screwed almost shut, his mouth twisted into a pre-crying pose, waiting for her to deliver the words, permission for the distress to start. She didn't keep him waiting too long, 'Zelgai made me spend the night with him and in exchange he set you free and he set me free.' Her voice was cracked and wavering. It was a strange voice that she hadn't used before, the result of trying to speak when her vocal chords and every muscle in her body were pulled taut with fear and anticipation.

Questions flew around his mind, stupid, naive questions that found their way out of his mouth, none of them logical, 'You spent the night with him where? What did you do? Where was I? Did he touch you?'

He fired questions one after another. Poppy knew that he wasn't grasping the reality of what she was trying to say, the facts wouldn't sink into his mind and become truth.

She made it clear for him. She wanted to spare herself the horror of having to slowly explore each aspect, figuring it was better to say it out loud and be specific, rather than answer one question after another until the details had been wrung from her, 'Pretty soon after we arrived at the house, they sent Miles away and I thought they were going to kill him. Zelgai told me that you were in the house and that he would set you free. I was so happy Mart and so grateful, I even said thank you! But it was a trick, he let me show him how happy I was that you were to be set free, then he told me that if I didn't sleep with him he would kill us both. He told me how he would do it and it was... horrible, terrible, even the idea of it was terrifying. I had no choice and that is why I am so bloody stupid, because I walked into that house completely innocent, thinking I could appeal to his better nature. He made me have sex with him Mart! You know how I can't stand anyone to touch me! He touched me and I can still feel his vile beard against my skin, no matter how much I scrub myself. I can still smell his breath just before I fall asleep. It was the worst thing that I could ever have imagined Mart, but I didn't imagine it, it really happened! It happened to me!'

She was screaming at him, talking too quickly for it to make a lot of sense. He sat looking at her with tears pouring down his face, his arms around his body. He looked like the Martin that she knew when he was a little boy. She wanted his arms around her, needed him to put his arms around her and tell her it was all over and it would be OK, he was taking her home and they would start over... But he didn't.

Martin could hear what she was saying, but it didn't make any sense to him. It was like watching TV when the words and pictures are out of sync and you have to concentrate on making it all match up. She was talking too quickly for him to take it in. There were two facts that swirled around settling on every surface of his brain, 'He told me that you were in the house' and 'He made me have sex with him.'

It was all he needed.

Martin cast his mind back to the day before his release. He had been dozing on the mattress when the door opened and in walked his old friend Man U. He was, of course, pleased to see him. He was always pleased to see him, someone familiar and friendly. Martin knew that he would never forget his small kindnesses that made the biggest of differences to him.

He was beaming as usual. Martin could always tell when he had brought him something, or had something really urgent to tell him; well, to try and tell him. This was one of those times. He bent over; a bit too close, personal space wasn't his speciality. He said, 'David Beckham.'

Martin nodded, 'Yes, David Beckham!' knowing that this could mean anything from soldier, to man, or footballer, or English, or any other number of bloke-associated words. It was what came next that now resonated.

'Victoria Beckham! Man U pointed at the wall over his head.

Without really knowing what he was getting at, Martin repeated, 'Ah Yes, Victoria Beckham!'

Man U was practically jumping up and down, he was really agitated, 'Victoria Beckham! Victoria Beckham!' Again he was pointing at the wall and then the window.

Martin smiled and nodded. Man U seemed satisfied, but the reality of what he was trying to say only dawned on him now. He was trying to tell him that David Beckham's wife was in the house; only David Beckham was him and it wasn't Victoria, but his wife, his Poppy Day. She was bricks away, feet away and he didn't know. He didn't know that she...

Poppy and Martin had been brought up surrounded by sex: her mum, always catching up on it with any bloke that she could get to hang around for longer than five minutes; the kids on the estate laughed about it; the boys at school bragged about it, some of them even practiced it. Their attitude, however, was prudish. A lack of liberalism meant that for Martin and Poppy, it was only ever each other. It was important that no other hand had touched his skin, no other eyes seen her naked. It was part of their commitment and a big part of what made them special.

On the day that Poppy became his wife he felt a shift in his world. He stood on the steps vacated by Courtney and her brood, looking at his mum and dad, who hovered on the edge of the crowd, not wanting to join in. The sour twist to his mum's mouth told him that she wasn't impressed with the day or her son's choice of wife. He didn't care; he knew the reality of his parents' life. What he and Poppy shared was beyond comparison, thank God. Martin felt a surge of joy as he held the hand of this woman that wasn't his mate, girlfriend or fiancée; she was his wife, the most amazing girl on the planet.

Yet, he had been in the house, lying on that bed, beaten and captive while his wife had been under that same roof, a few metres away, having sex with the man that had kidnapped him; the man that had taken away his normal life; the man that had beheaded Joel's dad.

The tears streamed down his face. He had never cried such desperate tears in his whole life. 'No, No...' he whimpered over and over as if, by saying it enough, he could erase it from his mind and make it all go away. Nothing that he had been through could have prepared him for the pain of her words. Poppy and he had only had each other; it was sacred, special.

She tried to reach out and touch him. He shrugged and flinched simultaneously at the very thought of their skin making contact. This made her stomach flip; she had to concentrate on not being sick. She tried to talk to him, tried to make him focus on her, 'I did it for you Mart. I did it for us. I pulled on my heart strings as hard as I could, but nothing happened. I tried Mart, I really did. I pulled and pulled, but you didn't come! I wanted you home and that was the price that I had to pay, I paid it Mart! I am still paying it! Mart please talk to me baby!'

Then he started laughing and Poppy didn't know what to say or how to act. He thought again about Man U and how it hadn't made any sense to him at the time, but it was now crystal clear, they had all known about it. His wife was in the next room with that bastard while he was laying there, his own fucking wife! He laughed because it was so horrendous, that if he hadn't laughed, then he honestly didn't know what he would have done. He thought about when she came to him that morning. He thought she was a dream, his angel, his beautiful Poppy Day and she had only minutes before left the bed... where she, where she had...

Martin tore around the room like a crazed thing, ignoring the pain in his ribs and the throb of his broken finger, shoving his possessions into a carrier bag and putting on his shoes. Poppy tried to get hold of him at one point, tried to physically stop him from leaving, but he made a noise not dissimilar to a growl, it was just like a growl. She shrank back on the bed. He left, crying and muttering to himself, as if consumed by madness. It was frightening and upsetting all at the same time.

Poppy didn't know how long she sat in that same position on that massive six hundred quid a night bed after he had gone. It was about two hours. She kept repeating the same logical argument in her head over and over, 'What had been the point? I did what I thought was best to get him home because I love him so much. I did what I had to do because I had no choice. It was the only way to secure his freedom and because of that I have lost him. It's all been for nothing, it's destroyed us.' It was poetic, ironic and very sad.

Martin hailed a cab; breathing deeply he fought to control the rage inside him, the like of which he had never experienced.

The phone rang, stirring Poppy into action, rousing her from her stupor. She thought it might have been Martin, she hoped it was Martin. It wasn't.

'Car is ready and waiting for you madam, come on down!'

'Oh Rob...' she cried into the receiver, there was no need to say anything else. He was in the room within what felt like seconds. He was suited, booted and obviously ready for the big day out. Poppy was sitting in her nightie with her hair still wet in places, no makeup, and her face streaked with tears. 'He's gone.'

Rob sat on the end of the bed. He didn't get angry or remind her that she was supposed to be hosting a press conference. It didn't matter to him that in an hour or so she would be keeping the Foreign Secretary waiting. He didn't mention any of it. He exhaled slowly as though they had all the time in the world. He took his hat off and raked his hair with his fingers,

'He'll come back Poppy, eventually.'

'How long is eventually?'

He didn't lie to her, or make some crappy comment that might have made her feel a little bit better for a little while. Instead he was honest, as she knew that he would be, as he always had been, 'I don't know love, but I suspect that he doesn't either. Neither you nor I can begin to understand what he has been through. The few people that I know that have been through similar or worse have come back changed, if they come back at all.'

Poppy knew that he was talking about Aaron.

'The thing is Poppy, Martin will be as confused as you are. There is no right way to cope with what has happened to him. He will have to figure it out in his own way and he will, eventually.'

'There you go again with your 'eventually.''

'It's the best I can offer I'm afraid.'

His company and words were much appreciated, but she couldn't see a glimmer of hope or a light at the end of any tunnel. She saw a black hole and everything she had counted on and thought that she knew was disappearing into it.

Martin sat with his hands clasped in the back of the taxi. His muscles bunched, his vision blurred. He had to get out of that room and away from her. He felt a mixture of fury and sadness. The only thing that he had ever been able to rely on had been taken from him. He had always felt like he and Poppy were in a little club, a team of two that no one else could touch. They lived in an impenetrable bubble; untouchable, unbreakable, he and Poppy Day.

Poppy was the one person in the whole world that he could trust. If you gave him a situation, any situation that you can think of, he would guarantee that he could predict how she would react, what she would do and say, how she would feel because he knew her. Or at least he thought he did.

He never would have thought or guessed that she... A small voice reminded him that she had no choice; that it was a matter of survival for them both and, of course, he believed her. It wasn't a case of not believing her. He couldn't imagine the situation that she was in, but he still felt really angry. Why did she put herself in that situation? Why didn't she take greater care? Take more people with her? Anything! He couldn't shake the thought that she could have done more, should have been more aware. If she hadn't been so headstrong and impatient...

It was a dilemma that raged in his head. All the things that he loved most about her, her strong will, her toughness and the way that she would go for it, whatever 'it' was, were also the things that made him the most angry now. He wanted to shout at her, 'What the bloody hell were you thinking?' He felt like a bastard because she had done it for him, for the love of him and, yet if he was being one hundred per cent honest, he looked at her after she had told him and he felt differently about her, not massively different, but a bit; enough. Martin couldn't reconcile that fact that she had broken one of their rules, whether she wanted or not. Spiritually they had separated and he couldn't see how they were going to repair the damage, or, even, if they could.

Rob made all the necessary calls to cancel their appointments. They could hardly have gone ahead, what with Martin having done a runner and not wanting to talk to or see his wife, and her still in a nightie, snivelling into a handful of Andrex. It was hardly what people were expecting was it? Not so much Lara Croft as Lara gone soft.

Poppy felt the weight of blame. What had been the bloody point? She had done something reckless and, as it transpired, pointless, because in the process of trying to rescue and preserve their love, their life, she had destroyed it, had destroyed them.

Rob stayed with her for a couple of hours. Poppy was grateful. She hoped that he would always be in their lives. She could do with someone like him to turn to, they both could. He suggested that she get out of the hotel and go for a walk, go home, go anywhere, other than sit and brood while staring at the six hundred quid a night wallpaper, lovely though it was. He was right, of course; it was exactly what she needed. There was only one place in the whole world that she wanted to go.

It felt wonderful to be walking up the path of 'The

Unpopulars', not like coming home exactly, but pretty close. Poppy hoped that, by doing the ordinary things that she had done before, she could get back to how she used to be. Back to normal, well kind of back to normal.

The door was opened by Bisma, who visibly flinched when she saw who it was. Poppy missed the open-mouthed smile that she was usually greeted with. In its place was the tight-lipped reluctance of someone who's faced with a political agitator whose image had been plastered all over the papers. It almost overwhelmed her. Poppy, wondered if this was how she was now destined to exist, with all those who had previously loved and liked her shunning her for undertaking a task to save the man she loved. How many more individuals would make her pay the price?

'Hello Bisma, how are you?'

The girl nodded, her eyes cast downwards.

Poppy decided to spare her any further embarrassment, 'Good…' she concluded as she walked down the corridor. She could feel beautiful Bisma's eyes on her back and wondered what she saw.

Poppy stood in the doorway and watched her darling nan sitting exactly as she had left her. She recalled the high hopes with which she had left this very room less than two weeks before. How she had changed in a matter of days; her spirit was raw and her trust in tatters. Poppy had envisaged standing before Dorothea in triumph, instead, she felt an overwhelming sense of desolation and despair at what she had endured and for what lay ahead. The relief at seeing Dorothea was wonderful.

Poppy didn't know what she had expected. The chances of her nan having got her nose pierced or taken up fire juggling were slim, but it felt as if she had been gone for a very long time, time enough for changes to have occurred.

They hadn't. She was still her old nan, sitting in the chair in her little room with her cardi wrapped around her, watching a crappy cookery programme on the telly with the volume too loud. Poppy stood and reacquainted herself with her look, her manner. She thought she was studying her unnoticed, when the old lady turned quite suddenly, 'You coming in then girl, or what?'

Poppy ignored the belligerent tone and sat on the plastic visitor's chair, kissing her nan's head as she passed, 'What are you watching?'

'Anything Poppy. I watch anything, any old rubbish to fill my time.'

'I have missed you Nan,' she held Dorothea's hand and watched as her skin wrinkled up under the pressure of her thumb. It didn't go back into place immediately, like scrunched up tissue paper.

'Of course you have love, because coming here and sitting in this shitty room with me every day is bloody wonderful...'

'It is wonderful for me. I love you. You are all I've got.'

'You got him back then?' Dorothea dismissed any sentiment by ignoring the words and cutting to the chase.

'Yeah I got him,' Poppy felt like she wanted to cry but didn't. What was the point? There was no way she could have told her nan about the price she'd paid, how part of her had been lost forever.

Nathan appeared in the doorway and stood waiting to be introduced. They smiled at each other. To their mutual shock Dorothea turned to him, 'Give us a minute please Nath...' before continuing, 'It was on the telly. I said to Mrs Hardwick, 'that's my girl. That's my Poppy Day. It wasn't any special bloody soldiers that got him back, it was my Poppy Day'. She told me to shut up and said

I didn't know what I was talking about! The old cow. But I did know, it was you wasn't it Poppy Day, just like we talked about? You went and got him back didn't you?'

'Yes Nan, you were right, that Mrs Hardwick doesn't know what she is talking about. I did go and get him back.'

'Did you take your mother with you?'

'Mum? No, no I didn't.'

'She wrote to me you know, saying that he was being well looked after and that if I wanted she would send me a photo, but I didn't bother. I couldn't see the point really.'

'Who? Mum? She wrote to you about what? Mart?'

'No Poppy! Why don't you listen? Simon's mother, his new mother. She said she'd send me a photo but I didn't reply. I knew there was no point; I wouldn't have been allowed to keep it anyway.'

'How did Mum feel Nan, about giving him up?' Poppy decided to pry, to grab the chance of salvaging a fact before it slipped through the net; something, anything that might give her a clue to her shitty childhood.

'She didn't know about him, no one did.'

Poppy sighed, another dead end, more frustration, 'I see.'

'Well, why should she? I never told her. I never told anyone, not even Wally. I'm sure he heard the rumours, but he wouldn't have cared, as long as he was fed and was left in peace to sleep... His dad was St. Lucian and he shone to me Poppy, like a bright light in a very ordinary world; made me feel special. Our baby was my secret, my lovely little secret. My Simon, my little boy, my beautiful baby, 'That Dorothea is no bloody good; we'll send her away for a whole year! We won't even write to her and ask her if her heart is breaking or if she is ready to come home, and when she comes back we'll have no mention of it in this house!' That's what my dad said Poppy.

I still hear it over and over. A whole year, Poppy Day, one whole year. It felt like a lifetime. No one came to rescue me and I was only in Battersea not bloody Afghanistan. I wasn't even allowed to say his name, not ever, not once, let alone have a bloody photograph. My little boy, my Simon.' She cried, sending her eyes instantly bloodshot. Dorothea's tears clogged her throat and muffled her voice. It was rare to see someone of her advanced years in such a release of emotion. Life experience had usually taught people in their eighties a certain level of containment, or was it that they had simply cried all their tears? Maybe any skeletons that were going to fall out of the closet had already fallen, been exposed and subsequently grieved over. Maybe, but not always.

Poppy rubbed the back of her nan's hand, holding it in both of hers. Her own tears came thick and fast then, 'It's alright Nan; it's all OK. It was a long time ago.'

'I know that it was a long time ago darlin,' but how Poppy? How is it alright? You never had a proper family. You never had anything at all; you were a poor little cow. Even though I loved you and your mum loved you in her own way, we were all so busy fighting our own demons that no one looked after you. I am sorry Poppy Day, I am so sorry my darlin' girl, but you have turned out wonderful! I'm so proud of you, and your mum would be too if only she would take her head out of her arse long enough to see what she's got. You're my whole world Poppy Day and I think the day that you stop coming here is the day that I will give up and fall over. There'll be no point because you are everything to me.'

'Don't talk like that Nan. I am not going anywhere. I'll always come and sit with you, always. I promise.'

'That's good for me to know Poppy Day, but I don't want you here when I have disappeared,' she was emphatic.

'What do you mean when you have disappeared?'

'You know very well what I mean. Like now, Poppy, I am here and I know that I am here, but often, in fact, more and more often, I am not here. I don't know where I go, but I know that I am not here. It's like I've vanished and the gaps between me being here are getting bigger and bigger until I won't be here at all and I will disappear. You know that, Poppy Day, don't you? Tell me that you know that because it is very, very important to me that you understand. I want to know that you understand.'

'I do Nan, I do. I know that one day you will disappear.'

'I want you to know that I would never choose to leave you, but I can't help it, and when I have gone I don't want you to waste your life sitting here with me because I won't even know it. It is the most terrible thought that you might see me and I won't know you. Promise me Poppy Day, that when I have gone, you won't come here, please don't do that to me, please!'

Poppy understood. She had never and would never lie to her, 'It's OK Nan, I *do* understand and when that happens, when that day comes, I promise I'll do what you want.'

They held each other tight.

Sixteen

Miles set up shop while Poppy looked on. Initially the unfamiliar surroundings of the hotel room gave an element of formality to their interactions. It didn't last long.

He thought it was funny that she was holed up in the flashiest hotel in London, a slightly better arrangement than she was used to of late, at least now she had room service. The rules of the interview had been established before his arrival. He understood how important it was that their story be told truthfully and openly in a way that didn't glorify any aspects, giving a respectful account of what happened to Aaron. It was also best for all that he interview them separately, considering the current circumstances.

He positioned a small microphone on the table top; twisting the plastic stand to ensure that it would be facing her throughout, 'Righto. Have you got everything that you need?' He used his index finger to push his black square spectacles up and over the bump on the bridge of his nose, as was his habit.

'Well I think so. I'm only going to be talking, so I guess apart from my gob I won't need anything else!'

'OK clever clogs. I meant, are you comfortable? Happy to start? In need of a bathroom break?'

She liked the way that he phrased things, most people would say, 'D'you need the loo?' or worse. Not him, he made it sound quite gentile, 'I'm fine thanks Miles. How about yourself? Do you have everything you need?'

He smiled, liking the way she responded to him, 'Yes, thank you. I have done this once or twice before.'

'Well pardon me. What's that? A tape recorder?'

'Yes. I record everything and only make brief notes as you talk. It allows me to concentrate on what you are saying and ask any questions without missing anything. I often use the recordings to edit my work at a later date.'

'I see. Well, let's get started shall we?' she rubbed her palms together, trying to muster an enthusiasm that she didn't feel inside.

'Yes. Right Poppy. I'm pressing record if you are ready?' She nodded.

Miles opened his notebook and unscrewed the lid of his ink pen, smiling, trying to reassure her, '...here we go.'

'How does this work? Do I just start talking?'

'Yes, I have some questions that I'd like answered, points we need to cover, but essentially just talk and be comfortable. If I need to direct things, I'll chip in.'

'OK,' Poppy swallowed.

'I know it's hard to get started Poppy, so why don't you tell me in one word what your life was like before this whole adventure started?'

'God, that's tricky. I guess my one word would be, uncomplicated. Actually, can I have two words? They would be uncomplicated and simple. Actually, I'm going to have three, uncomplicated, simple and boring. Don't think of this as a bad thing though, in fact, quite the opposite. Compared to what the last few weeks have taught and shown me, I now think that uncomplicated, simple and boring is a great way to live. I can imagine what you are thinking, that you'd rather have anything other than that. Well, you're not me. Is this OK Miles? Do I just carry on talking?'

'Yep, you're doing great, just keep talking...'

'Fine. I can do that. Some would say it's getting me to shut up that's the trick. Sometimes, when I think about what I've done and what has happened to me, it feels unreal, as though it has all happened to someone else. It's like I've seen a film or read a book that was so all-consuming that some bits of it have stayed with me and replay in my head. Sometimes I wish it *had* all happened to someone else. In fact, that's not true; I wish it all the time.'

'Can you explain what you mean by that Poppy?'

'Well, I'm still trying to get my head around the fact that life can be, ordinary. Then one or two things happen and POW! Your whole life is skyrocketed into extraordinary and everything you thought you knew or could rely on has changed. I keep waiting for things to go back to how they were before, back to normal, but I'm beginning to understand that this is it from now on, my new normal. I guess you could say it for any life-changing event couldn't you? Like having a baby, or losing a loved one. What was unimaginable one minute becomes 'normal' the next! Maybe not the baby thing so much because you do have nine months to try and get used to the idea, although having said that, I am twenty-two and I don't think my mum has ever got used to the idea. I think she is the exception. God, I hope that she is the exception!'

'You don't mention your mum much. Are you close?'

Poppy snorted her laughter, 'Err, no, not close at all. But I don't want you to think that my situation can in any way be filed under 'if only my mum had loved me more'. It's got nothing to do with her. I do try to take stock, if only I'd made a different choice, said yes, said no, said nothing, whatever. I've done a lot of that. Could I have? Should I have? What on earth was I thinking? It always brings me to the same conclusion; that there is absolutely no point. I think of it like my whole life; my world was put in a wok and thrown up in the air, and when it landed, it was different. I once read a poem or had it read to me, I can't remember which, about a man who spent his whole life looking at the floor. He walked bent over, looking at the pavement, studying the carpet and looking at his toes. Then one day, a bird called to him and he looked up. For the first time he saw trees, the sky and aeroplanes, the tall roofs of buildings, clouds and pylons, a whole world above his head. Similarly, when he got home, he looked up at the ceiling. He saw lights and cobwebs, all the detail that he had been missing. His whole world had changed because he looked 'up'. What fascinated me was that this man had a very specific outlook on the world, yet there was so much more all around him every day. If only he had looked up sooner! I'm like that man, Miles. I was walking looking down, studying my toes and now that I have looked up, I'm not sure I like the world that's above my head. Actually, if I could have one wish, it would be that I could go back to looking at the carpet. The poem never mentioned that, the fact that once you've look up, you can't go back to only looking down ever again, because it's always there. I now know there are things outside of my postcode and beyond my immediate horizon that I didn't know about before; not necessarily good things.'

'Surely it's a good thing that you looked up Poppy and that you widened your horizons, because you have achieved a lot? You must be proud of what you've accomplished?'

Poppy looked towards the tree tops of the park opposite at girls on horses cantering along the track, shiny haired, white sock-wearing girls, 'Am I proud of my achievements? No. No I'm not. I don't mean to sound curt, but that's the truth, that's the way I feel. There's no pride, just a feeling of stupidity; I was naive.'

'Maybe it was your naivety, as you put it, that enabled you to be so brave. Could it be that an awareness of all the possible danger might have made you think twice, altered your decisions? I'm thinking about a stunt man who used to jump across canyons on a motorbike. His manager used to tell him that the distance was less than one he had already successfully jumped, and it was only after he landed safely on the other side that he'd tell him it was so many feet further. There is definitely something powerful about mentally taking something in your stride, having the belief that it will all be fine because you are unaware of the dangers. I guess the defining question is; would you do it again?'

Poppy held his gaze, 'He raped me Miles.'

'What?' Miles stared at her.

She shook her head, unable to repeat it.

'Who?' his finger jabbed at his glasses, as though visual clarity could help him mentally. He focussed on the tape recorder, unsure if he should stop recording.

'Zelgai. He threatened to kill me. I'm sorry I didn't tell you before. I hoped never to tell anyone, but Mart knows and it's only right that you do to.'

'Oh no, oh Poppy... I don't know what to say.'

Poppy reached across the table and rubbed the back of his hand.

His words were both apologetic and self-reprimanding, 'I should never have taken you there, I...'

'No, Miles, you can stop that. It is not your fault. I would have found a way to get to him, with or without you, and in answer to your question; yes I'd do it again because I needed to bring my husband home.'

It was some seconds before Miles answered; he knew that her words would resonate in his mind for always, that bastard had hurt Poppy, 'I am so sorry, for you, for you both. It's the most awful thing. I had no idea. You are amazing Poppy. Martin is very lucky.'

'I'm not so sure he sees it that way at the moment.'

The two sat in silence, digesting the newly shared revelations.

'I've been wondering Miles, do you think prayers have to be specific? You know like, 'please send down a bolt of lightning and get this bastard off me,' or whether it's OK to keep them general, hoping that the person or thing that you are praying to will instinctively know what you need or want? I need to give it some more thought. I read an article that asked the question, 'does everybody pray?' The conclusion had been, no, not everybody prays. I don't believe that. I really don't. I think that believer or non-believer, in the right circumstances in everybody's life, everyone would pray. What else is there at that final moment, when you hover in that black space of total despair, when all that remains is the possibility of an outstretched hand, a little bit of hope?'

'Everyone I have ever met that has been in that position has certainly prayed. Call it whatever you like, wishing, asking, projecting, but essentially it's praying, so I guess if people pray, it's because at some level they believe that there is someone or something in existence to answer that prayer... You are shivering Poppy, are you cold?'

'No, I'm not cold. I can't help it. It doesn't matter how warm I am, when I talk about it, or think about it, it's as if I am cold on the inside, really cold and I can't seem to get warm.'

Miles swallowed to remove the ball of grief that had gathered in his throat. Poor Poppy, beautiful Poppy...

The Crickets' flat was stifling; Miles loosened his collar before placing the laptop on his knees. It was unbearably hot. The central heating was turned up despite the relative warmth of the day. He drew his long legs together within the confines of the armchair. A cursory glance around the living space revealed Poppy in every detail. It was a fresh, light room with the odd quirky accessory. A wedding photo on the mantelpiece showed the couple in their finery, sipping Guinness through a straw from a shared pint glass. They looked happy.

Martin flopped down on the sofa opposite, barefoot and unshaven, his eyes swollen and red. Whether from crying or an ailment it was hard to tell. His sweatpants were spattered with food. A stained tee-shirt with 'Herrick' printed on it, looked crumpled and slept in; it bore the whiff of sweat and stale beer. He looked in bad shape, 'Can I get you a drink?'

Miles guessed from the way Martin tilted the neck of the beer bottle in his direction that he wasn't suggesting tea or coffee, 'No, I'm fine, thanks.'

'Goodo.'

Miles registered the sarcastic tone; there would be no point in conducting the interview if the subject was confrontational, reluctant or too drunk, 'How are you doing Martin?'

'Peachy thanks Miles.'

'Martin, if you would rather not do this then I can come back another time. You seem a bit pissed off.'

Martin was quiet; he pulled his fingers through his hair, scratching at his scalp. He dug his toes into the carpet and chewed on his lip, 'Well Miles, I guess I am a bit pissed off. In fact, not a bit; a lot. It's a bloody living nightmare. Every night when I close my eyes while I'm sitting up in bed…oh did you know that? I'm too scared to lie down, how funny is that? I fall asleep, then I wake up almost immediately because I don't know whether I'm at home in my bed or still there, in that place. I'm afraid to sleep.

I try and doze during the day so that I wake in the light and it's not so frightening, but that's difficult. Having no real sleep pattern, no routine makes me feel confused. I'm frightened of something that doesn't exist, so how can I fix it? It's not the monster in the wardrobe or the spider in the bath, nothing tangible that you can look for, remove or plan against. I'm afraid of something that has already happened, so I can't prevent it. I'm scared shitless of a memory, so what exactly can I do about that? Bloody nothing, that's what. So, yes, Miles, I'm angry. I keep asking, why me? Not that I'd wish it on anyone else. My anger is mixed with guilt, what wouldn't Aaron and his family give to have him sat here feeling angry? Why did they kill him and not me? Who made that choice?'

'I don't know Martin. There are people that you can talk to...'

'Yes, yes I know; very helpful, good-natured people. Truth is, no one can help me Miles because it's something only I can figure it out. Not some do-gooder that wants me to go to a paint therapy class, or to keep a bad dream diary; it'd have to be a fucking big book!'

'These people are trained, they know what they're doing Martin, it might be worth...'

For the second time Martin's diatribe cut across Miles good intentions, 'I've heard about blokes coming back from tours and going a bit nuts. Those who've seen and done things that send them over the edge, but I thought I was different. I thought I was stronger, more together; more able to cope. The thing that's hardest for me to explain, is not how it's changed me physically, although what they did to me was pretty lousy, but how it's changed me as a person; how I am and how I think. It might not be immediately obvious to people, but I feel, I don't know what the right word is; jumpy. I've always been fairly confident that I could look after myself if I needed to, that I could defend Poppy. I've always been quite fit, but also because I've always lived where we live. All the local head cases and tough nuts are either people we were at school with or related to people we know. I felt protected, immune I guess. Since I've been back, I keep looking over my shoulder, waiting for something bad to happen. I don't answer the telephone or the front door, I'm hiding away. I was making a cup of tea earlier and my hand was shaking so much that I couldn't pour the water from the kettle. That made me feel even weaker, more edgy; it's a viscous circle.'

'It's going to take time Martin. You've been through a lot.'

'Haven't I just! I find it hard to make sense of it all. How could it be that one minute I'm living in the flat with Poppy, eating fish and chips on a Friday night, going to the pub on a Sunday lunchtime to catch up with my mates, following Spurs and then BANG! I'm captured, in a hot foreign place where I don't speak the language and I don't fully understand what the issues are. How did that happen to me? What did any of it have to do with me? How did I get mixed up in a war so remote from my life, so far from what was important to me personally? It's the sort of thing that you see on the news, not the sort of thing that actually happens. Maybe I shouldn't say all that stuff, but it's true. It's true for me anyway.'

'Do you think the army let you down?'

'No.' His answer was instant, emphatic, 'People might think that, but they can't imagine what it's like out there. The landscape, the culture, the way the insurgents are organised. It's very, very complicated and, having spent time out there and seen it closely, more closely than I would have liked, I'm not that much closer to understanding any of it or figuring it out. So, no, definitely not, I don't blame the army. I know how tough it is to get the true picture or any useful information. They would've been trying really hard, I'm sure of that. They would have done what they could. I had no idea they tried to rescue me. It would have made a huge difference to me if I'd known. I hadn't exactly given up on being found, but after a couple of days I began to have doubts. Your mind plays tricks on you, you feel constantly disorientated. I was thinking that maybe they didn't know I'd been taken; maybe they thought I was dead, so why would they bother looking for me? Your brain wanders, I thought the whole patrol could have been wiped out; no one would have been able to get back and tell anyone that I'd been taken, maybe they'd assumed I was dead. Maybe they had told Poppy as much... These options all feel plausible when you've all the time in the world to consider them. The only thing that gave me hope, real hope, was Poppy. I knew that she would be suspicious of my lack of contact, so, if nothing else, I knew I could rely on Poppy to raise the alarm, to tell someone something, even if it was just that I was a lazy bastard that needed to write to her more. I was pinning all my hopes on Poppy.'

The irony wasn't lost on either of them. Miles decided to steer the topic. He needed to glean certain elements of his story, 'Why don't you tell me about what it felt like to be incarcerated? Your experiences?'

'God, it's hard to know where to start. When I was confined to that little room, I became very reflective, as I guess most people would. With that glorious gift of hindsight, I kept repeating the fact that I should never have joined the bloody army; I should never have left Poppy on her own. I'm still sorry for that. I should have done things differently, told her things that I didn't know that I would have to tell her. Almost like instructions. That sounds patronising, but you know what I mean, in the case of 'x' do this and in the case of 'y' definitely don't do that. She probably wouldn't have listened though.'

They both laughed softly, knowing there was no 'probably' about it.

'I used to lie there, trying to work out which decision, which choices had led me to that place and time. What could I have done differently? I thought a lot about the garage where I used to work. I thought about the twat I used to work for, how he took the piss out of me for years. Then I started to think about what my life had been like. I was unfulfilled, bored and more than a little frustrated, but I also got to go home to my Poppy every night. I got to wake up with her hair spread over my chest every morning and, Jesus, compared to what I'd faced since joining up, it felt like a fabulous life. I just couldn't see that when I was living it, almost as if I had to throw everything away and go through hell to appreciate what I had before.'

'That's often the way Martin.'

'I guess. It's a harsh way to learn a lesson.'

Miles nodded and thought about the lessons Poppy had learnt.

'Every time I think about her, Miles, my heart beats too fast and my mind swirls. Part of me wants to run to her, hold her and part of me wants to run away from her, as far away as I can get. It's complicated.'

Miles felt the pull between his professional self that needed to remain impartial, gather the facts, and Poppy's friend, who wanted to give advice. The friend won, 'I think she needs you right now Martin.'

'Ah, well, therein lays the problem, my friend. I need

her too, but it's not that simple. I feel isolated, very alone and the only person that could make that go away is my Poppy, my wife. She would have made this all better. She would have listened to me, helped me and taken away my loneliness. But now she can't.'

'Why?'

'Because she has become part of it, she is mixed up in it. She was there and she was involved. She took away the one person that would have made this all better for me! She took that person away when she got on that plane, stepped into my world, and when she did what she did... I don't expect you to understand, I am not sure that I understand. In fact, I know that I don't.'

'She did what she did for you, Martin, and she would do the same again.'

'I wouldn't want her to do the same again Miles!' He was shouting, 'That's the last thing I want her to do!' Martin exhaled, trying to calm himself, 'Poppy and I didn't have to try very hard, we were truly happy and it was bloody magic. I trusted her. We had only ever been with each other. That was so special to both of us, very rare. We'd always rather be together than do anything else, absolutely anything. She is my other half.'

Miles was happy to note the change to the present tense.

'God that sounds crap, Miles, but it's true, she is. I love her beyond words. She is my world and every action that I undertake, every thought that I have, it's all about her. I'm always thinking about what is best for Poppy. That's why it's not a question of laughing it off and going back to how we were before. It's so much more complicated than that. I feel nervous about touching her, not only because of how she might react, but because I'm nervous about how I might react, how it might make me feel. I don't want to feel or think anything negative about Poppy, so I almost don't want to risk it. I don't know if that makes any sense. To be honest it doesn't make a lot of sense to me. I've got so much going on in my head right now Miles that I'm not a good person to be around. In fact you are the only person that I've seen. I'm not ready to face Poppy yet, not yet...'

Again Miles steered the conversation, 'Did you ever fear for your life?'

This made Martin chuckle, 'When I was moved from the original building to the villa, yes, I thought they were going to kill me. I was in pretty shocking order. I heard a sound that I was convinced was either a gun or blade being made ready for my execution; it was neither. It was the click of a car door, but I was convinced it was my end. That was a surreal day, one that will stay with me always. I was being pushed forward slightly and a hand went to the top of my head, it cradled my scalp as I was folded into the back of a vehicle. This made me laugh, they had been happy to beat the crap out of me and watch me fall and smash my face, but God forbid I might bump my head as I got into the car! It was a small car with a narrow back seat and the vilest odour imaginable. I could smell diesel, but also something else that I couldn't identify. It was like cigarette smoke but worse, stronger, like a mixture of cigarette smoke, cheap cologne and strangely, vinegar. I've been told since that it was the smell of heroin. I won't ever forget it. It permeated the sacking that was over my head. It made me wretch. At least one of the guards sat in the back with me. He kept the point of his gun in my ribs for the whole journey. I think the other guard was in the front seat; someone else was driving. They chattered in Arabic, I got the impression that they weren't talking about me. That might be a distortion, but I'd listened to enough of their language over the previous couple of weeks to distinguish the tones quite well, when there was conflict, anger or humour.

The chat in the car seemed to be more general, like three mates out for a ride in their heroin-filled, stink-hole of a car. It made me think about our car journeys as a kid, off to Clacton for a day out with Madonna playing on the radio. What would our chat have been? 'Would anyone like a mint imperial? Shall we play spot red cars? Or I-Spy?'

This made me smile behind my sack mask. I pictured the two thugs with their faces hidden, hands grasping their big guns, 'Oh my turn! I-Spy with my little eye, something beginning with... H!' Then I imagined the other two shouting out, 'Hostage!' as Madonna pouted about being a material girl. Maybe it was the residue of heroin in the car, maybe it got to me. It was bizarre that for the three of them they were simply transporting cargo, all in a day's work, whereas I'd gone through every human emotion imaginable, including contemplating, preparing for and expecting my own death. Despite the comedy of my situation, my heart continued to race. It was entirely possible that they were driving me somewhere remote to kill me. I sat tightly coiled in anticipation. Like I said it was bizarre; you can't imagine. I'm glad that you can't, it messes with your head.'

'Why did they move you?'

'I don't know. It's not uncommon if they feel you are attracting too much attention or any rescue mission comes close. The car pulled into a garage. I know it was a garage because it had that echoey quality and I heard the metal door clatter closed behind us. There was also that unmistakeable smell of diesel and old grease. The car door opened and the shouter and his gun-toting friend were on either side of me. I still felt quite confident; they had lots of chances to kill me, so I figured they would've done it by then. Why drive me into a house, or another building, only to kill me? Not when there were so many empty stretches of desert around, quiet and unseen. I thought of Aaron again. One of the guards led me by the arm and I let him, I didn't want to take another tumble. I mean, I had to make my stand, but I'm not stupid.

The house smelt cleaner than the previous one and seemed more solidly built. The floor was tiled I think, whereas, in the last building it had been compacted dirt, dusty and horrible. I heard a door close. It clicked as it shut tightly into the frame, a solid wooden door in a frame that it fitted. The doors of the first place had been rickety, like stable doors with bars across, slapdash and made with cheap materials, peasant housing. This felt very different, more like a villa.

I climbed some stairs and my arm touched a staircase, which was cold and felt like wrought iron. There were very few buildings like this in the area; it meant money. I was taken into a room and pushed down onto the bed. Thankfully they took the sack off my head almost as soon as we had arrived. I don't think I could have stood having that thing over my head for days like it was before. It still makes me shudder when I think of it. I looked around the room; there was a window, which made everything seem really bright. It was brilliant actually, to see light and white walls. The floor was covered with white tiles with a patterned border. The walls were rough plaster, painted white. There was a red and gold woven rug on the far wall and a few bits of furniture, a wooden chair and a little table under the window. The light fitting was a wooden chandelier. Compared to where I had been held, it was real luxury. The bed had a clean mattress but no bed linen. I didn't mind and wasn't exactly in a position to moan was I?

I was glad to be still and settled. Kalashnikov boy cut off my hand ties. I put my hands on my face gently to try and survey the damage. I couldn't tell which teeth I'd lost, my tongue was numb and swollen, so even though I felt the gaps in my mouth, I couldn't trust the information it sent to my brain. I ran my fingers over my bashed-up face and I remember thinking that it was a good job I was an ugly bastard before it all happened!

Poppy always joked that we were so close, we were like twins. She used to believe the theory that if one of us was ever hurt or injured, then the other would feel it. I've always thought that it was total rubbish. But I swear to God, I was lying on my bed and I thought I heard her call to me. Not calling me out loud, but in my head, if you know what I mean. There was something else. I did feel a pain, but it wasn't like I'd broken my leg or anything, it was as if I had a pain in my heart. I didn't know why at the time.'

Martin's tears fell freely, 'She was pulling her heart strings, Miles, and I couldn't get to her. She needed me and I would've gone to her, I swear that I would have found a way. I would have helped her, but I didn't know she was there or that she needed me. I was in the next room and I couldn't save her. I'd always promised her that I would be there whenever she needed me, all she had to do was pull her heart strings, but I couldn't be there when she needed me the most... I can't get it out of my head; she needed me and I didn't help her.'

Seventeen

'So, I think that's probably it then, is it Miles? Do you need anything more from me?'

'I don't think so Poppy. I've certainly got enough to start. I'll consult with you both as I go along, before a single word is printed to make sure that you're entirely happy with the content and the way that I've interpreted and portrayed things.'

'I trust you to do good things with our words Miles Varrasso; you are a great writer, a bloody good journalist.'

'Thank you Poppy. From one fellow journalist to another I take that as a great compliment.'

Poppy smiled, she liked being thought of a journalist, even if it was only pretending, 'It's like we have come full circle, isn't it? It's been weird talking about it, strangely healing in a way that I didn't expect it to.'

'Healing how?'

'I think mainly with regard to me and Mart. It's helped me to order my thoughts. I know that I love him. I've never doubted how much I love him, but now I know that we need to find a way to move forward, together. I don't think it'll be quick or easy, but I do know that we can't sit brooding in dark corners can we? I need to drag him out of whatever pit he has dug himself and we need to sort it out; otherwise, what was the point of going through all of that just to lose him now? That wouldn't make any sense would it?'

'No, it really wouldn't. How long is it since you saw him?' he wanted to prepare her for the state she might find him in.

'I haven't seen him since he left the hotel. When was that now? It must be about a week ago...'

'I've seen him a couple of times obviously, but he asked me not to tell you too much. It made me feel a bit disloyal, but I had to respect his wishes Poppy. I'm sorry to say that he wasn't in very good shape,' concern was etched on Miles' brow.

'It's OK, don't worry Miles, I'm going to find him right now. I'm pretty sure he's at the flat, but, wherever he is, it'll be a darn sight easier to find him in E17 than it was the last time I went looking for him.'

'How do you know that he will be at the flat?'

His question made her laugh, '...because that is where we live Miles! It's where we're from, and where our friends are. Where else would he be?'

Miles shrugged. The idea of limiting your whole world to one postcode was alien to him, however, when the prize was a girl like Poppy, he could almost understand it, 'You really love him don't you?'

She didn't answer immediately, but, instead, gathered her words and thoughts slowly, 'To say that I love him doesn't feel like enough. It's so much more than that, it's a perfect and pure love. He is my person and I'm his, we are meant to be. It's like all is right with my world when I am with him, I only breathe properly when I am near him. It's like my heart waits for him. He is my guardian angel and for once it felt great to be his, to give him a glimpse of what it feels like, when someone has got your back and will travel to the ends of the earth and go through anything to bring you home. That's what he has done for me my whole life. So, yes, Miles, yes I love him, I love him very much.'

Her words struck his heart like tiny daggers. In his head he heard the words he wanted to say; he imagined speaking them slowly, concentrating on not shouting, 'I love you Poppy Day! Even though you have never eaten anchovies and drive me crazy with your obstinacy. I absolutely love you!'

Instead, his words were muted, offered quietly, 'You are both very lucky and I wish you both every happiness...'

She smiled at him. There was affection in their stance; people might assume that they were brother and sister, the symbiotic trusting and the reciprocated affection.

Miles turned to his companion, 'I'll give you a lift.'

'Don't be daft Miles, I can jump in a cab. I am only going to the flat.'

'Well I know you can jump in a cab, jump on a plane... You can do anything Lara Croft but no, no, this time I insist.'

'Well, if you insist.'

'I do Poppy. I also wanted to say thank you.'

'What for? I haven't done anything. Oh God, Miles, you've got that look again. You are not going to go all soppy on me are you? I've seen that face once before when you were stood in my tent, blubbing like a baby girl.'

Miles laughed. He removed his spectacles and pinched the bridge of his nose, 'I want to thank you because you have done so much Poppy. You've been open, honest and generous with your story and your words. People don't always tell it from the heart but you and Martin both have, it's made all the difference. People will be fascinated by your triumph, by your determination and by your nerve!'

'Do you think so Miles? I worry that it's all a bit boring. I mean who cares what a hairdresser from Walthambloodystow has got up to?'

'I do Poppy. I care, and, if I care, then plenty of people will.'

'Well, if you say so. I mean you are, after all, the award-winning brain around here!'

'I think we both know that that isn't true, Nina Folkstok.

You're pretty smart yourself!'

'Very funny. It's your story too Miles; my intrepid rescue would have stayed an idea if it hadn't been for you. Are you glad we met? Has it been worth it? Or do you wish you'd never bought me a cappuccino? Or that you'd ratted on me at Brize Norton?'

'I don't think me ratting on you would have made the slightest bit of difference. You'd have found a way.'

Poppy smiled, knowing this to be true.

'...and yes, I am glad we met. You've taught me things Poppy, I like the way you look at the world. My mother says that you are never too old to learn something new.'

'Your mum's right. I didn't know sea horses were real until I was eight; I thought they were imaginary, like mermaids.'

'You mean mermaids aren't real? Jesus poppy, next you'll be telling me that the tooth fairy is a myth!'

'Funny guy! I'm just going to spend a penny – see you down there Miles.'

The phone on the bedside table rang. Poppy hitched her bag up onto her shoulder with one hand on the bathroom door handle. Miles looked at the phone, 'Are you going to get that?'

Poppy had no intention of loitering a second longer than she had to, she wanted to get back to her husband, 'Think I'll leave it. It's probably Rob; he's the only one that calls me here. I'll give him a shout later.'

Miles grimaced; leaving a ringing phone unanswered was as alien to him as not balling socks correctly or replacing a CD in its non-alphabetised slot, all acts that caused his OCD receptors to twitch.

'Miles, don't worry, I'll call him later. You're such a worry pants.'

'That's me, Mr Worry Pants!'

'You go ahead. I'll only be a mo. I'll see you down there.'

She reached for the bathroom handle. Poppy placed great faith in her intuition, but on this occasion, she was wrong. It wasn't Rob, but Martin on the other end of the unanswered line. As Miles closed the door of the hotel room, Poppy's husband began leaving his message, 'Pop... it's me. I understand if you don't want to talk to me, but I need to tell you that I am sorry baby. I love you Poppy. I love you so much. I'm sorry for leaving you like that. I felt so angry for all sorts of reasons; none of them seem to make any sense now. I was bloody useless and I wasn't there for you, the one time that you really needed me and I was only a room away... Please come home Poppy, come home so that we can talk. I love you. I'll be right here, waiting...'

Miles squinted as he walked into the late afternoon sunshine, it was a good day. As he pulled the key fob from his jacket pocket and walked to the driver's side of the vehicle, he was thinking about Poppy's words. He'd come to the conclusion that she was right; an uncomplicated life, simple and boring, without pain and heartache *would* be preferable.

It was almost simultaneous. As he pressed the button to open the door, so the man in the shadow pressed the small button on his little black box. The car exploded in a hail of fire and debris. Bits of metal, glass, wire and plastic that had only seconds before been recognisable as a car were reduced to an assembly of junk. A complex Mecanno puzzle, with each component fragmented and twisted.

People standing within ear shot of the blast dropped to their knees and held their heads in their hands, waiting for the fallout. The windows of the hotel popped, then flexed, before exploding into a million tiny prisms that flew through the air as shards of silver, seeking and embedding themselves in anything soft that would give them refuge, from clothing to flesh. The noise echoed in a ripple of sound waves that cracked the air, tearing it open, a hammer upon the peace of the day.

Following the blast, there was an eerie and disturbing silence that lasted too long for anyone to feel comfortable. For those embroiled, it was like watching a movie in slow motion. People saw blood trickle from new cuts and slashes, marvelling at its warmth and redness.

The hotel concierge laughed as his tongue slipped through a gap in his face that wasn't his mouth – which was now missing – seconds before being robbed of consciousness.

A student, on her way to a date at the cinema, teased her hair behind her ears. A split-second later, she was staring at her lower limbs, trying to understand why and how they were detached, before slipping into the swirling icy current of death.

A man staying at the hotel kicked the hand of his wife that lay alone on the step as he stumbled forward. He knew it was hers because of the distinctive engagement and wedding rings that glinted in the sunshine. She meanwhile, sat bemused and fascinated by her shortened arm; shock and adrenalin rendering her devoid of pain and understanding. Birds flew far away, and those that saw them go envied them their escape.

Miles Varrasso was no more. He was returned to matter; no part of him remained intact. He was deconstructed, destroyed, dismantled, obliterated and erased. Gone forever. A valid, full and young life wiped out by the cowardly single press of a small button.

As the spirit was wrenched from his body, it headed for

a leafy suburb in the West Country, where a middle-aged Classics teacher of Italian lineage sat at the desk in her study, preparing her class plan for the next day. When the news came through that would destroy her world and her faith, Claudia Varrasso would not feel her son's strong hands as they rested on her shoulders, giving her strength and inner warmth across two worlds, but he was there nonetheless, trying to draw her pain. A small white feather that had been dispatched from a jeans pocket had followed Miles' spirit. It would be sitting on the bedside table, waiting for her to discover in a day or so's time, and, not for the first time, it would bring a human in need great comfort…

'Miles! No! Miles! Please! Someone! ' Poppy's screams from smoke-filled lungs could be heard above the siren and shouts.

As he walked from the wreckage, the figure in the shadows pulled out a mobile phone. Neither a drop of sweat, nor a tremor of hand was apparent. Nothing to betray his action, he was cool and calm.

The telephone rang in Zelgai Mahmood's study. The mobile vibrated in Major Anthony Helm's pocket. The receptionist at eleven Downing Street punched a call through to The Right Honourable Tristram Munroe. Who knows what two of them heard? But for one, the message was succinct and chilling, 'It's done.'

Martin lay with his arms around his wife, she trembled inside his grasp. He held her even tighter, he knew all about shock.

Poppy recalled the first ever conversation held with the man that would become her dear friend,

'You won't make old bones like that Miles.'

'Who says I want to make old bones?'

'I guess maybe you don't. I just assumed that no one wants to die before their time is up, before they have finished. I think that would be the worst thing, time suddenly running out for you without warning...'

Lying on their marital bed, with her chest gently rising and falling against his arms, Martin's head stirred on the floral pillowcase. He couldn't think about the what if's, if he'd made the call a few seconds later, earlier... he was too busy enjoying the sensation of warmth against his skin. Martin inhaled the scent of her hair and closed his eyes. He felt at peace, never wanting to let her go, his love, his Poppy Day. Finally, he was home.

One Year Later

'Are you sure you don't want to come with me?'

'Positive. Peggy and I are going to have one last look around here and say goodbye. I'll drop her off with Jen and I'll meet you up there, Mart, like we agreed...' Poppy lifted the baby girl in the crook of her arm and placed a gentle kiss on her downy forehead. The baby splayed her tiny fingers, before resettling them against her dozing chest.

'Maybe you could come with me now and drop Peggy off later? Bring her to say hello? We could get a photo?'

'I said no Mart, please don't. Let's just stick to the original plan. There's no point,' tears pooled in Poppy's eyes, her mouth contorted, ready to cry. A promise was a promise.

'It's OK darlin', I understand. I just didn't want you to miss an opportunity that might not come again.'

'I can't help it, Mart. I don't want to see her. It's not her anymore. It hasn't been her for a long time.'

'You don't have to explain again Poppy. I was just thinking that once we've moved, it'll be harder to get up to see her. Bordon's not exactly got a tube station...'

Poppy pictured her new house in the Hampshire countryside. There was already a bird table and a swing in the garden and she couldn't wait. Martin kissed his wife's freckly nose and ran his finger over the mouth of his sleeping daughter, Peggy Alessandro, 'Bye my beautiful girls...'

'Your cap badge's wonky; can't have you at the Cenotaph looking anything less than perfect,' Poppy twisted the REME horse that glinted on her husband's beret. Martin wore his new regiment colours with pride. The transfer had been easy and in three days' time he would start to train as a mechanic. Before they left London behind, there was the small matter of the Remembrance Day parade to attend, as guests of honour, no less. It seemed, somehow, more poignant this year; not only because of what they had been through, but because of Aaron...

It was a quiet day, much like any other at 'The Unpopulars.' Twenty or so people that used to have lives, sat on squeaky vinyl seats, tapping the arms of the chairs with gnarled fingers in time to the *Countdown* tune. Balancing the odd cuppa and sipping the bitter liquid, trying not to think of a time when tea could be made in their own kitchen to their exact specification: a bit more milk, a bit less sugar, a favourite mug. A kitchen in a house where there were bills to be paid, calls to be made, grass to mow, groceries to fetch, the touch of human skin across the mattress at night. Trying not to think of a time when they had a life, before this...

They had been herded together for simplicity, fed and watered until a last breath took its toll on tired lungs. It would, of course, be for the best. They'd had a good innings and at least they never suffered. Never suffered? They had no idea.

'Nathan?'

'Yes my love?'

'There was someone that I wanted you to meet.'

'Oh right. Who was that Dorothea?'

'I don't know...'

'Well, I'm sure it will come to you.' He tried to change the subject, switch her focus, 'How about a nice cup of Rosie Lee? I may even be able to rustle up a couple of choccie biccies, but don't tell everyone, I save them for my favourites.'

'Am I your favourite?'

'Oh yes, you most definitely are.'

'Can you get my mum for me? I haven't seen her for a long time and I miss her,' Dorothea's breathing became irregular; she couldn't understand where her mum had vanished to.

'I'll see what I can do. Now, let's see about that cup of tea.'

Nathan looked up from the task in hand, 'Ooh look Dorothea, you have a visitor.' He and Martin shook hands, 'Wow! You brush up well! On your own soldier?'

Martin nodded, ignoring the slightly accusatory tone. It was hard to explain just how difficult it was for his wife.

Poppy wandered the small rooms in the flat that had always been home. She felt a strange pull in her chest, desperate to be gone from the concrete confines of E17, yet reluctant to walk away from the host of so many memories. She pictured Wally, asleep of course; her nan laughing in the kitchen; and she thought about her mum, Cheryl, who, having given birth to Poppy at sixteen, had been denied the opportunity to "ave a life' in her early years, and had been determined to "ave a life' since... actually, since as early as Poppy could remember.

'You have no idea Poppy what I've given up for you. I was going to go to sec-a-terriall college.' Poppy could hear her saying that throughout her childhood and teenage years. It was, of course, total rubbish, complete and utter crap. She never gave up anything for Poppy; she didn't have anything to give up in the first place. Instead, her daughter became, in her mind, the reason that she was not an air hostess, a croupier on a cruise ship or catalogue model. Why, generally, she had not set the world on fire, achieving all the things that she may or may not have dreamt about. It took the responsibility away from her; it was all someone else's fault. More specifically, it was Poppy's fault.

Poppy knew, however, that with or without her child in existence, Cheryl would rather have drunk, slept or smoked all day, than haul her hung-over arse out of bed. Poppy never told her this. What would have been the point? She smiled at her sleeping daughter and knew that she would be a very different kind of mum.

In every recollection from her childhood, Dorothea was present like bold wallpaper or a loud song on repeat. She'd displayed a particular brand of eccentricity that was a combination of comforting and funny. It was both of these things until the 'Dementia Express' quickened its pace. As Poppy grew up, Dorothea made her life as happy as it could be. She never tried to make up for Cheryl's shortfalls, but, whenever and wherever possible, she made her granddaughter laugh, making everything feel slightly better.

It used to puzzle Poppy that her nan felt no sense of responsibility for the way her mum was, as if she didn't understand how her daughter had turned out to be quite so useless. In fact, similar to her mum in that respect, both seemingly believed that you could opt out of responsibility and, therefore, culpability. It was only now she could see that Dorothea was fighting her own demons and was also cleverer than Poppy had thought, encouraging her granddaughter to be independent and strong. Silently pulling all her strings, wise enough to know that the one thing she did have to ensure was that Poppy could live without her...

'Hello there.' Martin called to Dorothea.
'You 'ere for me?'
'Yes, it's Martin, Martin Cricket.'
'Martin Cricket?'
Martin smiled, 'Yep.'

'Bloody stupid name. Ooh, I've remembered! I was just saying to Nathan, there's someone I want to introduce him to. It's a girl I think.'

'Now I've already told you Dorothea, the only girl I need is you,' Nathan again tried to divert her.

'I think she might be a relative, not of mine, of Mrs thingy's...'

Nathan turned away. Five months ago, the net had finally widened allowing Poppy Day to slip through the gaps, turning her from tuna to minnow in a matter of moments.

'Martin?'

'Yes darlin'?'

'Don't mention the girl to Mrs Whasername.'

'No?'

'No. It might make her sad. It doesn't make sense...'

'What doesn't, my lovely?'

'That girl, it's odd... I miss my mum. Can you get her for me? I don't know where she is?'

'I'll see what I can do.'

'I haven't seen my mum for ages. Can you get her for me? I need to tell her something, but I don't know where she is. She never came to see me you know. I was only in bloody Battersea...' Dorothea chewed her bottom lip and plucked at the buttons on her cardigan.

They were both silent for some seconds.

'Martin?'

'Yes my love?'

'What's the girl's name?'

'Her name?'

'Mrs thingy's special girl. What's her name?'

He placed her dry palm inside his hand and stoked her fingers, 'It's Poppy Day. Her name is Poppy Day...'

Acknowledgements

The writing and launch of *Poppy Day* has been fuelled by love and encouragement from everyone that I have encountered, thank you all.

I owe a big debt of gratitude to Brigadier Jim Drew CBE who got the ball rolling. Russell Thompson OBE who took a leap of faith and the wonderful Joseph Dublin and team at the Royal British Legion who brought Poppy to life!

My sincere gratitude to Stuart Higgins and all at Stuart Higgins Communications for your inspirational advice and unwavering support.

My thanks to the team at TIP ltd – working with you is a joy! (Mia – your dad can't draw!)

Thank you to John Miles, you are wonderful.

My brilliant parents Anne and Ken, who are always there for me and have taught me that nothing is beyond your grasp if you just reach high enough, you were right. I love you both.

The boys, Simon, Paul and Nicky, who inspire me with their humour and warmth. Love to their lovely other 'alves!! A big kiss to the legend that is Amelie Beth. Love to Jo, Luke and Alice!

My best friend Carol, who loves me even though she knows me! And whose daily dose of friendship and guidance makes my life better in every single way. Thank you for everything. You are right darling; it's the small things... HQ? Normal time?

Trixie – for telling me to 'Go for it!' and the hours she has spent reading and critiquing; thank you darling PT. Keep wading, I'll be waiting!

Katie Margaret – Love you to bits 'Princess'.

Our amazing boys Ben and Josh, who have put up with their mum being lost in a laptop for many hours and not moaned about my rubbish cooking (much!). Boys I am so proud of the young men you are becoming, so very proud. From the day you were born, you have been my anchor and my sunshine, you own my heart.

...and for the man who I would travel to the ends of the earth for, my wonderful Simeon an extraordinary soldier and an extraordinary man. The love of my life, my soul mate and my future. I treasure you every day xx

Poppy Day is written for all service personnel and their families who know the joy of loving and the pain of separation. One such serviceman was my grandad, 1457746 Corporal Josiah Ward (1922 – 2010) of 2715 Squadron RAF, married to my lovely nan; he proudly served his country. I loved him very much.